MW00773718

# THE
# PROCEDURE

## ELEA PLOTKIN

Copyright © 2022 by Elea Plotkin

All rights reserved. No part of this publication may be reproduced, distributed, or transmitted in any form or by any means, including photocopying, recording, or other electronic or mechanical methods, without the prior written permission of the publisher, except in the case of brief quotations embodied in critical reviews and certain other noncommercial uses permitted by copyright law. For permission requests, write to the author, addressed "Attention: Permissions" at Plotkinelea@ gmail.com

BookBaby
7905 N. Crescent Blvd.
Pennsauken, NJ 08110
www.bookbaby.com

Print ISBN: 978-1-66787-227-8
eBook ISBN: 978-1-66787-228-5

Printed in the United States of America on SFI Certified paper.

First Edition

The Procedure is a work of entertainment and should be read as nothing more. It is a work of fiction. Any resemblance to actual events or persons, living or dead, businesses, companies, events, or locales is entirely coincidental.

This novel is dedicated to my husband Andrew Plotkin, whose unwavering support for this creative venture made it possible, and to my sister Beth Anna Margolis, who inspired me to write.

# CONTENTS

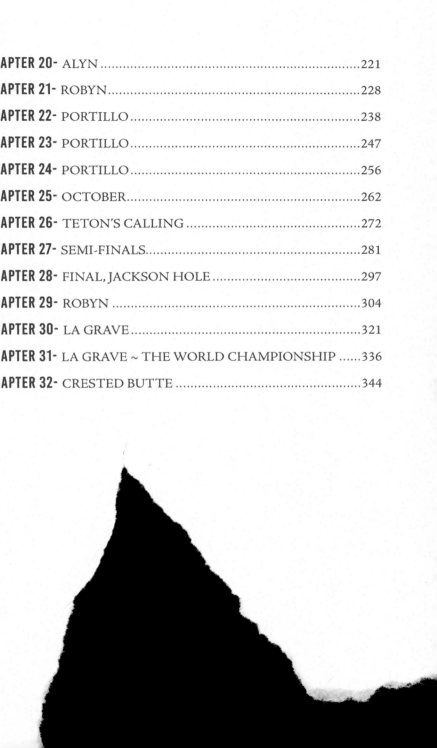

# CHAPTER 1
# SILVERTON

Finally, a break in the weather. For two days now, they had been holed up together impatient and bored, pacing around the rooms of the Gold Ore Inn, a tired but serviceable relic from the 1920's situated in the heart of Silverton nestled between an old saloon and antique apothecary complete with frontier façades and gas oil lamps dating back to the turn of the century. The rugged and remote mining town, perched ten-thousand feet above sea level in the San Juan Mountain Range of southwestern Colorado, was considered one of the most spectacular and challenging heli-skiing areas in the country, and one of the most dangerous, as well. Mostly off-piste, backcountry terrain, the alpine wonderland had all the qualities they lived for, for shooting video and practicing aerials on its notoriously steep, near vertical walls.

They had stayed in town while it snowed all night, then all the next day, fluffy white flakes coming down collecting in drifts and pillows two feet, then three feet deep; massive dumps of dry, light powder that the frozen, hardscrabble outpost was famous for. Now nine a.m., the snowfall had largely subsided and only a few lazy, thick flakes drifted to the ground. Light gray clouds still blanketed the atmosphere, but rays of bright sun peeked through the morning sky, promising a great day of skiing. The forecast was for intermittent sun and clouds, increasing wind late afternoon, temperatures in the low teens. After what seemed an interminable wait, an all-clear message came through from their heli-tour's pilot to the ski team, they could now be transported into the vast craggy wilderness, providing weather held.

The brawny AS 350 B3 sat poised, waiting at the base of Silverton Mountain, just off Red Mountain Pass. The pilot and his co-pilot prepared for the skiers to arrive.

Their drive up the pass to Silverton on Highway 550 Monday morning had been pure hell. A white- knuckle, near white-out blowing snowstorm had blown in to the region, turning each painstaking mile and icy, hairpin curve into an exercise of Hail Mary's and bargains with God to be a better person *I promise to make each day count if you please not let us roll off this mountainside and tumble five hundred feet to our deaths off this narrow road with no frickin' guard-rails, please God, not today God* kind of hell. Even Mason, who normally would have been chattering away like an excited Mynah bird, went quiet and slightly pale, holding his breath while the rest of them sat solemn and still, mouths grimacing, eyes closed. Whitney often thought these drives up the treacherous mountain passes were a lot scarier than skiing down their sheer mountainsides, which was saying a lot- considering they were all elite big-mountain, extreme skiers who barely flinched at the prospect of jumping off rock head-walls and vertical cliffs, skiing down pocket glaciers and icy, narrow chutes.

For ski aficionados, Silverton was about as close to Mecca as one could get. The area boasted some of the highest, steepest lines in the Rocky Mountains, unrivaled anywhere short of the Chugach in Alaska or the Tyrol in the Austrian Alps. Amidst its stupendously beautiful fourteen-thousand -foot peaks, one could lose themselves in the immense, snow- covered granite spires, hanging glaciers and open bowls in every direction. Only the most expert skier would dare attempt to venture down its avalanche prone faces, jagged rock outcroppings and densely forested basins.

On the road since late November, the team had been living out of duffel bags and backpacks, sharing bedrooms and bathrooms, tripping over each other's ski equipment and smelling each other's body odors as they toured the mountain west. Their adventures and escapades were frequently live streamed on social media and YouTube, they were stars.


After a breakfast of hot oatmeal and buttermilk pancakes in the inn's communal dining room, Whitney, Ian, Karis, Mason, Duncan and Alyn, the team's publicist piled into the gun metal gray Mercedes Sprinter to depart. Moments later, Shenti, their videographer, shuffled over to the vehicle with his equipment, breathing heavily as he hoisted himself inside. Trent, their coach and team director, sat in the driver's seat, per usual. The luxurious, oversize van was a major upgrade for the previously amateur skiers, who were accustomed to living on odd jobs and cold cereal. The Sprinter was one of many perks they enjoyed now as *paid* professional athletes sponsored by Consumco and all the company bestowed. The huge, multinational company was spending millions to promote the skiers, using their images and notoriety to advertise their own corporation's products and brand. Under its sprawling, powerful auspices, they were provided the best ski equipment on the market, the best vehicles for mountain travel, and the opportunity to train and heli-ski on the most massive mountains in North America as they prepared for the World Championship in La Grave, France.

They each found their seats and settled in.

Deftly, Trent steered the all-wheel drive through the just- plowed snow, parking it in a small lot beside the heli-tour's utilitarian, concrete storage and maintenance garage. Leaning around to face his charges all seated in rows behind him, he turned off the ignition, then spoke. Outfitted in heavy winter parkas, ski pants, wool hats and balaclavas, they looked like a band of survivalists ready for an arctic expedition. Four degrees Fahrenheit outside, his breath exhaled in frozen puffs. Spitting his words out tersely, he drilled, "Okay. Everyone be sure to check your equipment before you embark. Transceivers need to be fully charged- we'll be in avalanche terrain all day." Frowning in concentration, voice like granite, he added, "Alyn and I will take the snow machines over to the base of East Face and set up camp there. We'll meet you at the base of Hidden Valley over by the lake, near Exit Road, soon as you come down. We'll do two shots off the face, then swing over to the top of Apex with the helis and try for four shots off Billboard on Pope Face and West Face, if weather holds." Taking a swig of coffee from his cup in the van's center console he nodded at Duncan, adding abruptly, "Get that gear unloaded and over to the heli-pad, times a wastin.'"

With a quick push of the driver's door, he jumped athletically from his seat and strode purposefully towards the low concrete building to meet the outfitters guides and retrieve their backcountry snowmachines for their sojourn. Just as quick, Duncan hopped from his passenger seat and hurried to the back of the van, swinging open its over-sized cargo bay doors to unload their equipment.

Working fast and with practiced efficiency, he sorted through helmets, goggles, skis, poles, boots and backpacks, organizing everything before setting it on the snow- covered ground. Accustomed to the machinations of managing ski teams and all that went with it, he meticulously checked each skier's duffel bag to make sure every item was accounted for. Transceivers, ice axes, probes, shovels, crampons... The amount of stuff to keep track of was colossal. One lost glove could bring an entire day of filming to a halt and trigger an expletive- laced skier meltdown like none other. Consumco had hired him to manage the tour and all the logistics that went with it, including lodging, transportation, meals, equipment, and of course, the inevitable injuries and other untold crisis that would inevitably occur over the next ten months leading to the World Championship, next winter. Determined to do a great job, Duncan avidly dealt with whatever situation was thrown his way.

It was a major hustle, he thought internally, searching for a missing glove liner. One that required almost super-human diplomatic skills, an ever- cheerful temperament, and the ability to do expert ski maintenance and repair. Having spent most his young life practically living in ski shops throughout Colorado, outfitting customers and ski teams since he was in junior high, he came highly experienced in that department. Early on, he had established a reputation amongst local coaches in the state for being exceptionally good at smoothing out prickly burrs of conflict between skiers as they traveled together in the mountain west.

Highly temperamental athletes touring in tightly enclosed spaces for extended periods of time under stressful conditions in frequently shitty weather invariably led to problems, he reflected, grabbing some last-minute snacks from the cargo bay. On this gig, between the constant demands of Trent, their brusque and often tense leader, and their dour but incredibly talented videographer, Shenti, he was put to the task. He likened the whole endeavor to herding somewhat unstable and extremely high- strung cats. Keep the skiers warm and well fed, keep Trent from losing his cool, make sure Shenti made it into the helicopter sober. That was largely it. The rest was considerably easier.

Shenti, he considered, as he ferried equipment to the heli-pad, was probably the most challenging of the group. None the less, he had grown fond of the bearded, middle-aged man, an ex-Afghanistan war journalist who seemed oddly comfortable with the chaos and unpredictability of the whole scene, who generally went with the flow. Though Shenti was prone to periods of heavy melancholia with attendant alcoholic consumption, Duncan could usually find him when he needed to at the ski area's local watering hole; morose, over a tumbler of aged whiskey. His eyes briefly followed the videographer as the man climbed into the roaring helicopter, portly body crouched over, heaving his black canvas camera bags up into the metal bird's seating area, setting them down. The helicopter's cacophonous growl reverberated across the helipad, drowning out any conversation between the group. Everyone had exited the Sprinter and was grabbing their equipment, getting ready to board.

Duncan picked up Whitney's backpack, handing it to her. Helping her hoist it on, he adjusted the canvas straps, securing them into place. Above the reverberation of the heli, they began reciting a checklist, locking eyes.

Airbag pull-cord. Check. They nodded. Whitney slid her hand down her left side to make sure she felt its reassuring presence.

Avalanche transceiver, check. It was attached to her front chest strap, locked into place.

Probe, check. Duncan reached over, touching the folded metal pole inside her pack, just to make sure it was there.

Ice-axe. Check. Shovel with detachable handle. Check.

Water bottle. Check.

They continued like this for several more minutes. Satisfied she had everything, Duncan crouched down to check her ski boot buckles and make sure they were properly fastened. Switching her boot warmers on, he stood back up. He handed her her black Scott ski helmet, then attached a metal GoPro camera on top as she snapped the chin buckle together. It stuck up from her head like a Martian's antennae. "Don't forget to switch it on before you start your run," he reminded her, with an easy grin.

"I know, I know. Jeez, it's so easy to forget," she shook her head, chuckling. "I can't tell you how many times I've done that."

"I know. That's why I'm reminding you, kiddo," he gave her quick smile.

"Thanks, Duncan, I'll see you at the bottom," she lifted her arm, giving him a quick knuckle-five. Duncan was a gem, a late-thirties over-grown ski bum with a heart of gold, and especially protective of Whitney.

"Okay kiddo. You knock 'em dead," he told her supportively, handing her her new wide powder skis, the Volkl Deacon's with brand new Marker bindings. The company had delivered them to her just two weeks ago, he had checked her settings last night before loading them into the van. Set at 11, they would hold her boots in place without releasing no matter how hard she smacked the ground on a jump. They should be perfect. Last, he handed her her Atomic graphite ski poles, designed to absorb even the most jarring pole plants she could make. Grabbing hold of the two metal sticks, she lowered her new Oakley Flight goggles over her eyes and boarded the helicopter, ducking low beneath its blurry, whirling blades. Snow whipped up in powdery clouds, the sound of the hulking machine absolutely deafening. Placing her skis in the exterior metal rack, she hoisted herself inside, choosing a seat across from Shenti.

Giving him a friendly nod, adrenaline shot through her body in an explosion of pure joy and abject terror. Zinging through her blood vessels like an electric buzz saw, from the tips of her toes to the top of her skull, the jolt of chemical anticipation was so powerful it was almost painful to endure. Nearly unbearable, in fact. Willing herself to sit still while she waited impatiently for Mason, Ian and Karis to finish loading their gear and climb into the machine, she clenched her jaw and closed her eyes tightly. The feeling had recently started to plague her just after Robyn, her daughter, had been diagnosed with a seizure disorder. She wasn't sure why, but it had become increasingly bothersome and was starting to affect her ability to tolerate the helicopter rides they so often took.

The co-pilot handed them each black plastic headsets; each put one on and adjusted the head pieces listening intently for his instructions. Signaling for cross-check, the team made sure their seat straps were secure and buckled, then the doors closed. The pilot nodded affirmatively back at the co-pilot; they were off.

As the helicopter rose, Whitney felt the sway and weightlessness, the sensation of other- worldly suspension in a new medium, *air*; with no bottom, no sides, no platform nor means of *terra connection* with planet Earth. Like a dingy bobbing around on confused seas, she felt completely unmoored. The feeling in her gut only intensified as the heli swooped down for a moment like an elevator in free-fall, then rose back upwards like a raptor in flight. They headed purposefully towards a colossal wall of mountains, moving noisily over a densely forested basin. Flying towards the west wall of the ski area's boundaries like an oversize bird pursuing its prey, Whitney's jaw dropped open at the sight of the massive, serrated peaks and endless snow-covered walls. Gazing in stunned silence out the heli's snow- dusted windows, couloirs, crevasses, ice walls stared back menacingly from all directions.

"Ho-leeeeee shit," Mason's voice chortled wildly above the roar of the helicopter. Never one to hold back, he shouted, "I mean, loooook at that!" he was pointing to a 50 -degree face of fresh powder below them, practically levitating. His left knee started jiggling, uncontrol- lably. "I'm totally stoked, man!" he announced breathlessly, brown messy ponytail peeking out from underneath his helmet. Karis glanced over to him, speaking into her headset. "Whatsup Mase, they don't have this in Montana?" she coolly goaded him, sly grin under her balaclava. Long, blonde braids framed her high cheek- boned face, hung down to her elbows. They glinted metallically in the light coming through the frosted windows. She was a ski goddess queen.

"Oh wow, wow, no dude! I mean, … yes! we've got it there, but I don't get to places like this too often—look at all this snow!" he groaned happily like a man wallowing in a huge pile of ten- thou- sand- dollar bills.

Ian stayed quiet and shrugged his shoulders, staring out the win- dows, seemingly nonplussed.

Whitney couldn't help herself; she squealed out automatically with him. "I'm toootally stoked too! This is soooooo awesome!" She didn't mention that this ride was making her mad with fear. Couldn't say that. Very bad form. She had visions of herself falling to her death on the side of the mountain, rolling down the vertical cliffs inside the smashed helicopter, pieces of debris buried in the snow, body parts missing…. Then what would her family do? Mom and dad? Robyn? She shuddered, trying to bat away the incessant internal dialogue she had with herself all the time. Guilt. Fear. Love and addiction of the sport.

They were nearing the top of the Storm Peak; their pilot swung the machine around and began descending with a lateral rocking motion that induced a wave of panic in her as he approached the narrow ridge. High wind was making the landing more difficult, they could feel the machine fighting for purchase as it pushed them around. Snow blew up in every direction, visibility was almost nil. He announced over their headsets, "I'm not touching down, we'll have to hover here. Get ready to move out. Have fun kids," he added dryly, lowering the machine.

Hurriedly, Mason scooted off the seat and out the door, followed by Karis, Whitney then Ian, bodies hunched over as they exited the swaying metal bird. Grabbing their skis from its exterior metal rack, they fought the blowing snow and harsh gusts of wind swirling around the heli's rotors in a frenzied blizzard. Making their way over to a natural platform on the ridge, they paused a moment to watch the machine rise above their heads, then dip away. It turned again and hovered in place, preparing for their descents. Whitney could see Shenti's head briefly as he lifted his camera lens, pointing it out the open window.

Breaking snow, they trudged across the narrow ridge, making deep indentations into the fresh, two- feet deep powder. The four stopped at the edge of a steep cornice. Whitney saw the cornice gave way to an open couloir roughly ten feet across, between two vertical rock cliffs. Over the last several days, each of them had painstakingly inspected the backcountry ski area maps, choreographing their line and aerials. Of course, nothing was like the real deal, when they were actually *on* the snow, where things could go wrong a thousand different ways, the worst being avalanche, injury, or even death. Usually the first run was a "get to feel the terrain" run. Feel the condition of the snow. Was it crusty? Heavy? Powdery? Was there ice? Hidden hazards? Rocks, holes, crevasses? Once they understood the terrain, all hell would break loose.

Poised nearly two thousand feet above tree line here, above Gnar Couloir, steep walls of snow and rock emptied out into an open basin. Looking down the mountain face, they could see Duncan and Trent standing next to the snow machines near a make-shift station. Coolers, food, beverages, camera gear, other ski equipment set on a portable table for the excursion. Alyn was already hiking up the open snowfield looking for the best perch to take photographs as they came down. This week, she was writing a feature about Ian for Ski Magazine and needed some killer shots of him in mid-air.

Ian waited impatiently for Trent to notify him when the heli was ready. His walkie-talkie crackled in the background. The heli continued hovering off the mountainside. It would give a little tail-wiggle to signal exactly when Shenti was ready for the skiers' descents.

They each clicked their skis and poles on. Turning their transceivers and GoPros on, they adjusted their goggles then spread several feet apart on the edge of the drop. Ian would go first, then the others, one at a time, in ten- minute intervals.

Show time.

Ian shot straight off the ridge's edge, off a ten-foot vertical cornice into the narrow couloir. Rocketing down the 50- degree slope at lightning speed, his compact body made seemingly effortless dips and turns every seventy yards or so, carving just enough to check his

speed from sending him into the cliff walls as powder flew up gracefully behind him, leaving a flawless snake-like seam trailing down
the fall line. Catching the kicker off a rock cliff, he barrel-rolled forward off the edge of it, dropping into a full-in double twisting somersault on the first aerial, down a forty -foot drop, body a human
slinky. Whitney exhaled, watching rapt. Ian was pure liquid grace,
super-human. It was no wonder he was predicted to be the national
extreme ski champion next year, she thought, marveling.

Dropping into the powder, nearly disappearing an instant, he
popped up and kept flying down, making smooth turns with relaxed
ease. Next, he barrel-rolled off another lip on the side of a snowbank in an aerial maneuver, this time a loop side-flip, rotating
around his central axis like a curled -up earthworm and landing in a
spray of powder. Snow shot up behind him as he continued down the
widening bowl, out of the chute. Alyn aimed her Nikon's foot long
lens straight at him as he flew by, snapping multiple digital images.
Skidding over towards Trent and Duncan, he came to a full stop.

Next, Karis shot off the ridge and dropped into the couloir, body
a spring-loaded panther pouncing atop its prey, attacking the fall-
line with explosive precision. Each turn was a smooth calculation
that appeared effortless in its exacting execution and downward
trajectory, deceptive act of core strength and supreme control. An
almost seamless arc of powder flew behind her as she approached
the first jump, the same kicker Ian had taken. Launching off its edge
with a simple back-layout, she met the lower slope seconds later with
a perfectly timed landing. Dipping deep into snow for a second, her
body bounced back up. She was off, heading straight down the couloir, parallel to Ian's line. Meeting the raised snowbank, she shot off
the edge of it, twisting her body into a full 360- degree rotation, landing with a "whump" on the snow. Crouched down in a tuck position,

she bounced up a split second later, pointing her skis straight down. For the remaining hundred yards of the run, she stayed in a tuck position, skidding to a stop at the bottom of the basin to meet the group. Trent briefly turned to acknowledge her, then lifted his binoculars up again, eyes fixed up the couloir, waiting for the next skier's descent.

With a loud "whoooo hoooo!" Mason leapt of the ridge, landing in a spray of powder. Twenty feet below, his strong legs aggressively turned near the edge of the rock cliff, then dropped another sixty feet down to blast another hard turn on the opposite side of the chute. Body crouched low and forward and expertly balanced, shoulders hunched forward, he planted poles precisely along the way. Flying down the narrow shaft in one sleek, fluid motion he approached the kicker and attacked the lip straight-on. Exploding off it, he propelled himself into a back-tuck- double, unfolding out just above the snowy slope. Disappearing into a white puff of powder, he popped up like a spring- loaded projectile and continued straight down. Making a quick check-turn before launching off a snowbank, he performed a front-tuck somersault, landing in a spray of snow. Body crouched, Whitney watched from above as he skied down the face, marveling at his power and strength. She could hear whoops of ecstasy as he approached the bottom of the basin.

Wow, she bit her lip, determined. These guys are really going after it. Setting the bar high. No holding back this morning that's for sure, she thought, taking a deep breath. Crouching down, she pushed her poles into the snow propelling her body off the ridge in one swift motion. She headed straight towards the middle of the couloir. Making fresh tracks into the snow, she avoided the other's previous lines and spent powder. If she stayed in the middle of the chute, she would have the benefit of soft and forgiving thigh-high snow, could make small, abbreviated turns only when necessary. Checking her speed along the way, she maintained her line in the center, making a few extra turns. Low in the powder, crouched aggressive, forward, she allowed gravity to pull her down. Though on the very edge of falling, it was a gutsy move, one that no one else had taken.

At the edge of the kicker now, she felt a flush of apprehension. She planned to do a loop side flip, rotating around her central axis, but quickly decided to do a simple back flip instead. With a slight speed check approaching the kicker, she launched herself off the lip, entering the back tuck position. Completing the aerial, she extended her body a split second before meeting the ground. Leaning a little too far back on her skis, she dug her heels into the snow. Propelling her core muscles up and forward, she got back over her skis. In control now, she pointed her tips down the mountain and made several turns along the cliff walls, preparing her next jump. At the snowbank, she would do a 360, just like Karis. Play it safe, nothing more.

Though she had fully recovered from the previous jump, she didn't want to push it. Hitting the snowbank, she performed the full rotation, landing in a low, crouched position. Poles planting automatically, she flew through the snow, powder slough obscuring her vision. Feeling good now, she rocketed down the lower half of the couloir into the bowl, carving some wide turns at the basin. She skidded to a stop by the rest of her team. Trent lowered his binoculars as she approached, pursed his lips downward. Turning away, he pulled a bottle of water from his pack, took a long sip.

The helicopter was still hovering above, Mason called over to her energetically. "Hey Whitney! Way to go! Nice run!" Karis and Ian glanced over briefly from where they were standing, then resumed talking in low voices. Whitney took some deep recovery breaths and popped off her skis. Smiling back at Mason, she made an imaginary

"U" sign with her right forefinger, flashed two middle fingers up in a peace sign, "You too." The helicopter was approaching them now, lowering itself onto the basin floor. Trent trudged over and spoke with some urgency to Ian by the snowmachines.

Ian and Karis carried their skis towards Mason and Whitney and shouted above the heli's roar, "Trent wants us to do one more run. Wind is picking up at the top- weather is deteriorating. He said we'll come back tomorrow, ski the West Face when the conditions are better." They all nodded affirmatively. Black clouds were rolling in at the top of the ridge, ominous. At this altitude weather was always volatile, never static. A constantly shifting entity with a life all its own, it invariably dictated the day.

"Okay," they concluded, submitting. They could do one more run, that was all.


Back at the inn, Whitney took off her damp outerwear, hung it up in the locker room near the front of the building. She went over to the bedroom she was sharing with Karis to take a shower. Karis was in the common area talking with Shenti, both looking over video footage from that morning. Whitney peeled off her damp, long underwear and climbed inside the stall, relieved to be underneath the jets of hot water bombarding her aching muscles and sore calves. Efficiently, she shampooed her hair then rinsed it. Turning off the water, she stepped out the tiled stall. Grabbed a white towel, wrapped it tightly around her muscular torso. She studied herself in the fogged-up reflection of the small bathroom's vanity mirror, assessing herself critically. Dark brown hair, a little naturally curly, shoulder length. Brown eyes, dark brows; a little thick. Probably should pluck them again, she thought, idly. Features; average. Fair skin, a few blemishes. Probably should wear some make-up to cover them up, too, she considered. She wasn't as photogenic as Karis, she sighed, a little dejectedly. Karis was tall and lithe, all legs and long, highlighted blond hair. High cheekbones, perfect teeth. Cameras loved her, she was a darling of the media. She; on the other hand, was considerably shorter. Compact, *sturdy*. She dried her hair. She needed to check in on Robyn. See how her doctor appointment went yesterday, talk to her mom about the visit. Exiting the bathroom, she picked up her cell phone and dialed home.

"Hi mom," she spoke anxiously. "How is Robyn?" She could hear her mom take a deep breath before answering.

"Dr. McClellan saw Robyn yesterday; she wants her to come in early next week for some blood tests, discuss how she's doing with the current medication. She said at some point we'll need to do some scans of her brain to look for abnormal tissue, though she said the tests don't always reveal them, which is concerning," her mom informed her. "The doctor wrote a refill for her medication; I'll pick it up at the pharmacy tomorrow. I'm just hoping she doesn't have another seizure again soon; I worry about it all the time. Your dad is picking her up from school tomorrow to take her to violin lessons. I need to be at the store." She added, "we have a huge order coming in, the employees need help putting everything on display." Whitney could hear ache in her voice, she sounded tired.

"Thanks mom, you know how much I appreciate everything," Whitney swallowed, anxiously. "I'll call tomorrow, let me know if anything happens. I'm always thinking about you guys, 24-7." She told her briefly, "we're filming in Silverton again tomorrow morning, the weather came in hard this afternoon, we had to quit before we finished our set." Guilt flooded her brain. She shouldn't be here at all, away from her daughter she thought, frustrated. Conflicting emotions plagued her every time she considered her options. She needed the money from this tour, it largely paid for Robyn's medical care. The co-pays were brutal; medicine, lab tests so expensive… being away from her daughter was stressful, it bothered her continuously. Only several months ago she was recruited by Consumco to be part of this elite team, she was still struggling to adjust to the constant travel and relentless training schedule. Her parents contributed to Robyn's medical expenses and took care of her at their house. They all worked together so she could make an honest stab at the World Championships.

It was an imperfect arrangement, but one they decided would be worth it. Opportunities like this didn't come around every day.

The rewards for winning WESC, the World Extreme Ski Championship, were huge. A million dollars if she took first place, plus income she would earn from product endorsements, royalties, appearances and film offers. Her parents vehemently encouraged her to pursue her quest, but then unexpectedly Robyn had started getting sick, seizures starting almost imperceptibly, six months ago. They were just at the beginning of figuring out what was going on, trying to muddle through the next episode, the next doctor appointment.

"Will you put Robyn on the phone for me?" Whitney asked her mom.

"Sure, honey." She could hear her calling Robyn's name. Robyn spoke into the receiver a few moments later.

"Hi sweetie, it's mommy. How are you?"

Good, mommy. I'm learning Twinkle-Twinkle Little Star on my violin. Miss Abrams says I'm doing really good," Robyn answered breathlessly.

"Good girl! I can't wait to hear it! Can you play it for me over the phone?"

"Yesss! I will do that!" Whitney could hear her say excitedly, "Nana, will you hold the phone for me? Mommy wants to hear me play my song."

"She's going to get her violin," her mother said, over the receiver.

"Thanks, mom. I appreciate it."

"Here she comes, she's back."

Whitney listened intently. The sound of the bow moving across the strings came across her cellphone, a high-pitched, somewhat wobbly strain resembling the nursery song meeting her ear. Robyn stopped playing, she spoke into the phone again. "Did you like my playing, mommy?"

"Of course! I loved it. You are doing great! I can't wait to see you. I'll be home by next week and I'll watch you play it some more, okay honey?"

"Oh-Kay mommy. I love you."

"I love you too, sweetie. Be good."

Whitney tapped off the phone, set it down, put on her pajamas.


Trent's cellphone buzzed in his pocket. Bent over a table, he was studying a topo map of the San Juan Range, for tomorrow's filming.

Theodore.

Pressing the accept button, he held the phone to his ear, already dreading the conversation. A call from Theodore Hunt was never good.

His clipped, flat voice came over the receiver. Chief operating officer for Consumco, Theodore presided over an in-house marketing empire with carte-blanche from the CEO to do whatever he thought necessary to promote whatever they deemed necessary. And right now, apparently, he thought Whitney needed to perform better. He was calling from his Frankfurt office.

"I just received today's footage from Shenti. We can't use her shots, they're no good. This is the third time we've had to discard them," he stated, bluntly.

Trent's stomach knotted, anticipating the next salvo.

Theodore stated coldly, "We're not paying all this money for a skier who can't produce." Trent closed his eyes painfully as Theodore's voice railed over him. Ice, devoid of soul. "You told us she was the best, so we recruited her. What the hell is going on?"

Trent shook his head slightly, fighting for air in a vacuum of darkness. Outer space. He loathed Theodore but kept that to himself, locked in a vault where no one would know, his job depended on it. He told the man testily, "I understand. I'll deal with it. Don't worry."

Theodore continued, "We recently acquired 4tress. It's the largest insurance company in the world. Our New York office is expanding the advertising budget by a hundred million dollars. Homeowners, auto, life, disability... the works." He leveled, "our campaign's slogan is: 'Life is full of risk, but 4tress will protect you.' We need better footage of Whitney hurling herself off a cliff. I think you get the idea."

"Yes," Trent swallowed. This was where he was supposed to interject, tell Theodore that people were human beings, that they didn't always perform on demand, no matter how great they were at their craft. But he didn't, because he was such a flawed human being.

19

No one disputed Theodore; the man was an automaton, placed solely in his position to dispatch orders without feeling nor remorse.

And that was why they hired *him*, for which he was compensated very highly for.

They had had these conversations before, numerous times.

"You need to send her to Belcic," Theodore stated flatly, then hung up.


Karis popped her head in the doorway, she saw Whitney sitting on her bed. "Hey—Trent wants to talk to you. I didn't know if you were still in here. He's in the common area with Shenti." She went over to her bed and laid down on her back, stared at the ceiling.

Whitney sighed, taking a deep breath. She had an uneasy feeling about this. She remembered Trent's expression when she had skied to the bottom of the basin on her first run this morning. He had been frowning, a bad sign. With some trepidation, she left the room to talk to him.

He was in the breakfast area, hunched over Shenti's computer examining video footage from that morning. Shenti looked up and nodded at her, Trent straightened up and motioned to her. "Whitney, can we talk for a few minutes? he gestured towards the ski storage room door. They went over to it, he opened the wooden door and stepped inside, she followed him. He shut the door quickly, behind them.

"Do you want to tell me what's going on?" he stared at her intently, metallic gray eyes boring a hole in hers. Face tan and ruddy from years in the sun, with light-brown, short hair peppered with gray flecks, decades of skiing, climbing and cycling had given him a chiseled, athletic appearance.

"What do you mean…? What's going on," she stammered, uncomfortably. God, he intimidated her. She felt like a rabbit trapped in this tightly enclosed space, filled with ski equipment and damp outerwear. All the oxygen in the room suddenly evaporating.

"Do not waste my time and try to bullshit me, Whitney. I watch everything. I see everything. Ever since we started the tour at Crested Butte, I've been watching you hold back. Today you hesitated on the first jump, slowed down before the kicker- all those short turns down the chute. What the fuck?" he drilled her, harshly.

Stung by his words, her mouth went dry, anxiety engulfed her.

"…I, uh, I…I was nervous…just a little afraid," she stammered. There. She said it. Her mouth turned down, she looked at her feet, stared at the dust covered concrete floor. She waited apprehensively for his reaction.

"That's what I saw, Whitney. I saw you were afraid," he growled, pursing his lips. His brows furrowed. He took a deep breath, trying not to lose his temper. "Why?" he asked her, exhaling. Christ, now he had to be a goddamn psychotherapist too.

She exhaled; her voice wavered.

"My daughter…"

"Your daughter? Really?" he didn't compute.

"My daughter. She's six years old, she's ill. I don't want her to lose me, too. She already lost her dad."

"You're afraid of dying? Of getting hurt, is that it?" he frowned, chewed his lip, considering.

"Yes. Kyle died before she was born. Broke his neck in a moto-cross accident. His parents always tell me they hate what I'm doing, they're afraid she'll be left without a mother."

"Got it, Whitney."

She stared balefully at him, dejected.

He shot at her, "You are going to have to come to terms with this quickly, Whitney. I'm not here to hold your hand and help you through your problems. You have a lot of talent--strength, technique, showmanship-- but it's not enough if you can't put it all out there, every time, without holding back. You will not win the World Championship, or even the Nationals, for that matter, with *fear* standing in your way. That's a fact." He paused, staring at her. Evidently, he was waiting for her response.

"I hear you. I understand. I will try to manage it better," she pleaded. She didn't tell him about the helicopter rides. How they had started to terrify her.

"You are twenty-six years old."

"Yes," she squirmed.

"You'll be too old for this before long. Karis is twenty-one, Mason and Ian both twenty-two. You have another three, four years in the game. Maybe."

She chewed her lip, trying to suppress tears. He was really coming on heavy-duty. Ripping her a new one, as Kyle used to say.

Trent was not interested in having any losers. Period. Consumco paid him a lot of money to produce winners, and he had worked too hard, sacrificed too much to get to this level of coaching to let this little hayseed prevent him from earning his bonuses, salary. Some people in the ski industry might question his tactics, but he always *produced*.

"There is someone you can see who can fix your problem," he told her, measured.

"Who? What do you mean?" she frowned.

"A doctor. He has a simple procedure that eliminates the sensation of fear. You can talk to him about it."

Whitney stared at Trent aghast.

"You want me to….to have a…." she stuttered, outraged. She didn't even know what to call it.

"A procedure. That's all."

"What do they do?" her brows furrowed, distressed.

"You talk to the doctor, I'll give you his number. His name is Belcic. Give him a call," Trent replied curtly, handing her a piece of paper with a name scrawled on it.

"I can't do *that*," she hissed at him, repulsed, reaction visceral, from deep inside.

"Your choice. Think about it." He leaned forward and stared at her. "Obviously, you will not mention our conversation or anything relating to it, to *anybody*, ever. If you do, I will have you removed from this team faster than your head can spin off your vertebrae. Understand?" His eyes narrowed warningly.

She swallowed. Taking the folded piece of paper, she shoved it in her pants pocket.

"Yes."

She looked at him defiantly then asked bluntly, "Did the others have this…this procedure?"

He stood motionless for a moment, then turned on his heel and wordlessly left the room.

She slipped out the door after him and walked shaken, back to her room. Karis was still laying on the bed, scanning her cell phone. Probably reading all her press and looking at the photos of herself, she thought miserably. Now she had a massive headache forming at the back of her skull and her temples were starting to throb. Grabbing some Tylenol from her travel bag, she swished them down with a glass of water.

She and Karis had been rivals for several years on the circuit, Karis had risen from the ranks, the girl wonder from the Roaring Fork Valley, not far from Aspen. Beautiful, aggressive, she was a great skier who appeared utterly fearless on the steeps, competing against her in Colorado and the other western states. For the past three ski seasons Karis had consistently scored near the top, close to her. She had a history of comparing herself to Whitney and undermining her in the press. Now, they were holed up with each other, vying for a single spot at the World Extreme Ski Competition. The circumstances were predictably screwed up. Karis glanced over at her. "What did Trent want?" she asked curiously.

"Nothing much. Just wanted to talk about my strategy for tomorrow," she lied, quickly.

Karis sniffed. "*Your strategy*. How about, say, ten less turns?" she sneered mockingly, then turned on her side, away from Whitney.

*Stay calm. Don't let her get under your skin….*

"Listen Karis, I've got a terrible headache, I really have to go to bed now," Whitney told her tiredly, getting under the covers. She couldn't take it right now, didn't have the energy. She needed to unwind for a while, disappear under the hotel blankets and too-flat pillow after that horrible conversation with Trent. Shutting her eyes, she took some slow, deep breaths, then imagined herself walking alone along an empty beach with gentle waves licking her toes.... On soft sand.... somewhere in the Caribbean....

Mercifully, Karis didn't say anything more, she just got up and left the room, bored. Whitney tried not to berate herself, but it was difficult. A perfectionist, she always tried to please her coaches, do her best. The verbal exchange with Trent had left her feeling devastated. She would just have to do better.

Tomorrow will be a new day, she told herself silently. *I'll show him I can handle this.*

# CHAPTER 2
# SILVERTON

Whitney got up early that morning before any of her teammates, she hadn't slept particularly well last night and her conversation with Trent still lingered in her head like a bad hangover from the previous day. Groggy, still in her flannel pajamas, she walked into the communal dining room and made a cup of instant coffee, trying to clear her mind. Some plain granola sat inside a clear glass container on the buffet table with a stack of white porcelain bowls beside it, she helped herself to one and scooped some granola into it, then grabbed a small carton of milk in the mini-frig nearby. Pouring the milk over her cereal, she sat down at a square wooden table and started eating, already preoccupied with how she would approach today's skiing.

Still dark outside, the room was quiet and peaceful now, no other guests were awake yet. Unfolding her Silverton backcountry ski area map, she spread it out on the table. Studying the terrain, she examined the topography closely, calculating her best route down the West Wall, off Storm Peak. From what she could tell, the West Wall was a 50 -degree steep that had a series of huge rock buttresses jutting out of it, in no remarkable pattern. Halfway down the face, it appeared the jagged rock formations funneled the skier into one single narrow chute, named "Waterfall." Everyone would have to drop into it; there was no other alternative way down. Based on the map, the best spot for her aerial would be at the very top of the run, before she entered it.

At the base of the chute, the run continued through a forested glade, eventually dropping into a quarter-mile gully. The gully led to a narrow cat-track that took them to an open area where the heli would likely be waiting for them. She took another sip of coffee and made some mental notes.

Getting up to refill her cup, she left the dining area and wandered over to the inn's front door to look outside. Peeking through the worn, leaded glass windows she could see that more snow had fallen last night, it glowed luxuriously in the approaching dawn light. Already, Duncan was busy moving around outside, his lanky form waxing and sharpening their skis beside the front porch. Whitney noticed he would pause periodically to examine an open, red spiral notebook balanced on the porch railing and make notes on it while he worked. A meticulous technician, he kept a personalized chart for each team member providing their weight, height, boot size and binding release settings so their equipment was safely adjusted and ready for use.

Frequently, their skis would become scraped and gouged by sharp rocks and tree stumps that poked from underneath the snow. Right away, he would fill the gash with p-tex, then sand and smooth the bottoms. He sharpened their edges, waxed their skis, repaired their boots if they became damaged, and fixed whatever needed fixing. The performance equipment they used was designed to take a beating and protect them, it did its job. Each team member traveled with at least four pairs of skis and three pairs of boots for different types of conditions. Deep powder required a super-wide, flexible ski that could float on top the snow easily, icy crud and packed snow required a stiffer, all mountain ski that gripped the slopes with its metal edges. Consumco paid for everything, and it had to appear clean and sparkling for the constant promotional shots they took throughout the day. Duncan was continuously wiping things down between runs.

Whitney grabbed her blue down parka from the ski locker and went outside to join him. She sat down on the entryway's top step, idly finishing her coffee and munching an apple. Duncan wore a faded orange and black canvas parka with a "Steamboat" logo across its top lapel and a brown, wool beanie over his tousled sandy-blonde hair. She watched his breath freeze in the frigid air as he examined one of her skis.

"Didja like those Volkls yesterday?" he asked her affably, glancing up at her.

"I did. Really nice ski. Which pair should I use today?" she posed, considering.

"I think you should go with the Volkls again. We got more powder last night. They should work great on the West Wall," he replied, authoritatively.

"Sounds good."

Over the last several months she had gotten to know Duncan and enjoyed chatting with him when she had the opportunity. From Steamboat, Colorado, he had worked at the local ski shops there since junior high. A real mountain rat just like her, owners had hired him to set bindings, outfit customers with ski equipment, soothe young children with harried parents on vacation, be a general go-fer at their shop. Local ski teams relied on him to repair skis and boots, organize races, lend a helping hand on a volunteer basis.

28

Simply put, he would say, "I just fell into the life- I showed up." Summers, he worked at a fly- fishing store in Steamboat guiding out of state tourists on angling trips along the Blue River. An occasional construction job in town helped him stay flush until ski season started and he could resume work as a ski technician, again. He told Whitney he was single and hoped to live in Steamboat for as long as possible, he loved the place.

"Hey, while you're here, let's fit those new Rossi's for you," he suggested helpfully.

"Good idea," she agreed, nodding. Quickly, he went back inside the inn and retrieved the boots from the storage locker, unbuckling their metal clips. She stood up, then slid her left foot into one as he held it in place for her. She grasped the porch railing for balance with her other hand.

"Push your heel all the way back, that's it…" he told her. "Now push your calf forward." He snapped her toe clip closed, asking her, earnestly, "Can you wiggle your toes alright?" Whitney wiggled her toes up and down. "Yep, they're good," she told him. "Okay, let's do the rest now," he said, adjusting the remaining clips, snapping them down. "Does your foot feel comfortable?" he asked, adding, "we might need a custom insole for these, but let's see how you do with them today, first." Unbuckling the other boot, she stuck her right foot inside it, he made the same careful adjustments. With a chuckle, she told him, "I remember doing this for our own customers at our ski shop. My parents started me out with boot service, then put me on ski rental, then retail sales. I did inventory and all that kind of stuff, through high school."

"Your folks have a store in Crested Butte, right?" Duncan recalled. "The one on old main street? I remember that shop, from last time I was there. Nice store."

"It's across from Secret Stash Pizza. Olson Outfitters."

"Right…" he tilted his head up and smiled. Whitney asked him, curious, "did you ever do any ski racing, in Steamboat?"

"I competed in slalom on the Nastar circuit for a few years," he replied easily, "but never professionally. Didn't have that kind of talent, not like you guys. Never had the inclination to hurl myself down a mountain and off a forty- foot cliff. That's some crazy shit."

Whitney grinned, "I joined a local ski team in grade school, started out with slalom. In junior high, I wanted to do freestyle, so I switched to skiing with twin tips and spent all my free time at the terrain parks with the snowboarders, learning their tricks. We had a trampoline in our back yard, and I used to spend hours on it with my little foam skis doing somersaults and back flips. It wasn't until my senior year in high school that I discovered free skiing."

"You certainly did, I'll attest to that," Duncan commented. "Say, how's your daughter? She doing okay?"

Whitney sighed, contemplating, "Unfortunately, she's been having seizures more often, they seem to be getting worse. Our pediatrician says it might be epilepsy, but we need to run a lot more tests. I worry about her all the time, to be honest."

"Sorry to hear that, I hope they figure out what's going on, soon," he replied, sympathetically.

"Thanks, I appreciate it," Whitney told him, keeping her new boots on. "I better get inside and get ready to go. Thanks for all your help."

"You bet." He stood up again and began sharpening the edges of Ian's skis, wishing they could talk for a while longer. He liked Whitney, she was interesting, neat.

Whitney clomped back inside with her boots on, she almost bumped into Ian, coming out of the ski locker carrying his duffel full of gear.

"Hey Ian," she greeted him, genially.

"Hey," he answered neutrally, brushing past her. Heading over to the lounge area, he sat down to put his ski boots on. Black ear buds stuck inside his ears, he seemed completely unaware of his surroundings, lost in Ian world; with only minimal connection to planet earth and all the people and things on it. Whitney wondered what he was listening to. Mozart? Grunge? A motivational speaker? Who knew? His jet black mohawk stood straight up in pointy spikes, four thin silver hoop earrings hung from small to large down his earlobes. Upside- down silver arrows dangled off the bottom lobe. Slanted parallel lines along both front clavicles in the style of a Maori warrior peeked out from his neon- green and black pullover shirt. The black tatoos on his deeply tanned skin reminded Whitney of Tutankhamun, the Egyptian boy-God.

Alyn bounded energetically into the lounge and rapidly snapped a series of pictures of him with her Nikon. He barely looked up.

There was a large, jarring clatter as Mason entered the lounge and dumped ski his boots on the floor. He sat down to put them on. "Man, I did NOT sleep last night, that bed was hard as shit," he announced loudly, to no one in particular. Rubbing his eyes, he asked, "Hey-anybody have any sunscreen? I need some." Pulling his hair into a pony-bun, he snapped a scrunchie around it.

31

Karis materialized, carrying her equipment. Looking stylishly sleek and modelesque in her brand- new silver and white Spyder ski jacket, an expensive number that probably cost well over eight-hundred dollars, they shuffled into the Sprinter, taking their usual seats. Shenti in the very back, squeezed in with his equipment, and Duncan shotgun, as usual. As Trent drove them over to the heli-pad, Whitney gazed out the windows at the old saloons and hotels, restaurants and backcountry outfitters, admiring their western, fron-tier-style facades. Most were built at the turn of the century, when a gold and silver rush brought thousands of miners to the hard-scrab-ble, rugged outpost. She could totally imagine frontier women in long dresses and petticoats riding down the main street of town in covered wagons, cowboys in leather chaps.

A high lonesome whistle from the Silverton -Durango steam train echoed off in the distance, its plaintive sound a melancholy remnant from a by-gone era.

The weather had notably improved, a high-pressure system had moved in overnight, pushing away clouds and frigid temperatures. The forecast was for clear skies and only light wind. Because the West Wall was on the back side of Storm Peak, considerably further from the ski area's base, Trent, Duncan and Alyn would join the skiers on the helicopter ride over. It would deposit them at the bottom of the run first, then take the skiers up to the top of the ridge.

Try as she might to ignore her apprehension and anxiety about the ride, Whitney was unable to tamp it down completely. Her heart raced and her skin perspired as she looked out of the windows from her seat, the vast space between her and the snow-covered moun-tainside an almost unbearable sensation. She closed her eyes and inhaled and exhaled slowly, forcing herself to think of something else. Counted to twenty, then counted backwards, trying to disassociate from the actual act of being there…. When had this started to happen? she fretted, inwardly. Helicopters hadn't bothered her in the past, when she had skied in the Selkirks and Canadian Rockies, near Revelstoke. It had started when Robyn got sick, she realized, thinking back. Clenching her hands and teeth she muttered prayers to God as they descended towards a flat plateau near the trees, swaying buoyantly on the way down.

Soon as they touched ground, Trent, Alyn and Duncan exited the door and moved away from the burly machine. Lifting off again, the pilot headed up to the top of the peak. She thought of her daughter and how much she wished she could be just home with her right now, helping Robyn with her seizures and going to the doctor with her, instead of leaving that difficult task to her mom and dad.

The pilot interrupted her thoughts, speaking into the headset, "Okay folks, we're about to land. Check your gear, we'll see you at the bottom." Whitney gripped her seat, shuddering inwardly. She closed her eyes.

Mason and Ian both scooted out first, followed by Karis and then Whitney. Ducking down, they grabbed their skis from the exterior rack and began trudging across the narrow ridge, rapidly. Shenti stayed back, video equipment at the ready for their first shots down the mountainside. The helicopter rose again, hovering over the edge of the steep face, waiting.

They paused and stood for a moment on the ridge, turned their avalanche transceivers on. Surveying the expanse, they each selected their line down, plan of attack. The San Juan range was a regal cathedral of snow -covered spires and cliffs, rocky pinnacles, treed gullies and glades. Whitney inhaled deeply, taking in its magnificent grandeur. It was a place of transcendent beauty, an other-worldly realm. She had always loved the sensation of standing atop these mountains in the West, something so profoundly gratifying about it. If someone asked her why she risked her life to go there, she would try to explain that the scenery was part of the raison d'etre, itself. She could lose herself and her daily worries of life in the simple act of swishing down the mountain, absorbed solely in the snow and its every facet. The texture, bumps, dips, moguls, knolls and drops were a joyous playground of nature that communicated to her with every turn. A tango of love and pure joy. All else fell aside. Skiing was pure freedom.

Whitney watched as Karis dropped into the maze of protruding rocks and buttresses, her body flashing down between them in a series of deep dips and turns, swiftly disappearing in a cloud of deep powder, then reemerging to attack the next turn before skiing into them. Caroming between those lethal features before moving on to the next line, she effortlessly launched off a small cliff executing a single back flip then landed squarely on top her skis, legs slightly apart. Popping out of the landing, she leaned aggressively forward and kept rocketing downward, heading towards the chute. Rock wall on both sides converged to a narrow opening, extreme precision was necessary to enter its steep chasm. Crouching low, she made a quick kick turn into it, then dropped down further, out of sight.

Whitney looked up towards the helicopter, the sound of its rotors echoing off the mountainside. Shenti's lens was pointed straight at Karis. Mason was groaning in apparent ecstasy as she descended. "Whhhoaaah, ooooaaah, look at that!" upper body swaying, bobbing back and forth with her every turn. Inwardly, Whitney wondered if Karis had done the medical procedure that Trent had alluded to last night. It could well be possible, she thought, suspiciously. Ian's gaze followed Karis, nodding as she exited the chute and swished down to her next aerial, a single helicopter 360 with legs in a crisscross position. A poof of light powder shot up around her as she landed once again on top her skis, kept flying. Now she was in the trees, form weaving between the tall, snow- covered pines. Every turn around them was executed with lightning-fast movements. Whitney no longer could see where she was, she had disappeared far down into the shadowed gully.

Ian turned to Whitney and gave her a sharp nod. Trent had just radioed up to him, she was next. A tinge of apprehension washed over her body, concerns about Robyn's medical problems and last night's exchange with Trent both weighing on her mind. She scooted to the edge of the ridge and dropped in, body crouched and spring-loaded, sinking deep into the powder as it met her thighs, engulfed her torso. Shoulders forward, knees loose, hips rotating, she flowed easily down the fall-line, making only light pole plants along the way. At the first rock buttress, she carved a single turn and moved beyond it, ready to meet the next one as it loomed before her. This one was much larger, but she rotated her weight and swung alongside it effortlessly, pointing her tips down. Now she was preparing for her jump. She would do a front one-and-a-half, adding a twist before the landing. That should up the ante, she thought, inwardly. With a perfect in-run into the kicker, she flawlessly performed all the elements of the aerial and landed atop her skis with a solid, balanced whump.

Re-engaging with the fall-line, she cruised straight down, poised to enter the chute. Heading into the funnel, the rock headwalls closed in on her. With a quick tailslide, she kick- turned down into the opening. Instantly, she felt the back of her ski scrape rock. Her ski released from her boot, she was launched into the air. She completely

lost control. No purchase, no contact with the ground, she was falling, falling, falling… her poles flew away from her, completely air
borne. She felt her body touch snow and her other ski eject, she was
catapulting down the near vertical chute. Shutting her eyes tightly,
she tucked her head between her legs, hearing her helmet hitting
rock…. Now she was tumbling, accelerating, going faster and faster,
boots scraping against more rock, ripping the metal clips right off
them. *She was going to die.* Internally, she said goodbye to her mom
and dad, her little Robyn. *I'm sorry, I'm sorry, I'm so very sorry*, she
told them silently, submitting. A lifetime spent on the mountains
had finally caught up to her. She would be maimed, paralyzed, anni-
hilated by what she loved most.

She felt her body come to a miraculous stop. A soft, forgiving
cradle caught her balled up form. She was swinging up and down,
up and down… bouncing within it like an elastic band. Something
encircling her legs and torso was holding her in place like a fireman's
trampoline, too. She opened her eyes in disbelief, shocked to find
that *she was still alive.* Could move her legs, arms, her hands…

A small group of stunted pines had aborted her fall. She was dangling, suspended on the face of the mountain, still swaying slightly
up and down. Unbelievable! She touched her face, flapped her arms
around and kicked her legs. Seemingly, they were all intact. Did she
have internal injuries though? Was she bleeding anywhere? Had she
suffered a concussion? Weirdly, she felt okay, other than the fact she
was in profound shock, almost in a fever-dream. This was the worst
crash of her entire career, bar none. Until this very moment, she had
not truly comprehended how bad a crash could be.

Mason and Ian were skiing down to her from above, they had
located her poles and were bringing them over. "Holy shit, Christ
all mighty that was fucking epic!" Mason shouted at her. "Are you

okay?!" Skiing towards her, he reached out for her hand in the pines. "What a total yard-sale! I got one of your poles. "Let me help you out," he insisted, scooting up next to her.

Ian handed her her other pole, then skied further downhill to search for her ejected skis. He located them at the base of the chute, one stuck inside a tree well, the other fifty yards away, half-buried in a two-story shrund of snow. Gathering them, he took off his own skis and hiked back uphill to Whitney and Mason. Both extricated her from the tangled branches and helped her back onto the precariously steep slope. Propping her up, she clicked into her ski bindings and shakily, awkwardly, balanced against them. Once she was back in her skis, she and Mason side-slipped slowly downhill in tandem while Ian hiked beside them, trying not to pitch forward and tumble, himself. Ian announced, I called Trent and ski patrol, they'll get a snow machine here soon as possible, get you to the helicopter ASAP."

"I think I'm okay," Whitney announced breathlessly, voice sounding oddly far away, uncertain. She had seriously gotten the wind knocked out of her sails.

"No, no, you've got to be checked out for injuries right away," Mason told her, agitated.

They escorted her down to the very bottom of the chute. Ian snapped his skis back on, Whitney skied gingerly beside them, making slow, careful turns. Getting to a more level spot near the glade, they waited with her until a ski patrol wearing a bright red and black coat appeared twenty minutes later. He towed a rescue litter behind his snow machine. Racing over to them, he called tersely, "How is she?"

"I'm alright, I'm okay," Whitney told him. "Took a hellacious fall, but I'm okay," she tried to reassure him.

"You need to get checked out at the ski-patrol station," he stated insistently, preparing to take her back on the litter.

"Really, I'm alright. I'll ride back with you, on your back seat. I'm not lying on that sled," she told him, shaking her head "no". Internally, she was absolutely terrified by the experience. It would take her awhile to recover, she had been rocked to the core. In those horrifying moments of falling, she had seen her own demise, seen Robyn's sad face, realizing her mother was gone from this earth.

"Okay then," the ski patroller answered, conceding. Strapping her skis and poles onto the litter, he helped her onto the back seat of the snowmobile and climbed back atop the machine. Gunning the engine, they took off in a flash of speed, heading to the bottom of the gully. The helicopter was already whirling its blades, waiting for her. She flew back to the base with the rest of her team.

"Follow my finger," the EMT held his forefinger in front of her pupils, tracking each of her eyes. She followed it back and forth. "Okay. Tell me, what is the date today?"

"January 27, 2022."

"Good."

"Who is the president of the United States?"

"Joe Biden."

"What is your full name and birthdate?"

"Whitney Ann Olson, May 22, 1996."

"Good. I need you to take a deep breath. Then I want you to cough. He used a stethoscope and listened to her lungs. "Do you have any pain?" He was worried about broken ribs, among other things.

"No, I feel okay."

"Let's check for bruises," he said to her, intently. The nearest hospital was almost a hundred miles away, he would do a perfunctory examination before he sent her away on a helicopter. She seemed to be fine, but he had to be sure. "Let's have you remove some clothes; you can lay on the cot. I'll come back in a few minutes, and we'll have a look." He handed her light sheet, then walked out of the first aid room, closing the door behind him.

Whitney unbuckled her ski boots and pulled them off. Seated on a hard chair in a room filled with emergency medical equipment, she looked around at all the bandages and braces. A blood pressure monitor and cardiac defibrillator sat on top a cabinet counter along with a bunch of other papers and miscellaneous objects. She laid down on the cot. The EMT came back in. "Let's take a look, shall we?" he said. Examining her skin, he found no major bruising except for a few unimpressive darker spots along her shins. "Were these here before today?" he asked her, concerned.

"I think so," she answered, looking down at them. They were pressure bruises, where her shins met her boots.

"I see a light bruise on the top of your right thigh." He palpated it. "Do you feel any pain?"

"No, not much, really."

He had her sit up and then did a series of response tests along her body with his rubber- tipped reflex hammer.

Afterwards, he informed her, "Everything appears to be normal. You were extremely lucky today, Whitney, I must say. You need to take it easy for a while. Stay here for a few hours and we'll keep an eye on you. If you are feeling alright, you can go back to your hotel and rest. But if anything changes at all, if you become dizzy, have vision problems, blurring, trouble with balance, any type of pain or headache, shortness of breath, blood in your urine, you must call us immediately, okay?" he handed her a bottle of water. "Stay hydrated and call me later tonight, after you leave, just to check in. I'll give you my card."

She replied, "Okay, I will."

"Can I ski tomorrow?" she followed, anxiously.

"I don't recommend it. I think you should take a day or two off, just to be careful. If you have any kind of medical issues, we don't want to push it. If anything develops over the next day or so, we can address it. You shouldn't risk skiing too soon."

Whitney fell silent, sighing. "I get it," she replied glumly. Inwardly, she was relieved, she wasn't ready to get back on the snow yet.

"Sorry to say," he looked at her sympathetically.

Then he blushed, slightly, "by the way, would you do me a favor?" he countered, "Could you autograph this for me? I would love that," he told her, pulling out a SKI magazine from one of the counter drawers and handing it to her. There was a picture of her on the April 2021 cover.

"I would be delighted to," she answered him, mustering a grin.

"Hey, thanks a lot. It's not every day that I get to hang with the top extreme skier in the country in own my examination room. I can't wait to give this to my son. He's a huge fan," he added, a little bashfully.

"Do you have a Sharpie? A pen?" she asked him, politely.

"Oh yeah," he shuffled some papers around and found one, then handed it to her.

"What's your son's name?"

"Mikah"

"How old is he? Does he ski?"

"He's twelve, and oh my God, does he ski. We live up here, he wants to be just like you and Ian. A star."

"I'm not sure I recommend it," she told him, half-jokingly.

Signing it in scrolled cursive, she wrote: Mikah, follow your heart and follow your star, ski the big mountains, ski the big gnar! Good luck, Whitney Olson.


Already three o'clock in the afternoon, Whitney hung around the ski-patrol building bantering with other ski-patrollers as they came and went from the building. By five o'clock, she decided to go back to the inn and get something to eat. Someone offered her a ride there, but she declined, preferring to walk back herself and get some air. She called Duncan, just to check in. "Hey, I'm doing fine. You still out on the slopes?"

"No, we're back. My god, how are you doing? You okay?" he exhaled, worriedly.

"Yeah, they checked me out. All systems functioning," she told him, ruefully. "By any chance can you swing over here to ski-patrol and bring me my snow boots? They're in the ski locker and I need them to walk back over."

"Sure thing, no problem. I'll run them over there right now."

"Thanks. Could you also tell Trent that I'm absolutely fine, I plan on skiing, day after tomorrow."

A pause.

"Uh, sure thing, I'll give him that message," he hurriedly grabbed his coat and left to go meet her.

Arriving shortly, he walked back to the inn with her, carrying her skis. The two-story inn was only a half-mile away from the ski-patrol building, down the main street. She discussed the crash with him, describing the event in painstakingly, excruciating detail. "I don't see how this could have happened," she told him, ruminating, "My settings were set at 11, right? The ski shouldn't have popped off."

Listening intently, he frowned.

"What could have happened?" she pressed him, further.

He took a long breathe, chewed his lip. "Honestly, I don't know. I mean, the binding was set at 11, it shouldn't have released under normal circumstances. But then again, if the back of the ski impacted the rock wall that hard, it could have… I suppose," his brows furrowed, thinking.

"Will you check the settings on them when we get back?" she asked him, anxiously.

"We'll check them right now," he stopped walking and stood still. Holding her skis in front of him, he peered closely at the bindings. A shadow darkened across his face, he looked perplexed.

"What's wrong?"

"They're set at a 4."

Something had gone very wrong. He could not have done this, he agonized, confusedly.

"I swear on a stack of Holy Bibles I did *not* do this. I did not," he stated, adamantly. Resolute.

Whitney stared off into space, barely noticing the buildings or the vehicles, the people walking down the street with their families and their friends, laughing and talking. She felt ambushed.

*Someone* had done this to her.

# CHAPTER 3
# SILVERTON

Trent sat across from Whitney at the breakfast table, his face was grim, his mouth in a frown. "How are you feeling today?" he asked her, directly. They were alone.

"I feel fine. Really. I'm fine."

"I looked at the footage. You're lucky to be alive," he stated flatly, not mincing words.

"I realize that," she exhaled heavily. He was studying her, eyes boring a hole into hers.

"We're done here in Silverton, we finished filming yesterday," he informed her, succinct. "We'll be leaving tomorrow, going to Summit County for the next three weeks to do more training. You should go home and see your daughter. I think it's a good idea. Clearly, this is all becoming too stressful for you to handle."

"Did you talk to Duncan?" Whitney said, outraged. This was not fair. Not fair, not fair, not fair, she fumed, utterly pissed.

"He came and talked to me yesterday, Whitney."

"Someone changed those release settings on both my skis!" she spat, in a torrent of anger.

"Listen, I don't know what happened, Whitney. Mistakes happen; you had a terrible fall. It happens. We're in the business of terrible falls, Whitney. That's why you have to be a hundred percent on your game." He went on, grimacing, "We talked about how you have been holding back with your skiing the other day; that is precisely what can cause these types of accidents. A slight hesitation, a miniscule change in your reflexes- those things will really mess you up. I want you to go home and take some time off," he said with finality.

"That's it? You're not going to try to figure out what happened with my bindings? *Who changed them?*" she shot back, angrily.

"Go home. Take some time to regroup."

She shook her head and dropped her shoulders in defeat, totally frustrated. This wasn't right.

Trent stood abruptly and took a deep breath. "I'm just glad you're okay, Whitney. We'll talk next week." He strode out of the dining area and went outside to help Duncan move all their equipment into the Sprinter.

Distressed, Whitney sat and stared at the walls, stewing. Heart pounding, she chewed her lip, trying to calm down. She took some deep breaths.

Karis ambled in the room and walked over to the buffet. Taking a container of yogurt out of the refrigerator, sat down across from her. "Sorry about your fall yesterday. I feel terrible for you, it must have been terrifying," she offered disingenuously, eyes blinking with an insincere gaze.

"Do not pull your "make-Whitney-feel-crazy-bullshit on me," Whitney replied warningly. Irritated, she stood up and bussed her table, departing the room. Typical Karis tactics. She tried to ignore them.

Karis pulled out her cellphone and scrolled down her screen, nonplussed. Looking up momentarily, she called after her, "By the way, Alyn has decided to do a feature on me while we're in Summit, she figured you'd be away." She glanced back down at her screen, ate a spoonful of yogurt absently.

Whitney walked back to their room to pack, enraged. Dammit. When had Alyn spoken with Karis? she fumed, grinding her teeth. Karis had come back to the inn late last night, maybe they had talked then. Anyway, there was nothing she could do about it right now. Just go home and chill. Take some time off, be with Robyn.

Oh, the glamour and glitz of fame, she shook her head, sighing ironically. She had almost fucking died, and now this.

Alyn tapped the door and popped her head into the room. "Um, Whitney, do you think we could talk for a moment?" she asked, carefully.

Whitney whirled around, a bit warily. Now what...

"Uh, sure. Where do you want to talk?" she asked Alyn.

"Here is fine. May I come in?" she countered. Entering, she sat down on Karis's bed, laptop by her side. Lean, willowy frame, she was in her mid-thirties and of Chinese- American descent. With almond shaped blue eyes and straight black hair cut in a sleek, shoulder length A-line, she reminded Whitney of a swan. Perfect bangs framed her graceful, long neck.

"I'm sorry about that horrendous crash yesterday. Thank God you're okay. Shenti showed me some video, it was unspeakable. How are you doing, now?" she inquired, levelly.

"I'm okay, just dealing with the aftermath, you know," Whitney answered, sighing. "Trent told me to go home, take some time off, regroup." She added bitterly, "my bindings were pooched. Set at a 4.

**45**

I have no idea how that happened. They ejected when I entered the chute, when the tail of my left ski smacked the rock."

"I saw it on the footage."

"Yeah, it was a nightmare. Listen, I have to get going, finish packing," she told Alyn, upset.

"Whitney, I did get some fantastic shots of you at the top of the run, and of your first aerial," Alyn reached out, cautiously. "And I'll use them for my next promo piece when we get back together in two weeks. It's just that I'll be in staying in Summit County with Karis and it's a convenient opportunity for us to finish her feature for Alpine Magazine. I have a deadline."

"I understand, I get it." Whitney shrugged and continued packing.

Alyn stood up with her laptop, departing the room. Well, she tried to hand the young woman an olive branch…these athletes were so temperamental….

Whitney paused packing, watching Alyn leave. Maybe she should get her hair cut like hers, when she got back to Crested Butte, she thought. She dismissed the idea right away though; her hair was too frizzy for the cut. *Bummer.*


Leaving Silverton, the ride back down on highway 550 to Ouray was equally as treacherous as the drive up, they proceeded slowly on the narrow, winding turns. The snowplows that ran up and down the steep pass all night had thrown hard, icy chunks along the sides of the highway, making it even more challenging to navigate. CDOT, the Colorado Department of Transportation, made herculean efforts to keep the pass open, clearing the avalanches and slides that invariably crashed down onto the road and covered the highway all winter. Still, it was like sliding down a luge on a white ribbon of death.

As they approached the last steep hairpin down to the deep box canyon, Whitney turned to Mason, sitting beside her, humming an indistinct tune, mentioning to him, "I remember when I was in seventh grade, my family camped at Amphitheater Campground for a few days. It stormed like crazy. We had to sleep in the car, lightning was everywhere. It was wild." She pointed to the campground, now buried completely under snow, mountains rising straight up from it. Mason nodded, earnestly. "Yeah, we had had storms like that too, back in Missoula. *Massive.*" He coughed raggedly, Whitney turned her head away, then asked him, conversationally, "didn't you go to college there?"

"Yeah, I went for one year," he replied, sounding glum. "University of Montana. Thought I'd try business school. My folks have a home construction and remodeling business in town. Figure I'll probably work for them after I finish this gig. Or whatever you call this thing," he laughed a little sheepishly. "Do this while I'm still young and still can. Get it out of my system. My older sister Madeline is the responsible one in our family, not me," he added, admittingly. They fell silent for a spell.

Trent needed to stop for gas and fill up the Sprinter's tank. They drove through Ouray's old historic mining district, past the frozen waterfall near the campground, past the hot springs. Then pulled into a small gas station. Duncan hopped out and went inside the convenience store to get coffee for everyone. He brought back a tray of cups and handed them out.

Shenti shuffled out of the vehicle and stood near the station's front doors, smoked a cigarette. Whitney absently watched him take rapid puffs, out her window.

Apparently, when one has been embedded in Afghanistan for the past fifteen years, the last thing they worry about is setting off a gas explosion, she mused idly.

Karis and Ian sat close to each other in the row in front of her. Both wore earbuds, listening to who- knows -what, eyes vacant.

Trent finished filling the tank. He wiped down the front and back windows, then cleared snow off the brake lights. Jumping back into the driver's seat, he started the engine. Preoccupied and silent, as usual, he pulled out of the station. Duncan turned to them from the front passenger seat, informing them, "We'll be staying at an Airbnb in Summit County. I got us booked in a six- bedroom place in Frisco." They all nodded perfunctorily, acknowledging.

The ride was mellowing them out. Mason and Shenti had started to doze off, Whitney could hear Mason's soft snoring beside her. Even when he was sleeping, he was noisy, she thought to herself, slightly irritated. Drowsy, she rested her head against the window and stared off at the passing snowfields and ranches, then drifted off, too.

They pushed on towards Gunnison, passing miles of empty graz-ing land and barbed wire fences, old homesteads and cattle ranches. Small towns with single gas stations, convenience stores, an occa-sional frozen reservoir. Saying goodbye, Trent stopped in the park-ing lot of the Colorado Mountain College in Gunnison and dropped Whitney off next to her Volkswagen Taos, where she had left it, unat-tended for the past six days.

Provided by Consumco, she could keep it for as long as she remained in the top five female extreme skiers in North America.

If she lost rank, she had to relinquish the vehicle. The sponsor gift was crucial, she couldn't afford another car. Transferring all her gear out of the Sprinter, she hoisted her skis onto the Taos' ski rack, then locked it down and climbed inside. She would drive the rest of the way back to Crested Butte, alone.

Within forty-five minutes, she arrived home in the mountain community, pulling the car into her parent's driveway. Their modest, refurbished miner's house greeted her on the edge of town, near the base of Kebler Pass. Her folks had bought it almost thirty years ago, before prices went stratospheric and got so expensive only rich people could afford to buy one.

Transplants from Colorado Springs, they had made the move to Crested Butte when she was a toddler so they could backcountry ski, hike, and start their own business. Their store, Olson Outfitters, gradually became a de-facto basecamp for locals and tourists alike, who shopped there for their high- quality climbing equipment, ski gear, outdoor clothing and chance to commune with other fellow alpinists and intrepid adventurers.

Many of the ski patrollers, ski instructors and mountain guides who worked at Crested Butte ski area had also worked at their store at some point in their lives and knew the Olson family well. Whitney practically grew up inside the store and skied regularly with their employees. When she was six, the local ski-mountaineering legend, Hans Reinhart, took her under his wing and taught her how to ski heavy, ungroomed snow, how to negotiate steep drops and chutes without falling. He had encouraged her to follow her passion for skiing, always with a kind word and ready smile.

With him, she was able to stretch her wings and push on to the next level of difficulty without inhibition or fear of reprisal. She had loved his grizzled, lined face and words of wisdom as they ripped it up on the snowy slopes. Almost seventy-nine now, his unbridled zest for the sport had inspired her for as long as she could remember. A reassuring presence in her life, he often shared stories of climbing Mt. Blanc and skiing down it when he lived in Austria before settling in Crested Butte. He would tell her, "You can sit around, watch TV your whole life, or go out and live it."

And it was skiing the steeps that made her feel most alive.

A close family friend, sometimes Hans and her would sit for hours at her house, watching his old film footage of extreme skiing pioneers like Anselme Baud and Pierre Tardive scale the massive peaks around Chamonix and ski down them twenty-five years before the sport even made waves in the United States. And then Whitney would show Hans her own videos of young, extreme skiers like Chris Davenport, Shane McConkey and Glen Flake in movies like the Blizzard of Aaaahs, and Steep. He would shake his head and marvel in disbelief as their bodies catapulted off cliffs and rock headwalls, flipping and twisting through the air like Chinese jin.

"Mommy, mommy! Mommy's home!" She heard Robyn shriek when she turned her key in the front door. Robyn ran up and grabbed her thighs and squeezed them hard, closing her eyes. She was wearing a purple tutu and had glitter all over her face.

"Hi sweetie!" Whitney crouched down and embraced her. "I'm home, luv bug," she gave her a kiss and hugged her some more. Robyn grinned happily. Her face was framed by a mess of light brown hair and smudged with finger paint, smelling of Elmer's glue.

"We're making a ballerina picture with finger paint and glitter," her mom said, walking out from the kitchen. "I got her the outfit at Walmart, in Gunnison." She walked over and gave Whitney a hug. "It's good to see you. How was the trip? Did you get all your filming done?" She looked a little puzzled to see her.

Whitney bit her lip.

"We got it all done. Everyone else went to Frisco, but I wanted to come home." She didn't tell her about the crash. Too awful, there was enough to worry about.

"Robyn has an appointment with Dr. McClellan day after tomorrow. We'll go together," her mom stated, walking back into the kitchen.

"Good idea, I need to get up to speed with everything," Whitney told her, heading towards her bedroom, duffel bag in tow, suddenly exhausted. She needed to lie down. Instead, she said to Robyn, "Why don't you play me a song on your violin sweetie, show me what you learned from Miss Abrams."

Robyn ran quickly into her bedroom and brought out her three-quarter sized instrument, a loaner from the school. Excited, she stood in front of Whitney and scratched out "Mary Had a Little Lamb," her round face and brown eyes a picture of concentration.

"Beautiful! You are a wonderful performer. I loved it!" Whitney clapped her hands in applause.

Cindy turned towards Whitney. "Miss Abrams scheduled a little performance for the students on April tenth. I hope you can make it."

"I'll try. I'm not sure where we'll be, I'll look at the tour schedule," she said, feeling guilty. While she was here with her family, she would try to be present, but her mind was already flitting to her teammates in Frisco, cohabitating, collaborating, moving ahead...

"Where's dad?" she asked, distractedly.

"He's at the store. Big weekend, skiers are descending from everywhere. We just got a lot of snow; the word is out." She added, "I need to help him with customers tomorrow morning."

"That's fine, I'll watch Robyn all day."

"Thanks. Let me know if you need anything. All her medications are in my bedroom, top dresser drawer. School starts at eight a.m., she needs to be picked up at two p.m.," her mom reminded her.

"Right," Whitney exhaled, closing her eyes in concentration. First grade. New schedule.

*Whiplash.*


In the morning, she made Robyn breakfast. A scrambled egg and piece of toast, some cut up pineapple.

"I love these eggs, mommy, they're good."

"Thanks, luv bug." She needed to give her her medication. She hurried into her parent's bedroom and found the bottle of lamotrigine. Dr. McClellan had said the medicine was for controlling her seizures. They were still figuring out what the best dosage and blood saturation level for her. A moving target, it had to be continuously monitored.

"Here; take your pill, baby," she handed Robyn a glass of water, carefully watching her swallow it. "Good job," she smiled at her, apprehensive. What would happen to Robyn? Would she be alright? Thinking about the potential medical possibilities was truly frightening.

"How 'bout we go visit Grammy Luann and Grampa Jake then go get an ice cream together at Third Bowl after school today?" she twinkled at Robyn, trying to act upbeat.

"O-Kay! Mommy!" Robyn squealed, happily.


Kyle's parents lived out on a fifty- acre ranch outside town off highway 135 between Gunnison and Crested Butte. The wide- open spaces in the rural mountain valley had provided a perfect place to ride moto cross, something Kyle had zealously done every day after class, in high school. Determined to compete at the national level, he practiced the airborne tricks and jumps on his prized dirt bike, hell- bent on attaining his goal. Senior year, he and Whitney started dating heavily, drawn to each and their shared passion for extreme sports. They both understood each other; had so much in common growing up out in Gunnison County that they fell into an easy partnership, fueled by adrenaline sports and love of the out-doors. Marrying the summer following graduation at Crested Butte Highschool, surrounded by family and friends, Whitney got pregnant right away.

At the same time, ski industry reps and filmmakers had begun to court her, sponsors like Red Bull, K2, Rossignol, Visa all clamored to have her aboard. Her name was out, the girl-wonder from Crested Butte who skied the steeps like a boy. They wooed her with products and film offers, travel and cars. When they asked her to be a spokes-person and ski in films, she jumped at the opportunity. College could wait. She hid her pregnancy from the press, figuring she'd have the baby and then get back into training soon as possible.

Kyle had been practicing a back lay-out off a kicker at the dirt bike track near Taylor Reservoir on August third when he crashed.

Broke his neck instantly; didn't linger, thank God. He had caught some gravel with his front wheel off the launch and slid, going into the jump. Just enough to torpedo his trajectory and cause him to lose the proper height and balance over his bike. The jump was incomplete, he landed on his head, bike on top of him.

It was a nightmare, everyone shell-shocked, everyone trying to deal with the grief. She went home to her parents and gave birth to Robyn in December and spent the next several months with the baby, just trying to recover from losing Kyle and the crushing heartbreak. Her parents helped her take care of Robyn, and then told her she needed to get on with her life. She could start school, pursue an undergraduate degree in something, or join the circuit and ski professionally. They would help raise Robyn at home.

She chose skiing, her oxygen.

Luann and Jack were not happy about it at all. Understandably, they worried that she too, would get killed, and then Robyn would be parentless. Whitney always felt guilty when she related to the two, their displeasure at her choice was evident and ongoing. To say she felt conflicted about it was a major understatement. Balancing on a tightrope between life and death, every time she went out on the mountain the pressure and fear of leaving Robyn alone weighed on her like a fifty- ton freight train. She *had* to be successful, she had to be tough, she had to prevail. At the same time, she was expected to be feminine, to be *attractive*. It seemed like twice as much work to be a female competitor, and twice as much responsibility.

Despite Luann and Jack's obvious disapproval, she always drove Robyn out to see them when she came back to Crested Butte. Robyn loved her grandparents, and they loved her.

# CHAPTER 4
# CRESTED BUTTE

"Tell the lady what flavor you want," Whitney prompted Robyn. They were at Third Bowl, standing inside the quaint, locally owned craft ice cream parlor in the historic district. A freezer with rows of ice cream containers ran almost the full length of the cozy, barn-like room. Robyn stood on tiptoes, peering up at it, she could barely see over the edge of the long, white display case. Whitney read some of the selections to her from the rotating menu board. "There's lavender-blueberry, lemon cheesecake crunch, toasted coconut caramel, coffee chip, strawberry...."

"Strawberry!" I want strawberry! Robyn interjected, excitedly. "May I have sprinkles?" she asked her mom, imploring.

"She'll have strawberry on a waffle cone with sprinkles," Whitney informed the lady, smiling. Ordering some coffee chip in a bowl for herself, they grabbed some napkins and brought their ice cream to one of the little tables placed informally in the room and sat down. Local artwork and ski memorabilia decorated the walls.

Whitney sat across from Robyn. Robyn licked her cone happily, sprinkles and pink melting cream dotting her face. Some dripped to the floor.

"Don't get that on your jacket," Whitney reached over and wiped her chin with her own napkin, reflexively.

"Thanks for taking me here, mommy."

"You are *so* welcome, luv bug. How was school today? What did you learn?"

"I learned about vowels. Mrs. Hennessey is teaching us how to read."

"Wonderful! Can you tell me what the vowels are?" Whitney prompted her, lighting up.

"Yes. They are A, E, I, O, U, and sometimes Y," Robyn beamed, proudly.

Whitney smiled back at her, a stab of maternal pride and adoration coursing through her body. *Her daughter*, brilliant and alive, adorable and cute. Kyle would have been smitten, she reflected momentarily, a lump catching in her throat…

She told Robyn, "This afternoon we'll read together. I bought a new book for you today."

Robyn suddenly slumped over; her cone fell to the floor. Eyes shutting, she went completely limp. Whitney shot out of her seat, almost knocking over her chair. Grabbing her daughter, she held her so she wouldn't hit the floor. Ice cream lay in a sad pink clump, melting on the aged barnwood planks. They stayed still for several awful moments, her own pulse racing a million miles per second.

Robyn's eyes fluttered open. They looked empty and unfocused, pupils dilated.

"It's okay, honey, it's okay. I'm here, mommy's here with you. You're going to be okay. Just take some deep breaths, you'll be alright," she reassured her. They waited, suspended, Robyn's eyes refocused, she looked at Whitney. "My ice cream's on the floor," she mourned, stricken.

"It's okay, sweetie, you had a little seizure. I'll get you another one, later. Any flavor, okay?"

Robyn's mouth sagged, she whimpered. Whitney consoled her sympathetically, "Let's go home now, shall we? We'll snuggle and read a book together, okay? I'll bring you some ice cream in bed."

"Okay, mommy, I'm tired," she slid off her chair holding Whitney's hand. They made their way out of the building together. Robyn needed to rest, would likely develop a headache, nausea. Whitney needed to stay by her side, supervise her every breath.

In the morning, Whitney drove Robyn and her mom to Gunnison for her medical appointment with Dr. McClellan. The pediatric clinic was located just off the highway in a new, modern development inside a cluster of non-descript, light grey concrete buildings. Robyn would miss class again; Whitney called the school to notify them.

Dr. McClellan was a mid-forties, fit, light-haired woman with a kind and thoughtful demeanor, she consulted with them after Robyn's examination. They sat in her small linen-colored office, sprinkled with a few family photos, a small potted plant, and conversed.

"Robyn is experiencing what I would characterize as "tonic" seizures, a condition that can result in momentarily lapses of muscle strength, consciousness, and sudden stiffening of the body, arms, legs," she explained to them. "She does not appear to be having convulsions, which is very encouraging, at this point. Sometimes children outgrow this condition. If we continue to keep her on the proper dose of lamotrigine, or a similarly effective medication, we can moderate the effects of her seizures in such way as to prevent her condition from progressing and becoming much worse." She elaborated, adding, "It could be a genetic condition, a result of some type of chromosomal abnormality, or something else of a different origin, which is what we will try to determine over the next several months. It will take time. These types of seizures are not cured overnight, but rather an ongoing, complex medical condition that requires careful testing and continuous monitoring." She gazed across her desk at them as they digested the information, waiting for their response.

Whitney swallowed. "What is her prognosis? What is our next step?"

Dr. McClellan replied, "We will run an EEG to record the electrical activity in her brain, as well as do a functional MRI scan to get a dimensional image of her brain to look for structural problems. We may do a CT scan to look for scar tissue, tumors, or malformed blood vessels as well. This can be done either in Grand Junction or Colorado Springs, depending on the specialist."

"Tumors?" Whitney's heart skipped a beat, her stomach knotted painfully.

"We always check for them, as a matter of course. Statistically, it is much rarer in children, but we will check, just to be thorough. There is a condition called tuberous sclerosis; tumors that grow in multiple organs of the body, brain, skin kidneys, lungs, heart. They can trigger seizures. But as I said, it is far less common, so please don't assume that that is the cause of Robyn's seizures. We will do all the routine examinations first, and move through everything systematically, as I explained," she nodded, reassuringly.

Whitney and her mother nodded, listening carefully. Robyn was out of earshot, in the clinic's playroom, down the hallway from the doctor's office.

"Do you think she might need surgery?" Whitney asked her, worriedly. *Oh my God, the bills, the medical expenses...*she cringed.

"I cannot rule that out, Whitney, but for now, we will keep her on this medicine, that is the correct path. I will review her blood lab soon and get back to you. We may need to alter her dosage; I will let you know." The doctor smiled, then inquired, "how is Robyn faring at school?"

Cindy stepped in, "I consult with her teacher and school nurse regularly, they are aware of her condition. They've told me she shows signs of developmental delay in language and social skills to some degree… I do worry about that," she finished, gravely. Whitney nodded, heavily.

"Of course, understandable. That's not untypical for these seizure disorders in young children," Dr. McClellan replied. "Hopefully, the lamotrigine will help prevent those problems from getting much worse. In time, when she improves, she should be able to recoup many of the skills she may have lost."

Whitney asked her, concerned, "What about physical activity? Is it dangerous? What exactly should we be doing?"

"She needs to stay active, but she has to be careful, insofar that if she had a seizure while playing outside on a playground, or riding a bike, or anything of that nature, she could fall and hurt herself," she answered, frowning. "You'll have to take extra precautions. I would categorically avoid swimming. Drowning is of major concern."

"Skiing is out of the question? I imagine," Whitney posed, regretfully.

"Not completely, but it would have to be done in an extremely controlled environment, with careful oversight, and with the expectation that a seizure could happen and that you would have to respond to it, immediately. So, I think skiing would have to be extremely limited, perhaps only with you or your family members, close to the base, and on very gentle slopes...I realize this must be difficult for you to hear, Whitney," the doctor said, sympathetically.

Whitney nodded, saddened. How she would have loved to teach Robyn to ski.

"Thank you for all of your help, we really appreciate it," Whitney and Cindy stood up, nodded at her graciously. They left her office to get Robyn, take her home.

Whitney called Trent that night after dinner from her bedroom. She spoke furtively.

"I've thought about what you said. About the procedure," she told him, holding her breath.

Trent was silent on the other end, waiting for her to continue.

"I need to talk to you more about it. I think I've decided...." Her voice wavered slightly, "I think I should get it done."

A long pause.

She heard him inhale tightly. "Alright, Whitney. I'll get in touch with Dr. Belcic tomorrow, let him know. I'll call you back soon with more information."

"Alright then," she exhaled, flood of nervous anticipation coursing through her body. She set down her cellphone, feeling almost faint.

Robyn needed the money, she needed to stay on the team. The decision seemed logical.

Life had a way of forcing one's hand.

# CHAPTER 5
# CRESTED BUTTE

Seven a.m., she rose early to prepare Robyn for school, slightly disoriented from sleeping in her childhood bed after being away on tour for a month. It took several moments to remember where she was, the sensation always unnerving when she came home between trips. Her parents had already left the house to go work in the store, they would be there all day waiting on customers, doing bookwork and sales until the last person straggled through the front door to return their rental skis and they closed for the night. During high season, they stayed open late to accommodate after-dinner tourists who strolled the main street, shopping for last-minute t-shirts and hats to commemorate their visit to Crested Butte.

A plethora of other small retailers clustered around the old town center, competition for their business was fierce. Whitney's folks worked long hours to keep Olson Outfitters afloat and their employees well paid. Though extremely popular in the small community and well loved, the store had never been an especially lucrative endeavor.

Robyn was still sleeping, her head resting on her pillow, hair and blankets a messy lump. Whitney rummaged around the kitchen, looking for bread and peanut butter, jam and plastic baggies to make a sandwich for her lunch. She cut an apple into thin slices, adding some baby carrots and celery sticks to the mix. Searching the pantry, she found a box of graham crackers and put a few into another baggie, packing everything into Robyn's lunch box. She went into her bedroom to gently prod her awake.

"Time to get up and get dressed, luv bug. School today," she cajoled, cheerily. Groggily, Robyn scooted to the edge of the bed and yawned, stretched her arms while Whitney scrambled around the room putting together an outfit, helping her get ready.

Where was Robyn's other shoe? Dammit, where did it go? Whitney crouched down on the floor and looked under her bed. Where the hell was it? *Shit!* "Robyn, where did you put your other shoe?!"

"I don't know mommy!"

"Well, we have to find it! Go look for it honey, try to remember where you took it off." Now the clock was ticking. School started in forty-minutes. Grabbing Robyn's hairbrush, she took some scrunchies off her dresser.

"Robyn, you have to brush your hair!" her voice rose louder, getting agitated. Robyn was running around the house, still searching for the shoe. "Let's do you hair now! I'll help you find your shoe in a minute," she yelled from the bedroom.

"Okay, mommy," Robyn returned and dutifully stood in front of her. Whitney started brushing with quick, brisk strokes through the unruly mass, dividing it into two pigtails. "Ouch! Mommy! that hurts!" she cried out a fretful reproach.

"I'm sorry sweetie, mommy's in a hurry!" *Okay that's done, let's find that shoe…*Sweating now, Whitney raced madly around the house, finally locating the lost shoe inside Robyn's rubber snow boot by the front door, near a pile of shoes. Relief flooded her body. Oh jeez… *boots that go over children's shoes….! A* revelation. They had to get going.

She helped Robyn put on her mittens and knit wool hat; the ones with the reindeer on them, *oh shit, she forgot to give Robyn her medication!*

"We need to go back to the kitchen honey; you need to take your pill before we leave." They raced back to the kitchen, Whitney grabbed a glass and filled it with water, handing it to her. She rushed into her mom's bedroom and grabbed the prescription bottle from her top dresser drawer and came back, giving a pill to Robyn. Robyn swallowed it hastily, then swung her elbow around accidently knocking her lunch box over. The latches popped open, the sandwich and baggies spilled to the floor, carrots and apple slices a colorful splat. Squatting down together, they gathered up the food and shoved it back into the box, racing back to the front door again.

Frazzled, Whitney nearly forgot to put her own parka and snow boots on. Six degrees outside, frost clung to the front porch steps. They walked out to the narrow sidewalk, snow piled high on the side of the road, patches of ice everywhere. There was a frenetic quality to the community, skiers and shoppers scrambling for parking spots, places to idle on the narrow, crowded streets as they hastily grabbed coffee and bagels to go before hitting the slopes. Crested Butte, the town's namesake, loomed two thousand feet above village. Covered in snow, it's near vertical face stood sentry from the valley floor.

Robyn's grade school, a simple, low, brown brick building, was only a half-mile away. Almost there now, they trudged past a series of old miners cabins and simple ranch-style homes that had been transformed into four- million-dollar estates and charming bed-and-breakfasts. As they rushed to the school's front entrance, the first bell began to ring. Whitney accompanied Robyn down the hall-way to her classroom, she needed to speak with her teacher, Mrs. Hennessey.

Mrs. Hennessey stood at the classroom door cheerily greeting her students as they shuffled in. Seeing the two of them, her face lit up. "Good to see you back! How is Robyn doing?" she smiled brightly. Whitney replied, slightly breathless, "She's doing well, thanks! I wanted to let you know that she had a doctor appointment yesterday. She should be back in class now, going forward."

"Good, good! Glad to hear it," Mrs. Hennessey smiled warmly.

"Thank you for all your help. Robyn loves school, and she loves you too," Whitney told her, sincerely.

"She's a special little girl," the teacher gazed down at Robyn maternally.

Whitney explained, "I'll be picking her up for the next two weeks after school. I'm on a short break from my tour-- I just wanted to let you know."

"Very good. Glad you're back. Robyn's been talking about it for a while, she's excited to see you again."

A tinge of guilt zinged through her, she tamped it away towards the back of her mind, a coping mechanism she had developed over the past six years as a single parent and competitive skier.

After dropping off Robyn, she walked back towards her parent's house, savoring the familiar scenery, the small-town, rustic vibe. On the way, she decided to stop at their store to say hello to her dad. Gone for over a month, she had scarcely spoken with him, save a few times, mostly on the phone. Usually at the store from morning to night, he stayed there until closing while her mom went home mid-day to take care of Robyn.

Nearing the end of Main Street, she entered the store, a hum of activity greeted her. Several employees turned their heads excitedly; she was a local celebrity.

"Hey! It's our hometown hero, Whitney's back!" someone called out loudly. A few customers looked over at her, curious about the buzz. A woman came over and eagerly asked her for an autograph. She cheerfully obliged, grabbing a Sharpie next to the register and signing the back of her ski helmet. Tom, her dad, was in the back end of the store, helping a young man fit a new ski boot. She headed over to them. Her mom was behind the counter, folding a t-shirt a customer had just purchased.

"Thought you might come by," a familiar, crusty voice greeted her warmly.

Whitney whirled around, "Oh my god! Hans!" She gave him a big hug. "So glad to see you!"

"Wouldn't miss it, wouldn't miss it. Your mom and dad told me you were in town for a little while. So, how's the tour going?" He sat on an old wooden stool, next to the cash register.

She bit her lip, considering. If she told him about her crash in Silverton, it would invariably get back to folks. They sure didn't need the extra worry, so she answered Hans brightly, though obliquely, "It's going well. Consumco is treating us like royalty, I can't complain."

"Excellent! You keep up the great work, Whitney. You have no idea how proud I am of you," he told her, emotionally.

"I owe it to you Hans," her eyes suddenly welled up. A widower, Hans was looking older. His beard was scruffier, his eyes a bit more wrinkled and rheumy, he moved a little slower these days. How time was flying by. She stood by the register and chatted with him for a while longer…

At two p.m. she got a call on her cellphone from Trent.

"I spoke with Belcic. He'll be expecting you a week from tomorrow, on January 24. You'll need to pack some regular clothing and prepare to stay at his clinic for a week. In Belgrade," he stated, brief.

*Belgrade?* Where the hell was Belgrade? She didn't even know.

"It's in Serbia," he must have read her mind. Uncanny.

"Consumco will have a private jet for you at the Gunnison Airport at seven in the morning," he explained. "You should arrive by six a.m. the next day. They'll have a driver waiting for you at the tarmac, he'll take you to the facility."

"*Jesus,* how long will I be there?" Whitney swallowed; this was serious. She thought she would be driving herself over to University Hospital in Denver or somewhere closer by. *Belgrade?*

"You'll be there for a week, then the company will fly you back to Gunnison. You can drive out to Frisco to join us, afterward."

*Jeez.* This was happening quickly. She would have to tell her parents she was leaving a week earlier than she had originally anticipated. Robyn would be extremely disappointed, she realized, reflexively.

She asked Trent nervously, "Do you really think I should do this?"

"I think if you want to stay competitive, yes, you should do this," he stated, firmly. "You have incredible potential, Whitney, but your fear and apprehension is impeding your ability to ski as well as you should. I'd like to see you compete in the World Championship next February- even win the event," he added, voice set. "In my opinion, no one skis better than you do, when you're on your game," he finished, convincingly.

Part of her wondered if he had said the exact same words to Karis. She brushed the thought away quickly.

"Alright," she swallowed nervously. "I'll be there."

"Good. I'll text you your itinerary. Consumco will have all your paperwork, you won't be charged for a thing. All you need to do is show up," he hung up dismissively, discussion over.

Whitney exhaled, her mind swirling. She needed to pack. Get some cash... notify Mrs. Hennessey... talk to her folks. No, she couldn't tell her parents about the procedure, she wasn't allowed to tell anyone, she remembered, wide-eyed. She would make something up.... tell them that Consumco was sending her to Belgrade to do a special promotional appearance for a new product they were selling.... that they needed her to meet with their company reps... yes. That sounded plausible, she thought, running the fabrications through her head.

Trent frowned and set down his phone. Mission accomplished, he exhaled, relieved. The procedure would be a game changer for her, he knew, with certainty. It had been for him, he reflected, not without bitterness. Though life turned out differently than he originally planned....

Back in the 'nineties, he was living in a little village called Cesky Krumlov in the heart of the Sudeten with his bike-racing buddy, Lech, in the Czech Republic. They had a cramped apartment on the banks of the river that snaked through the fairytale-like historic town where they spent their days cycling along the rolling countryside and endless back roads. He had traveled there to join Lech the summer after his own near-death accident in Bozeman, trying to get back in condition for the North American Extreme Skiing Competition in Valdez, Alaska, that following winter....

Sophomore year, middle of February, he still winced at the painful memory; he and Travis had finished their classes for the day at MSU and left campus to go ski the back country at Bridger, just a few miles from Bozeman. Both competitive downhill racers, freestyle maniacs, they welcomed a change of terrain where they could just free-ski and do aerials on the steeps with wild abandon, their true passion. They had brought all their avalanche equipment with them, but in the end, it didn't matter. A fracture slab broke off at the top of the ridge on their second run down, its ferocious power mowing down every tree and living thing in its path. Including Travis. Unlucky, Travis had been skiing dead-center on the slope and the tsunami of snow barreled over him in a crushing wave, burying his body instantly in a coffin of white cement. Trent had been hit by the avalanche as well, but he was on the edge of it and was able to ski, or rather, surf the avalanche further down until it too, slammed upon his body throwing him into a chunder not unlike being swallowed by a forty-foot ocean wave and spin-cycled to death. Spitting him out at the bottom of the slope on a wide basin, partly submerged but miraculously still alive, he was able to keep breathing. Initially too stunned to even respond, he had somehow mustered the instinctive wherewithal to radio for help. His leg was broken, among other bones; that was excruciatingly apparent. Turned out to be the left femur, revealed later by the X-ray at the emergency room when they airlifted him to Bozeman. Had three broken ribs, cracked L-2 and L-3, and a fractured left shoulder.

Search and rescue tried in vain to dig Travis's body out from underneath the snow and save him, but he had already died of blunt force trauma and asphyxiation by the time they finally got to him.

Trent's own life had instantaneously changed. After spending four months in Bozeman recuperating, he decided to quit college and go to eastern Europe instead; meet his friend there and build his body back up, all over again. Lech's cycling pack were like rabid animals, covering hundreds of miles a week, pushing hours and hours a day through the Czech countryside, single- minded in their quest to qualify for the Tour de France. Muscular and strong, seemingly indefatigable, they churned out brutal rides, week after week with almost super-human endurance and no apparent fear of crashing. He would try to keep up with them, which was nearly impossible, out of their league. But he did learn something, which came as a big surprise. Lech confided to him one day in broken English, "We don't dope, that's old news, that's over… We've got something much better." Trent's antennae shot up, interested, "We go to a doctor—a neuroscientist, he's in Prague. He's doing research… works for the military…I had the procedure- it took away my fear… I'm much more focused, energized… perhaps you should contact him too.…"

Trent drove to Prague the next day, Dr. Belcic eagerly agreed to meet with him, interested in his predicament. "I was a ski racer, I want to compete again, but I had a terrible accident," he told the distinguished doctor, confiding his trauma about the avalanche and broken bones. Dr. Belcic was very receptive, explaining to him, "I can eliminate the PTSD you have from the event and reduce any fear you have about skiing itself, but I cannot fix the residual physical damage in your body from the actual accident. If you choose to undergo the neuro- surgery here at my clinic, you think it would help you, I would be happy to include you in my program." He assured Trent, "There would be no expense for you to participate, our country's military is funding my research and development."

The doctor went on to share more information about the efficacy of the procedure, how he thought it would eventually be used to help soldiers around the world with PTSD and other psychological impediments, how it could help athletes cope with performance issues. Trent found the exchange to be extremely compelling, a godsend, in fact. Throwing caution to the wind, he decided to go ahead and do it.

Afterwards, he stayed in Prague to recover, then flew home to Montana. But that winter, back on his skis, he knew his freestyle career and dream of winning Nationals was over. His body instantly informed him of that soon as he attempted his first, basic aerial on the snow.

What lay in his future was coaching, he realized that day, with clarity.

# CHAPTER 6
# BELGRADE

Heart aching mournfully, like the strings of Robyn's violin playing a sad song across her chest, she hugged and kissed her daughter goodbye with assurances that she'd be back, she would see her in just a few months. Her parents nodded understandingly, they were intimately familiar with the demands and contractual obligations that a sponsored skier had to their company.

"Love you guys, thanks for all your help, I couldn't do it without you," Whitney embraced them gratefully on her way out the door, her carry-on suitcase in tow. Climbing in her Taos, she made the solitary drive out to Gunnison airport at five-thirty a.m., allowing plenty of time for delays in the frigid, winter-gray, dawn light. A sleek Gulfstream 650 sat solitary on the runway, waiting for her.

The pilot and co-pilot greeted her as she boarded the plane. Conversing with the attractive redheaded flight attendant, the only additional crew traveling with them non-stop to Belgrade, they paused mid-conversation. She escorted Whitney to her seat; a buttercream, leather work of art that reclined all the way down, near the window. Graciously, she offered Whitney a cup of fresh hot coffee.

Would she like a pastry, some orange juice? she inquired, as they departed.

Whitney sat down, stunned, speechless. *They were spending a fortune on her,* she thought. A shiver of apprehension and anticipation rippled through her as she settled into her seat, imagining what lay ahead. Could she do this? She *was* doing this, she chewed her lip, surreally. She could win WESC. Over a million in cash prizes, endorsements, film royalties…. she could pay for Robyn's medical care and avoid debt…reimburse her parents all the money that they had spent….

This could be the solution to all her problems.

Soon after the Gulfstream effortlessly, smoothly lifted off, she drifted into a liminal state of sleep and awareness, dream and torpor as they glided through the atmosphere, enveloped in a sea of clouds and occasional bright sun. Then complete darkness. Occasionally the flight attendant would reappear again with a delicious hot meal and hot towel. She would sit upright and eat, then doze back off in a pleasant, relaxed fugue.

Interesting how flight completely divorced one from reality and all constructs of planet earth… as though disembodied, suspended in some alternative state that wasn't exactly human, she mused, languidly.

Finally, she felt the plane descend in altitude; sensed they were approaching Belgrade, the city revealing itself through the gray and bleak winter sky. The tops of cathedrals and office buildings appeared barren, no foliage nor greenery buffered their urban angles and edges. They were cruising over the confluence of the Sava and Danube rivers on their final approach towards the sprawling airport.

Whitney gazed out the window across the landscape, anxiously breathing in the new environs. Serbia. Land of the former Yugoslavia, of conflict and strife; land of Russian influence. She shivered, unconsciously.

The plane touched down; she sighed easier now, they rolled along the tarmac, coming to an abrupt stop. The pilot continued taxiing to a low gray building that looked like a hangar and then came to a second, final stop, killing the engine. Now she sat up alert, waiting for permission to deplane. She saw a large, black SUV pull up, not far from where they were parked. Clearly, it was for her, the man in the driver's seat sat smoking a cigarette with his window rolled down.

She stood up and began stepping down, surreally, off the plane. The attendant handed her her suitcase and the man climbed out of the SUV and opened the back passenger door for her. She got in, he closed it without a word and stepped back into the driver's seat, looking bored. Then they were off, speeding through the streets and neighborhoods of Belgrade. Speechless, she gazed out the darkly tinted windows in a detached, out-of-body torpor, jetlagged, disoriented.

They arrived at the medical facility and pulled up to the front entrance. Whitney gazed across the formidable hospital complex. Huge buildings and parking lots, multiple towers and clinics filled the compound. A woman rushed outside to greet her, escorting Whitney inside the glass double-doors. A male attendant checked her into the facility, and then guided her down a hallway to a clean and modern guest quarter. A twin bed and a simple dresser sat inside it.

"Your meeting with the doctor is at three this afternoon," he told her, his voice imbued with hourly routine.

Bleary-eyed and dazed, she hung up her a few pieces of clothing, then fell into bed for some rest.


"Come in, come in," Dr. Belcic stood up and greeted her as she tentatively tapped on his office door that afternoon. It was a spacious, airy room which bespoke success and gravitas, clearly, he was a very important man. He gestured to a chair and sat down across from her at his large, modern desk. Glass tables and windows, modern art and tasteful upholstery all communicated knowledge and education, money and influence. A scientist and neurosurgeon, pioneer in his field, he fervently believed that someday the larger medical community would embrace his research on fear and its counterproductive, unnecessary psychological and physiological impediments. They would come to appreciate the benefits of his procedure, its applications.

He had tremendous pride in his work and his staff. The Czech government had discontinued his research program almost fourteen years ago, claiming there were too many complications associated with the procedure for their military personnel. But he had proved them wrong. He had picked up and left, kept going, continued refining his methods. The Serbs were only too happy to have him; they understood the value of his work and his genius. Though they couldn't provide the steady stream of money for his research like he had previously enjoyed, they allowed him the freedom to do it with minimal government oversight and interference.

Fortunately, Consumco had become a much needed and timely source of revenue, his relationship with the company treating their elite, sponsored athletes a huge financial supplement to his regular medical practice and program. The manufacturing and advertising juggernaut spent millions a year grooming their skiers to win competitions and promote their vast array of products and services. That most serendipitous encounter with the American, Trent Resnick, twenty years ago had been the answer to his prayers.

Whitney gazed across the desk. The doctor was mid-sixties, she guessed, with a tuft of white hair and rather full, gray and white beard. Silver framed glasses balanced across the bridge of his nose, she could see his intelligent light blue eyes behind the bi-focal lenses. Trim, he wore a tan cashmere sweater over a black turtleneck, with brown tweed slacks and comfortable, stylish leather loafers.

Giving her his full attention, he gazed a few moments at her. There was much to talk about.

"I am sure you have many questions, Whitney, but first, if I may, I would like to learn about you. Would that be alright?" he asked her, directly. Though he had a thick Czech accent, he spoke English extremely well. Better than most Americans, she thought, looking at him, still dazed.

"What is it that you fear most, Whitney?" he asked her pointedly.

A pause. She considered a moment, then answered simply, "I fear becoming paralyzed from skiing, or dying, and leaving my six-year-old daughter motherless."

"What do you fear even more, or as much?" he prodded further, intently.

She tilted her head, the answer escaping her lips. "I fear not being able to ski, not being able to engage with my sole purpose and passion, which is to ski competitively and win. Skiing is my life. Without it, I am lost."

"Hence, the duality of your very existence, I see," he commented, thoughtfully. "Your coach told me about your fall. Do you believe you developed post- traumatic stress syndrome from that?" he inquired, frowning.

"I don't know. I haven't skied yet, since."

"I will explain to you how fear affects us, Whitney, in layman terms," he stated, simplifying his terminology. "Fear is an innate, subconscious response to any stimuli that presents any type of threat to us. It protects us from doing things that could be harmful to ourselves, even kill us. We experience "fight or flight," chemical surges that allow us to instantaneously react to a potentially dangerous event. It begins in the amygdala," he explained, picking up a model of a human brain and a silver pointer on his desk, then tracing it along the hard, plastic replica, covered with blue and red squiggles, lines and symbols, "and it becomes an electrical impulse that travels through our neuropathways and communicates with other regions of the brain. For example, the pre-frontal cortex, and the temporal lobe." He kept going. "These areas create the emotional and physical responses to the stimuli. Now, in normal circumstances, this is good, very necessary. However, in the case of someone who has experienced a traumatic event, or multiple traumatic, life-threatening events, the neuro pathways can become overly stimulated and unable to calm down. Then the patient experiences chronic stress, PTSD, anxiety disorders, phobias. Over time, these can become very deleterious, as it takes the human body a tremendous amount of energy and stamina to combat the continued strain of chronic sleep deprivation, stress and fear." He took a breath, "Fear is often expressed as actual physical pain, the two are indelibly related," he paused. "Do you have any questions?"

"No," Whitney replied, mesmerized, she was speechless.

"All right, then. We continue." He leaned towards her, across the desk, still holding the brain. "Our strategy is to locate the precise locus of fear within the cortexes and transect the neuro- electrical impulses before they arrive there."

Whitney swallowed, staring wide-eyed at him and the plastic brain, completely transfixed. She asked him tentatively, "um…does it hurt?"

"We use a technique called minimally invasive gamma ray, an almost microscopic sized instrument which we can manipulate inside the brain while imaging your brain in real-time," he replied. "You shouldn't feel anything, really, with the exception of some slight discomfort as we thread the device up your nose into a pin-hole size opening underneath your cribriform plate. You will actually be awake and quite alert all throughout the procedure, as we will need to communicate with you while we stimulate pathways and search for their exact loci. We will do this," he went on, "using computerized imagery as we trigger your fear, utilizing a virtual- reality ski immersion apparatus that simulates real-life, extreme skiing experiences."

Whitney inquired warily, "What about side-effects? Are there any?" To say she was concerned was a gross understatement. She was quite terrified, naturally.

"An excellent question, one that anyone in their right mind would ask," he responded, leaning forward. "With all the advances in neuro- surgery now, we can pin-point loci and transect with minimal damage to other existing structures. It is unlikely you will experience side-effects, however, not out of the question. Sometimes patients feel a shift in their emotional senses as they adapt to the change in fear perception, in other words, since they are less fearful, they become less inhibited, less anxious. Typically though, it is subtle, and the patient will gradually adapt to their new base-line emotional state. Nothing is risk free, however. You will have to determine whether this is acceptable and worth the risk, yourself."

It sounded pretty nice actually, Whitney thought, suddenly relieved. Who wouldn't want to be less anxious? Her terror dissipated, she relaxed more, breathed a little easier.

She asked him cautiously, "What about recovery? How long will it take?"

"Typically, it will take several hours to recover from the procedure. Normally it is an out-patient procedure and patients go home the same day," he answered. "However, our arrangement with Consumco requires you stay here at the clinic for at least five days under observation in case there are any complications. We also need you here so we can run a battery of fear- simulation virtual-reality ski exercises to check the efficacy of our procedure. Do you have any additional questions?" he looked at her, patiently.

She frowned, "well, what I wonder, is, um…" she tried to ask artfully, but then just blurted out, "isn't this uh…. just cheating?"

Dr. Belcic smiled, "another astute and worthy question, Whitney. What we are talking about is manipulating emotions. If I made you feel happier, or more sad, or more concerned, or more affectionate, would you consider that to be cheating?" He paused, then explained helpfully, "I'm not giving you an ability that you don't already have, I'm just allowing your existing ability to be revealed."

"Oh…" she pondered. That made sense, the logic was undeniable.

She couldn't think of anything more to ask him, all in all, every-thing seemed reasonable. The fear she initially felt, had waned, she sensed she was in excellent hands. And so many others had evidently had the procedure before her, too. Somehow, leaving Belgrade with-out having it done did not seem like an option...

Dr. Belcic nodded. "If you have any more questions, I'll be here until six p.m. You can just knock on my door. Any one of my nurse assistants can help you with any questions you might have, as well. We have scheduled your procedure for tomorrow at one p.m." he informed her. "You will have an MRI and CT scan at eight a.m. in the morning, then surgical prep. Just try to relax and get a good night's sleep. Everything will be fine."

*Wow.* Whitney blinked, eyes widening. Everything will be fine. Would be fine.... This was...was....

Mind blowing.

# CHAPTER 7
# THE PROCEDURE

A t six a.m. she was woken by a woman wearing light blue hospital scrubs entering her room, wheeling a cart with a tray of scrambled eggs, toast and fruit compote on it for breakfast.

"No coffee today, I'm sorry," she greeted Whitney cheerily in broken English, sliding the cart next to her bedside. "When you are finished, you may put on this gown," she placed it beside Whitney. "I will come get you. Yes?"

Whitney nodded foggily, still waking up. Surprisingly, she had fallen into a deep slumber right after dinner last night, as though she had been shot. The flight to Belgrade and the intensity of meeting with Dr. Belcic yesterday had been exhausting. Hungrily, she ate the toast and scrambled eggs, then put on the light blue surgical gown.

A medical technician escorted her down a long, beige corridor to a room filled with high-tech imaging equipment. She explained to Whitney, "To create the 3-D images of your own brain's anatomy, we will fuse two-dimensional images from MRI and CT scans with our own state -of -the- art computer program, allowing Dr. Belcic to immerse himself right into your brain and all its tissue and vessels.

He will be able to fly through them, so to speak, using virtual reality to assist him." She elaborated, "This will allow him to map out your anatomy and practice your procedure before the actual surgery itself, so that it can be accomplished relatively quickly and with extreme accuracy."

She instructed Whitney sit down on an imposing, grey leather medical chair. Swinging a rather large, white metal apparatus, all rotating arms and appendages, she moved it around and above her head, adjusting it continuously with computerized assistance. "Dr. Belcic designed this piece of equipment," she mentioned casually. "Now," she stated, "I need you to take a breath and hold still. We will take a group of images, then do our other scans."

The morning progressed with more examination rooms and more brain scans, a lunchbreak in her room again, standard blood draws and urine samples. They checked her blood pressure multiple times, then prepared her for the actual procedure itself. Swabbing and disinfecting her skin and nasal passages, they gowned her again in fresh, clean hospital garb and encouraged her go to the bathroom one last time. Nurses and medical personnel moved through the clinic, busy and preoccupied. Other patients occasionally passed by along the corridor, their voices a hum of words and whispers inside the busy practice.

At precisely one p.m. she was escorted to a large surgical room on the far corner of the clinic. Dr. Belcic was waiting with two other assistants.

"Hello, Whitney," he greeted her with a convivial nod. Face almost entirely obscured by his blue surgical mask, cap and goggle-like eyewear; blue fabric draped over his entire body like a graduation gown. His assistants were similarly attired. An imposing array of high-tech medical equipment filled the modern room. It looked like the inside of a space shuttle, Whitney thought, inwardly. Bright overhead lights flooded the area, gleaming off the many metallic surfaces. Machinery, computers and screens glowed and flickered somewhat eerily, she shivered. He gestured to the chair, or rather, the reclining bed-chair. His assistant began fitting an Oculus virtual reality headset over her eyes with a silicone seal.

Now she was engulfed in darkness. She felt herself being reclined to a semi-upright position, the whir of the electric recliner a pleasant and surprisingly relaxing sensation. Someone placed a padded, snug feeling apparatus around her entire head to keep it in a stable position. Next, she felt an almost imperceptible sensation of something being threaded up her nasal passageway- a tickle, a bit of pressure. Dr. Belcic's voice entered her ears, slightly far away. "Before we begin the procedure, we will check to make sure that you can hear my voice above the ambient sound of your virtual- reality headset. Are you ready?"

"Yes."

A snowy mountainside immediately flooded her vision, all her senses. She was surrounded by glaciers, peaks, rock and sky. She could hear the wind blowing, feel her skis on the snow, feel their metal edges sliding and scraping against the uneven surface.

"Can you hear my voice clearly? Dr. Belcic asked.

"Yes," she replied.

"Can you see the image clearly in front of you and also hear the sound?"

"Yes," she answered, exhaling.

"I am going to give you some instructions. Please listen to me carefully."

"I am listening," she said, entirely alert.

"You will experience typical skiing activity, interspersed with frighteningly realistic, dangerous moments on the mountain which should induce a normal fear response," he said. "When you feel frightened, you must tell me. Use the word "Fear," okay?" he instructed. "As we move through the procedure, I might ask you if you smell something, or if a memory or picture comes to mind. Or perhaps an emotion. It might be sadness, happiness, anger- anything at all. I will be stimulating different neural pathways in the different lobes of your brain and those emotions and sensations will override what you are experiencing on your virtual screen. Do you understand?"

"Yes."

Dr Belcic put his headset on and positioned himself in front of his computer screen, the microscopic endoscope would feed the imagery to him as it moved through her brain in a pre-programmed sequence. With the click of a button, he could initiate the stimulation and transection. There would be only two, perhaps three transects necessary.

"We will begin, Whitney."

Suddenly she was skiing, a beautiful blue-bird day, the swish of her ski's back edges cutting through groomed, packed snow on a smooth, easy run through an open glade, only a few other skiers in her midst, they looked like intermediate skiers, perhaps vacationers and their children, all out for the day to enjoy the slopes and then go back to the lodge and drink cocoa…now she was dropping down the hill towards a gentle gully, still easy-breezy, she hadn't skied this mellow for quite a long time, she thought to herself, as she cruised along the soft, forgiving snow…a child suddenly skied right out in front of her, cutting her off, she was skidding to avoid hitting him, her right ski catching a patch of ice, she was losing her balance, losing control, her other ski caught an edge and she was skiing right towards a tree on the side of the run, about to smash into it…

"FEAR!" she yelled. Jeez. This was realistic.

Now she was hiking up a snowy ridge, carrying her skis up to the top, the wind was howling, she was about to put her skis back on and ski down and…she suddenly smelled cigarette smoke, foul, acrid odor assaulting her nose like an unwanted intruder.…

"I smell cigarette smoke," Whitney announced out loud, wonderingly.

"Good," came Dr. Belcic's muffled reply.

She was strapped on her skis and began floating down knee-high powder, soft clouds of snow spraying off the back of her skis as she effortlessly turned and dipped, turned and dipped, carving wide serpentine curves down a pristine open basin of untracked snow…a cloud rolled in, suddenly obscuring her vision, the light becoming instantly flat. She couldn't see the snow very well now, her depth perception impaired… what had just seemed so glorious and wonderful was actually the edge of a giant cliff and she was launching off it--irrevocably airborne, moments from her certain death.…

"FEAR!" she shouted instantly. God almighty, this was too real!

"Very good," came the immediate reply.

They gave her a reprieve, she was walking into a ski lodge now, her ski boots crunching against the snow, she took them off and sat down at a wooden table outside on the deck, she was looking out at the mountain peaks, sipping some hot cider, all the other skiers eating lunch, taking photos, drinking beers, talking…she felt so sad, an overpowering urge to burst out crying came over her, she began sobbing…

"We've located that particular pathway," Dr. Belcic said dryly. Someone dabbed her cheeks with a tissue. A little moisture seeped below her VR headset.

Once again, she was back on the slopes, this time though, getting on a chairlift. She began heading up the mountain, forty feet above the ground. The chair began to swing back and forth a little bit, the wind pushing it ever so slightly. There was no cross bar to hold on to. The wind picked up more, and a sudden, unexpectedly powerful burst jolted the chair, snapping it off the cable, she was tumbling down.... down....

"FEAR!" She screamed. I can't take much more of this she grimaced, clenching her buttocks like a ten-dollar watch, sweating like a pig.

"We're almost finished," Dr. Belcic reassured her.

Someone removed the headset and nasal tube, the cranial apparatus and other assorted implements, she sat back for a few moments and just exhaled.

Dr. Belcic told her, "You might feel quite tired for the rest of the day. I suggest you just get some rest, try to sleep. Our nursing staff will check in on you intermittently to see if you need anything. Tomorrow you can take it easy, get back to your normal self." He added, "We will meet later this week and run some efficacy tests, those should be less stressful for you."

She nodded and slid off the chair, feeling slightly wobbly. A bit like walking on flat ground right after bobbing around in a boat out in the ocean, she thought. Dr. Belcic's assistant helped her slide into a wheelchair and pushed her back to her bedroom, saying, "I know you can walk, but we do this just in case you get dizzy. You did great, by the way." He helped her stand up and then get into bed. "You'll feel better tomorrow, I promise."


Morning came, she woke up feeling rested and well, surprised at how quickly she recovered from the procedure. Someone brought her breakfast, then lunch, she watched some Serbian TV which was totally incomprehensible; sat around and looked through some Serbian magazines which were also incomprehensible, then eventually got up and took a warm shower. Browsed her cellphone apps, wandered around the hallways a little bit, peeked into waiting rooms… looked for some magazines, anything to read, in English. Someone handed her an American Vogue, she went back to her room and reclined in bed, holding it.

Karis.

There she was. On the front page, posing in extravagantly over-the-top Versace ski wear. Long, gorgeous blonde hair flowing out from her exquisitely made-up face like a lion's main. High-fashion tall and leggy body contorted in an impossibly alluring pose, she was holding a brand- new pair of Rossignol skis, like the queen of Versailles. She looked amazing.

Whitney's chest deflated, all existing air exiting like a popped balloon at the end of a birthday party. She tossed the glossy magazine across the sterile room in frustration, fuming deliriously, *I have got to make a hair appointment! Soon as I get back to Frisco!* It would be her very first stop. Probably should get eyelash extensions too, she told herself, feeling grossly inadequate.


On January 29 she had an appointment to meet again with Dr. Belcic. He was waiting for her, seated behind his imposing desk.

Today he had on a black turtleneck sweater and grey herringbone jacket. "Whitney, have a seat." He took his glasses off and wiped them down with a lens cleaner, then put them back on, assessing her. "I think you are doing exceedingly well; all our post procedure tests have turned out just as I would have hoped. How do you feel?" he asked, leaning forward, crossing his arms, listening.

"I feel...I feel...." Whitney looked around the room, trying to gauge her feelings, her eyes wandering across the abstract paintings and stacks of textbooks, I actually feel fine," she replied, looking back at him. It was true, she felt entirely normal. Perhaps a little less anxious, more relaxed, "I feel less anxious, more relaxed," she clarified, after a few beats.

"The effects of the surgery typically take about a week to kick in," he said, using the American terminology. "What you will experience is a gradual decrease of the fear impulse, until it all but disappears during highly stimulating events. I have denervated the pathways that would normally trigger it. Now, you need to be aware that there could be some unpredictable emotional side-effects during the transition. I'll be sending you home with an enantiomer nasal spray that will counteract these sensations if they should occur." He picked up a small vial and showed it to her. "A single squirt up into the nasal passages is all you will need. It is very powerful, and, I might add, undetectable in the blood stream. Only use it if you absolutely feel you need to, as it has tachyphylactic properties, meaning it only works in the short-term, and becomes less effective as you use it. Understand?" He handed it to her.

Whitney swallowed, nodding. She sure hoped she wouldn't need it. Whatever it was.

"What is an…an enantiomer?" she struggled with the pronunciation, looking at the vial, warily.

"It is a three- dimensional molecular structure with two identical appearing molecules that are mirror images of each other, with opposite R and S designations, a duality that co-exists within the molecule, akin to your duality as a mother of a young child and a professional extreme ski competitor….to use the metaphor, if I may…" he answered airily. "In my research I inadvertently discovered a neuropeptide that will stimulate emotional sensations somewhat like oxytocin, a neuropeptide that is responsible for maternal behaviors. At the same time, it will nullify your fear denervation. In other words, if you use it, you will experience fear as acutely as you did before surgery."

"Oh…I see," Whitney digested the information, barely understanding it. She did not see.

"If you have any questions, you may reach out to my staff, we are happy to help you," he smiled, benignly.

"Thank you," Whitney replied, puzzled. She thought everything was fine. Now, she was supposed to carry around this… this bottle called, she squinted at the label, ANTm3. A little peevishly, she put it in her pocket.

In two days, she would be leaving Belgrade. Consumco had scheduled her for seven a.m. flight to Gunnison Municipal Airport on the Gulfstream. Once they arrived, she would drive home to Crested Butte, check in on Robyn, pick up her ski equipment, then drive all the way back to Summit County to meet her teammates, in Frisco.

The prospect seemed daunting, but Dr. Belcic's staff reassured her, she'd be just fine.

# CHAPTER 8
# FRISCO

The road up Monarch Pass seemed to go on forever, mile after mile of steep, unrelenting grade that climbed endlessly, with no apparent summit in sight. The Taos' transmission growled and shifted, first into third gear, then into second as it labored up and up, fighting tough as they entered the thin, high-altitude air. Like a triumphant trojan horse, it rallied to the top, passing the other cars, far ahead. Whitney pressed the gas pedal to the floor and kept her foot firmly on it, wanting to get over the pass before sunrise. A dusting of light, powdery snow covered the road, the just-rising sun reflecting off its frigid surface in a glowing ribbon of white. She had left Crested Butte in a fit of haste at the crack of dawn, only going home last night to see Robyn, grab her stuff and get some sleep. Loaded with ski equipment and a determination to make it to Frisco before noon, she saw only a few vehicles on the desolate stretch of highway, leaving Gunnison.

At the top of the pass, she reflexively decelerated, the stretch of blacktop on the other side a notorious trap frequently coated with black ice in the frozen, shaded shadows of the forest. Three years earlier, she had slid uncontrollably on it in her old car, nearly careening off the mountainside. Monarch Pass had given her the heebie-jeebies ever since. Today though, it didn't bother her in the least, she felt remarkably relaxed driving over its crest. Descending the other side, she stayed in second gear along the six percent grade between the mountains, passing the Monarch Ski Area Day Lodge on her way towards Salida. At the highway's junction, Whitney turned and headed north, parallel with the Arkansas River and Collegiate Peaks. The brawny group of fourteeners loomed overhead along the river valley to Buena Vista.

She stopped in Buena Vista to get gas. The historic western town, renowned for its hot springs and massive mountain views, had a little diner that sat off the highway in a small, non-descript truck stop. She paused for an hour there to have breakfast. Over a plate of blueberry pancakes, she called the Pink Columbine Day Spa in Frisco to schedule a hair appointment.

"Pink Columbine Day Spa and Salon this is Chiffon speaking," a breathless, feminine voice answered.

*Chiffon?*

"Yes, um…I would like to get my hair cut today. I'd like to book a morning appointment, say, around eleven? Would that be possible? Whitney asked her, hopeful.

"Uh, let me see… we have Mervette available at eleven-thirty, would you like to schedule that for today…?"

"Yes, yes. And I need color. Can she do color?"

"She could do color; we need to schedule that for…uh, that would take us to two-thirty p.m…."

"Yes, let's do that. And I need my eyebrows waxed….do you do eyelash extensions? Whitney held her breath, giddy.

"Yes, our esthetician, Indra can do those for you. Did you want to schedule that as well?"

"Yes, YES!" she answered, emphatic.

There was a pause, she could overhear Chiffon speaking to someone.

"Indra says she can get you in at two-thirty today. Just so you know, eyelash extensions take two hours. Would you like me to schedule that for you too? May I please get your name?"

"Whitney Olson."

"Oh my *God!* Whitney Olson? The skier?" Chiffon's voice rose excitedly.

"Uh, yes."

"Is there anything else we can do for you?" she asked, voice skittering. She was levitating.

"I think I would like to get my nails done too."

"Of course, of course! I can get Ambergris this afternoon. She can do acrylics, is that what you want?"

Whitney pondered, uncertain. "Um, sure- that would be great." She asked Chiffon, "do you have a make-up artist there? Someone who can, um... show me how to put make-up on the right way?"

"Of course, of course! Cree can do that for you. Would you like me to schedule that for you? Is this the same day?"

"Yes. I want the works. Everything."

"Oh-kaaaay, this is going to take us until about eight p.m. tonight. Is that okay?"

"Yes."

"We'll look forward to seeing you at eleven- thirty, then. Thanks for calling."

Whitney finished breakfast and tapped her cellphone off with satisfaction. Now, on to Leadville… Back in the Taos, she drove another hour, arriving at the hardscrabble old mining town perched ten thousand feet above sea level. With a population of three thousand inhabitants, the town's historic main street was filling with cars, bustling to life as residents and visitors alike prepared for a day of winter sports in Eagle or Summit County.

Just another rollicking morning in the Colorado Rockies, Whitney thought to herself as she passed through the center of town. She dropped down the twisting highway towards Copper Mountain, one of her favorite ski areas in central Colorado. Bursting with incredible terrain, its snow-capped peaks surrounded her every turn. They beckoned enticingly. As she descended towards I 70, she shifted to lower gears along the steep grade, passing the Climax molybdenum mine. The sun shone brilliantly out now, blue sky electrifying.

Turning East on the freeway, she zoomed twelve more miles to the Frisco exit, then motored directly into the town's central business district. As usual, Frisco was a riot of activity, skiers tromping around the sidewalks and streets, buses full of tourists and children heading to the slopes; everyone rushing to Keystone, Breckenridge, Arapahoe Basin. She parked her car on the street and walked into the salon.

They finished her cut and color first. "Oooooh I like it!" Mervette crowed, admiringly. She stood behind Whitney in front of the mirror, their reflections shining back like a Jackson Pollock painting. Whitney had told her she wanted a drastic change. An urban, punk rock style like Debbie Harry during her CBGB days in New York City. With magenta color. And lime green highlights on the tips, framing her face.

Whitney looked at her reflection, barely recognizing herself.

"I really like it too. You did a great job." She studied her profile from side to side. Wowee. What a change.

Ambergris sat across from her and painted her nails a lovely magenta color that matched her new hair color. Obviously thrilled to be doing them, she asked Whitney if she could take a picture of the lacquered works of art for her Instagram account. It was *such* a special honor to work with *the* Whitney Olson, she cajoled. Whitney obliged. "Thank you *soooo* much," Ambergris told her, excitedly.

Next, Whitney went into a fluffy room with Indra, who peeled off all her extraneous hairs down to the last microfiber. Indra held up a mirror for her to see. "Your brows are *AMAZING!* she announced, emphatically. Whitney looked back at herself dubiously. What had once been a thick, bushy mess of eyebrows had now become thin, slanted strips that reminded her of Spock, from Star Trek. Indra spent another hour and a half gluing single, black false eyelashes onto her eyelids. It felt like she was wearing a furry tarantula on her face. All in all, she was coming along nicely.

Just wait Karis, here I come, she did cartwheels around the room, mentally.

Indra brought her over to Cree, who was waiting for her in a different part of the spa. Racks of make-up- facial creams, blushes, liners, glosses and glitter in every imaginable shade lined the walls.

"Let's do a purple eye shadow that sets off your hair color," Cree suggested, enthusiastically. Lining Whitney's eyes first with black gel, like Amy Winehouse, she added, "Here, I'll show you how to do it."

They spent the next hour applying artful dabs of pink and purples, highlighters and contour.

Cree stood back, gazed at her handiwork. The change was truly audacious, you had to admire it.

*Transfiguration,* Whitney thought, gazing at her own reflection in the mirror. She was really going to shock her teammates, she giggled internally, looking forward to it.

Chiffon tallied up her bill. A stack of make-up, a hair-straightening wand, a special bottle of shampoo and conditioner and vial of brow wax sat on the counter. Now eight-fifteen p.m., the place was preparing to close soon. Whitney grabbed some adhesive pink rhinestones off the display rack next to the register for her nose and eyebrows, before paying the final bill.

"That will be fifteen hundred dollars," Chiffon stated, sliding her visa card through the machine briskly.

*Yowzer.*

Whitney gulped, telling her, "Please add in three hundred dollars for tips, too."

Chiffon cooed, "Thank you so much! You look *fantastic*! Come see us again soon."

"*Thank you,*" Whitney exclaimed giddily, sliding out the door with her bag of new products, feeling a little like a fugitive on a murder spree.

She climbed back into her Taos and drove to the Airbnb, a large house on a cul-de-sac not far from the business district. The Sprinter was parked in the driveway, taking up most of the compact space. She parked on the street and went inside. Everyone was sitting around a rectangular pine coffee table in the lounge, eating pizza.

Duncan almost dropped his slice of pizza when she walked through the front door. Eyes widening, he blinked repeatedly. She had done something radical to her hair. He barely recognized her.

"Holy shit! Is that Whitney!? Mason threw his pizza down on the table, stood up and began Moon- walking backward. He crouched down, struck a ninja pose, fluttered his fingers rapidly. "Whitney has CHAAAANGED!" he chortled, careening around the room, raucously.

"Your stylist did a *terrible* job," Karis glanced up briefly, assessing. She looked back at her phone, took a bite of pizza.

*Witch.*

"I like it, I think it looks good," Ian commented. Whitney stared at him, shocked. *Did he just speak to her?* OMG.

Trent gazed at her with a glint in his eyes. She detected a small smile playing at the corner of his lips.

Alyn was eating some crust, she stopped chewing. "Whitney; let's get some photos of you soon. Say tomorrow? I *love* the new look!"

Shenti wandered into the lounge for a second slice, shirt partially unbuttoned, hair disheveled. Stopping in his tracks, he stroked his beard and squinted. "Is that *you* Whitney?" he mumbled, perplexed.

"JUST for your information, it *is* me," she announced to them all indignantly. "It *is* Whitney, and I'm going to bed. It's been a *very* long day." Grabbing a slice of pizza, she went to look for her bedroom, duffel bag in tow. Tomorrow she would go skiing. Alone, by herself. Just like Dr. Belcic suggested she do.

She was the new and *improved* Whitney. Everything else could wait.

# CHAPTER 9
# WHITNEY SKIS A-BASIN

L ike some strange dream she had but then forgotten, the procedure in Belgrade receded from her mind and she put the whole
disturbing episode behind her, intent on moving forward and
getting back into training with her teammates. Trent hadn't said anything at all to her about the trip, acting like the event never occurred.
His only comment to her as she retreated to her bedroom last night
was "tomorrow I want you to go to A-Basin and ski by yourself, see
how things go," demeanor making it abundantly clear that the topic
was closed, he was done with it, full stop.

Now, she was standing in a lift line at the base of A-Basin waiting
for a chair to whisk her halfway up the mountain. The intermediate runs would be perfect for getting her blood flowing and muscles
activated before skiing the expert runs at the top. In an hour or so,
she'd be ready to ascend to The Beavers and Montezuma Bowl where
she could ski the back bowls, evaluate any changes in her technique.

Arapahoe Basin boasted some of the highest terrain in the country and was legendary amongst local skiers for its authentic down-
home vibe and alpine terrain, without all the commercial trappings
that came with the larger, tourist-oriented resorts. Whitney loved the
challenging ski area like mother's milk; tonic for the soul, comfort

to her heart. Not only for its formidable steeps, but its stupendous views and sweeping vistas that spanned across the Continental Divide. When she departed out the front door this morning, Trent reminded her to start out easy. "Make some turns, see how it goes. Don't push too hard until you get a feel for your new risk tolerance."

Standing at the top of the chairlift now, she gazed over to the East Wall. The concave, nearly vertical face rose dramatically above the lower basin in a massive amphitheater of snow and jagged rock, candy to her eyes. With a push off her poles, she skied over to its belly and dropped into one of the many runs below. Her body immediately fell into an easy rhythm, hips and knees absorbing every miniscule change in the snow's feel and texture. Cruising easily down a powdery untracked line, she floated like a bobbin, effortlessly responding to the slope's varied bumps and features. Immediately, she sensed a shift. A lightness. She felt more agile. It was like…like she was free of *mind* and merely following her instinctive *self,* liberated from apprehension, anxiety or inhibition. She felt completely at ease and totally confident.

Taking the chairlift up again, she skied over to a different intermediate run right beside it, joining a group of skiers on their sojourn down the meandering, groomed slope. Perfectly balanced and in control, she carved broad turns through the snow sans resistance, sans strain. The energy previously expended to *resist* gravity, to *resist* the fall line from her subconscious fear of falling seemed to have melted away. She felt a purity of movement that was entirely unshackled from that most inhibiting of impediments, *fear.* It was unlike anything she had ever experienced before.

Straightening her skis, she crouched into tuck position and shot the rest of the way down like a bullet released from its chamber.

*Dang.* This was feeling *good!*

Time to stretch her wings. Catching the chairlift back to the top, she traversed across Lenawee Ridge, and headed over to Montezuma Bowl. Here, the crowds of skiers had thinned out. She was entering the back side of A-Basin and its ungroomed, natural steeps. Inhaling deeply, she took a few moments to gaze across the Rockies' spires and forests, deep valleys, blue sky, then murmur a prayer of gratitude to the mountain gods. The majestic peaks appeared to go on forever, their timeless beauty a lofty reward for those lucky enough to venture up to these most dramatic of places.

Pushing off her poles, she dropped into the wide- open bowl and began making broad, gentle turns down the untracked face. Shoulders and knees falling into their familiar pattern, absorbing the dips and troughs, skis brushing the snow beneath the surface, she responded to each tactile variation with an automatic, effortless adjustment. Exhaling methodically, she allowed her body to let go and accept the continuously changing sensations without analysis or *thought.* Skiing between a cluster of rock headwalls and stunted pines, she glided down the slope like a gentle mountain stream following gravity to the bottom.

A buzz of excitement zinged through her, the shift in her skiing already apparent. Catching the Montezuma lift to the top of the Lenawee Ridge again, she traversed farther across the ridge towards a more isolated spot. Dense stands of pine, aspen and untracked snow beckoned invitingly. Here, she turned up her mojo considerably. Skiing through the knolls and natural features, she popped off some kickers, zig-zagged through trees down a hidden, shaded gully.

Something akin to adrenaline, though tranquil in its countenance, coursed through her body like rocket fuel, igniting her zeal.

*Sweeeeet!* Her inner cheetah was back and starting to roar.

The next run she selected was at the farthest end of the ridge, away from the main area, where people seldom ventured. Traversing across the entire ridge, she picked her way through trees, exposed rocks, logs and heavy, untracked snow. At the very edge of the ski area's boundary now, she had a wild and untamed stretch of heaven to herself. From this idyllic perch, she could see the serrated peaks of the Gore Range and Holy Cross wilderness like a picture-perfect postcard from Nepal or Tibet. Taking a deep breath, she inhaled the crisp, clean air then dove into its beckoning, untamed pool. Independent and free, untethered, unbound, she ripped down the fall line like a person possessed. Catapulting off a series of uneven knolls, descending at breakneck speed, she executed a single, then double- front flip off two consecutive rock headwalls. Popped off a kicker near the base of the run with an iron cross 720, sticking the landing with a solid whump on the snow. At this point, she felt totally, insanely, invincible. *Was this what it felt like to be a man? she wondered, awestruck.* The mountain was her bitch, she owned it.


Late afternoon she returned to the house, utterly spent but totally enthralled. Trent, Ian, Mason and Karis were sitting at the rectangular oak dining table, next to the kitchen. Three 12-packs of neon green, aluminum cans were stacked like a rock cairn in the center of it, Trent called over to her, droll. "We're having a meeting, Whitney- come join the party."

Hanging up her parka in the laundry room to dry, she left on her ski pants and sweater and went over to join them. True to form, Ian had his earbuds in, eyes closed, listening to who-knows-what. Karis was scrolling her cellphone, obviously bored. Mason was munching cashews, tossing them into his mouth like a seventh grader. She pulled out a chair and sat down.

Trent looked over at her, pointing, "This is Consumco's newest sports drink. AcyDgreen. It's made with watercress, lime and kiwi," he said, informing her. "We're supposed to promote it. Each of you is gonna taste it and say something useful. Got it?" he stated, all business.

Mason yanked a can from the top of the stack and pulled back the tab. Taking a swig, he swished it around his mouth, noisily. "Tastes like donkey piss, but less filling!" he announced, setting the can back on the table with a bang.

"I don't care if it tastes like horse's ass, you're gonna pitch it." Trent shot at him, irritated.

"Yes, coach."

"Whitney?"

She reached for a can and pulled back the tab, taking a sip, gingerly. "Um, I think it is…quite acidic, but someone would probably enjoy it," she offered, diplomatic.

Karis glanced up from her phone, gave her a withering look.

"Karis." Trent barked.

She set her phone on the table, selected a can, took a careful sip. "Ummmm… It's not what I would personally choose to drink… but I *will* tell my friends in Aspen about it. They might buy it for their parties and stuff," she sniffed, disinterested. She picked up her phone again and continued scrolling through it.

"Ian."

He pulled an earbud out of one ear, blinked his eyes, startled. "Did you say something?"

Trent pursed his lips at him, exasperated, "Here's how it's gonna work. When you finish your run, Alyn's gonna hand you the can. You're gonna pop that tab off and throw that sucker back like it's the best goddam beverage you've ever had in your entire frickin' life. And then Shenti's gonna shoot the clip. Understand?" he inhaled pointedly, frowning.

Ian nodded.

They all nodded, agreeing.

"Karis, would you kindly show us how it's done?" He said flatly, giving her a look.

Standing up with an exaggerated sigh, she set her phone on the table again and took a can. Popped open the tab and struck a suggestive pose, hips thrust out, chest tilted up. Flipping her long, golden tresses with the back of her hand, she raised it to her mouth and took a long, satisfied gulp. She flashed a blinding, toothy smile and exclaimed breathlessly, "There's *noooothing* I love more than AcyDgreen after a *killer* run down the mountain!"

She sat back down, picked up her phone.

Trent nodded, lips down. "And that, my friends, is how it's done," he stated, with satisfaction.

Karis scowled. "I have to take this call. It's Sven."

Trent frowned, "This meeting is adjourned. FYI we are flying out of Eagle airport Monday for Prince Rupert. Plane departs at 9:50 a.m. Be packed and ready to go," he stood up from the table, leaving them.

As Whitney left the table, she overheard Karis speaking to Sven Nordigren, her Swedish boyfriend. World Cup downhill racer with Adonis-like looks, she periodically hooked up with him when they were on the same continent. "My parents are soooo superficial. All they care about is money, status and winning. I *hate* them!" she lamented on the phone. Moments later, Whitney heard her fervently tell him, "My mom and dad said that if I win WESC they will buy me a new Range Rover! Isn't that *awesome?*"

She made an exasperated sigh, headed towards her room.

Alyn caught her in the hallway. "Hey- could we do some photos of you this afternoon? I'm starting to write your feature for Outside Magazine. I'd like to start your interview too," she proposed, quickly.

"Of course. I'll get ready right away," she told her, instantly excited. "How 'bout we meet on the deck in an hour?" She needed to wash, style and blow dry her hair. Apply her new make-up and attach a rhinestone to her left nostril; another above her right eyelid. This would take some time.

Her cellphone rang. It was her dad. He didn't call that often; it must be serious. "Whitney, I just wanted to let you know Robyn is having some trouble with her medication. Not terrible, not like that, but she's been feeling a little nauseated. We had to keep her home from school yesterday. Just wanted to let you know... I didn't want to worry you, but your mom asked me to give you call." She cringed. Her dad was a peach, always working, always taking care of the family. Now, he had to deal with this problem. Originally moving to Crested Butte in order to spend more time outdoors, he had essentially ended up doing childcare and running basecamp instead. She replied hurriedly, "Dad, thanks for letting me know. Listen, I need to do a promotional thing with Alyn right now, can we talk later?" she asked. All this medical stuff would have to wait, she was too busy.

"Sure, honey, of course. Take care," he replied, hanging up.

Alyn was waiting for her on the deck outside the kitchen, with her Nikon and a bag of lenses. Whitney grabbed a can of AcyDgreen on the way out the sliding glass doors to meet her.

"Let's take some shots with the new product, okay?" Alyn told her. "How 'bout some fun poses. Try squatting down and balancing the can on your head," she suggested, holding her camera and aiming it at Whitney. "Great!" she stated, enthusiastically. "Let's try some others," she clicked away, rapidly. Whitney moved around with the can, trying to be creative. "Why don't we go out front of the house. Bring your skis," Alyn proposed. "We'll get some shots of you in tuck position with the can balanced on your back, or your helmet." Whitney nodded, agreeing. They left the back deck, Whitney grabbing her boots and skis from the mud room. They shot another round of digital photos near the driveway.

Finishing the session, they went back inside and sat down in the lounge. Alyn opened her laptop and began asking Whitney questions. How was she feeling about her prospects for competing in the Nationals? How was her training going? Where was her favorite place to ski?" She typed away.

Then she pivoted and inquired casually, "I understand you have a daughter with some health issues, how is that impacting your career?" she glanced up, momentarily.

Whitney caught her breath, surprised. She hadn't anticipated this question. Robyn's condition was something she downplayed, even concealed from her team. She didn't want them to think that she wasn't completely focused on her training or that it detracted from her ability to travel and do all the promotional work.

Alyn looked at her expectantly, waiting for an answer.

She responded, measured, "My parents and our pediatrician have things very well under control. In my opinion, it's not an issue. We communicate about her medical needs when I'm on the road, it's not something that affects my training." There. Enough said, she thought internally.

Alyn led with the next question, "You changed your make-up and hair style dramatically this year. What prompted you to change your look?"

Oh jeez, another trap, Whitney thought, sighing. What was she supposed to say? That she was perpetually insecure about her appearance? That she never felt like she could measure up to Karis's effortless beauty? That she was constantly worried Consumco would let her go because of her average looks? *Even though she was the top-ranked female freeskier in the whole country?*

Somewhat evasively, she tried to sound nonchalant. "I just felt like it was time for a change…just thought I'd step out of my comfort zone and have a little fun with fashion, that's all," she answered, lightly.

Alyn could tell she was fibbing; she gave Whitney a cynical look. Usually able to cajole information from interviewees with disarming ease, she knew when she was being gaslighted. And right now, she was being gaslighted. As a journalist who had acquired skills long ago working for the Seattle Times in investigative reporting before being hired by Consumco to write fluff pieces for the company full time, she recognized the signs. She paused, annoyed. Whitney asked her lamely, deflecting, "Do you have any aspirations yourself, Alyn? I mean, besides doing work for Consumco?" she added, fidgeting.

Alyn shrugged briefly, she replied, "Well, I've always wanted to write a book, I suppose," mouth flat, ending the interview. She got what she was going to get, the rest was superficial prattle. Clearly, Whitney was holding back. The question was, *what* was she holding back? And why?

Whitney jumped up quickly and went into the kitchen, rummaging around for a snack. While she ate, Alyn uploaded the digital photos to Consumco's sports Facebook page for publication, she would send the other AcyDgreen promo shots to Tik Tok, YouTube and Instagram later this evening. By tomorrow, the images would have over twenty million hits.

She had been around Whitney long enough on this tour to read between the lines, understand her ambivalence about sharing information about her daughter's medical issues. That was understandable. But there were other things to talk about. It was apparent that Whitney was shutting down. She wanted to know more about Whitney's increased assertiveness, her feelings as a single parent and athlete, why she seemed so worried that her equipment was being tampered with. Intuitively, she knew there was more behind the surface, that she was missing something important.

## CHAPTER 10

# WHITNEY AND KARIS SKI PARK, AT COPPER

Eight in the morning, Trent sat waiting for them in the driver's seat of the Sprinter, warming up the engine in the driveway. Whisps of white exhaust belched from the van's tail pipe, dissipating into the frigid air. Grabbing her gear bag, twin tips and ski boots, Whitney hurriedly lumbered down the front walkway of the house and stowed everything into the van's cargo bay, climbing inside the back seat behind Trent and buckling her seatbelt. Silently, they waited for Karis. Fifteen minutes went by, Trent exhaled impatiently, taking sips of coffee from his travel mug and fiddling with the defrost buttons. Karis finally materialized, looking utterly fabulous in an elegant, dove gray and creamy beige quilted Bogner ski jacket with form fitting, matching beige ski pants with gold zippers and hardware on the waistband. *Must have cost at least twenty-five hundred dollars,* Whitney sighed internally, trying to warm her cold, stiff hands over the back console heater. Maybe she should go over to Vail tomorrow and buy a new Bogner jacket, she considered, fretting. If she had one, she would look more Instagram worthy, more *hot…* it might even increase her number of followers, her influence….

Too expensive, she dismissed the idea glumly. The gorgeous ski-wear was completely out of her league. Clearly, the apparel was only provided to Karis because it looked so great on her. If she wanted to own her own Bogner, she'd have wait until she made a lot more money, she sighed, resignedly. Maybe if she won Nationals….

With a clattering heave, Karis shoved her equipment in the cargo bay and then climbed inside, taking a seat behind Whitney in the last row. "I'm freezing my ass off back here, could you turn up the heat?" she spat.

Trent's shoulders tensed. A pause.

"What do you say," he stated, voice flat as a pancake.

"*Pleeeeeze.*"


The parking lot at Center Village was already overflowing, Trent steered the Sprinter into a private lot for guest Medallion members, coveted parking privilege another convenient and expensive perk that Consumco provided the team. Here, they were able to get a prime space near the area's base and walk right up to the village ski lockers, thirty yards away.

Still barely communicating, save a few monosyllables, the three lugged their equipment towards the entrance, snow crunching under their boots. Bracingly cold outside, their breath swirled out in frozen, white puffs. Already the main village was swarming with tourists and locals, crowds weaving around the ticket windows and ski shops, children pouring outside for snowboard and ski lessons with instructors in tow. Friends were yelling at friends, skiers buzzed around the crowded gondola station and lift lines in a happy, excited madhouse.

They walked briskly into the ski locker building to get ready. Setting her canvas duffel bag on a well-worn wooden bench, Whitney extricated her winter gloves and helmet, then looked for her goggles.

*Where were they?* she fumed, chewing her lip. Rummaging through all her accessories, she searched for the critical piece of eyewear amidst the tangle of scarves, wool hats, packs of orange chemical warmers and aluminum water bottles. Alarmed, she dumped everything out of the bag onto the floor, picking through all the items. They were nowhere to be found. Trent and Karis had already finished getting ready and were standing near the exit door, waiting for her.

*Dammit!* she cursed under her breath. Without her goggles, she'd be snow blind in two hours.

She'd have to purchase a new set, that was her only option. Frustrated, she called out to Trent and Karis, across the room. "Go ahead to the terrain park without me. I'll meet you guys later... can't find my goggles- must have left them in my car," she waved them off, disconcertedly. They shook their heads in dismay and departed, leaving her alone.

Hurriedly, she left the room with her equipment and joined the throngs of skiers, tromping in her ski boots to the closest ski shop she could find. Scrambling around a bustling shop, she scanned the display racks for a replacement. A salesperson came over to help. Unlocking a long, glass display case full of goggles and lenses, he offered her assistance. She bit her lip, upset. A new set of top end Oakley Flight's with all-season lenses would set her back almost two hundred dollars. Worth every penny, one of the finest goggles out there, she rued spending the money. She needed to conserve every dollar for Robyn's medical care. Spending this amount on a different pair was infuriating.

"Looks like we don't have the Oakley's in stock," the young man told her regretfully, searching through the rows of colorful goggles in the storage drawers, below.

*Shit!* Why spend money on a set she didn't want, especially when Consumco would just send over the Oakley's next week? Reluctantly, she selected an inexpensive, off-brand goggle just to get through the day.

"Better try them on, see if they fit," he suggested politely, pointing to a large mirror on the opposite wall, obviously not recognizing her. And why should he? She barely recognized herself after that wild flight of sanity at the Pink Columbine Day Spa, last week.

Pulling her helmet off she tried them on, standing in front of the mirror. The sight of her magenta hair and green highlights startled her. She looked like a flamboyant sea creature emerging from the ocean floor with dark, purple eyeballs.

Against her better judgement, she handed the young man her Visa and paid for them, thanking him profusely for his help. She'd just have to adjust to the new, smaller lenses as she practiced this morning. More than a little frazzled now, she grabbed her skis and poles and rushed towards the chairlift.

Waiting in the queue for twenty -minutes, she finally slid onto a chair and skied off at the top, eventually locating Trent and Karis half-way down the terrain park, busy talking to each other. She absolutely hated starting a training day like this, discombobulated, trying to catch up.

"You're *sooooo* late," Karis hissed at her, shooting Whitney a disdainful look.

Whitney raised her gloved right hand, made a clawing motion in the air, like a cat. "Meow," she snarled back at her, exasperated.

Trent rolled his eyes, chagrined. "Okay you guys, let's warm-up on some rails and half-pipe," he told them, annoyed. He would ski beside them both in the terrain park, analyzing every move. When they reached the bottom of the run, they would ride the chair up together, multiple times.

Whitney put in her earbuds and turned on some tunes, trying to get focused. Foster the People and David Bowie's Greatest Hits instantly flooded her head as they zipped down the hill, heading into the zone. Crouching down, she popped onto a rail and slid sideways then dropped back onto the snow, rotating her body 180 degrees. Skiing backwards, she prepared for the box. Instantly she switched back around and slid along the hard surface laterally. Then she dropped back onto the slope, her twin-tips rotating once again. *Shit!* These goggles were messing with her timing. Not only were the lenses smaller, they lacked the clarity she was accustomed to. Unnerved, she was just going on instinct now, trying to adjust to them as she skied. The situation was adding a whole new layer of difficulty and danger, she grimaced, aggravated. The last thing she needed was an injury caused by a piece of unfamiliar equipment.

Slowing down a bit, she performed a series of 360's on the surface of the snow, raising her left leg high in the air like a ballet dancer's pirouette. Approaching the enormous half-pipe, she aligned her skis and crouched low, entering the pipe. Swooping down and across it, she popped off its lip, rotating a full 360 degrees in the air. Spring loaded and gathering momentum, she dropped back in and

swooped across to the other side, launching off its lip with a back tail
-grab and switch rotation, getting big air. Scooting across the hard,
icy surface again, she spiraled downward, executing multiple tricks
and grabs all the way to the bottom. The sound of Karis's twin- tips
scraped the snow, not far behind. Trent observed them intently, binoculars raised to his eyes.

Taking gulps of cold, dry air, the three caught the triple chair
back up, Trent sat in the middle, impassive, DMZ zone between
North Korea on his left side, and South Korea on his right. They
pulled some energy bars from their parkas and chewed them med-
itatively, gazing out across the fir- covered mountain and glittery
white slopes. Overhead, the sun blazed bright and clear, the sky a
preternatural blue.

Sliding off the chair, they skied over to an area where enormous
mounds of snow had been artificially configured into massive ski
jumps cascading down the mountainside in fearsome waves. Only
the most experienced and exceptionally skilled freestyle skiers would
dare utilize them. The area was largely devoid of skiers, providing
plenty of room for them to practice. Trent skied first, stopping at the
middle of the slope, then traversing offside to select a perch to best
watch Karis and Whitney perform their aerials. Per their usual routine, they were to move away from the landing zone and wait for him
to ski over and consult with them, following each successive jump.

Trent signaled up to Whitney. He wanted her to perform a front
flip, twist.

She turned into the hill, hips down and knees bent, preparing
the inrun. Popping off the lip, she gathered air before tucking her
knees to her chest and rotating forward; arms near hips, turning

upside down, adding a twist. Four seconds went by. Unfurling her torso, extending her legs, she contacted the ground, staying balanced and forward, completing the aerial. She waited on the side. Trent skied over to her.

"Not bad, not bad! You need more energy on the kicker though, more extension before initiating the flip, okay? The judges will be looking for height. Try to enter with more speed on the next jump, think five seconds, instead of four, okay?" he stated, evaluating her.

She nodded, affirmative. The goggles she purchased were making it hard to tell precisely where the kicker was, throwing her timing off. Normally, she had exceptionally good depth perception and proprioception, years of gymnastic lessons and hours spent on her trampoline instilling a strong sense of where her body was in space and what exactly it was doing when she did an aerial. But this morning, everything felt a little different, off. Not wanting to make excuses though, she resisted the urge to complain. She'd just have to suck it up, do better.

He signaled Karis next. Immediately she took off, svelte form racing down the inrun, entering the jump with impressive extension and speed. Airborne, her front flip twist had excellent elevation, she bobbled only a slight bit on the landing, legs slightly apart. Recovering quickly, she stopped on the slope waiting for Trent's feedback.

"Your left arm was a little forward in the rotation and your weight shifted to your left ski, creating an imbalance on the landing, forcing your right leg to over-compensate and bobble" he told her, lips pursed. "Try to keep both arms in the exact same position while you're in your tuck, okay?" he added, exactingly.

Karis nodded rapidly, gulping air with deep breaths.

They set up for the next jump; this bad boy was considerably larger.

Trent instructed; "I want you each to perform a back layout. Four elements to remember: Maximum extension off the kicker, legs together, arms extended symmetrically, clean landing. Got it?"

They nodded in concentration, rapt. At this high altitude, both were giddy with anticipation as the adrenalin and difficulty level ratcheted up. The back layout was an aerial they both relied upon to impress judges during competition and accrue points for showmanship. Both were very good at it. If Whitney wanted to get a higher score than Karis, she'd have to add a full twist, an additionally dangerous element.

After completing their back-layouts and sticking their landings, they waited for Trent's signal above the final jump near the base of the ski run.

A double- back flip, tuck. Whitney's heart skipped with excitement. To her surprise, she had no anxiety nor apprehension about the challenging maneuver. Despite the eyewear, she was feeling incredibly confident-- quite fearless, in fact. She could tell the procedure was really kicking in.

He signaled for Karis to go first. Pushing off with determination, she entered the inrun and popped off the kicker, hurtling herself backwards to execute each rotation. Slightly short on lift, she was unable to complete the entire second rotation and straighten her torso before landing. Without sufficient height, she came down too low and slammed her poles hard into the slope, her heals digging into the snow. Leaning backwards, she skidded on her backside thirty yards down the hill, careening to a stop. One pole bent in the middle, both metal sticks went flying across the snow. She lay on her right side, arms splayed. Trent skied over to her, giving her a few moments to recover. Helping her up, he admonished her tersely, "Not enough lift, Karis. Too slow entering the flip, knees need to come up faster, kiddo."

Glowering, she bent over, trying to catch her breath.

He turned his gaze uphill, signaling Whitney.

Taking a deep breath, she skied downhill and flew off the jump, aggressively slapping her knees up to her chest. Rotating backwards, she spun quickly in a tuck position twice, counting to six. Planting her skis back onto the snow, she reestablished her balance atop them instantly, extending her torso up to a near standing position. Relaxing her shins, she flexed her knees in a forward stance, sticking the landing. *Bingo*.

Trent nodded, affirmative. Thumbs up.

That was the best you were going to get from him, Whitney knew from experience.


Even though both women were in extraordinary condition, physical and mental strain from the grueling practice set in. Quadriceps and calves burning, cramping painfully, their energy began to flag. Despite their bruises and pulled ligaments, they kept up the relentless pace all afternoon, Trent driving them harder and harder until they were nearly delirious with fatigue.

By three p.m., totally exhausted from the intensity of the practice and meeting Trent's demands, the afternoon culminated in a Karis meltdown when he stormed at her, "You need to concentrate harder and keep your head in the game- you're losing your edge." Hearing that, she refused to do the last several jumps and instead sulked on the sidelines red-faced and angry while Whitney finished her final set. Both had taken multiple falls and bruised their tailbones; Whitney hyperextended her thumb. Mood volatile and dark, Karis angrily slammed her poles into a garbage can on their way back to the van.

When they got back to the house, Duncan rushed outside to help them unload their ski gear and clean out the Sprinter. Whitney immediately went through her car and searched for her goggles. Not finding them there, she went back inside and continued searching everywhere else she could think of. Finally, to her relief, she located them in the laundry room, wedged down between the washer and dryer. Apparently, they had slipped off the top of a machine.

She didn't recall bringing her goggles inside yesterday after she returned from skiing.

Had she? She wracked her brain, trying to remember. Maybe she did. *No, I didn't... I did not....*

Her cellphone rang. Luann. Gingerly, she answered it.

"Whitney, I wanted to talk to you about Robyn, I really think you should be home with her, I spoke with your mom, I understand she's been having some problems with her medicine... Don't you think you should be here with her right now? Honestly, if Kyle were alive, I'm sure he would be very upset...we both know that. I wanted to talk to you about this...it's really bothering me," she took a breath.

Oh jeez, Luann could really lay the guilt on thick, Whitney grimaced, inwardly. She *could not* do this to her anymore, she'd had enough. Indignantly, she retorted, "Luann, I would appreciate it you backed off a little. My parents and our pediatrician are handling things very well." Adding, "I think that Kyle would have wanted me to keep competing, if you want to know the truth." Luann sputtered a second, then hung up in a huff. Normally, she was extremely deferential to Luann, intimidated by the domineering woman. But today was different, she felt *emboldened*. It felt good to stick up for herself. Unfazed, she started packing for their Prince Rupert flight. They were heading to Bella Coola tomorrow.

Duncan came back into the house, carrying her ski boots. He stopped at her bedroom door. "Hey, did you see you tore off your battery pack on your right boot?" he showed her. Sure enough, the metal pack was hanging off the side with the electrical wires ripped apart. She peered at it, dismayed. "Don't worry-I'll run into town and get you a new one before we leave tomorrow," he reassured her, quickly.

"Thanks Duncan, I really appreciate it…probably can't buy that thing in Bella Coola," she replied, gratefully.

Duncan, the guardian angel.

"How did it go today?" he asked concerned, leaning against the doorway. She looked spent.

"Pretty typical. Trent worked us like rented mules. I almost broke my thumb," she showed him her right hand.

"Let's get some ice on that rightaway," he told her, heading into the kitchen. "Maybe take a little Ibuprofen, it should help with the swelling."

"Yeah, good idea," she called back to him, gratefully. He was already looking for a bottle in his first aid kit.

"Where'd Mason and Ian go?"

"I think they went out for a beer when they got back from ski-ing," he answered from the kitchen.

Whitney caught up with him at the refrigerator. She lowered her voice, "Hey, did you happen to see anyone open my car doors this morning? Or last night, by any chance?"

He looked puzzled. "No, I didn't. Why? What's wrong?" he asked, brows furrowing.

"Just wondered, that's all. I was trying to figure out how my Oakley's ended up in the laundry room. I don't remember putting them there." She knew she sounded daffy.

Trent walked in the kitchen. "Hey, Whitney, you looked *good* out there today," he offered robustly, grabbing a can of AcyDgreen from the frig. "Duncan. I need you to go find Shenti," he ordered. "I have no idea where he is. I need to talk to him before we leave. Would you go look for him?" his voice trailed off his shoulder as he strode out the room. Christ. This group was like lassoing cattle all day long.

Duncan nodded. "I need to go, I'll talk to you later, he told Whitney, hurriedly. "Keep that ice on your hand for fifteen- minute intervals over the next several hours, okay?"


She went back to her room to finish packing, she needed to load up her car before bedtime so she could get up in the morning and drive to the airport, meet everyone else there before departure. Karis was taking a shower, she could hear the water running in the bath-room, down the hall.

Karis's room was right across from hers. Her door was open, a pile of toiletries and clothing spilled across her bed beside her duffel bag. Whitney glanced over. Glimpsing a little vial, she peered closer. It looked like the same one that Dr. Belcic had given her in Belgrade.

Sitting in a pile of lotions and soap, make-up and shampoo, she almost didn't see it.

Furtively, she tiptoed across the hall to get a closer look. Picking up the vial, she quickly examined its label.

ANTm3. The plastic seal was still shrink wrapped in place, obviously never opened. She set the vial down like a live grenade and darted back to her room.

Karis *had* gotten the procedure, just as she suspected.

# CHAPTER 11
# BELLA COOLA

D ropping into the fjords of Bella Coola was like sinking into a bowl of white clam chowder in a freezing cold afternoon by the sea. The Gulfstream 650 was flying on instruments now, only the tips of the toothy pinnacles and jagged peaks of British Columbia's Canadian Coastals were visible through the heavy cloud and fog. As they descended, Whitney was able to see more of their craggy spires and glaciated walls, their endless waves of snow-capped mountains and desolate valleys. 3.25 million acres of pure, backcountry bliss.

Situated between the Kitimat Range to their north and the Pacific Range to their south, she got a glimpse of Mt. Saugstad, flanked by both arms of the Bentinck Inlet and Mt. Waddington, the tallest peak in the entire province. In a few moments, the Gulfstream would touch down onto the single air airstrip beside the massive inlet flowing inland from the Johnston Strait and the rugged, remote coast of the Pacific Ocean. All eyes were fixated out the windows as the plane descended in altitude and prepared for landing.

Largely inhabited by the Nuxalk, an indigenous First Nation tribe known for its expert wood carvers and painters, gorgeous ceremonial masks, totem poles and native jewelry depicting animals, salmon and sun deities, the region was also famous for its big mountain skiing. Whitney looked forward to visiting some art galleries while she was there and learning more about the area. Duncan had arranged for them to stay at the historic Tweedsmuir Park Lodge for the next eight days, she hoped they would have some extra time to explore the area together.

They had departed Eagle County Airport in Colorado at nine a.m. that morning, only stopping for an hour at Vancouver Airport to check in with Customs and Immigration and refuel. Now late afternoon, the sun was quickly disappearing behind a blanket of fog hanging over Bella Coola like a ghostly shroud. Darkness would soon approach, they were so far north. Nestled inside the Great Bear Rain Forest along the Atnarko River, in a protected biosphere of old-growth cedar, fir, moss and fern, the remote outpost was unlike any other place Whitney had ever traveled to ski. Bella Coola Heli-Sports was sending two mountain guides over to meet them on the tarmac, soon as they touched down.

The Gulfstream rolled to a stop on the empty airstrip. Whitney had dozed off on the flight, still sore from yesterday's aerial practice at Copper Mountain with Karis and Trent. Duncan had given her some Ibuprofen and a small icepack to hold on the plane, but her thumb was still slightly swollen and an unhappy, bluish gray. Right now, all she wanted was a hot shower and hot meal and a chance to call her mom to find out how Robyn was doing. She wondered if they had gone to Colorado Springs and done the brain scans that Dr. McClellan had ordered.

On the flight to Vancouver, Trent had sat down beside her in one of the plush, leather seats for several minutes, pleased to inform her that her photos with AcyDgreen had been a huge success on social media, yesterday. It was one of the rare moments she had seen him really smile. Soon as Alyn had posted them on Instagram, the company experienced an uptick in sales and bump in profit. She was amazed to hear that she had influenced the market, altered the value of their stock, not believing how quickly it happened.

"Guess they liked your new hairdo," Trent added, grinning uncharacteristically. He stood up and moved back to his own seat.

On the plane, Alyn handed her a new issue of Outside magazine she just received from Consumco's marketing division. "You might want to read it," she suggested, offhand. "Your feature should be coming out soon."

Whitney glanced at the cover. Ian was doing a mule kick off a thirty- foot cliff in Silverton, his interview on page twenty-eight. Trent seemed very satisfied with Ian; Alyn noted. He appeared happier with Whitney lately, too. Generally moody and inscrutable, he was hard to read and even tougher to please. But something had changed. Alyn couldn't quite put her finger on it, she just sensed *something* had shifted.

The Gulfstream rolled to a stop on the empty airstrip. The engine cut and the doors opened. Duncan immediately lept from the cabin to assist loading bags, equipment, skis into the two white, 1-ton vans the tour company sent out to meet them. The muscular, mid-thirties guides, Shane Pietla and Alex Ahrens enthusiastically introduced themselves to everyone, eager to finally meet the team. They all piled into the vehicles to drive back to the lodge, thirty minutes away.

Highly skilled professionals, Shane and Alex would be facilitating the team's heli-tours for the duration of their stay. The plan was to meet tomorrow morning right after breakfast at the lodge for orientation, discuss the exact locations the crew wanted to ski and shoot video.

The weather was turning into absolute crap, unfortunately. Shane and Alex warned them on the way over that it might be a few days before the helis could fly. "You could be sitting in the hot tub and playing ping-pong for a while until the weather clears," they told the group, apologetically. Mason chuckled happily, said that sounded just fine, he could use a good, long soak. Trent had grimaced, dour. Consumco wanted more video soon as possible for their AcyDgreen promotional campaign and he absolutely hated delays, they never reflected well on him. And it was never a good to have Shenti unoccupied for long stretches of time, especially in bad weather.

Whitney had her own private room at the lodge, thank God. Sharing space with Karis had become increasingly uncomfortable, she wasn't sure she trusted her. And the thing with the procedure was making her feel a little weirded- out lately. Trent had told her she couldn't talk about it, but how was she supposed to act like nothing had happened? Or pretend like nothing had changed? She often wondered if Mason and Ian had the procedure as well. Or was it just her and Karis? and if that were the case, why would they be the ones pressured into doing it? Odd. She chewed her lip, puzzled by all the secrecy and unanswered questions.

Could it be because they were female? she considered, not wanting to go there...Better to stuff that horrible thought into the mental incinerator, she shuddered, the implications were too disturbing...

Lying in bed, head on her pillow, she flipped open Outside and began reading Ian's interview, surprised to find herself drawn into the candid and revealing feature, she knew so little about him.

Alyn: You began skiing at a very young age. Can you tell us about that?

Ian: Well, it was by default, really. There was nothing else to do. My dad worked in Guest Services, just a fancy way of saying he was a line cook and custodian at the ski lodge's restaurant and bar, up at Mt. Baker Ski Area, when I was five years old. He used to drive me up there in the middle of winter so he could go to work. Told me to find something to do, keep myself busy while he flipped burgers and cleaned the bathrooms. Mom had a drug addiction, abandoned us when I turned four and dad got custody of me… So anyway, I would wander around the ski area, looking for things to do all day while he worked. Got myself some gloves and ski pants, hats and goggles in the lost and found bins and found some ski poles…The folks who ran the ski shop got used to seeing me around the store, scrounging around for things to use. Guess they took pity on me. "Oh, there's John Karoliks kid…" They gave me their old equipment, stuff they were going to throw out, anyway. I'd take anything--short skis, long skis, snowboards, whatever. Didn't matter. Dragged it all outside. Found some old boots that barely fit me, then just scooted around, trying to imitate what everyone else was doing. That's how I learned.

Alyn: You said your mother abandoned you…?

Ian: She had problems, you know, never got a handle on them. Moved back to Seattle- I'm not sure *where* she is, actually… I haven't heard from her in over seven years. Once in a blue moon she calls me, if she happens to have a cellphone or is sober. Dad moved us up to Glacier, Washington. We lived in a little old cabin at the base of

Mt. Baker, in the North Cascades. He took care of me. That place was burly, dude. I mean, you could go up to Mt. Baker, Mt. Shuksan, and get into some real trouble—huge, burly backcountry, deep, heavy snow, steeps like none other... it was the birthplace of extreme skiing before extreme skiing was even "a thing" ...I figured if I could ski up there, I could ski anywhere... Making the transition to the Chugach or the Alps was easy...

Alyn: When did you start developing as a real big-mountain free-rider? How did that evolve?

Ian: I was just snowboarding and skiing up at Baker every weekend, sometimes tagged along with the regulars there, a group of guys my age from Mt. Baker High School. Some were instructors, some were even ski patrol. We'd go shred the gnar in the steeps above Austin Pass, really rip it up good outside the area's boundary. Build our own jumps, do tricks, do massive aerials like there was no tomorrow... sometimes there *was* no tomorrow, if you know what I'm sayin'...."(*laughs, ruefully*) Anyway, word gets out, "Hey, there's these guys who are fuckin' awesome up at Baker, you should see the shit these guys are doin'!" Someone starts shootin' video... this guy from Bellingham, Mt. Vernon, I can't remember his name...Anyway, the video gets out, the next thing you know some dude from a film company is trying to get in touch with me and get me in his films. That's how it evolved. Then Consumco came a knockin' at my door.

Alyn: How did you manage high school with all this going on, at the time?

Ian: I never fit in with school at all, the teachers said I was "spectrum," whatever the hell that means. Couldn't concentrate, didn't want to be there, just wanted to be up at the mountains, skiing the steeps. Down in the real world, it sucked. Up here in the snow, I exist.

I belong. I can fly with the eagles… (*Makes flapping motion with his arms, then entwines them like a human corkscrew*).

Whitney closed the magazine and shut her eyes, the soft patter of rain outside her window lulling her to sleep. She pulled her blankets over her head, cocoon-like, in her little room.

In the morning, Shane and Alex discussed plans for their tour as they sat in the spacious central lounge constructed of northwest coast timber, decorated with Nuxalt artwork. Cedar beams lined the high, vaulted ceiling, and enormous, vertical windows looked out across the sixty- acre compound. Cloud and heavy fog blanketed the region, a combination of rain and snow had started falling. A large map of the surrounding mountain ranges hung on the wall, in front of them.

Alex explained, "We'll be taking the Bell 212 up to Munday Glacier, day after tomorrow. There should be a break in the weather by then, forecast is for twenty degrees Fahrenheit, partially clear with intermittent snowfall expected late in the afternoon. Be sure to pack your skins, ice axes, crampons and avalanche equipment along with your other gear. We'll provide food and beverages, of course." Earlier, Trent had informed Alex that he needed ski-mountaineering footage of everyone hiking up Glory Couloir and then skiing down it, Consumco wanted shots of them drinking AcyDgreen in resplendent jubilation at the bottom. Alex went on, telling them, "The heli will drop us off on the glacier, then we'll hike the remaining 2500 feet up to the top. There's an extremely steep pitch at the top of the couloir. You'll be able to put your skis on once we get to the rock ridge, at the summit."

Whitney stared out the window. The weather seemed to be deteriorating, not getting better. All she could see now was white mist, a dreary bog. Her mind drifted as Shane and Alex went on about the snow conditions and the tour. She had neglected to call home last night, falling asleep instead.

After the meeting and lunch in the lodge's dining hall, she called her mom. Cindy told her, "I took Robyn to Colorado Springs for the CT scan and the MRI yesterday; we're still waiting for the results. Dr. McClellan said it will take some time for the radiologist and the other doctor- I think his name is Dr. Halpurn-to get back to us. I'm hoping we hear something by tomorrow," she added, sounding worried.

"How's she been with the medication? Is she still nauseated?" Whitney asked, frowning.

"Sometimes she is, other times she's dizzy. She missed her violin lesson this week, poor girl. Mrs. Hennessey stopped by the house, just to check in on us. She brought Robyn some schoolwork so she could keep up with her class. That was awfully nice of her," she added, then asked Whitney, "by the way, how is it up there in BC?"

"Wet. Foggy. We're supposed to climb up Glory Couloir tomorrow and ski down it, but the weather is socked in… I'm not sure, maybe it will clear up by then. Is Robyn there? I'd like to talk to her."

"Sure. Hang on, I'll get her."

Whitney waited a moment, she heard Robyn on the other end.

"Hi sweetheart, how are you?" she asked, concerned.

"Hi mommy! Grandma took me to a big hospital yesterday."

"I know. You are a big, brave girl. The doctors are all trying to help you feel better, okay? They're doing these tests and giving you medicine so you can feel better. I know you have a tummy ache and sometimes feel a little dizzy, but you have to be strong."

*Have to be strong*? What was she thinking? Whitney berated herself, inwardly. Robyn was only six years old. She didn't have to "be strong." Why would she say that to her?

"Okay mommy, I will."

Cindy got back on the phone. "She's such a good sport about all this. By the way, her violin recital is on April 10th, just reminding you in case you can go. Hopefully, she can participate."

"Got it, mom. Don't you think I already have enough pressure with all this? I don't care about her violin recital right now, for god's sake," Whitney said, exasperated.

*Jeez, why did she just say that to her mom? What was wrong with her*? Whitney bit her lip, frowning.

"I don't know why you are being such a pill, Whitney," her mom replied, testily, surprised to hear her daughter respond that way. It seemed totally unlike her.

"I have to go mom. Love you," Whitney told her automatically, feeling disjointed.

"Be careful up there, Whitney," Cindy replied, voice strained, hanging up.

"Be careful up there…"

The words hung in the air, an oddly anachronistic phrase from a different time. Or life.

Completely incompatible with her existence as an extreme skier for Consumco, they hardly registered in her brain.

What registered with Karis? Whitney wondered suddenly. Was *she* afraid of anything?

She thought of her unopened ANTm3.

*No.* Karis was not afraid of anything.

That was a scary thought.

# CHAPTER 12
# BELLA COOLA

The brawny Bell 212 helicopter sat waiting for them like a velociraptor spoiling for a prize fight on the Tweedsmuir Park Lodge heli pad, its long rotors a spinning blur of motion, engine roaring with a deep thwump thwump thwump across the snow- covered ground. Clouds of white swirled blizzard-like around the machine as it waited for them to exit the lodge's front doors and whisk them away. Designed to move swiftly and with style, the Bell could comfortably carry up to twelve passengers inside its spacious lair and was the most frequently utilized helicopter for skiing in Canada and Chile. With a maximum cruising speed of 120 knots and maximum range of 238 nautical miles, it was one of the sleekest heli's Whitney had ever seen.

Each skier handed Shane and Alex their mountaineering skis before clamoring aboard, the guides placing them inside the heli's exterior metal rack. Securing a seat and strapping in for the twenty-minute flight, everyone stowed their backpacks, duffel bags, food in the cargo hold to distribute weight evenly and allow for safe lift. The pilot and co-pilot busily checked their instruments and spoke to each other over their headsets, preoccupied with the required safety check and their morning flight plan. A sense of urgency permeated the air, as conditions were projected to deteriorate after one p.m. They had only a five- hour window in which to land on Munday Glacier, hike up Glory Couloir, ski down it, complete their filming, fly back to the lodge.

Shenti looked a little peckish getting on the heli, sharing that he had heartburn all night after eating a steak that was too rich for his digestive tract and unfortunately following it with Banana's Foster. Alyn was helping him attach his safety strap, he couldn't manage the buckle by himself. Trent sat beside her, tapping his foot impatiently as they both fiddled around trying to snap it closed. Mason and Ian were sitting across from each other, faces obscured by helmets and balaclavas, Whitney and Karis moved to opposite ends of the cramped cabin, taking extreme care not to make eye contact.

Today, Karis was wearing a white Arctic North ski parka with matching white pants, white and black Smith goggles and a silver Yeti helmet. She looked fabulous.

Another outfit from her sponsors no doubt, Whitney thought, enviously. How she managed to pack all her coats and accessories with their limited luggage capacity was remarkable, given she had so much stuff. This morning, she had barely remembered to put her make-up on, stick a rhinestone on her left nostril.

Her own beauty routine was much too haphazard, she fretted inwardly. She really needed to be more consistent…

Was Consumco giving Karis preferential treatment because she was so beautiful? Her competition stats weren't as high as hers, that was a fact. On the other hand, she was a fierce skier who moved a lot of merchandise, she chewed her lip, broodingly.

*Stop it with the jealousy. Stop!* she admonished herself, feeling ashamed.

Alex and Shane did a final check to see all the equipment was loaded, then climbed on board taking their seats at the front near the cockpit. The sound of the helicopter drowned out all attempts at conversation, the powerful machine preparing to lift off.

As they ascended and hovered briefly over the pad, Whitney gazed across the gorgeous property, surprised to have no butterflies nor anxiety about leaving terra firma. No obsessive fixation about her impending demise, no concern about every conceivable disastrous outcome. Delighted, she found herself enjoying the glorious moment in its entirety, enjoying the loft above this ocean of snowy peaks, cotton-candy clouds, granite spires and desolate valleys, sans fear.

Absolutely liberated, she looked around the cabin at her companions and smiled, joining the group's blasé expressions as they made their way towards Munday Glacier.


Nine inches of new snow blanketed the white glacier in a sea of flat light, surrounded by snow- covered slopes off in the distance. Thick clouds obscured the still-rising sun. Accustomed to the typically clear blue skies of Colorado and its light, powder snow, Whitney gaped at the remote and unfamiliar alpine landscape, its saturated atmosphere and heavy moisture content, so frequently near precipitation. It seemed the clouds could swallow them up in their ephemeral maw, never to be seen nor heard from again. The thought didn't bother her particularly, it was just an observation.

Alyn was already taking photos of the group standing near the helicopter, as Duncan, Alex and Shane unloaded gear from the stationary, now quiet machine. Shenti wandered off from the group to smoke a cigarette. Alex called out tersely, "There's a crevasse fifty yards ahead, I suggest you stay where you are." Turning his attention back to the group, Shenti stopped trudging in the snow and lit up on the spot, gazing around, nonplussed.

When you're used to Helmand province, falling into a crevasse is probably no big deal, Whitney mused inwardly, glancing at him. She trained her eyes back to the guides.

Shane was informing them, "We'll need skins for the first thousand feet to the base of the couloir. After that, we'll hike. Make sure you have your crampons accessible in your packs. You'll all need your ice- axes, it can be icy at the top." He looked over at Karis, who was attaching a leash to the handle of her axe, "Don't use a leash," he reminded her, curtly. "If you fall on your axe, it could really injure you." She nodded then detached it, putting the leash back in her pack's side pocket. It was unlikely she could self-arrest with the ice-axe, anyway. The couloir was so steep it would be almost impossible, especially with a pack and skis on her back. He knew it, she knew it, they all knew it. Braids hanging beneath her silver Yeti helmet, she looked chic and distractingly attractive, even in twenty pounds of outwear. On Alex and Shane's radar, she was affecting their hormones, try as they might to act nonchalant, professional around her.

Poor Sven had a lot of competition wherever she went, Whitney thought, wryly. Seven thousand miles was a lot of space in a long-distance relationship. Especially if you were Karis Ryburn.

Trent would be staying down at the helicopter with Shenti and Alyn. Soon as the team arrived at the top of the couloir, they would get back inside the machine to hover over the skiers and begin filming.

Alex spoke next. "Check your transceivers, make sure they're on. Last check for go-pros, water, hand warmers, probes, ice axes, crampons." They all nodded, affirmatively, he took a final gaze. "Okay, let's go." Forming a loosely spaced line, they spread out behind him, Shane in very back, following the group. Setting off across the glacier, they broke snow, lifting their heels up pushing forward in their Scarpa boots and mountaineering skis. Each planted poles, methodically making their way towards the base of Glory Couloir. Alex occasionally shared some highlights about the terrain.

"We get cold, dry air from the east, mixing with moist, warmer marine air from the west. The snow quality is a mix of both, averaging thirty-four meters a year in these mountains," he told them. Mason interjected, regaling him about how badass the peaks were up in Montana and Wyoming; how he should go there someday to ski. Alex dryly replied that he used to guide on the Tetons before moving to Bella Coola, coughing. Whitney cringed. She attempted some light conversation with Ian, who was right in front of her. "I read your interview last night… it was really interesting," she offered, with repartee. The comment was met with silence, followed by a slight acknowledgement in the form of an "uh…. yeah." She fell silent again, trudging behind him. They had traversed across half the glacier already, Alex announcing that they would arrive at the couloir in twenty minutes.

Still extremely cloudy, a hint of sun glowed through the atmosphere, warming up the air, ever so slightly. Steep mountains loomed magnificent and white around the group; rock and treetops poked from the snow; an occasional raptor glided across the colorless sky. Quiet as a tomb, the terrain was a desolate wilderness unlike any place Whitney had ever skied.

At the base of the couloir now, they detached from their bindings and attached skis and one ski pole to their backpacks to carry uphill. Everyone took out crampons and attached them to their ski boots, preparing for the ascent. Following a few sips of water, a bite of an energy bar, they hefted their packs on and secured the straps in place. Each person held onto a single ski pole for leverage and carried an ice- axe for purchase. This time, Shane took the lead. They entered the couloir in loose pairs, Karis and Ian behind him, Mason and Whitney, just below. Alex stayed a little further down, at the back. Two striated walls of granite enclosed the team on each side that became narrower and narrower as they climbed. Halfway up the fifteen-hundred- foot chasm, twenty feet wide, they kicked upward, smacking the front of their boots with the sharp pointed toe, into the snow. Pushing up higher and higher, the walls became steeper and narrower with every laborious step.

Alternating kicks into the wall of snow with each leg, Whitney found herself breathing hard, concentrating on the singular task of staying balanced atop her burning legs and aching torso. Using her arms to pull herself up, ski pole clutched her right gloved hand and ice axe in her left, she thrust both implements into the wall in rhythmic tandem with her boots. Hard ice lurked beneath the surface, clumps of snow were breaking off and rolling downhill, beneath her. Glancing uphill, she could almost see the very top of the couloir now, a ridge of uneven, jagged rock, looming above. There, they would stop and attach their skis. Karis's right leg was to her left, near her head, the crunch of her boot smacking the snow, the sound of her labored breathing punctuating every step.

Whitney yanked her ice-axe out, poised outward a moment before thrusting it back into the snow. Suddenly Karis's right foot slipped down and hit her left hand, knocking the ice-axe from it.

The metal handle cartwheeled down the slope and disappeared into the abyss. Whitney gasped, the sudden loss of the axe taking her by surprise. Instantly, she leaned forward, pushing her weight onto her right ski pole, trying to regain balance. Karis seemed unaware of what had just happened. Whitney shouted, "I lost my ice-axe!" Alex yelled up to her instantly, "Hang on! I'm coming up to you! I'll get your other pole. Use it instead!" Quickly, he grabbed it off her pack and handed it to her upside down so she could drive the pointed end into the snow. Expecting to find her in a panic, she looked at him calmly without missing a beat and continued climbing up. Driving her boots in and hoisting herself up the last several yards to the ridge, she heaved herself onto a ledge.

Shane, Ian and Karis followed, slinging their packs off on the ledge. Mason and Alex came from behind, hoisting themselves up to join them. They all sat, gasping for air. Whitney caught her breath before speaking. Anger flooding her body, she lashed out at Karis in fury. "Don't you *ever* climb near me again!" she spat out, shaking with rage. She had an urge to rip her apart, throw *her* ice-axe off the couloir. This was too much. The chick was a menace, a total headcase.

Trent would have to do something now, she clenched her jaw, trying to hold it together. Alex and Shane looked alarmed, aggrieved, not sure of what to say. Usually, clients didn't act this way. The weird thing was, neither of the two women were acting normal. Whitney hadn't seemed frightened when her ice-axe tumbled down, and Karis didn't seem to care a single bit about it, when it occurred. Shane radioed Trent, telling him uncomfortably, "We're up at the top, we'll be coming down soon. Uh, Whitney lost her ice-axe, would you see if you can spot it somewhere at the base?" They all sat on the ledge.

Fifteen minutes went by, the heli moved in their direction and began hovering over the couloir, waiting for them to descend.

"Who's going first?" Shane posed. Mason clicked his bindings on. "I'll go, man." He took a couple deep breaths, lowering himself back onto the snow. With a couple hopping kick- turns he skidded laterally from side to side. Then pointing his ski tips down, he let gravity carry him, making only occasional short turns to the bottom. Whoops of glee trailed behind. The heli hovered overhead, Shenti's camera poking out the window. Next, Ian dropped in with a series of short kick-turns at the top, rocketing down then disappearing, compact form a colorful, flying jeti on the ribbon of snow between the rock walls. Shenti expertly shifted his camera, filming him. Karis and Whitney followed, with equal zeal.

Later, the guides talked amongst themselves, Alex telling Shane, "I've never seen anything like it. Women who ski like that-- totally insane. Just jumped off the ridge and hurtled themselves down, made only a couple turns… totally audacious. *Who* does that? They shook their heads. After the run, they had all rendezvoused at the base, imbibing the AcyDgreen as instructed, trying to look properly jubilant, invigorated.

But the day left them frazzled and perplexed. Something had just seemed *off*; they couldn't put their finger on it. The weather had deteriorated as predicted; it began snowing soon as the heli lifted off from the glacier. Back at the lodge, they all regrouped to discuss plans for the next several days, but it seemed unlikely they would be able to ski at all, as conditions were becoming too unstable. Wind and rain were blowing into the region from the Pacific, the fog obliterating all visibility.

Whitney followed Trent into the ski storage room at the lodge, shutting the door behind her.

"You heard about what happened up on Glory Couloir. She kicked my ice-axe out of my hand. I could have died," she seethed, her voice shaking with anger.

He stood, impassive, listening.

"I spoke to Alex. He believes it was an accident," he frowned. "I checked the GoPro video on his helmet with Shenti to see what happened. Her leg slid off the slope, it hit your left hand. It was an unfortunate accident, Whitney. I can understand your anger, but you need to let it go," he finished, lips turned down.

"I don't care what you *saw* on the video, she kicked my hand." Whitney persisted, infuriated. This was outrageous. Fucking intolerable.

"Listen to me Whitney," Trent's voice lowered warningly. "I told you, I think you can win WESC. I believe that. But Karis is an integral member of this team and Consumco will see that she stays on. I advise you to back off and let this go, before it affects your ability to ski and work with the group in a productive fashion. Understand?" He crossed his arms, deliberately.

What he didn't say was that Karis was a marketing juggernaut for the corporation, that she could do just about anything and get away with it. Worth a fortune to the company, she influenced millions of followers to purchase make-up, insurance, soft drinks, and more. Notwithstanding, Whitney was the best female extreme skier in the country, with honest street creds and the best chance of winning WESC. Somehow, he had to keep the two out of each other's hair.

Whitney took a deep breath, trying to calm down. The stakes were too high to push this conflict any further. For Robyn's sake, she needed to back off.

"Alright. I'll let it go," she relented, "but I think she's dangerous." Turning away, she left his orbit, feeling totally depleted. Trent wasn't doing anything to protect her, and she had no room to object. She'd just have to be more careful around Karis, she told herself. Keep her distance, watch her back.

# CHAPTER 13
# BELLA COOLA

Typically, the end of February could be an excellent time to ski the Canadian Coastals, but right now the weather was simply not cooperating. A combination of maritime rain and freezing-then- warmer temperatures was creating a sleet-like wet snow that made conditions miserable at the lower elevations and heli-skiing in the higher elevations all but impossible. All tours were delayed until the current weather system abated and the skies cleared. Trent had already spoken with Duncan about cutting their stay short in Bella Coola and flying up to Valdez instead. Now Duncan was on the phone and internet trying to secure lodging and heli-tour reservations in the port city of Alaska, on the fly. Consumco's pilots were on standby, waiting to hear back from him on when to return with the Gulfstream to transport the team.

Whitney stayed in bed until nine-thirty a.m., luxuriating in semi-wakefulness in the comfort of her own private room. Sleep had been fitful, the emotionally charged conversation with Trent and his indifferent response to her appeal yesterday replaying in her mind over and over like a record needle skipping in place on the same song. How someone could be so unempathetic was baffling. Utterly mystifying. His message had been loud and clear though, he would defend Karis no matter what she did, she was too valuable to the company for him to confront.

She wondered. Was he was receiving money from Consumco to protect Karis, knowing her vicious proclivities? He must know what she was doing, she pondered, dejectedly. He couldn't possibly coach at this level and not see what was happening in front of his eyes. Unless, perhaps, he was deliberating ignoring the obvious for his own purposes, she considered, cynically.

She would just have to protect herself; it was that simple. Protect her equipment, steer clear of Karis, keep her mouth shut. Clearly, it was necessary if she hoped to get through this tour without more confrontations with either of them.

Still groggy, she got up and put on some cotton leggings and a t-shirt, then left the cozy room for a late breakfast in lodge's dining room. The staff had left out a large bowl of cut -up cantaloupe and fresh blackberries, a tray of homemade pastries sat on a wood buffet table adorned with woven Nuxalk textiles and painted designs. Artisanal pottery plates were stacked on the buffet, she helped herself to some fruit and baked goods, then found a seat inside the cedar-planked dining room for a quiet meal.

Finishing the delicious breakfast, she filled her mug with more hot coffee and brought it over to a cushy chair in the guest lounge by the river-rock fireplace. A small table lamp sat next to it, she sipped her coffee and collected her thoughts, mentally reviewing her day. Call home… find out about the scans. Pack for tomorrow…

Alyn ambled into the lounge, holding a mug. Seeing Whitney, she came over. "Mind if I join you?" she asked, sitting down on the plush burgundy sofa near her in front of the fireplace. "I heard about what happened yesterday on Glory Couloir. Glad you're okay," she commented, taking a careful sip.

"Yep," Whitney took more sips, remained quiet.

Alyn led, casually, "What do you think happened?" she looked at Whitney pointedly, ever the investigative journalist.

"It was an accident. That's all. Dropped my ice-axe, no big deal," she replied, gazing off to the side.

"Riiiiight." Alyn stretched the word out sardonically and continued drinking her coffee, staring at the dancing flames. Obviously, Whitney wasn't talking. Her thoughts flickered to Karis, about their recent interview and her conversations with the young woman. What she had learned about her since she began doing publicity for Consumco throughout this tour. The Ryburn family seemed to be one of wealth and social climbing, her father a successful venture capitalist, her mother an Aspen socialite, both involved in a multitude of fundraising and civic activities within the splashy community. They owned a lavish home in the Roaring Fork Valley surrounded by celebrities and Davos types, a whirlwind of fancy dinners, events and paparazzi-like snapshots in the Aspen Times. Karis had two siblings, an older brother who owned some type of tech company having something to do with equities trading, an older sister who was an international business attorney, already partner in some prestigious New York law firm. Karis grew up skiing at Snowmass and Aspen, the ritzy ski areas virtually out her front door. A natural athlete who took to the slopes as a toddler, she immediately showed promise at a very young age. Her parents supporting her with gymnastics classes and ski lessons, ski teams and competitions through grade school, junior and senior high. She became a stand-out downhiller and free-skier by the time she was seventeen. A local celebrity, she modeled clothing and jewelry for exclusive boutiques and hotels around Aspen, her finely chiseled face gracing the covers of Aspen Magazine and other mountain periodicals. Their glossy and refined images bespoke wealth and privilege, athletic prowess and beauty. Karis had confided to Alyn that her parents paid her a bonus every time she won a competition or received a modeling contract. It was how they incentivized their children- who all seemed vying for their parent's approval, based on the conversation. When Consumco sponsored Karis, they acquired a gold mine. Someone who could launch their products into the stratosphere with her long blonde tresses, green eyes and perfect complexion.

Whitney interrupted her reverie. "I think we're flying to Valdez tomorrow afternoon. Would you room with me? I can't share a room with her, you know. She might kill me in my sleep," she looked away again, towards a window, distracted.

"Of course, I'll let Duncan know...hey, how is your daughter, by the way?" Alyn asked her, taken aback. What did she just say? ... *Might kill her in her sleep?* She did not appear to be joking.

"She's doing alright, we have some tests this week. As a matter of fact, I need to call home, find out what's going on. Thanks for asking," Whitney stated flatly. She glanced back at Alyn, blankly.

Alyn stood up. "I'll catch up with you later," she departed, taking her cup back to the dining room and leaving it on a table. Strange conversation. Something about Whitney had changed, she noted. Karis, on the other hand, had been a wolverine since the day she started this tour and was always difficult to relate to, claws and bared teeth her normal state. Hard to understand these people, they lived in a different world.

Still seated, Whitney called home. Surprisingly, her dad answered. Normally he would be in the store right now, helping customers. He told her, "I'm at the house right now with your mom. We're talking about Robyn. Dr. McClellan called this morning. Evidently, they found some abnormal tissue formation around her occipital lobe on the MRI. The doctor described it as being diffuse, rather than focal, which is to say," he struggled with the medical jargon, paraphrasing, "which is to say... that they didn't find a tumor, but the tissue isn't normal, it may be triggering her seizures. She still wants us to continue with the medication, though she mentioned that she may need to change it if the seizures originate in the occipital lobe. It's going to take time to sort this out, she'll need more tests ongoing. And the doctor in Colorado Springs...Dr. Halpurn," her dad took a breath, "thinks we may need to take her to Children's Hospital in Denver to work with the specialists there. We'll let you know what they tell us, soon as possible." He finally paused. Whitney swallowed, trying to digest the words. With a catch in her throat, she asked him, "has Robyn had another seizure since I left?"

"No, not since your last visit," he answered, exhaling. "She's actually back in school today, we brought her in so she could have a normal day." Cindy got on the phone, joining him, slightly breathless, "Hi honey, I'm in contact with the doctors, we're waiting to hear what they want to do next. It should be soon. Try not to worry."

Whitney wasn't worrying. Things would work out. Why her parents sounded so agitated, so upset, was beyond her. Right now, she needed to get packed, get ready to fly out tomorrow she thought, detachedly.

"I need to pack, we're leaving tomorrow. Going to Valdez, the weather's terrible here," she told them, voice distant.

"What's going on?" her mom pressed, "Aren't you staying in Bella Coola?"

"No. Too much fog, it's a complete white-out. Do you need me to come home?"

"No, you stay with the team. We can manage for now. However, we did get a bill in the mail yesterday. Eight thousand, two hundred dollars. I think insurance will cover a large portion of it, but I wanted to let know. You'll need to send a check to the lab when we find out what the balance is."

"Yes, of course, mom," Whitney's chest constricted. "I'll call you guys tomorrow before we leave, okay? Thanks for all your help, as always," she hung up.

Staring at the fireplace, mesmerized by the glowing embers and flickering flames, she chewed her lip, deep in thought. Duncan ducked into the lounge. "Oh, you're here," he brightened, glancing around. "I just wanted to let you know we're scheduled to depart tomorrow, three p.m. How are you doing? he asked, curiously. Hair smoothly brushed, she hadn't applied any rhinestones, or black eye-liner, or purple sparkly eyeshadow to her face yet this morning. She looked a lot more like her normal self he thought, a little relieved.

She glanced up, smiling suddenly, "Good! I'm fine, thanks." She was always glad to see Duncan.

"Good. Good! he replied broadly, walking into the lounge to join her. "Hey, I've got a little time to kill. Want to play a game of Scrabble?" A stack of board games sat on the shelf near her. Checkers, Yatzee, chess, waiting for a rainy day. He tried to act nonchalant, giddy with the prospect of hanging out with her.

"Sure. That would be great. Let's play! I haven't played scrabble in like, ten years," she told him, enthusiastically. It would be nice to have a distraction. Forget about all the problems back home for a few hours. He was just so easygoing, so *nice*.

Sitting down on the sofa, he set up the square board on the coffee table in front of them and began organizing his letters, studying his words. Whitney crossed her legs in her chair and leaned forward, studying hers. Going first, he opened the game with the word 'Grape.'

"Sixteen points, not bad…" she wrote down his score on a piece of paper.

After several moments, she put her letters down with the word 'Plug' then scored it.

He chuckled, "Fourteen points, not too shabby…." he shifted in his seat leaning forward. Gathering his letters, he placed the word 'alikes,' on the board, pluralizing the word 'plug.'

"What kind of word is 'alikes' Whitney laughed indignantly. "Use it in a sentence!" she goaded him, playfully.

"I alikes you," he answered, easily.

She laughed, "that's so scabby. Okay, I'll let you have it. Twenty-two points with a double- word score for a word that isn't a word." It felt good to laugh out loud, she couldn't even remember the last time she had done that.

Duncan grinned. "The modern language is a fluid thing, you know. By the way, how is your hand?" he asked her, concerned. "I heard about what happened yesterday on Glory Couloir. Losing your ice-axe. Jeez, that must have been scary."

"It was an accident," she showed him her hand, holding the palm up so he could examine it. The tissue at the base of her thumb was still slightly puffy and blue. "I was holding the axe with this hand, and I think my grip on it was just compromised, to be honest. One thing leads to another, unfortunately Karis's boot kicked it right off. I managed to get to the top without it, though."

Duncan shook his head, "thank God you're okay." He would have felt terrible if something bad happened to her.

"I'm fine," she shrugged, putting down her word. She put 'look' in front of 'alikes,' stringing together one whole new word.

"Lookalikes? What kind of crazy word is that?" Duncan laughed out loud. "Use it in a sentence."

"It lookalikes we're in for more clouds and rain," she replied, voice deadpan.

"Very good. Excellent grammar, I must say. You got me back with that one," he grinned, laughingly. His heart was doing strange things, it seemed to be skipping around like a pogo stick on steroids.

He jumped up, looking at the time. "Wow, I can't believe we sat here for two hours already. I gotta get our equipment ready to load in the vans tomorrow. Maybe we can finish this game later, okay?" he told her eagerly.

"Sure, no problem. It was fun," she nodded. Standing up too, she inadvertently brushed against his body, a small jolt of electricity skittering through her spine, a surprise. "I need to finish packing," she stammered, flustered. She hadn't even considered dating or hooking up with any other guy since Kyle died, her energy focused exclusively on taking care of Robyn and skiing. Both were all consuming, no room for anything, nor anyone else...

She had thought. But Duncan, he was different. There was a connection between them, she could feel it.

She wondered if he felt it too.

Best to put any feelings she might have aside though, she told herself, sternly. Now was not the time to get involved with anyone. Especially Duncan. Things were too complicated, too risky. She had to stay focused.

# CHAPTER 14
# VALDEZ

From her window, an awe-inspiring amphitheater of frozen glaciers, snow- covered peaks and waterfalls appeared from the
mist to greet them as they flew towards the eastern fjord of
Prince William Sound preparing for landing. Utilitarian buildings,
container ships and oil tankers that made up the port city slowly
revealed themselves in the dim light. Whitney squinted to make out
their shapes as they neared the Valdez airstrip, the airport's ground
control guiding the Gulfstream gently to their final approach. Some
turbulence bumped the plane, rocking it sideways. Like a rubber ball
skittering across a basketball court they rapidly descended, the pilots
tersely cautioning everyone to remain buckled up before touching
down.

They would have a final customs and immigration check at
the airport before transferring to the Best Western that Duncan
had made reservations at, his harried calls for lodging yielding five
separate rooms with two kitchenettes near the outskirts of the city.
Valdez heli-sports would meet them at the hangar, drive everyone
to the hotel following the four-hour flight. Trent was still hashing
out the logistics of their ski tour with the highly esteemed Alaskan
outfitter as they approached the runway.

For extreme skiers, the Chugach conjured the essence of free skiing, the very pinnacle of *steep*. In the early mid-nineteen nineties, world free-skiing champions Doug and Emily Coombs, both legendary pioneers of the sport, established Valdez as a haven for heli-skiing worldwide. After guiding people there for over seven years, they eventually left the region and moved on to Verbier for less dangerous terrain. Too many close calls with avalanche and other mishaps compelled them to leave the burgeoning industry they had developed in the state; other outfitters stepped in to take up the charge, their legacy living on. No other range came close to providing the near vertical pitches, the velvet powdery snow that the Chugach had, and no other place offered access to such vast swaths of untracked, unexplored lines. With up to a thousand inches of snow a year, Valdez had become the official mecca of steep, the unofficial mecca of death.

Theodore insisted Trent get close-up footage of everyone exiting the helicopters atop a knife ridge while they were in Alaska, he wanted the dramatic imagery for Consumco's ongoing AcyDgreen and 4tress advertising campaigns.

Trent informed him it would require two helicopters; one to shoot video from above, the other to deposit the skiers onto the ridge. Essentially, they would be relaying their skiers from the base, rotating two at a time with the guide as they skied down the mountain. Theodore told him to have Whitney, who had stronger command of skiing steeps than Karis, to ski the hardest pitches with Ian, and have Karis, who he wanted to protect, ski the easier pitches with Mason. He made it clear that Karis was their prize, she couldn't get injured. Trent attempted to reason with him, venturing, "Whitney's our potential World Champion, Theo, I think they *both* should be protected."

"Just follow orders, that's your job," Theodore stated, dismissively.

*"Got it,"* Trent had acquiesced, tightly. This had all the earmarks of a potential blow-up he predicted, and the only upside to the whole unsavory decision was that the two would be riding in separate helicopters, skiing down different mountains.

Well, it would keep them out of each other's way, he sighed, trying to look at the bright side.

Shenti would send video in real-time to Consumco, they could use it for whatever products they wanted. Lately, Trent had found him up late at night chain smoking cigarettes while editing for the mega-sponsor, said it reminded him of working near the battlefield, in Kabul.

The van pulled up to the front doors of the Best Western, an attractive two-story, rectangular building with a parking lot that wrapped around its sides and abutted another hotel, fast-food outlet. They had driven through town, a snow-covered wonderland of frozen roads and frozen water, icicles hanging from building awnings, surrounding peaks an amphitheater of white. Arriving twenty minutes later at the hotel, they were tired but stoked, everyone excited to be there, Valdez the ultimate big-mountain destination every skier dreamed of; the big leagues.

Alyn lugged her duffel bag down the hallway to the simple but comfortable room she would share with Whitney, taking stock of their new home base. Each had a queen bed; they shared a dresser and bathroom. A rectangular window overlooked the parking lot. From its limited vantage, she could see the fjord in the background, its urban tangle of rugged trawlers and fishing boats moored at the sprawling marina. Hulking oil tankers lumbered out in the water.

The room's walls were light tan, with matching cotton bedspreads. A petite desk sat near the closet's double doors.

Whitney was still carrying her equipment into the room, the sound of her snow boots tromping across the carpeted floor, heavy thuds. With two pairs of skis, poles and boot bag banging against her leg, she looked like a Sherpa heading up the Himalaya, bulging backpack laden with at least fifty pounds of gear. Alyn frowned. Normally Duncan took care of all this, put these items in storage. What was going on?

"I'm keeping this stuff in our room," Whitney announced. "Do me a favor. *Do not* let anyone in here, period. Full stop." She set everything on the floor, leaned her skis and poles up against the wall.

"Uh, okay…" Alyn replied, puzzled. She watched Whitney go back outside and retrieve more items, outerwear, helmets, set them on her bed. She announced abruptly, "I'm going out for a while, want to come?"

Alyn considered, a moment. Tired from the flight, which had frazzled her nerves, she needed to work on Mason's interview for Rock and Ice magazine. "Where are you going?" she asked, curious.

"Just down the road. There's a bar n' grill I saw when we first got here. I just need to get out. Get something to eat, have a drink," she replied. "You're welcome to join me."

"Thanks, but I think I'll stay here," Alyn told her, unpacking. She got out her I-pad.

Whitney's cellphone chimed with a text from her bank, she entered her password. Apparently, Consumco had just wired six thousand dollars into her checking account, an unexpected bonus. Must have been for her AcyDgreen photos that Alyn posted this week she sighed. Thank God. The money would help cover Robyn's CT scans, MRI's.

She left the Best Western, the minus 14- degree temperature knocking her breath away the moment she stepped out its double front doors. Walking down the narrow road to the bar and grill, cars and trucks whizzed by, splashing dirty snow up from their tires. Ten minutes later she walked into to the gritty establishment, her eyes quickly adjusting to the dark interior. There was a long, well-worn bar with what looked like local patrons sitting and drinking at this hour, the bartender busy pulling beers and mixing drinks. Shenti was at the far end, nursing a whiskey sour, hunched over, smoking a cigarette. He seemed lost in thought, she decided not to bother him. She found a booth at the far end of the dingy room with hard, brown Naugahyde seats and a scratched, well-worn wooden table. A plethora of initials were carved into it, she sat down. There was a bottle of ketchup, salt and pepper shaker, menu. Above her head was a large plastic silver and pink singing salmon that burst out absurdly into "Whole Lotta Shakin' Goin' On" intermittently. Hard rock music filled the background. The place smelled like hamburgers and French fries, wet sock. A pool table was in the backroom, walls plastered with neon beer signs. Some people were playing a game, laughter erupting periodically.

Sometimes she really questioned what she was doing in a joint like this, why she was sitting at a table with a singing salmon instead of at home with Robyn, where she probably should be. Guiltily, she remembered Luann's comments, once again feeling pulled apart in two opposing directions, the sensation most acute when she was eating a meal by herself, among people who were probably wondering what a single woman like her was doing there. *Couldn't be good, couldn't be good… must be a terrible mother…* They didn't know that she was trying to take care of her daughter, trying to have a career, trying to *follow her dream.* There was a surreal quality to it all; the procedure, the travel, the six days here, the eight days there; the forgetting what town or hotel she was in...the eating and drinking things she normally wouldn't... the dealing with Karis's sociopathy... Trent's mercurialness...

She ordered a drink. Vodka tonic. Double. The waitress brought it to her table, she ordered a platter of deep- fried halibut fish and chips. Alcohol doing its magic, she settled into her booth and gave a long exhale. Food arriving, she took a bite of deliciously hot, crispy battered fish, antidote to all that plagued her, permitting her brain to pleasantly unwind into a fugue of greasy pescatarian goodness and carbohydrate...

A sound. Automatically, she turned towards it, a chair crashing onto the floor. Shenti was lurching backwards. A rough, mid-forties looking man with a bald, shaved head and tats was pushing him to the ground, his whiskey sour splattered everywhere. The sound of breaking glass...What the hell was going on?

"Don't fuckin' tell me Afghanistan was a disaster, mother fucker! I was fuckin' there, you asshole! We did the job we was sent to do, kept this country from more Al Qaeda for twenty fuckin' years!" the man slurred. "I saw children and shit blow up too, so shut your fuckin' mouth!" Inebriated, he took a swing at Shenti's head, though widely missing it, it landing in the air. Jesus, what the hell did Shenti just say to him? Whitney fumed. She got up from the booth and strode over to them both.

"Leave him alone, please. Get the fuck away from him," she stated to the man, alcohol the multiplier of the procedure. She was superwoman.

"Who the fuck are youuuu?" he sneered, lurching unsteadily towards her.

"I'm fucking nobody. Just leave him alone," she threatened, menacingly. People were staring at them, mouths open. Some were hooting uneasily, the air charged.

The man took a swing at her, missing. Instantly she leapt onto his body and wrapped her legs around his torso, arms and legs squeezing his stomach with all her might. They toppled to the floor together with a crash, a table fell over. Now the man was pinned beneath her, she was sitting on top of him, ready to take a swing. Shenti lurched towards her, yanked her away from him, yelling, "Get off him, Whitney! NOW. Let's GO!" Whitney climbed off the man, heaving. He lay on the floor curled on his side, in a stupor. "Fuckin' *girl*! What the fuck!" he moaned, a tad admiringly.

Whitney grabbed her parka and threw some money on her table on their way out, helping Shenti through the door. Right eye bruised, his lip was bleeding. Probably hit the table and cracked it open when he fell, she realized. They both stumbled unsteadily down the snow-covered road into the freezing night air. Heading towards the marina, they sat down on the edge of the pier overlooking the icy water. Whitney handed him a paper napkin, ketchup on it.

"Jeez, Whitney. What's wrong with you? You could have been killed," Shenti admonished her, shaken.

"What am I supposed to do? Sit there and eat fish and chips while you're getting attacked by some maniac?" she retorted, gasping into fits of laughter uncontrollably, almost rolling on her side. For some reason the situation seemed riotous. She fell silent and stared at the seiners and trawlers, their nets full of orange and white buoys spilling over their decks. Shenti gazed up at the luminous mountains cocooning the city, sentinels, in the frigid air. He dabbed his lip with the ketchupy napkin. "All I said to the guy was, in the end, we left them there to die like we always do, and what did we accomplish?"

Whitney considered, foggily. Her own problems seemed minor, in comparison. A little perspective never hurt, she thought, trying to maintain focus. Perhaps her problems weren't so bad. Awkwardly, she patted him on the back, trying to make him feel better. Shenti spoke, "that man had every right to be pissed off at me, he suffered from the war, I'm just a shitty drunk. I should have just kept my mouth shut." Whitney sighed heavily, dimly contemplating her freezing breath in the near-black air. They huddled for another thirty minutes until the effects of the alcohol wore off, then stood up and shook their frozen limbs, walking back to the hotel together.

Alyn finished taking a shower and was in her pajamas, ready to go to bed. Retrieving her toothbrush, she was down to her last micro-squeeze of toothpaste. Whitney probably wouldn't care if she used some of hers, she considered, absently. Picking through Whitney's light blue nylon travel bag, she searched for some paste amongst a jumble of dental floss, moisturizer, lip balm. A small white vial fell out onto the bathroom sink counter, rolling into the sink. Picking it up, she peered at the label, squinting. The simple, white label had only several letters on it: ANTm3. Unopened; the plastic protective seal was still in place. Curiously, she peered closer. Was it some type of anti-aging cream? She read the label carefully, searching for a product description or application, finding nothing at all on the container. Odd. She put the vial back in the toiletry bag and swished it around with the other items, furtively. Squeezing a dab of Whitney's mint flavored toothpaste on her brush, she finished cleaning her teeth and went back over to her bed, climbing between the covers. Restless, she chewed her lip. Whitney had been acting paranoid and more aggressive, no doubt about it, she considered, thoughtfully. Bringing all her equipment in the room like she was afraid someone might tamper with it, obsessively checking her bindings and boot buckles, avalanche gear, even her clothing.... Something was up. Hesitantly, she made a call on her cell phone, even though it was quite late.

"Harris?"

"Hey, Alyn, how are you," his voice met hers with a jovial familiarity, always glad to hear from her. They had worked together for years in the newsroom at the Seattle Times as investigative reporters, well before she decided to leave the newspaper business and do freelance sports journalism, instead. He was still with Gannett, doing similar work writing political editorials, after she left. "Good to hear from you! What's up?" he inquired. He hadn't talked to her in over six months.

"I need you to do something for me. Get some information, if you could."

"Okay..." She could hear him drumming his fingers on something in the background, as was his habit.

"See what you can find on Trent Resnick. Ski coach. I think he's from Bozeman. Single, not married, to my knowledge. Just let me know if anything pops out at you. Oh, one more thing. See if you can find anything out about ANTm3," she asked him, frowning a little. "ANTm3?" he repeated, carefully. "What is it? A drug?"

"I don't know, I have no idea- that's what I want to find out. One more thing," she added, "let *me* call you. No texts, no email, we did not have this conversation, okay?"

"Got it."

"Thanks Harris, I'll be in touch," she hung up, quickly.


Shenti and Whitney got back to the Best Western, he seemed sober and relatively okay. She left him in the foyer to go get ice for his eye. His room was on ground level, she headed down the hall to find the ice machine. Passing Ian's room, his door swung open, she almost bumped into Karis, exiting it. *What the...?* Whitney flashed, inwardly.

Completely ignoring Whitney as though she were a ghost, Karis sauntered towards the end of the hallway and turned the corner.

*Was she sleeping with Ian now?* Jeez, nothing should surprise her. Stupidly, she always felt like she was the last person to learn these things. Sven might be a World-Cup downhiller, but Ian's star was rising fast. Soon he might be earning more money in endorsements and film royalties than just about any other skier out there. Like any good social climber, Karis was just keeping her options open, she imagined.

Maybe she wasn't sleeping with him. Maybe they were just hanging out together, she shrugged her shoulders, sighing. Who knew? What started as a simple quest for fish and chips had turned into a very weird night. She located the ice machine and dumped some inside a plastic laundry bag, then carried it back to Shenti, who was still waiting for her in the foyer. He held it to his forehead, above his swollen eye. "Thank you, Whitney, I'll be fine. Get some sleep now, okay?" he implored her.

She went back to her room and climbed into bed, closing her eyes to the occasional hum of the building's furnace fan, the sound of Alyn's breathing.

When the sun came up, bright rays peeking through the window's blinds, Whitney rose and walked down the hall, knocking on Mason's door. Desperate to make coffee, his room had the larger kitchenette. After several long moments, he finally opened it, long hair in a disheveled tangle, eyes unfocused and crusty. Uncharacteristically quiet, he immediately disappeared back into his bedroom and shut his door. She searched the cupboards for ground coffee to assuage her mild hangover, alcohol not really her forte, she seldom drank. Trent knocked on the door a few moments later, she let him in.

He stood in front of her next to the stove and pulled out his cell-phone, holding it up in front of her. She squinted at it.

"Look familiar?" he asked, voice deadpan.

Someone had snapped a photo of her in the bar last night, legs wrapped around a man's body, magenta hair flying around her face, lipstick smeared askew. Shenti was mid-way off the floor, his arms reaching out for her. Apparently, their altercation had made the local news.

"Young woman assaults *veteran* in Valdez bar. A rather alarming caption, I'd say. Shit, Whitney, that was *aggressive*." A smile played on the corner of his lips.

"That's not me," she told him flatly, pressing the coffee pot button on. "You're lucky he's not pressing charges." "He frickin' *liked* me. Shenti was in a bind, so I helped him out," she stated, shrugging.

"I'll say. Listen, I'm not reporting this to Consumco, but you need to cool your jets a little, next time around." He changed the subject, all business. "By the way, I'm putting you in the first heli tomorrow. You and Ian will be skiing the steepest pitches. Don't do any aerials, keep it simple. Concentrate on staying forward and use a shorter pole, it will help you to stay balanced through the slough. Ski the spine and try to stay above your slough, it should fall to either side. If it feels like the mountain is giving way, it probably isn't, that's the typical thing that happens up here. We'll have the heli hovering right above you and a guide skiing right behind you monitoring everything, so stay cool." He finished, "Ian will be skiing with you too, in case something happens. I'll keep Karis in the second heli with Shenti and Mason. You're going to do great."

She nodded.

"Check in with Duncan before you leave in the morning, he'll have a radio for you."

"What time do we leave?"

"Nine a.m. The guides will pick us up out front. Have everything ready."

"Got it," she nodded, sipping her coffee.

Trent poured himself a cup of the steaming liquid and then headed out the kitchenette. Whitney was a tough cookie, he thought inwardly. That dust-up at the bar last night was minimal by his standards and probably wouldn't go anywhere beyond the local news. He doubted people cared anyway. This was Alaska.

# CHAPTER 15
# VALDEZ

Her interview with Mason last week hadn't yielded much new insight into his mind, but she went through the motions dutifully and began writing the feature. Rock and Ice was a less conventional publication and they liked grittier content, Consumco wanted the piece submitted for publication by Friday. She rose early and sat up in bed with her I-pad, getting some work done before departing with the team this morning.

Alyn: You mentioned you grew up in Missoula, went to college there as well. Can you tell us about how you began freeskiing and why you decided to leave University of Montana before graduating?

Mason: I grew up fifteen minutes from Snowbowl, my family would go there all the time, they put me in snowboard lessons when I was five years old. Basically, I spent my childhood in the terrain park and never left. It was like a second home. I'd go there every day after school until the sun went down, then ride the town bus back to our house, for dinner. After ski season, I'd skateboard and do parkour, just to get the energy out. My parents said I was hyperactive- it was either do sports or take Ritalin, *(Laughs)*. In junior high I joined the diving team to develop my aerials, figured it would help with terrain park. Then when I was fifteen, me and my buddy

Shawn Cauffman went to Airborne Eddy's ski camp at Mt. Hood for a week and I watched these guys from a distance climb out of helicopters and ski down these massive, untracked steeps like friggin' warrior kings. And I wondered, (*pauses and throws his arms up dramatically*) why am I here on my snowboard when I should be on skis, doing what they're doing instead? I switched to freeskiing and never looked back, *never* looked back man, the rest is history.

History, Alyn sighed, looking through her notes. Not exactly World War Two or the Declaration of Independence, but there had to be something interesting in this pile of detritus.

Alyn: It's no secret that you've struggled with alcohol and drug addiction in the past, is that what compelled you to leave school and join Consumco?"

Mason: They recruited me sophomore year, I was winning every competition in sight. Western division free-skiing finals, national semi-finals, North American finals. The only person better than me is Ian Karolik, and I'm gonna give him a run for his money at the World Championships, he knows that. But Ian's the man, he's *the man*, my hat is off to him. I'm honored to be touring with the guy, I mean, I learn something from him every time we ski together. And Trent's great, he's so supportive and easy to work with. I'm a lucky guy, dude, livin' the dream. I stopped drinking when Consumco started sponsoring me- left college with a shitload of debt, probably owe the school sixty grand, but I'm bringin' it down, bringin' it *dowwnnnn*...

Alyn paused. Had he been drinking when she did this interview? the thought occurred to her. She continued typing.

Alyn: Can you tell us about the next six months and where the training tour is headed after Valdez?

Mason: Next stop, summer skiing in Portillo. We'll be in Chile for two months, I am totally stoked beyond stoked, Aconcagua, here we come. Two months of Andean bliss, DUDE! (*stands up, starts air-skiing, whistling through his teeth, making whooshing sounds, enters tuck position, then sits down again and howls for several seconds.*) We have the national extreme skiing competition second week of January in Jackson Hole, and WESC starting first week of February in La Grave. I promised I'd take my sister with me, she's the responsible one in my family. Did I mention that? I think I mentioned that.

He had to be tripping the light fantastic, Alyn thought wearily, closing her I-pad. She'd finish this later. She needed to get dressed, have some breakfast, prepare for her day out in the Chugach with the team. She would be outdoors all day, taking notes at the base of Thompson Pass while everyone was in the helicopters, skiing.

Two black vans with the business logo 'Valdez Heli Tours' waited for them in front of the hotel, freezing white puffs of exhaust billowing from their tailpipes in the sub-zero temperatures, frost collecting on their windows. The back cargo doors were open, Duncan and the two guides were already loading equipment into them. Backpacks, boots, poles, and skis sat piled in their bays. This excursion required large chemical body warmers and extra warm layers; hypothermia was just one of the many hazards. Whitney wore her polar fleece long underwear, she hoped it was adequate. The sun was out, crystalline clear skies promising a day of exceptional skiing. Everyone was spilling out of the hotel with a buzzing intensity to take on the Chugach. Whitney handed Duncan her skis and equipment she lugged down from her room, he looked at her curiously.

"Why didn't you let me keep your equipment? I'm storing everything in my own room while we're here, it looks like a ski locker," he told her. "I could have checked your skis, got everything ready for you."

"I'm not so sure about that," she snapped at him, "look what happened in Silverton. Don't want a repeat of that." He looked crestfallen. She seemed out of sorts. Agitated, he noticed with concern. He had heard about the altercation at the bar, Shenti had come to him for Tylenol and some bandages, late last night.

"We need to do an equipment check together before you get on the helicopter," he told her firmly, stowing her bags in the van. "I have your radio. I need to check your transceiver, your GoPro--have you checked everything yourself?" he asked, brushing aside her words. She nodded affirmative.

"Good. We'll check it again, just to be sure. I'll be in your heli by the way, so if you need anything, let me know."

Whitney climbed into a van, Shenti was already in the back seat, she sat down beside him. Mason and Alyn got in next and sat in front of them. Mason was unusually quiet, barely saying two words at breakfast in the hotel. Duncan had gone to the grocery store and ubered back with bags full of bread, lunchmeat, cheese, yogurt and fruit, she had consumed it with them in the kitchenette. A small dining area was near the lobby, Karis and Ian were eating breakfast there when Whitney came down to the meet the vans.

The outfitter would be doing an orientation once they arrived and prepared to embark. A woman climbed in the van's front seat, she turned around to great them. "Good morning!" she chimed cheerily, a smile lighting up her face. Mid-thirties, rosy cheeks, freckles, she had light brown hair. "My name is Heather Wynn, I'll be one of your guides, today. We'll be driving up the Richardson Highway towards Thompson Pass for fifteen miles, the heli's are parked there. While we make our way there, I'll be giving you some information about today's tour." She went on, "We are super excited to be guiding your team, it's an amazing honor for us to ski with you guys. We're totally thrilled!" Her eyes sparkled.

"So, here's the plan," she studied her clipboard, "Ian, Whitney, Duncan and I will be in Heli 1; our pilot will be taking us up to Loveland Peak and dropping us off at the top. This is a fifty-five -degree pitch, 6000 feet of vertical drop. When we first start out, I want you to proceed slowly, make some turns and test the snow to see how the slough is responding before you begin your descent. I'll go first and see what the conditions are like and then radio up to you. I have instructions from Trent that Whitney will proceed first. She will ski to me, then Ian should follow and join us. Once we have ascertained the quality of the snow and the slough, Whitney will proceed first, staying on the ridge line. Ian will ski parallel to her, then I'll follow fifty yards behind. Guess they don't want me in the video," she quipped, good natured, then went on, "When we arrive at the bottom, the heli will meet us. My understanding is that your videographer needs to switch heli's in order to film the other group. So, wait for instructions, and we'll coordinate that before we embark." She continued, "that group will be skiing Mile 27 Peak, we'll hover over them for filming."

Heather examined her notes a little closer. This tour was more complicated than most but that was to be expected. She made a mental note to ask Whitney for her autograph when they finished skiing today hoping to have a chance to talk with her. She had read an interview about Whitney recently, learning that she had a young daughter with medical problems who lived at home with her grandparents.

She wondered how Whitney managed to deal with single parent-hood and the grind of professional ski touring at the same time. Must be tough, she thought, sympathetically. Most people couldn't do it.


Two A-Star 350 B 3 helicopters sat off Richardson Highway at mile marker 15, rotors spinning, surrounded by an endless ocean of pristine white peaks, glistening in the morning sun. The thwump of the heli's rotors echoed across the Chugach, breaking the silence of the alpine kingdom. The vans pulled off the side of the road to a huge staging area. People were already congregating near the snowcats and snowmachines, setting up food and beverage stations for the day. Apparently, word was out, because several groups of bystanders had shown up to photograph the team as they exited the vans. Trent had a distaste for spectacle, he frowned at the sight of them. Heather apologized, brightly, "the locals love to watch the skiers here, it's like Mardi Gras."

Trent, Shenti, Mason and Karis did a safety check near Heli 2 with their guide, Scott Burke, a mid-forties, super- athlete decked out in North Face outerwear, carrying Atomic skis. They got on board and waited until Heather's group boarded Heli 1. The pilots did their cross checks, snow swirling about the machines like a win-ter squall. The relay was on. They rose from the ground and were whisked up to the sky, entering a sea of cliffs and couloirs, chutes and spires, ice fields and hanging glaciers. A realm where unexplored and untouched mountains still existed, inaccessible by human beings except by helicopter. Whitney gazed out of the window in sheer wonderment. What a privilege it was to see this divine and beautiful wilderness, she exhaled. She felt utter calm and peace, a sense of pro-found gratitude for this glory, this opportunity. Duncan looked over at her and she nodded at him, smiling behind her balaclava, sharing the unspoken yet intimate bond of the transformative experience. Words were unnecessary, the moment spoke for itself.

They were over Loveland Peak now, the heli lowered itself above a narrow knife ridge. She could see the other helicopter not far away, starting to hover in place above the west face of the mountain, waiting for them to disembark. Heather nodded, speaking through her headset. "Almost ready folks, check for loose clothing, check your equipment, watch your step." The pilot hovered on the ridge, they climbed out, crouching low, grabbing their skis from the exterior rack. Blowing snow met their faces and pelted them with a barrage of icy particles, force of the wind and engine momentarily pushing them off balance. Whitney fought the elements, holding her ground. The group moved away from the heli as it rose up and off, depositing them on the rocky ledge. Like a speck of dust on another planet, dwarfed by the behemoth mountain range where she now stood, she stared down into the steepest, meanest, vertical drop she had ever seen in her entire life.

She knew, intellectually, that she should be terrified, but her mind didn't seem to register the situation in that manner. Dispassionately, she took stock of the snowy face, disappearing into a seemingly vertical abyss. Heather's voice broke through her reverie. "Ready for safety check. Please start with me," she commanded Ian and Whitney. "Tranceivers, on. Radios, on. Check your airbag. Probes; check. Go-pros, on. Please check your pole straps and goggles, make sure they're secure. Check your boots. Check your bindings, please. Make sure they are secured. Do not ski to your left, off the spine. Avoid skiing below your slough. Stay at least five more millimeters forward in your stance, it will help with balance. Remember, we will make a group of short turns and then stop to access the conditions. Ready?" she finished. They both nodded.

Heather found it remarkable that she was instructing the two top rated extreme skiers in North America how to ski Valdez powder. A former freeskiing champion herself, she had been guiding in Valdez for over five years since she moved here with her husband and young daughter. Excited, she disappeared off the edge of the ridge and skied a hundred yards down, then waited for them.

Whitney took a deep breath and entered the precipice, snow falling away from her skis like water as she made several turns. It almost seemed like surfing, though she had never surfed before. It was like trying to stay above a rolling wave trying to pull her underneath, the snow constantly cascading beneath her as she carved more turns down its flow. She met up with Heather and stopped, they waited for Ian. He skied down a moment later in a series of turns, evaluating the formidable slough. Joining them, he stopped. Heather spoke, asking, "Are you ready?" Heli 2 hovered above them. Trent held binoculars at the window, watching. Shenti began filming.

Whitney pushed off her poles, floating and dipping, poles forward, skiing the foaming surf. Snow falling away like water beneath her, cascading down the succession of rippling pillows along the spine, her expert turns carving cleanly down the mountain neither sliding nor skidding. It was the longest run of her life, twice as far as the longest vertical drop she had skied anywhere in the lower forty-eight. Her mind emptied of all else but the execution of this single task: To produce an elegant and simple line that conveyed the joyous beauty of skiing that even someone who had never stood on a pair of skis before, could appreciate. Vaguely, she sensed Ian on her right side, skiing a slightly behind her. Heather, somewhere above. The three finally arrived at the bottom of the mountain, the heli still hovering above them. When it landed, Shenti and Trent exited the metal bird greeting them, exuberant. "You nailed it Whitney!" Trent congratulated her, beaming. "You totally slayed it!"

They continued to do runs throughout the day, Whitney alternately sitting in Heli 2 watching Mason and Karis ski Mile 27 and Pyramid Peaks, hovering above as Shenti filmed the two descending the 45- degree faces together. Getting stunning footage, the images were beautiful.

Looking at the video later at the hotel, Whitney could see that her and Ian had skied a monster. Loveland Peak and Mile 27 was the difference between surfing an eighty- foot wave like Mavericks and a forty-foot wave, somewhere in the Pacific. Shenti had congratulated her, impressed. "I'm sending this off to Consumco, Alyn can use the stills. I'm sure they'll want them for everything. You really knocked it out of the park this time, kiddo.

Whitney had smiled, surprised, swelling with uncharacteristic pride. "Thanks, Shenti," she told him. Underneath his gray beard and gruff demeanor, there was a pool of emotion, love for his craft. He obviously cared deeply about the quality of his work and his film, whether it was skiers going down mountainsides or soldiers on the battlefield. She would call her folks later tonight and tell them about her day and send some photos. They would be amazed.

Trent found her sitting in the hotel's dining area, sipping some hot apple cider. It was almost six-thirty p.m, she was about to go upstairs and have some food in the kitchenette, eat dinner there, maybe Alyn or Duncan would join her. Trent slid into a blond wooden chair across from her near the beverage dispensary, folding his arms, looking slightly pained. She waited. These types of encounters were rarely good, she braced herself for landing.

"Here's the good news. No, the *great* news. Consumco loved the footage today. I spoke to the director of marketing; they want to use your images for their new insurance company." Sing-song, edgy, he intoned, "It's a dangerous world, but 4Tress is here for yoooou... etcetera, etcetera. They're going to give you a five- thousand -dollar bonus." He paused.

"And..." Whitney gazed at him levelly.

"And... they want you to lose fifteen pounds, they think it would look better on camera," he winced. "You know, the camera adds fifteen extra pounds, that kind of bullshit, I told them you were a strong athlete and doing great, your weight was not a problem.... I mean, look at the footage, you can't argue with that, right? But you know how these suits are, they haven't a clue, all they care about is dollars and image and that kind of crap."

"You're friggin' kidding me."

"Uh, no."

"And do they tell Mason to fucking wash his hair, or pop his zits? Or Ian to stop wearing so much eyeliner and shit all over his face?" she lashed out, aggrieved.

Trent exhaled heavily, tilted his head, frowning. Judging from what he could tell, the procedure was making her more assertive, she didn't seem remotely afraid of him anymore. Perhaps some unintended fallout they hadn't anticipated....

"Jesus Christ, I'm going upstairs now, I'll see you tomorrow, Trent. Thanks for all the bang-up news," she told him, shaking her head in frustration. She got up and walked out, feeling completely derailed.

Slipping into her room, she sat on her bed and stared at the walls, leveled. *Damn them!* No matter how hard she tried, how hard she worked, these vampires just wanted more blood. If she went on a diet, it would totally mess with her concentration and stamina, she just knew it.

She called home, no one answered, she left a message.

"Hi guys, just checking in, I need to find out how Robyn's doing. I need to get Dr. Halpurn's number, I wanted to call him about Robyn…. We had an amazing day, I was going to tell you about it-hope you're all well, I'll call later," she spoke, trying to sound cheerful. She hung up, sighing. Maybe she should take tomorrow off and try to catch up on everything at home. It was nearly impossible to stay on top of things medical while she was out skiing during the day.

Well, she'd just have to lose the weight, she conceded, bleakly. There wasn't much alternative, if she wanted to stay on the team.

# CHAPTER 16
# VALDEZ

She texted Trent, soon as she woke up, Alyn was still asleep, in the other bed. "I need to take today off. Have to contact Robyn's doctors and my insurance carrier, get updated on her care. Can't ski today." He wouldn't be pleased, but she had no choice.

Shuffling out of bed, she went to the bathroom, used the toilet, then turned on the shower waiting for the water to heat up. Stepping into the stall, blasts of hot water struck her body, the chill of winter washing down the drain along with all the soap and shampoo. Her thoughts migrated to what Dr. Belcic had said to her the day before she departed his clinic in Belgrade. "Some patients experience a change in their emotions after the procedure, the ANTm3 can help with that during their transition to a new baseline state..." Something like that, she couldn't remember his exact words. At the time, it was all a blur. She just remembered him handing it to her, suggesting that she use it if she thought she needed to. Did he say it lasted twelve hours? A whole day? Three days? Again, she couldn't remember. Unfortunately, she had been so thoroughly discombobulated after the surgery much of what he said went right over her head.

Her baseline state had most definitely shifted, she concluded. The altercation in the bar and Trent's comments about it were a real wake- up call, that was for sure. Normally she wouldn't have reacted the way she did, fighting so aggressively. Her emotions were simply *off*.

Stepping out of the shower, she reached for a towel and dried off, wrapping it around her torso, steam filling up the room. She stared at the mirror, gazing at her reflection. Maybe she *should* try the ANTm3, she considered thoughtfully, biting her lip. Digging through her toiletry bag, she found the narrow, plastic vial in the bottom. What did Dr. Belcic say about its application? Take one whiff into each nostril? The transparent cellophane protective seal was still snuggly in place, she retrieved a metal nail file from her bag then stuck the pointed tip into the seal and tore it off quickly. Flipping the small, white cap off the top, she held the tip up to her nose. Closing her left nostril with her opposite finger she gave a quick squeeze and quickly inhaled. Cold spray entered her nasal passage, hitting the back of her throat. Switching nostrils she inhaled again, tasting the not-unpleasant substance as it peppered its way down and into her sinuses. Apprehensively, she put the cap back on the vial, and placed it back in her toiletry bag. Would she feel anything? she wondered. How long would it take? And how would she know if it was even working?

Below the sink, she found a small blow-dryer. Plugging it in, she began drying her hair. The green-colored strands near the front of her face were already starting to fade a little, they looked like two washed-out grayish fronds hanging over her cheeks.

Probably should get a touch -up at a salon when she got back to Crested Butte next week, she frowned. This style needed way too much maintenance…. What was she thinking?

Brushing on some mascara, she applied her purple eyeshadow and then stuck the pink rhinestone adhesive to her left nostril, studying her face critically. Did it look like a real piercing? Or like she just glued it to her nose? Did she look like she was trying too hard? Was her lipstick too dark? It looked slightly garish under the fluorescent light. Maybe she needed a different hue… Hair dry, she opened the bathroom door and slipped out quietly to get dressed, trying not to wake Alyn. Still in bed, she was beginning to stir, her breath becoming shallower.

Everyone else was probably waking up right now, Whitney thought. Getting ready for skiing in the Chugach with Heather and Scott today…

A text chimed on her cell phone, Trent. "Go ahead and take the day off, Whitney, we'll talk later." With a sigh of relief, she left the room and walked downstairs to the cozy dining area on the main floor. Bright lights and square tables with padded wooden chairs met her eyes. Hot breakfast food was displayed on the long countertop against the far wall, she helped herself to a mug of black coffee from a stainless dispensary and placed a fresh apple and cup of plain, lowfat yogurt on her paper plate. Eyeing the warm blueberry muffins longingly, she sternly restrained herself.

No muffin for her, she thought sadly. Losing fifteen pounds was a tough order. Dieting was terrible for athletes. Funny how the word diet started with the word *die*, she thought, irritably.

What next? Would they want her to get a face lift too? She sat down at a table forlornly with her own meager breakfast.

Chewing her apple, she scrolled down her phone contacts. Dialed Dr. McClellan's office. A receptionist picked up the line. "May I please have Dr. Halpurn's office number?" she requested. The receptionist answered politely, "Please hold while I get that for you." A pause. "Here's the number. Is there anything else I can do for you?"

"Um, yes, would you please have Dr. Mc Clellan call me today? I'd like to speak with her, thanks."

She took a bite of yogurt.

"Of course, I'll transfer your message," the woman replied. Whitney hung up, then dialed Dr. Halpurn's number. A voice message came on, a myriad of choices and extensions meeting her ear as she listened to the phone. Selecting his medical assistant's voice mail, she left a message, asking him to call her. She sipped her coffee, queuing up her insurance company's website to learn more about her health care plan. Without her computer, it was difficult to navigate the entire screen, only bits of pages were visible on her phone. A plethora of word- salad confronted her; qualifiers, disclaimers, adjuncts and conditions, all beyond her capability to fully comprehend. From what she could tell, every procedure and lab test had a thirty-percent co-pay until she reached a threshold of seven thousand dollars and after that, she was fully covered. Hospital fees would be reimbursed after she reached a twenty-four- thousand- dollar threshold and if expenses surpassed three -hundred- thousand dollars, then major medical would kick in. Catastrophic health insurance might be necessary to cover the remaining amount....

Robyn didn't *have* catastrophic medical insurance she thought, alarmed. And neither did she. What if something happened to *her*? Here she was, worried about Robyn's potential medical bills, but what if *she* fell off a cliff while she was skiing and broke her neck? Or became paralyzed? What *then*? How would she pay for everything? Heart pounding, she started to perspire. Scanning the website further, she tried to calculate Robyn's actual expenses, but it seemed impossible at this juncture. Until the doctors submitted their requests for approval for any procedures to the insurance company, there was no real way for her to ascertain how much everything would cost. Besides, she realized, it was possible Robyn might require ongoing medical care for years and she wouldn't know the full amount for a very long time.

Still staring at her phone, Ian and Karis entered the room, laughing. Ian nodded a brief hello to her, Karis glided by without a glance. Grabbing some coffee and sweet rolls, they sat down together at a corner table and began eating and scrolling their cellphones. Ian had on a geometric black and white ski sweater, the colors accentuating his black mohawk, black eyeliner. His right eyebrow was pierced with a silver bar sticking through it with two black metal balls on each end. Karis wore a form-fitting, ice- pink pullover with a matching ski jacket and fox-fur collar, hair in two long braids, blonde highlights glinting off their surfaces. Honey- colored lip gloss reflected off her shapely mouth. Both looked Instagram perfect. Karis lifted her phone and snapped a selfie of herself holding the sweet roll, mid-bite. She texted it to Ian.

Whitney stood up and bussed her table, then walked over to the hotel's lobby, finding a spot to sit beside some potted plants near the window. She stared outside, deep in thought. Several minutes went by, she watched Heather and Scott pull into the parking lot with their vans and swing them around to the building's front doors, under the canopy.

Duncan rushed outside to meet them, toting skis and bags of gear. The three paused to chat for a few moments, then went back inside and carried out more boots, skis and duffel bags. Sky clear, air freezing cold, piles of snow sat in the medians where the plows had deposited it early this morning. Duncan hadn't noticed her standing in the lobby, she backed away from the window, uncomfortably. She still felt guilty about snapping at him yesterday before they went heli-skiing. In a bad mood, she had just lost her tongue, lost her filter. Though he seemed surprised by her outburst, he hadn't responded, ever the diplomat. She wished she hadn't been so abrasive to him; he didn't deserve it. She made a mental note to apologize to him, later today.

Her phone rang. Dr. Halpurn. She moved towards a hallway looking for a quieter place to talk. There was an empty computer room for business travelers, she opened its door and slipped inside, taking a chair. His voice came over the receiver, sounding staid.

"Hello, this is Dr. Halpurn, is this Whitney?"

"Yes, thank you for calling. I'm up here in Valdez, unfortunately I wasn't able to meet you in Colorado, I'm on a ski training tour with my team," she answered, apologetically.

"Your mom told me about what you are doing. Sounds exciting, it must be freezing up there, I imagine," he dispensed with small talk, moving on to Robyn. "I have been in contact with Dr. McClellan with regards to our initial CT and MRI of Robyn's brain, I'm sure you have questions about everything, I wanted to speak with you. Seizure disorders are extremely complex medical conditions, and we're at the beginning of the process, so to speak. Your daughter's MRI revealed some abnormal tissue in the occipital lobe, which is a helpful clue to the origin of her seizures, however not the final story, there is much to investigate. We will need to do a series of EEGs over the next several weeks to get a more complete picture of what is happening inside her brain. I have already spoken to your mother, we'll be scheduling Robyn's appointments soon." He paused.

"It would be helpful if I had more details about the actual seizures, from you. Often, it is hard to elicit information from young children about what they are experiencing, at the time. Do you know if Robyn has visual hallucinations?"

Whitney drew a breath, considering, "I don't know, to be honest, she hasn't said that she uh, sees anything… um, strange." She should have asked her that question, she berated herself inwardly, already feeling inadequate.

"Bright colored balls, circles in her eyes? Flashes of light, loss of color, visual distortion?" Dr. Halpurn probed. "Has she made any reference to these events, at all?"

She chewed her lip, thinking. What was it that Robyn had said to her a few months ago after a violin lesson? she tried to remember, "she said the lines on the music page were wavy… they bothered her."

"Interesting. That could be a sign of dismorphopsia. Let's talk about physical sensations. Does she experience tinnitus or vertigo? Headache? he asked, methodically.

"I'm not sure about tinnitus, but she says her head hurts, she gets dizzy, nauseous, she vomits afterward. Gets really tired, and has to rest," she answered, distressed.

"Those are typical symptoms in the ictal phase, following a seizure. Can you tell me if she noticeable changes in her eye movement, forced closure of her eyelids or head movements? Jerking?" he persisted.

"Yes, she has that, I've seen those things, a number of times," she replied, frowning.

"Are you aware of these events occurring at night, during her sleep?"

Whitney reflected, she had been home so little, she hadn't spent a night watching Robyn sleep. Had her mom seen anything like that happen at night? she would have said something to her. She told the doctor, "Not that I'm aware of," slightly unsure.

"Does she exhibit loss of consciousness or convulsions?"

"I haven't seen convulsions, but when I was with her during her last seizure, I think she might have lost consciousness. We were sitting at an ice cream parlor, eating ice cream, and she almost fell off her chair. Maybe it was from vertigo- I just don't know. But we were able to walk out of the place afterward and walk home together."

"This is all extremely helpful, Whitney. As I said, we will be exploring the numerous possibilities and pathologies of Robyn's seizures, it is very much a process of elimination to determine what type of disorder she has and its pathways in her brain. A number of cortical malformations can present as occipital epilepsy, too numerous to go into at this time; but we will arrive at a diagnosis."

Whitney asked him, agitated, "will Robyn be alright? Can you figure out what is going on and cure it? She won't have this forever, will she?" she added, anxiously. "What does cortical mean, exactly? Is her vision in danger?" she persisted, on the verge of hysteria.

Dr. Halpurn paused, she sensed he was collecting his thoughts before answering, his voice measured, "At this time, our strategy is to see how she responds to the medicine she is currently taking and see if the seizures diminish or disappear over time while still pursuing neuroimaging and testing to determine the pathways and precise origins of the seizures themselves. If she does require an occipital corticectomy, our experience suggests that the consequences to her visual function may be less severe than you would imagine, that she has a very good chance of a positive outcome. As we progress through her tests, we will be able to pinpoint the cause of her seizures and provide more specific information."

She swallowed, a lump forming in her throat. "How long do you think this could take?"

"It depends. It depends on our clinical findings and what they reveal. I understand your desire to move quickly and get this over with, Whitney, but we must be absolutely sure we are making the proper assessments before doing any type of invasive procedures whatsoever. It is a painstaking process, and we have to be patient. It could take several weeks to several months, depending on the results of our testing. It could take more time," he added, "depending on if her seizures increase in frequency and duration or decrease in frequency as she responds to her medication... in which case, we would want to continue the medication and avoid surgical intervention. Theoretically, that could be six months to year, as we evaluate her progression. Does this make sense?" he asked her, patiently.

"Yes, it does," she answered, fretful.

"I'm sure you'll have many more questions along the way, that is to be expected. You are welcome to call my office anytime, Whitney. I hope we have an opportunity to meet soon. I'll be in contact with Dr. McClellan regularly, she can also provide information along the way."

"Thank you so much for explaining all this to me, I really appreciate it," she told him, gratefully. "It's all very confusing, to be honest."

Confusing. It was incomprehensible.

"It is," he replied, sympathetically. "I understand it's very difficult to watch your child go through this, as a parent. You are doing all the right things though. We'll get to the bottom of things- hang in there, alright?"

"Thanks again," she repeated, the corners of her mouth wavering. They both hung up at the same time. She glanced at her phone; nine forty-five a.m. Everyone had probably left by now, likely getting on board the helicopters, she imagined, a tad regretfully.

Later in the day, she called her mom. Three in the afternoon, Robyn should be home from school by now, having a snack. There was no answer, she left a message.

After her conversation with Dr. Halpurn she had called Dr. McClellan, left another message, waited for a reply, wandered over to a convenience store for a sandwich, went back to her room, took a nap.

Propped up against the back of her bed, she called her mom again. She picked up, Whitney could hear water running, dishes clattering in the background.

"How are you, honey?" she asked Whitney, concerned.

She envisioned herself fighting with the man at the bar, inhaling the ANTm3, arguing with Trent, starting a new diet, worrying about Robyn; she took a breath, answering brightly, "I'm fine, mom. I spoke to Dr. Halpurn this morning, he explained a lot of things to me and was very helpful. He said you were scheduling an EEG soon. Thanks for doing that. I should be back home next week, I can probably go with you."

"Did Dr. Halpurn tell you about the seizure checklist that he gave me?"

"No, didn't mention it. What is it?"

"We have a chart to take notes on Robyn's seizures. Duration, time of occurrence, eye, facial, body movements, vomiting, headache, dizziness, nausea…" Cindy replied, answering. Whitney could tell she was reading off a medical list. "We need to keep very careful records to see if her medication is working."

Whitney told her, "Dr. Halpurn said that Robyn may not need surgery if the medicine works. But she might need it if the tests reveal other things. This is so confusing. I can't believe it takes so long to figure this out. I'm totally stressed about this."

"I know, honey, I understand." Her daughter sounded more like herself, Cindy thought internally, relieved to hear her acting like a normal person coping with her child's illness. For the past month or so, she had been acting detached, remote. Maybe she was finally processing what was happening to Robyn, becoming more emotionally involved…

"How is dad?" she asked, reaching out.

"He's good, he's good. You know, working hard…the store is super busy now, height of ski season. We've got a big sale coming on next week with old inventory- we're making room for next season's new equipment. Hans came by to say hello, by the way. Asked how you were doing."

"Sweet. Tell him hi, next time you see him. I should be home next week for a few months, believe it or not. Once we finish up in Valdez, everyone is going back to Frisco to train through April until we leave for Portillo, in June. I've decided I need to go home and train by myself, instead. I want to work with Zokas at the gym and practice skiing with Hans. Would you tell him that, when you see him?" she spilled out in rush, suddenly.

"Sure, of course. I'm surprised to hear this," Cindy paused, puzzled.

"I just decided, mom. I need to come home."

"Well, let's see…let's see how things go," Cindy replied, cautiously.

"Okay, I will. Is Robyn there right now? Can I say hello?" she asked, plaintively.

"Let me get her on the phone."

Robyn's voice came over the receiver.

"Hi sweetie, it's mommy. How are you today?" Whitney asked her, cheerily.

"Good, mommy!"

Whitney's chest tightened, thinking of her conversation with Dr. Halpurn. Would Robyn have normal vision? Could she go blind? The thought was petrifying. "Listen honey, I'll be home next week and we can be together. We'll go out for ice cream, play games, watch Little Mermaid, okay?"

"Yay! I can't wait to see you, mommy."

"Me too, sweetie. I love you so much! Huggies."

"I love you too, mommy. Huggies back."


Not until five p.m., when everyone came back from skiing and they all were seated together in Mason's room eating an impromptu spaghetti dinner, did she realize that she *did* feel differently on the ANTm3.

*Empathetic.* She felt more empathetic, there was no doubt about it.

But she also felt more anxious, and more fearful. Talking to Dr. Halpurn and her mom today about Robyn had been fraught with fear and anxiety. While Trent, Ian, Karis and the others were bantering about their adventures in the Chugach today, -the drops, the slough, the views, the heli rides, her mind was elsewhere, worrying about insurance claims, medical bills and surgical complications.

After dinner, she helped Duncan do dishes in the little kitchenette. They loaded the dishwasher and hand washed the pots and pans, wiping down the table and counters. Mason disappeared to his bedroom, Ian and Karis went out somewhere together. Trent stayed behind with Duncan and her, sat in chair, studying some maps.

"Sorry I snapped at you yesterday," Whitney apologized, putting some dishes in the cupboard.

"Apology accepted," he replied easily, with a lopsided grin. "No big deal," he added, opening the refrigerator and placing a bowl of leftover spaghetti inside it.

Trent broke their repartee, stating out loud, "Tomorrow, Ian, Mason and Karis will be doing cat skiing on Sapphire Mountain. Whitney, you and I will do some one-on-one together. We'll take the snowmachines up Thompson Pass and glacier ski with Scott and Heather. Practice your rope skills. Be prepared to depart by eight-thirty a.m. and bring all your climbing gear." He folded the map and stood up to leave the room.

"Sounds good," she answered, automatically. She turned to Duncan. "By the way, I never found my ice-axe after our climb up Glory Couloir. Do you have another one I could use?"

"I'll get you one, don't worry," he told her reassuringly. He always brought extra gear on their excursions; skiers were always losing things, there was so much to keep track of. She asked him, "which skis do you think I should use tomorrow?"

"Bring your Atomics. They're great for mixed conditions. You'll get a little of everything up there--ice, crud, powder.

"Thanks," she smiled, folding a kitchen towel and hanging it on the oven door. Doing dishes with Duncan was about the closest thing to normal these days. In fact, it was a pleasure. She almost wished they had more to clean up, just so she could hang out with him a little longer.

Though he was thinking the same thing, Duncan kept it to himself. Maybe there would be a time when he could express his attraction to her, but it would have to wait.


Tomorrow, she'd tell Trent she needed to go back to Crested Butte and train by herself for the final month of ski season so she could take care of Robyn. He'd just have to deal with it, she sighed, dreading the conversation. For some reason, she was feeling intimidated by him again. Speaking with him was a landmine of traps and snares, verbal acrobatics and jedi-mind tricks. The man was expert at keeping people off- guard and on the defensive, it was how he manipulated them to get what he wanted. To ask for a concession that made her appear less than committed to the team, her training, was going to be rough. He would not be pleased.

# CHAPTER 17
# VALDEZ

Skillfully, Heather steered the van up Thompson Pass, checking her mirrors every so often to glance behind her at the two shiny black and red Polaris Voyageur snowmachines sitting side by side like praying mantis, trailered behind them. Thick nylon straps restrained the machines in place, the vehicle climbing higher and higher in elevation every minute. Three degrees Fahrenheit outside, early morning sun was breaking through the scattered clouds, sending beams of light reflecting off the frosted windows. Trent, Whitney, Duncan and Alyn sat quiet gazing out at the massive, snow-covered peaks sweeping down to the gray, arctic sea in giant, serpentine waves. Scenic grandeur at every turn, they traveled behind Scott and the rest of the team towards mile marker 27, where they would rendezvous with the other guides at the base of Sapphire Peak.

Heather fixed her eyes on the road, the trailer jostling noisily over crusty lumps of icy snow as it swayed loosely back and forth. She explained over her shoulder, "We'll be going to a glacier at an area called Tones Temple. It's six miles north of Sapphire Peak, we'll take the snowmachines up there with Scott while your other teammates cat-ski with Jonah and Carli." She went on, clarifying, "We'll have to abseil down a couloir to get to there- you'll need your harness and crampons. There's fixed rope, it shouldn't be too difficult. Scott will meet us at the base of the glacier with a snowmachine so we can relay up and down the route several times. Then we can practice self-rescue inside a crevasse later this afternoon if you like," she added, helpfully.

Trent leaned over to Whitney, "I asked Heather and Scott to take us somewhere we could practice fixed- rope ski touring. La Grave is mostly off-piste skiing. You'll be confronted with via-ferrata type climbing just to reach the runs. And if you're not prepared for it, you're basically out of contention," he added, explaining, "The Europeans are accustomed to this style of skiing in the Alps, but the Americans aren't. We don't have those kinds of technical routes at our ski areas. Consequently, we're at a major disadvantage, which is a serious problem. Their judges will assume you can handle their routes, which is why we need to practice," he finished, frowning.

Whitney swallowed. This was why they were doing one-on-one, Trent needed to coach one person at a time, it was too dangerous to take multiple people all at once. She assumed Mason, Ian and Karis would alternate climbing inside the crevasse with the guides over the next several days.

Heather pulled the van off the highway to a parking area at Mile Marker 27, right behind Scott. The trailer bumped loosely over icy potholes and grooves, she expertly swung around and came to a stop. A few other skiers were already there, unloading equipment. The snowcat was parked in a snowfield, twenty yards away from the pull-off. A buzz of anticipation filled the air as they scurried around the parking area, getting ready. Shenti and the others tumbled out of Scott's van and paused momentarily to take in the environs.

Scott quickly went over to Heather to confer, then hopped onto her trailer to back the snowmachines off, their cacophonous roar piercing the mountain solitude like chainsaws in a library. The two started hauling gear from the vans to their sleds, packing down coolers full of sandwiches, snacks and beverages for the excursion. Scott grabbed a box of energy bars, handing them out to everybody.

Whitney donned her gloves, goggles, balaclava and switched her boot warmers on. Before leaving the hotel this morning she had painstakingly inspected all her equipment, Duncan had done the same as he loaded it into the van. Everything had appeared in good working order. She trudged over to the solitary blue Sani-can sitting at the edge of the parking area to relieve herself, Karis followed from behind, sidling up to her.

"Trent told me why you didn't ski yesterday," she stated, conversationally. "Said you're not committed to the team. Said it would be better if you just quit, went home to take care of your daughter," she hissed, voice icy. Stepping in front of her, she blocked her path. "We need someone who can train with us every day, help the team. You're just a liability," she snarled, venomously.

*Ambushed.* Whitney clenched her teeth, restraining herself from responding. *Don't react.* She's just trying to psyche you out. *No way* had Trent said those things, she told herself internally. Uncanny though, how Karis could intuit her insecurities. She kept her face forward, refusing to make eye contact. Karis turned away abruptly and headed back to the vans.

Shaken, Whitney stepped into the Sani-can. *Did that just happen?* She shook her head, taken aback. Fricking bizarre. What was *wrong* with that woman?

Frozen butt, she exited the structure and walked back to the vans. Karis was already trudging towards the snowcat with her skis to join the others congregating around the boxy, treaded vehicle. Behaving as though nothing out of the ordinary had happened, she smiled and greeted the skiers as they all boarded.

Heather and Scott were still unloading gear from the van's cargo bay, sorting through carabiners and rope. Crampons, ice-axes lay in piles. Trent was busy lugging duffel bags over to the sleds. He looked happy for a change, glad to be getting some physical exertion.

Finally, an opportunity to do some climbing and skiing he thought, with relief. He'd spent too much time standing at the base of the slopes and inside helicopters with Karis, Whitney, Mason, Ian, trying to navigate their interpersonal conflicts. Too much time dealing with Shenti's temperamental moodiness and Mason's goddamn problems, in private. The kid was drinking again, he was sure of it. Probably doing drugs, too, he fumed. And Theodore was driving him up a wall as well, constantly asking him for footage that was unreasonable, dangerous. Putting his skier's lives at risk. He tried to explain to the man what a reasonable request was and wasn't, but the guy was daft. Wanted Ian to wear a wing suit and fly down the mountainside, holding a can of AcyDgreen while Shenti filmed him. What a douche. Said he had seen someone do it on TV and thought it was *super cool*. Like it was perfectly reasonable to ask Trent to make that happen. Like anyone could just put on a goddam wingsuit and launch off a mountainside without having their brains splatter across it, bigtime. Honestly, these execs in New York and Frankfort had no idea how dangerous this shit was. Just keeping his skiers in one piece was becoming a major ordeal now, they had become so demanding. He chewed his lip, growing more agitated. A person could prepare their whole life for a competition, be the best in the world, but it only took one bad run, one bad day to take them out. An injury, a mental breakdown, an avalanche- he knew that better than anyone else.

Skiing today would do him some good, he thought ironically. Help him burn off a little steam.

Before getting on the snowmachines, Scott and Heather gathered the team to give an impromptu lesson about the climbing gear, its application and usage. Whitney stood listening politely. Already familiar with the information, she had been climbing with her dad and other local alpinists in Crested Butte since junior high. Often, she practiced on the Crested Butte Community Center's climbing wall when she had the chance. Nonetheless, it was always helpful to review safety procedures, given an opportunity. Trent listened politely as well, appreciating their attention to detail. Heather and Scott were doing an excellent job, he thought, consummate professionals. Years of technical climbing in the Tetons, Sawtooth and Bitterroots had given him a lot of perspective about guides. Some were better than others, he had seen them all.

Whitney considered telling Trent about her run-in with Karis a few moments ago, still stung by the vicious encounter.

Better not, she quickly decided. He might get angry at her for bringing it up, and they needed to get going this morning without the drama, without delay. Best to let it go, she conceded, trying to push the unpleasant exchange out of her mind.

Alyn was looking at her and Karis strangely, sensing real tension between the two. *What was going on?* she wondered, puzzled. Something must have happened this morning, she just hadn't caught it.

Trent climbed behind Heather on the backseat of the snowmachine and grasped the sides as she gunned the engine. The muscular Polaris growled ferociously and shot uphill like a rocket, sled
in tow. Whitney climbed behind Scott, and they followed loosely
behind, roaring through the deep powder. Cutting tracks through
newly fallen snow, they whipped across the gigantic snowfield, racing towards a treed gully. Heading up into the shaded mountainside, they steadily gained elevation. Following Heather as she wove
through embankments, trees, fallen logs and rock outcroppings,
they zoomed along for another forty-five minutes, finally arriving
at a high, snowy ridge. Here, views of the towering peaks seemed to
go on forever. Gasping with awe, Whitney yelled to Scott above the
engine, "This is freakin' amaaaaaazing!" Scott yelled back jovially, "I
know! I never get tired of it!" They raced a little further, he killed the
engine, stopping. "We're here," he announced exuberantly, swinging
his body off the machine.

Heather and Trent roared to a stop beside them, joining the two.
The four conferred. Scott announced, "Heather will take you down
the couloir and ski with you, I'll take the machine down and meet
you guys at the bottom of the glacier. We'll leave one machine up
here."

Poised by the sleds, they extricated rope, backpacks, skis and
poles. Scott handed Whitney and Trent their safety harnesses, they
put them on, adjusting the straps. Donning crampons, transceivers,
they attached their skis and poles to their packs. Now it was time for
their safety check. They stood together and went through the drill.

"Transceivers, on. Check." Heather stated.

"Ice- axe, check. Shovel, check." She continued, "Probe, check."

"Crampons, secure. Check." They nodded, faces obscured by goggles and balaclavas, helmets.

"Do you want me to turn on my GoPro?" Whitney turned to Trent.

"Might as well. You never know what footage you're gonna want to keep." he answered, automatically.

"Okay. Let's do our harness check," Heather announced, inspecting each carefully, making sure all their straps and clasps were properly attached and secure. "We're ready," she stated, nodding. They began trudging towards the edge of the ridge. Whitney followed her as she peered over the side of it, eyes scanning the narrow, nearly vertical chasm below. She could barely make out the rope dangling down the cliff wall, inside the ice encrusted chute. She got a glimpse of it running laterally, across the other side, disappearing beyond her sight. A shiver of apprehension ran through her.

Heather crouched down and clipped onto the rope, lowering herself over the edge. "I'll lead. Whitney- you follow ten feet behind, okay? Trent, you follow Whitney please," she instructed, firmly. "Use your crampons and ice-axe for purchase, we'll abseil slowly. Only proceed after you have double-checked your carabiner at every rung," she reminded them, scooting down into the couloir. Whitney knelt and clipped on, her skis and poles shifting her weight, backpack pulling at her sides. Vision obscured, she dangled her legs down into the abyss, feeling her way off the ledge. Ski boots clanging against the striated rock, she inched down, gripping the rope with one hand, her ice-axe with the other. A film of sweat flushed over her skin. Nerves. This was not good, she ruminated, trying to bat away the unwelcome sensation. Heather called up to them, "When you get to the horizontal fixed rope, cross over to the other side. I'll meet you there."

Ignoring the vertical drop hundreds of feet below, Whitney concentrated solely on her descent. Taking methodical steps downward, she kicked her crampons into the ice and snow and thrust the tip of her ice axe into the couloir's wall with every step. Trust the rope. Trust the rope, she kept telling herself over and over, repeating the words inside her head, willing herself to stay calm. Breath whiffed out in frozen puffs around her face, she could hear Trent's grunts echoing above her. He was working hard too, she realized.

It took about twenty minutes to get down the vertical portion of the rope, they both arrived and began moving laterally across it, bodies plastered against the surface of the couloir. Heather waited for them, motioning ahead. Following the rope, they continued traversing the icy rock face, practically hanging off the mountainside. Trepidation flooded Whitney's body, she almost panicked. *Must be the residual effects of the ANTm3*, she told herself, taking more deep breaths. What else could it be? She had been fine all month long, and now this. *Don't say a word*, she steeled herself, grimacing. Trent was right behind her; he couldn't know what was going on inside her head.

She was almost there! Heather waited for her, standing on a level platform of snow. Whitney exhaled with relief, shimmying over. Standing beside Heather, they waited for Trent. In several moments, he joined them. Still breathing hard, the three surveyed the glacier.

Heather radioed Scott to notify him their location; his voice crackled back over the device, affirmative. Removing their harnesses and crampons, they stowed them inside their backpacks, took a few sips of water. Unclipping their skis and poles, they set them on the snow and snapped into the bindings.

"You follow, stay right behind me," Heather told them, authoritatively. "There are several crevasses on the south edge of the glacier, you'll see the light blue fissures. Be sure to avoid skiing anywhere near them. Further down, there are several seracs, we need to stay at least forty yards away from those, as well. Sometimes they break off- not a good place to be if that happens," she added, warningly. "If I stop skiing, you need to stop immediately, in case we encounter any issues with the route."

Trent and Whitney both nodded affirmatively, acutely aware of the hazardous obstacles she was describing.

"Okay, let's go." Turning on her edges, she began skiing leisurely down the thirty-degree slope. Whitney followed twenty feet behind. Soft snow rested on hard crust beneath it, she could hear the scrape of ice underneath her skis as she carved turns in tandem with Heather, matching her pace. They passed by some bergshrunds, skiing around the massive piles of windswept snow and ice with plenty of clearance. Enormous walls of white snow, rock cliffs surrounded Whitney's peripheral vision, an endless sea of sky and sun, reflecting off their glinting surfaces. Scale was *different* up here in the Chugach, she marveled. Features that looked close by were actually very far away. What appeared a small obstacle became a gigantic structure as they got closer to it. She was but a speck of dust in this vast, arctic landscape.

Heather paused, sliding to a stop momentarily, Whitney and Trent quickly halted beside her a few seconds later. She pointed to a distant spot. "See that crevasse?" They looked over towards a gash of translucent snow slicing across the glacier, its blue and black void visible, menacingly below. "If you get closer, you can see the bottom. It's about twenty feet deep. There's a little water flowing down there, it's shallow, like a rocky sandbar," she informed them, they nodded back at her. "Scott's probably waiting for us by now," she said, pushing off her poles, skiing down further. They cruised easily behind, passing jumbles of ice and uneven terrain as it funneled to the bottom of the glacier. Scott was sitting on his snowmachine munching an energy bar, his deeply tanned face smiling broadly as they approached.

"How was it up there?" he called out, enthusiastically.

"Great! Really nice run! Getting to it is no picnic, but the rest is a breeze," Heather laughed merrily. Trent and Whitney nodded in agreement. Aside from a few moments of mild terror, it *had* been fun, Whitney thought, wryly. And, beautiful... she had been completely transported, temporarily forgetting about Robyn's medical problems and all that went with it.

"Do you guys want to take another stab at it?" Heather turned to Trent and Whitney. Trent replied, "Definitely. He glanced at Whitney, "I could tell she was uncomfortable. She should do it again, but alone. She needs the practice." He stepped out of his skis. Whitney pursed her lips. She thought she had hidden her discomfort well. Had she been *that* transparent?

"Hey, it's okay to have a little fear," he told her dryly, "It's what keeps you alive."

She wasn't supposed to *feel* fear anymore. Wasn't that the whole point of the procedure? *Just how long did this ANTm3 last, anyway?* she chewed her lip, frustrated.

"Yup, let's do 'errrrr again," she nodded, drawling the words out like John Wayne, ever the good sport.

Whitney and Scott climbed onto the Polaris, Heather and Trent stayed behind with the cooler of food and beverages for a leisurely lunch on the glacier.

At the top of the ridge, Scott handed her a radio. "I'll stay up here and stay in communication with you. I won't leave until I know you've arrived at the base of the glacier. If you need any help, let me know. I can assist you quickly, I've done this route about a hundred times," he reassured her, upbeat. "We've never had any problems. The glacier isn't avalanche prone, just so you know. Your coach wants you to go it alone, says you'll be confronted with something like this in La Grave. I'm sure you'll do fine."

Whitney swallowed. This was the test. She knew it would come to something like this. One-on-one. Trent would be watching closely to see how she handled it.

"Tell Trent I'll be beat our time down by thirty minutes," she told Scott. "Ask him to start timing me right now, okay?"

He grinned. "Okay, you got it." He radioed down to him.

Striding quickly to the ledge, she clipped her harness onto the rope and dropped into the chasm and began descending, moving with a swiftness stoked by adrenaline and pure indignation. "*Here I come, I'm num-ber one*, she repeated, clenching her teeth, muttering. She scooted downward on the rope with rapid precision, methodically unclipping and reclipping her carabiner with a determined click. Wasting no time, she spread eagled across the traverse, slamming her ice- axe and crampons into the headwall, crabwalking along the rock and ice, until she arrived on the glacier. Surprisingly, she felt far more confident this time, invigorated by the challenge. Removing her harness, she yanked her crampons off, then took a swig of water, throwing everything back into her pack. Hoisting it back on, she snapped into her Atomics and was off. Using Heather's previous broad, sweeping tracks to guide her, she raced down the glacier, abbreviating the line of their descent by a good twenty minutes. Now she was in a tuck position, flying.

Heather and Trent looked up from their sandwiches in surprise. Trent grinned, he tapped his stopwatch, peering at it.

"You were faster than anyone I've ever coached, Miss Whitney. *Very* impressive! We'll see if Karis can beat your time. Would you care for a sandwich?" he asked her solicitously. She grinned halfway, shooting him an exasperated look. He chuckled out loud, taking a bite.

Scott came back down and joined them for lunch, it was nearly two p.m. now. They took the snowmachines up near the crevasse and parked them, unloading all the climbing gear onto the snow.

Heather extracted a new, lightweight, PETZL kit designed for crevasse self-rescue, handing it to Whitney. "This is what you'll be using in La Grave," Trent informed her. "We'll practice Prusik technique here for the next three days while everyone rotates through this glacier tour."

"Sounds good," she replied, earnestly. He seemed to be in an unusually good mood this afternoon. Perhaps this was the time to ask him about finishing her season in Crested Butte.

"I need a favor, Trent," she posed, voice turning serious. *Might as well get to the point.*

"What's that," he clipped, instantly tense.

"I need to finish up the season back home, in Crested Butte," she spilled out. "Robyn needs me. She's having serious medical problems. She may need brain surgery, for all I know. I'll work with a trainer at the gym, I'll ski with a coach every day- I'll do everything I need to do- just without the team." She held her breath.

"No."

"No? Just, *no*?" she exclaimed, infuriated. "You saw how I did today, I can *do* this. *I have to do this,*" she insisted, chest constricting painfully. Pent-up angst welling up, she pressed him harder. "You don't have a child, do you? If you did, you would understand how important this is. I *promise* you I will do everything possible to make this work. And I *will* go to Portillo, but I need to be with my daughter now," her voice rose angrily.

He responded sharply, "I am responsible for your training. And Consumco will not approve it. Your sponsorship requires you train with the team."

She exploded. "You know what? They can go fuck themselves, for all I care! I did their fucking *procedure*. I *changed* my fucking *hairdo* and *went on a starvation diet*! They are not going to destroy my daughter too," she stormed at him, totally pissed.

Uh oh. Now the dam had broken. She was putting it all out there…totally out of control… Mt. Vesuvius spouting hot lava…. He'll probably fire me right now, she thought wildly.

Silence.

He scowled for a moment, looking at her like he might blow a gasket, but then took a long breath, considering. "Trent, *please. I have* to win WESC," she pleaded. "I have no choice. It's the only way I can pay for her medical bills. Please let me go," she implored, quietly.

"Okay. I'll talk to Consumco. You go home," he told her, acquiescing.

"Thanks. I will make this work," she reassured him, tearing up.

"Okay," he turned away brusquely. Couldn't handle the emotion. *Christ, women.* And where the hell did she learn to curse like that? Sounded worse than a sailor with a bad case of scurvy.

He had to admire her though. *No one* stood up to him. She was turning out to be one tough fire- cracker, he thought. Did a great job on the glacier today, too.

*One-on-one.*

Well, she just made a slam dunk, he thought. Maybe she *could* train at home and still survive....

# CHAPTER 18
# CRESTED BUTTE

Past her bedtime, Robyn ran to the front door as Whitney opened it, shrieking with excitement. "Mommy's home! Mommy's home!" She had flown back to Eagle County after their last day of skiing in Valdez, making the four- hour drive back to Crested Butte early that evening as dusk turned to dark sky. Cindy and Tom let Robyn stay up late waiting for her, even though tomorrow was a school day. Wearing cute cotton pajamas with little pink elephants all over them, hair slightly damp from her bath earlier that evening, she wrapped her arms tightly around her mother, hugging her.

The effects of the ANTm3 had not entirely worn off. During the flight back to Colorado Whitney had experienced distinct moments of heart-pounding anxiety as heavy turbulence above the Alaska Range battered their plane. Dropping, skittering across the windy mountain range, even Ian and Mason had turned green and clammy. Six days out since she had first inhaled the chemical, she shut her eyes, closed her hands into a tight fist, willed herself to stay calm as she stoically stared at the back of Trent's seat for the remainder of the flight. When they finally taxied to a complete stop in Eagle, relief washed over her flesh like rain on desert flower, she nearly kissed the ground. The sun was starting to set behind the high-altitude plateau.

The drive across Tennessee Pass at dusk, then Monarch Pass in total darkness conspired to make the sojourn even more hazardous than usual. At least in daylight, she could see the hairpin curves, oncoming truck traffic and lonely miles of snowy highway leading to Leadville and Gunnison. At nighttime, however, the drive was more like reading Braille, accomplished largely by feel and memory of the road, rather than by vision itself. By the time she arrived home, she was exhausted.

Trent and the rest her teammates had piled into the Sprinter to drive to back to the rental house in Frisco. On the way out to the airport's parking lot, Trent informed her, "We'll be skiing at Arapahoe Basin through April. We need to talk during the week about your training. Call me," he added tersely.

"Don't worry, I'll call you," she reassured him, grateful to being going home. She had already gotten in touch with Hans and Zokas, her personal trainer in Crested Butte. The two men were precisely the kind of people she needed at this juncture. Nice, supportive, cheerful.


Whitney hugged Robyn back tightly, nuzzling her pink cheeks and damp hair. "I'm soooo glad to see you, bug! Tomorrow, you can tell me everything. Show me what you're doing in school, play me a song on your violin." She turned to Cindy, "I'll need that checklist from the doctor so I can keep track of things too, mom."

Cindy nodded, "By the way, your dad got in touch with Hans. He's tickled pink and wants to help you. But you'll need to pick him up at his place, he can't drive anymore. They took his driver's license away last year when his eyes turned bad."

"That's fine. I'll call him tomorrow," she replied. Coming home always made her feel a little disoriented, like an astronaut hurtling back to Earth in re-entry. Disturbed and disconnected, it took at least several days for her to adjust to the new routine around the house.

"We got a copy of SKIER Magazine yesterday. Guess what— you're on the cover!" Cindy crowed, striding into the kitchen and grabbing it off the counter. "That's my baby, that's my girl," she handed it to Whitney, proudly. The picture was of her inside Glory Couloir, climbing up the chasm, ice-axe in hand, skis strapped to her back.

Alyn must have taken it before Karis knocked it out of her hand, she considered, silently. The caption on the cover was in bold letters: Whitney Olson- Extreme Skier, Single Mother Extraordinaire.

Her heart sank. *Torpedoed.* Her efforts to downplay single parenthood with Alyn had clearly bombed, the magazine's caption said it all. She wondered how Consumco would respond, expecting the worst.

Oh well, screw them, she thought, suddenly weary. I'm tired of pretending that I don't have a child to raise; pretending like I'm not affected by her medical issues. She brought the magazine into her bedroom, laid down and began reading Alyn's article dispassionately. Snippets of it caught her by surprise.

*Whitney Olson continues to push hard, never flinching at the next challenge, never backing down from the next super-human endeavor. Despite caring for her young daughter with severe medical problems, she continues to ski and train with the best athletes in the country, holding her own as a top contender for next winter's World Extreme Ski Championships in La Grave, France....*

Reading further, now she regretted she didn't divulge more about how conflicted she was. It was about time women raised these issues, she realized. She should have been more honest, talked about how hard it was to raise Robyn and keep competing, keep skiing at this level. Shared how at times she thought she should just quit the circuit, get a regular job, stay home and care for her daughter. Instead, she had downplayed the challenges, trying to make things seem effortless so her sponsors wouldn't think she was compromised by motherhood. Idiotic, she thought. She was only human, after all.

Maybe if she was candid about being a mother and a competitor, more female athletes would speak out. Maybe they might receive more support and acceptance, she brightened, with alacrity.

Her phone pinged, a text from Alyn. "Your feature is blowing up! Go to SKIER Facebook and read the comments. You're like Joan of Ark."

Whitney scrolled the site, shocked by the feedback.

"It's about time female athletes could talk about childrearing and still pursue their goals!"

"Whitney Olson, you rock! Keep up the great work on behalf of all us moms!"

"Thanks, Whitney for sharing what it's really like… Keep up the fight!"

There were literally hundreds of comments coming in, she couldn't keep track of them. Wow! she blinked, totally surprised.

A ping from Trent. "Your interview seemed to really strike a nerve… Since I let you go home, I'm starting to look like the *good* guy. Hey, imagine that. Consumco is figuring out how to capitalize on this- like they've been championing mothers all along…Congrats on the article, kiddo."

Trent. Aloof, exasperating Trent. Maybe there was a glimmer of humanity in there *somewhere*, she mused wryly.

She woke up early the next morning, helped Robyn get ready for school, going through the medical checklist with her before walking over to Miss Hennessy's class.

"Do you see any blotches or lines in your eyes? Notice anything that doesn't seem normal when you look around?" she asked Robyn, carefully.

"I see lines on my schoolwork and my music notes are wavy. They're hard for me to read."

"Okay." Whitney made a check. "Do you think it's getting worse, or better, over the last several days?"

"It's getting worse, mommy."

She cringed. "Okay, you can tell me the truth, honey." She could see from Cindy's notes that Robyn's last seizure had occurred two weeks ago, her checkmarks went across the chart. Nausea, fatigue, rapid eye movement. The medication seemed to be helping somewhat though, in so far that her seizures hadn't increased in frequency over the past four months since she began taking it.

But her hallucinations and visual problems were deteriorating, based on what Robyn was telling her. *That* would indicate that the medication was not necessarily working as well as it should be…. Whitney frowned. This was complicated, confusing, hard to decipher.

Each week, she was supposed to apprise Dr. Halpurn and Dr. McClellan about any changes. Robyn was scheduled for another EEG in Colorado Springs, two weeks from now.

They stood by the classroom door, hugging goodbye. Miss Hennessey greeted them. "It's nice to be back, Whitney told her. Thanks so much for all your help with Robyn, I really appreciate it."

"My pleasure," she smiled. It's good to have you back, Whitney. Robyn's been excited about you returning, she always talks about you," she added. "We'll see you this afternoon."

Whitney pulled her Taos up to Han's driveway. The old miners house at the base of Kebler Pass was looking a little tired, she noted. Abandoned flowerpots sat despondent and unused on the front porch, the wood planks were starting to sag and needed re-staining. Ever since Han's wife Marta, had died of cancer eleven years ago, the place hadn't been quite the same. She was the one who had kept it looking like a shiny penny, with fresh flowers, trimmed shrubs, a small vegetable garden.

Hans hoisted his skis onto the car's ski rack, put his ski boots and duffel bag in her back seat, climbing in. He moved slowly, taking time to lower himself into the seat, his back and hips obviously tight and arthritic. He turned to greet her, chuckling. "I'm not as flexible these days, the old knees and hips aren't like they used to be." Eyes crinkling, he smiled, glad to see her. She looked different--it was the hair color, he realized. An odd magenta color...The cut was different too, but he kept his opinion to himself.

"Thanks for doing this, Hans," she leaned over and gave him a quick hug. "I really appreciate it."

"My pleasure, my pleasure, what else am I going to do with all my time? I get up, I plan my next meal, I take my walk...Now I get to work with the best skier in the world. Say, how 'bout that! Saw your picture in the magazine yesterday, at the store. Stopped in to say hello to your dad. He was so proud of you, nearly jumped out his boots." He chuckled again. "Hey, did you know I get to ski for free now? I'm so old they gave me a lifetime pass. Can you believe it? I probably won't need it for very long though, if you know what I mean…" he sighed heavily, looking out the window.

"Hans, you're going to outlive us all."

"Hmm… Listen, Whitney, I've been thinking…what we need to do."

"What?" she turned her face briefly, hands on the steering wheel. They were already passing the forest service road to Oh Be Joyful Campground, just ten minutes from the ski area's base.

"We need to study every map we can get our hands on of La Grave. Memorize every route. I'll go to the library and look for them. Bring them over to your place."

"Hans, I can get them online."

"Online. Humph," he snorted, disdainfully.

"We can get SAT photos; I'll download them."

"SAT photos?" his raised an eyebrow. "What the heck are those?"

"*Satellite* photos."

"Whatever happened to a damn piece of paper? He retorted, frowning. "I want a map I can hold in my hands. You need to under-stand the *scale*. *See* the mountains. Memorize every single headwall, buttress, glacier and chute."

"Okay, Hans, you try and find those maps," she nodded. "Maybe our library has something."

Steering the Taos into a parking space, they stopped and got out, Hans slowly straightening his body, bones creaking in protest.

Whitney unloaded his equipment for him and carried hers, they made their way across the parking lot, breath condensing in the frigid air, ski boots crunching against packed snow and ice. Swarms of skiers were heading towards the gondola to start their day. A few local lifties waved enthusiastically over to them. "Hey Hans!" they shouted, broadly. "You're more famous than I am around here," Whitney teased him.

"That's because I'm the oldest known human on skis," he laughed, gruffly.

Getting into the gondola, they exited at the top and caught another chair further up the mountain. Hans suggested, "Let's hike over behind the Butte- there's always a stash of untracked snow there. No one else is up here yet, we'll have it all to ourselves."

Skiing off the chair, they traversed across the ridge as far as they could, to the area's roped boundary. Whitney drew a deep breath, inhaling the fresh pine scent and clean air. She took a second to savor the blue sky, glorious peaks and valleys, forested glades. This was what she loved most- the beauty and tranquility of nature. Hans paused.

"What is the most important thing there is, Whitney?" he asked her, suddenly serious.

"Winning," she told him, automatically.

"No. It is not. *Robyn* is the most important thing. The relationship you have with her for the rest of your lives. Get your priorities straight. Until you understand that, you will not be able to ski with the type of freedom you need," he stated, insightfully. "Because right now, you ski with shackles. Shackles of desire, of grasping, of obligation, of necessity. And those are impediments. They impair your clarity of purpose, your individuality, your *creativity*, as a skier. It is important to win, but it is *not* important to win. That is the duality of sport that I really want you to focus on. Will you do that, Whitney?"

"Yes," she nodded, with gravitas. Like a Bodhisattva, Hans was full of wisdom and enlightenment. She had always respected his point of view.

"Okay. Good. Next lesson." He paused. "Look all around before you ski this hill. Take in the entire geography of the terrain, all its features. The topography, its bumps and curves, its shape, the surrounding ridges and mountains. Right now, you are only seeing it from this perspective, from where you stand, as you gaze *down* the slope. Now imagine yourself in a helicopter, seeing it from *above*. The judges will judge you on your creativity of line. Its fluidity, its beauty, how it looks in the context of the entire mountainside. You need to think of your run as one continuous, connected entity, not a series of separate aerials or parts," he continued. "For example, when you watch Ian ski, he creates an entirely seamless line that is completely harmonious with the natural features of the terrain. His aerials look effortless."

She absorbed his words, taking them to heart.

He went on, "You must memorize La Grave's mountains and visualize yourself descending its faces, every day," he advised. "You cannot emulate someone else's style; it must be solely your own. The best athletes, musicians and dancers create their *own* style. The judges recognize and reward that. You must ski for *yourself* -no one else. Not Trent, not me, nor your parents. And do not think of yourself as student anymore. You are master," he finished. He unzipped a pocket on his old navy parka, pulled his small field binoculars out. "You go ahead, Whitney, I'll meet you at the bottom."

She nodded, then pushed off her poles, knees loose and forward, dropped into the heavy, deep untracked snow. Shooting between a stand of aspen, she emerged onto a small ridge, then shot further into an open glade, catching air off a protruding knoll, performing a 360. Landing the jump easily, she popped up, swiftly carving a long, clean line to a section of gullies and dips, swiveling through them like a human slinky. Hips quiet, poles planting furiously, knees absorbing the punishing impact, she caught air again on the last bump, executing a spread eagle. Legs apart, then back together, she landed with a firm thwump over her skis, instantly setting up for her next aerial. Hans was skiing down the edge of the run holding his binocs, watching every move. Launching off a large buttress into a tuck position, she rotated into a back one-and-a half and set the landing with expert precision, then continued down at breakneck speed.

The girl was on fire.

At the bottom, she waited patiently for Hans to descend. Slowly, deliberately, he skied down to her.

Whitney expected him to say something, but he was oddly quiet. He suggested they ride the lift again, they shuffled over to it, sitting side by side. The old double chair puttered slowly towards the top, taking its time. Ponderingly, he spoke. "Quite frankly, I've never seen you ski quite like that before," he stated, puzzled, his voice raspy from the cold. "It's as though you have *no* fear, no fear at all," he added, facing her. "Do you *have* any fear?" he asked, concerned.

She considered, silent a moment. No, she did not have any fear at this moment. The ANTm3 must have completely worn off, she realized. It had taken almost eight days. She answered Hans, nonchalant, "Um, I don't really feel afraid of jumps anymore, I can make the inruns much faster now…we did a lot of training… on that, this winter… at Copper," she added, obliquely.

"I see." Hans stated, gravely. Silence hung between them; the chairlift swayed slightly in the breeze. Pillows of snow had collected on the branches of the Douglas firs, weighing them down. The entire glade was dusted with glistening white powder. A bluebird cackled defiantly, through the trees.

He spoke, again. "Did you ever hear the story about the frog?"

"No, Hans," she replied, sighing. "What frog?"

"Once upon a time there was a little frog," he began mildly. "Then the man put the little frog into a pot of warm water and said to him, "here, little frog, you will be fine. Just stay and relax, okay? So, the frog stayed, feeling comfortable… Then the man turned up the temperature a bit more, it got hotter inside the pot… Now, the frog sensed it was getting hotter, but it decided to stay anyway, it figured it could handle it. Then the man turned up the temperature even higher…. The frog got so hot, it boiled to death. By that time, it didn't have the strength to jump out."

"You're point is…." she asked him, half-smiling. Hans liked using analogies and metaphors, it was part of his charm.

He told her, dead serious. "You have become desensitized, Whitney. I don't know what happened to you, but I fear for you. You could become that frog, if you're not careful."

She swallowed, a lump in her throat. *Desensitization.* It was one of the biggest killers of alpinists, every year. Hanging off a cliff in sub-zero temperatures on an avalanche- prone face becomes entirely normal. The person takes greater and greater risks, not appreciating that the odds of survival are going exponentially down with every belay, aerial, or run they make. Pushing the limits, until one day, they've simply pushed too far.

"I understand what you are telling me, Hans." She couldn't tell him about the procedure. And how manic she was from the ANTm3. How she was utterly fearless one minute, then totally anxious the next.

"Good. Think very carefully about it, please. Robyn and your family are the most important things in life, not winning. Or killing yourself. Agreed?"

"Yes." *But winning was how she could pay for things. And keep doing what she loved to do most.*

It was a conundrum.

"One more thing, skiing does not define everything about you. Whether you win or lose, you have value as a person. As a mother. Your kindness, integrity, work ethic…. *those* are the attributes that comprise the totality of who you are. Not just the skiing and competing," he told her, with compassion.

"Okay. You make me sound like Mother Theresa. Which I'm not," she laughed, ruefully. "But I sure appreciate your kind words and support, Hans. They were in awfully short supply from my coach, my teammates."

"I understand. Say, I have an idea. Why don't we just ski for fun, Whitney. You need to enjoy life more. Laugh a little, have a good time," he posed lightly, shaking his head.

Whitney laughed out loud, relieved. Hans was psychic, pure magic. He had come out here in these cold, harsh elements to help her, despite his ailments. Someday he would be gone, she realized.

A tear formed in her eye. She would truly miss him.

# CHAPTER 19
# CRESTED BUTTE

Excited to receive Whitney's call, Zokas immediately set up a training schedule three days a week with her, nine a.m. to noon at the Crested Butte Community Center. They met in the glassed- in foyer at the entrance of the building Monday morning, a huge smile breaking across his face as she walked through its front double doors. "You're back! What a surprise. I didn't expect to see you again this soon- thought you'd be in Summit County," he exclaimed, giving her a big hug. He almost didn't recognize her; her hair style and make-up were so dramatically different. She looked like a different person.

"I thought I *would* be in Summit, but I needed to come back and help Robyn," she told him. "She's having more medical problems, unfortunately. Trent let me come back until we leave for Portillo in June," she explained, setting her duffel on the concrete floor. "I'll be training here with Hans for the next three weeks until the end of the Butte's ski season, then drive back and forth to Summit to train with the team."

"Sorry to hear about Robyn," he replied, sympathetically. "After you called, I went ahead and designed a new training program for you. You'll be working on core strength, cardio and flexibility. We'll practice aerials Monday mornings at the pool. I've reserved time for us at the diving board between six and seven a.m.," he smiled. "It's great to see you."

"Thanks, that all sounds really good," Whitney responded, automatically. An exceptional athlete, Zokas had won the national diving championship in Greece before moving to the United States to start his sports trainer career. He had visited Colorado as an exchange student in high school and fallen in love with the Rocky Mountain lifestyle after learning how to downhill ski and rock climb in the state. After finishing his kinesiology degree in Athens, he returned to Crested Butte to set up shop. Whitney had met him in her family's store when he stopped in one day to look for hiking boots. Striking up a lively conversation, they had become fast friends, training together before she was recruited by Consumco. Ever since then, they had kept in touch.

Energetically, he told her, "We'll start on the climbing wall, I've got two hours reserved for us. Did you bring your all your gear? Your backpack, ski boots, skis?" he asked her.

"Yes indeed." She pointed at her bulging duffel bag. "It's all there. The skis are on my car. Should I bring them in too?"

"Yes. I'll meet you at the climbing wall," he told her, grabbing her duffel bag, hoisting it on his shoulder.

Loping back outside, she retrieved her skis then carried them to the far end of the cavernous building. Long, dangling ropes hung off the enormous climbing wall, harnesses and climbing equipment lay strewn about the enclosed space. While she knelt to buckle her boots, Zokas placed a fifteen- pound weight inside her backpack, then attached her skis to it. The pack would simulate the sensation of actual ski mountaineering while she climbed. Hoisting the unwieldy bundle onto her back, she clipped into her harness and put her ski goggles on. He spotted her on the rope, from below.

"Go up fifteen feet, then move laterally across to the other side," he directed her, pointing left. She followed his instructions, heaving herself up the multicolored wall as she grasped the holds with glove- covered hands. The entire surface was covered with different size, oddly shaped synthetic rocks, she could barely feel them underneath her hard, plastic ski boots. Her feet slid around searching for purchase, the sensation not unlike climbing an icy mountain with crampons. The extra weight in her pack was rapidly fatiguing her, taking the wind out of her sails.

Zokas yelled up, encouragingly. "Okay! That's good! Climb laterally back to the center, then go ten feet higher! You're almost at the top! When you get there, stop and catch your breath for a minute before you climb down," he added, looking up at her. She was breathing quite hard now, the burn was on. Gritting her teeth, she pushed further up.

When she rappelled down, Zokas expertly spotted her, feeding out rope. Landing with a little hop to the padded floor, she leaned over, gasping for air.

"Okay, okay, Laaate's discuss," his stated, his Greek accent starting to emerge, haltingly. A mop of thick, curly black hair fell in front of his eyes, he swiped it away. "You are not breathing well, Wheetney. You're losing too much energy. Take more prolonged, deep inhalations, like this," he demonstrated, standing beside her. "Let's practice together," he started counting methodically. "One, two, three, four, five. Now stop. Hold, one second. Now- slowly exhale and count to five. One, two, three, four, five. That's better," he exclaimed. "As you ascend, control your breathing to conserve energy. Okay?" he stated, firmly.

"Okay. Got it. Let's do the climb again," she set her lips, determinedly.

They stayed on the climbing wall for another hour. Afterward, Zokas took her through a series of sustained yoga stretches to prepare her for the cardio portion of their training session. They moved to the indoor track encircling the perimeter of the gymnasium, the sound of men's shouts and basketball slamming against the backboard echoing through the cavernous building. Together, they alternated jogging and sprinting for twenty minutes until their lungs and leg muscles burned. Walking around the track to cool down, Zokas grinned, satisfied. "Good workout today, Whitney! Keep at it."

Late that afternoon she drove to the grade school to pick Robyn up from her violin lesson. Miss Abrams met with her when they finished. Speaking in low voice, she told Whitney confidentially, "Robyn is trying hard to prepare for the recital, but she's really struggling with her piece. She's having difficulty reading the manuscript… she says that the lines are squiggly, that the notes move around… I just wanted to let you know."

Whitney nodded, listening, "I appreciate your feedback. Her doctors say those are symptoms of her seizure disorder," she replied, frowning. "She'll be getting an EEG in two weeks, hopefully we can find out what's causing the problem. In the meantime, we'll just do what we can. I don't want her to feel any pressure to perform. If she's able to participate, that's great. If not, well, that's okay too."

"I think that makes sense. She's a delightful student, I'm happy to help her any way I can," Miss Abrams told Whitney warmly. She handed Robyn her music books. "Don't forget these," she reminded her. "I'll see you next week, okay?"

They left the empty building and walked out to the Taos, Robyn carrying her violin case.


"Hey sweetie, I thought we'd drive out and see Grandma Luann and Grandpa Jack this afternoon. They'd like to see you. Maybe you could play your piece for them." Whitney remarked, clipping her seatbelt on. Robyn was gazing out the car window. Snowflakes were forming on the windshield, heavy grey clouds moved over the mountains into the valley. "Okay mommy," she replied, fidgeting in her seat, clutching her music books. Whitney drove towards Gunnison, open fields and grazing range stretching out for miles, accumulating more snow. Light was rapidly fading behind the valley walls.

When they arrived at the sprawling property, cluttered with farm equipment, piles of baled hay underneath layers of snow, Luann ushered them inside the single-story, brown ranch home. She started a pot of fresh coffee, quickly slicing four pieces of white devil's food cake and putting them on some plates. Jack lumbered into the kitchen to join them, they sat down at the round, oak table. "You changed your hair," Luann stated, sans decorum.

"Umm, yes."

"How long are you back for?" she asked Whitney, directly.

"I'm back for almost two months, then I leave for Portillo," Whitney told her, uncomfortably. Jack nodded, listening. She looked like a city girl now, not the girl from Gunnison County that Kyle had married, he thought, internally. Too much make-up, strange looking hair. Whitney glanced at the farm kitchen's walls, pictures of Kyle from grade school through senior high hung in wooden frames, his handsome face gazing out at them. The last one at the end had a small, hand-crocheted heart beneath it that said, "Rest in Peace, our hearts are with you forever, Beloved Son." She frowned sadly, averting her eyes, it was too painful to look.

They all took some bites of cake. "How 'bout you go do some coloring in the front room," Luann suggested to Robyn, gently. Sliding off the chair, she went into the darkened living room, got her crayons and sketch pad from the oak bookshelf and set them on the antique coffee table. She sat down on the carpeted floor and began drawing.

"I'd like to know what's going on with her medical care," Luann turned to Whitney. "I've been calling your mom every week now to get information. Frankly, I'm worried."

Whitney set her fork down and chewed her lip, sighing. She wanted to get up and leave, take Robyn with her, she had no patience for Luann's annoying queries. The subtext that she was deficient in taking care of Robyn.

*What is wrong with me?* she berated herself, internally. *Luann's her grandmother, for God's sake. Was it the procedure?* She had to do better. Going through her mental files, she tried to say the right thing. She offered politely after a few beats, "Would you and Jack like to come with us to Colorado Springs for her EEG.? I can pick you up on our way there. Or, if you like, you could drive yourselves. You could meet with Dr. Halpurn, participate in the consultation. Would that make you feel better?" she finished, diplomatically.

"Yes," she and Jack responded instantly, obviously relieved. Whitney looked over towards Robyn, she was hunched over her sketchpad, drawing a horse with a barn next to it. Suddenly, her eyes fluttered, facial muscles went slack. Head tilting to one side, she dropped her crayon. It rolled off the table. Her hands and arms went limp. Whitney's chest seized, she ran into the room, grabbing Robyn. "She's having a seizure!" she shouted back at them.

They both rushed over and lifted her onto the sofa to lie down. "I'm calling Dr. McClellan's office right now," Whitney started dialing. *Shit!* It was after office hours; a voice message came on. She quickly left her number, requesting a return call ASAP.

Robyn's eyes fluttered open. She stared out, unfocused, unaware of her surroundings. "Robyn!" Whitney commanded, urgent. "Robyn! Can you hear me!"

"Yes…" she replied, weakly. She looked up at Whitney, Jack and Luann, bewildered.

"Let's get her a blanket. She can stay here," Luann told Whitney. "I'll sit with her. You wait for the doctor's call. Agitated, Luann ordered, "Jack, go get her a pillow and some water," lips pursed.

"Mommy, I have to throw up."

"Okay, luv. I'll get you a bag," Whitney ran into the kitchen, looking for a bag. Jack rushed in to help her find one. She bolted back with it.

"Okay, luv, you let that icky stuff out, you'll feel better," Whitney held the bag. Robyn vomited into it, her face wan, drained of color. "Good girl, that's it- you did good, it's okay," Whitney soothed, stroking her sweaty scalp.

"She's likely to have a headache soon, do you have some Tylenol?" Whitney asked Jack, tersely.

"Yep, I'll get her some right now," he strode into the bathroom, bringing back the bottle from the medicine cabinet.

Luann sat beside Robyn on the sofa. "You rest, honey. You'll feel better in a little while," she crooned, softly.

They all sat with Robyn. Within a matter of minutes, she was asleep. A call came in from Dr. McClellan, she and Whitney spoke, tone serious.

"You'll need to bring her in tomorrow, we need to see her first thing in the morning," she informed Whitney. "Robyn may need to go to the neurology clinic, in Colorado Springs."

# CHAPTER 20
# ALYN

Without her own car, which was parked at her small condo in Capitol Hill, Alyn was consigned to walking everywhere in Frisco or taking an Uber if she needed a lift. Consumco had flown her from Seattle to Summit County, where she had first joined Trent and the team when she was originally hired. The rental house in the small, bustling ski town had become a home-base of sorts, though she seldom stayed there more than several weeks in a row.

Back from Valdez now, she would stay with the team through the end of May. The company had extended her contract to do more promotional work for them, they seemed to like her photography and editorials, which were garnering a lot of media attention and boosting sales. The town was centrally located within a cluster of sprawling Colorado ski resorts; Keystone, Breckenridge, A-Basin, she could literally see their steep and winding runs cascading down the mountainsides from her bedroom window, just several miles away. This morning, Trent and Ian had already left to practice aerials at Copper Mountain. Karis and Mason had gone to Keystone to do cat- skiing, departing in Karis's shiny, blue, Volkswagen Tuareg, a gift from Consumco she kept parked beside the Sprinter. Shenti was nowhere to be seen. Alyn assumed he was either still asleep or wandering around Main Street by himself, poking into bars and having a drink.

She stayed in the house alone, finishing up her writing. After lunch, she went back into her bedroom, locked her door and called Harris.

"Hey, I finally got a chance to get back to you," she kept her voice low. "Were you able to find out anything about the ANTm3?" she asked him, surreptitiously.

An air of puzzlement filled his voice, he replied slowly, "This is the strangest thing, Alyn. I searched the Physician's Desk Reference through the last ten years; nothing showed up. I googled every pharmaceutical company I could think of, every medical product, vitamin, supplement, herbal remedy imaginable-nothing showed up there, either. I combed the internet for *anything*. It doesn't show up as an illicit drug, which is what I started to think it was, after having no success. Perhaps it's an acronym for something else… a foreign substance, maybe. Are you sure that's what it's called?" he prodded, quizzically. "Was there anything else on the bottle that provided any other clue? Could it be a skin care product or something?"

"I guess that's possible," she chewed her lip, considering. "Although I don't think so." She asked him, "Did you happen to discover anything about Trent that might be of interest? Every time I ask him to do an interview for one of our magazines, he refuses to participate," she shook her head. "He's incredibly secretive."

Harris's voice was thoughtful, "When you told me he was from Bozeman and was a competitive skier many years ago, I searched through the town's archives- college and local news articles, going back over twenty years, before this stuff was even printed on the internet. I contacted the Bozeman Daily and asked an employee to do a search for me. Said I was interested in writing a feature on the history of Montana skiing, how local skiers shaped the industry, blah blah blah...."

"And..."

"Well, interestingly, this woman was able to find some articles that had been written about Trent right around the time he was training for the National Extreme Ski Championships...this was before WESC had officially been established, back when he was apparently an undergrad at Montana State. Anyway, I digress..." Harris continued, "he and a friend of his had been backcountry skiing at Bridger and were both caught in an avalanche. His friend died at the scene, but he survived. The article said he was extremely injured- broken back, pelvis, ribs, etcetera. He dropped out of school and went to the Czech Republic to live with a friend in Cesky Krumlov, a guy named Lech Javurek. Apparently, Lech was a cyclist who was training for the Tour de France at the time, and helped Trent get back on his feet. Let him cycle with him and his teammates to rehab..."

Alyn interjected, "Where is this going? I know you well enough that it must be leading somewhere," she added, dryly.

Harris chuckled over the phone, "yes, it is...So I googled Lech; turns out he competed in the Tour de France but was disqualified during the race, along with several other teammates. Keep in mind this was almost twenty years ago, and the records are sketchy.... not a lot of detailed information, but anyway, from what I could gather, their urine tests showed traces of a drug that was linked to a military lab outside of Prague. Not the typical steroids or things they often find in bike racers urine, but something much different, a neuro-stimulator of sorts. And much of what I read was based on rumor and speculation, just what the other competitors and journalists were saying, based on conjecture... nothing was confirmed. And of course, the government categorically denied any involvement whatsoever." Harris went on, "but what I found interesting were the anecdotal comments from the other cyclists--that the Czech team was taking extreme risks, going too fast around turns, bordering on out-of-control cycling, using aggressive tactics against other competitors, and that kind of thing."

"Interesting," Alyn commented, pondering. "Did you find out anything about the military lab, at all? About the government programs? Anything printed in periodicals, online?" she fished around, perplexed.

Harris considered, ruefully, "I would need to be able to speak Czech find someone in the country who had access to far more information than I am capable of procuring, I'm afraid."

She sighed, "I'm sure that's true. I'm probably sending you on a wild goose chase for nothing, Harris."

They were silent a few moments, she could almost hear him thinking out loud, fingers drumming on his desk with a click, click, click. "Okay, let's work this backwards," he suggested, finally. "Can you think of any place your team members or Trent has traveled to since you started working with them?"

"We've traveled all over the place, Harris. That's all we do. Travel and ski and shoot video."

"Okay. Name everyplace you've gone together."

"Silverton, Colorado. Bella Coola, British Columbia. Valdez Alaska. We'll be going to Portillo, Chile in June. Then Jackson Hole and La Grave France, next winter. After that, my tour of duty is allegedly over.

"Have any of your team members traveled anywhere else at all, alone? Specifically, has Whitney gone anywhere by herself? Maybe outside the country?"

She thought back, contemplating, "well, I know they do promotional appearances occasionally, though lately they've just been training like crazy and we're always together. A few months ago, however, Whitney went to Belgrade for a promotional blitz—I guess some sponsors were opening some new stores there... as a matter of fact, I think Karis went there too, right before I began working for Consumco. She mentioned it to me, I had almost forgotten."

"Belgrade."

"Yes, I think it was for ski apparel, they sent them there as spokeswomen. For the company."

"Serbia. They sent them to *Serbia*. Doesn't that strike you as odd?" he mused, droll.

"Hmmm, I don't know."

"That strikes *me* as odd."

She sighed, "I think we've hit a dead end, unless you can find someone who speaks Czech. Or you want to pursue this further, which is unnecessary and probably pointless, at this juncture," she exhaled, frowning. "I miss working with you sometimes, Harris. We had fun together, didn't we?" she added, chuckling. "I remember when you figured out who was paying off the county coroner to cover up those nursing home victims in Tacoma and all hell broke loose. Most people would have given up on that investigation a long time ago."

"You know me, I'm like a dog on a bone. Can't resist a good mystery."

"Yup. Listen, thanks for shootin' the breeze with me, Harris, it's good to talk with you again," she told him, glancing at her watch. It was already past three p.m.

He chuckled back, "Hey, my pleasure. Give me a call in three weeks or so. You never know what the cat might drag in."

"Sure. Will do. Bye."

Throwing on her winter coat, she laced up her Gore-tex boots, grabbed her purse and left the house. Walking over to Frisco's main supermarket to purchase some shampoo and other items she needed, snow crunched underneath on the sidewalk, chunks of gravel and ice tripped her up along the way. Cars crawled by, searching for parking spots along the main drag, people looking for a place to eat and drink, apres ski. Traffic was jammed at every intersection, rush hour in the heart of ski country. Entering the supermarket's wide double doors, she grabbed a shopping basket and started down the aisle, searching for toiletries.

Familiar voices met her ears, coming from the next aisle over. She paused. Mason and Karis were in a heated exchange by the beer cooler. It sounded bad. She peeked around the aisle near the spices and herbs and spotted them standing together, arguing. She ducked back quickly, listening.

"I don't give a shit about your god damn money, or your parent's goddamn money, *I want out!*" Mason snarled at her angrily.

"You sure seemed to like our money for your fucking student loans and drugs," she spat back at him, sounding enraged.

"Fuck you! I'm done, I'm out! Goggles are one thing; this other shit has gone too far," he yelled at her, his voice carrying across the store. Alyn peeked around the aisle again, he was jamming a six-pack back into the beer cooler furiously. "I'm walking home!" he shouted at Karis over his shoulder as he stormed away, pony-tail bobbing around beneath his wool ski cap.

Karis stood and opened the cooler, retrieved the six-pack. Nonchalantly, she strolled to the front of the store, paying for it.

Alyn drew back out of sight like a crab to its shell, watching as she casually departed through the front doors.

Alyn stood still a few moments, collecting herself. Their argument had a surprisingly vicious quality to it, she thought. They had seemed to almost come to blows. Clearly, something was very wrong between the two. She exhaled and considered tactically, sometimes the best thing to do was nothing, nothing at all. This was one of those moments, she told herself. She would stay clear of the battlefield, out of the line of fire. Just observe, listen and wait. No telling what would happen between those two down the road, she thought, predicting it wouldn't be good. Someone was going to get scorched.

Walking back to the house, Mason's angry words kept ringing through her head. "*I want out...*

*Out of what?* she wondered, suspiciously.

# CHAPTER 21
# ROBYN

A lab technician in Dr. Halpurn's neurology clinic wearing a pin on her lapel with the name Kim Jameson on it ushered Robyn and Whitney down a long, wide corridor towards an adjacent wing inside the busy hospital. She held a medical chart, blonde hair pulled into a neat ponytail. Gesturing towards an empty room, she informed Whitney pleasantly, "We'll be in here today- you're welcome to sit over there," pointing to a chair in the corner. To Robyn she said kindly, "let's have you sit on this big chair- I'll help you up, okay?"

Climbing onto the chair, Kim smiled at her, reassuringly. "I promise, nothing will hurt. You'll hardly feel a thing- except for me touching your scalp while I attach some metal discs to it," she added, twinkly. Robyn gazed up at her wide- eyed, skinny legs dangling off the padded chair covered with a white paper sheet. "Pretend I'm putting sticky gum drops on your head, okay?" Kim told her cheerily.

"Okay," Robyn nodded bravely, then asked solemnly, "What is an EEG?"

"Excellent question! The letters stand for "electroencephalogram," she replied. "It measures and records your brain's electrical signals and gives us information about your brain's activity.

Your brain has specific wave patterns when you're awake and when you're asleep. We can learn more about them when do this test," she explained patiently. Robyn nodded, digesting her words seriously. Kim smiled, "I might ask you to relax and close your eyes at some point- or look at some bright lights. Or breathe differently, okay? That way we can see what your brain is doing during those tasks." She turned towards Whitney, "This will take about an hour and fifteen minutes. You're welcome to stay, if you like," she offered. To Robyn, she said, "I'll have you lie back now so you're more comfortable." A soft, whirring sound emanated from the chair as it slowly reclined.

"Okay," Robyn told her, lips turned down, looking a little worried.

"Dr. Halpurn should be in soon," Kim stated, moving around the room with practiced efficiency. Sliding a complicated looking piece of medical equipment beside Robyn's chair, Whitney watched as she attached electrodes to Robyn's head.

"You're doing great," Kim reassured her, cheerfully. Robyn smiled bravely.

An intense wave of DeJa'vu hit Whitney, nearly knocking her off her chair. She was back with Dr. Belcic again while he stood beside her in his surgical chair, altering her brain… speaking as he worked, asking her questions…. It seemed like a lifetime ago, buried far away, back in her psyche. She tried to push the image aside as it surfaced, wanting to forget it. Confusedly, she observed Robyn, her emotions yo-yoing between intense anxiety and detached dispassion for her daughter; the reaction becoming more recognizable to her as she lived with the unpredictable side effects of the ANTm3.

Luann and Jack were waiting patiently in the lounge of the neurology clinic, only Whitney had been permitted to accompany Robyn into the examination room. They had accompanied them to the clinic, driving behind Whitney in their white, Ford F150 to Colorado Springs, stopping along the way for occasional potty breaks and a quick lunch along the four- hour drive. She had been surprisingly grateful for their companionship; Jack's stoic face a reassuring presence in her rearview mirror as they covered the hundred and seventy miles of winding, treacherous mountain highway over Monarch Pass, Poncha Springs through heavy, wet snow. A spring storm had dumped more than a foot last night, slowing their progress along the desolate Arkansas River Canyon and rolling hills of Fremont County in the early, frozen hours of the day.

Whitney's thoughts drifted momentarily as she sat watching Robyn and Kim. Perhaps Luann and Jack would be more receptive to her skiing career if she allowed them to participate in Robyn's medical care she considered, with new awareness. She focused on Robyn again, who looked dazed and groggy, eyes fluttering shut.

Dr. Halpurn entered the room wearing a white lab coat, he quickly greeted them. Tall, grayish-blonde, short hair, brown eyes, he appeared to be in his late forties, trim, all business. "Good to meet you," he shook Whitney's hand then joined Kim as she worked, commenting, "You're in good hands, I see we're underway here…After we complete her EEG, we can meet in my office and go through the results, answer any questions you might have." She nodded quietly, watching him and Kim scrutinize the data coming in near Robyn's chair.

Afterward, Kim brought Robyn to a children's play area in the clinic to wait, do some coloring, have some snacks while Dr. Halpurn, Whitney, Jack and Luann talked in private. Getting right to the point, he informed them, "Robyn's brain shows some abnormal activity with certain types of stimulation. In order to get a more complete picture of what is happening inside her brain during the day and at night, we'll need you to do a prolonged EEG at your home, as well." He added, "my staff will provide the equipment and information you'll need in order to do that, before you leave today."

Luann looked at him anxiously. "Will she need surgery?"

He addressed her, measured. "Surgery remains a possibility, depending on the progression of her seizures and their origin. However, there are many effective avenues for managing seizure disorders before we go down that path. Most children improve significantly with medication and even some dietary modifications." He went on, "I'll consult with Dr. McClellan about increasing Robyn's lamotrigine dosage, we'll see if that helps decrease the frequency and duration of her seizures. We may want to put her on a ketogenic, low carbohydrate diet which contains more fats if the medication alone doesn't achieve our goals. You can meet with our dietician later, while you're here."

Jack fidgeted in his chair, frowning. Unconsciously. Luann wrung her hands, distressed. Whitney absorbed everything calmly, emotions flat. They would be here for at least several more hours this afternoon, she thought. She should make hotel reservations nearby. It would be too late to drive back to Crested Butte safely, with all the snow.

Dr. Halpurn addressed Luann, continuing empathetically, "I understand your concern, and to answer your question further; if these therapies don't work, we can try others as well. One being vagus nerve stimulation." Explaining further, "resective surgery is typically only done when the region in the brain is very small and doesn't affect speech, hearing or movement. It's something we would avoid doing unless it became absolutely necessary. We'll continue to do CT and MRI in conjunction with EEG, monitor the tissue in her occipital lobe in case it develops lesions that should be removed."

"Thank you for all the clarification," Whitney told him, gratefully. Luann and Jack could hear first-hand what she was dealing with now, relieved. She sighed, turning to them. "I'll make reservations at the Wyndam Suites nearby, we can spend the night there and drive home tomorrow."

Including them in Robyn's care was the right thing to do, she admitted to herself. They deserved to be involved. And Kyle would have wanted them to be included, too.

Dr. Halpurn stood up from his desk. "The National Epilepsy Foundation has a chapter in Colorado that is very supportive of families going through this situation. Would you like their contact information?" he asked kindly.

"Yes, definitely," Whitney replied. Picking up a pamphlet, he handed it to her.

School on weekdays, violin practice afternoons, Robyn settled into a routine over the next several weeks with Whitney home by her side, monitoring her medication and side effects, consulting weekly with Dr. McClellan. Her recital piece, "Air" by Haydn was finally starting to take musical shape, after numerous setbacks and struggles to read the manuscript. Whitney listened to her practice as she sat at their kitchen table studying the La Grave ski area maps, conferring daily on the phone with Trent.

The at- home EEG equipment Dr. Halpurn had provided them revealed nighttime electrical spikes in Robyn's brain, confirming there was more seizure activity than initially thought. Luann offered to drive the device back to Dr. McClellan's office in Gunnison, saying conciliatorily, "I don't mind. It will give me something to do while Jack chases cattle." Whitney thanked her, grateful for her help. She and Robyn would do homework together in the evenings, then play crazy-eights or checkers afterward. Sometimes they baked cookies in the kitchen, making a mess then cleaning it up. Cindy was able to leave the house more often, go to work with Tom at the store while Whitney watched her.

While Robyn was at school, Whitney skied with Hans in the morning and trained with Zokas in the afternoon. Trent phoned her every day.

"How's it going with Hans?" he would ask, not knowing Hans was seventy-eight and hardly skied at all anymore. Mostly, they sat on the chairlift and talked. He would stand at the top of the slope and watch her ski down, then make low-key suggestions and observations about her technique and form. They would huddle together at his table, studying maps and satellite photos of La Grave for hours on end, him quizzing her on every conceivable route down the notorious mountain she might encounter.

She told Trent, "It's going great! Hans is making me ski hard. We're *killing* it."

"Good. I want you to come to Frisco, ski A-Basin with us next week."

"Okay. Happy to."

"By the way, have you lost weight?"

"*Oh yes*! seven pounds."

"Excellent."

Zokas had her doing wind sprints on the indoor track and diving at the Community Center pool every week, now. She had developed greater endurance, core strength, her aerials had become more refined under his coaching.

"Your dad dropped off a Petzl kit this morning for you," he told her one morning. "You need to practice prusik knots, be able to use the equipment without any problems, if necessary. We'll practice using it until you can do it in your sleep, okay?"

"Okay, Zokas, you're the boss," she told him. She would practice tying the loops, hoisting herself up the roped pully system under his watchful eye. Lug her backpack and skis to the top of the climbing wall, as he fed her rope from below.

"Control your breathing, Whitney!" he would call up to her, lapsing into Greek, "You are-ah gating so mucha better, Wheetney! You like-ah wonderwooooman!"

April tenth, the day of Robyn's violin recital arrived. Miss Abrams set up folding chairs in the school's choir room for the event. Parents and students filed in for the performance as she handed out programs, directed people to their seats. A baby grand piano sat at the front of the room, decorated with fresh flowers and an elegant white, silk throw across the top, for the occasion. A long buffet table sat at the side of the room with a punch bowl and platter of cookies for the reception, following the program. The sound of violins being tuned and children rushing back and forth with excitement filled the air. Parents snapped photos; everyone was dressed up in their nicest clothes. Whitney had bought Robyn a fancy blue satin dress and shiny black Mary Janes and fixed her hair up into a bun. Tom and Cindy, Jack and Luann sat in the front row, near the piano.

"I can't do this mommy!" Robyn turned to her suddenly, petrified.

"What!?"

"I can't perform! I don't want to!" Robyn shrieked; her face turning white.

"You *have* to! You *know* your piece, *you've played it a thousand times, you sound great!*" Whitney exclaimed, voice rising.

"No! I can't do it." Robyn declared, mouth set. She bolted out the choir room door, running down the hallway. Miss Abrams watched them, distressed. Clearly Robyn was having a meltdown, she fretted. Performance anxiety, poor child.

"Robyn! You come back!" Whitney shouted at her, aggravated.

"Nooooo, mommy." Tears were streaming down her face.

Whitney chased her down the hallway, catching up with her near the lavatory. "You get back in that room! You be strong! Be tough!" she demanded, eyes flashing.

Robyn crouched down to the floor, Mary Janes, new dress, violin, a crumpled heap. "*No!*"

"Alright then, we're going home." Whitney stated angrily, marching her down the hallway. "*Come!*"

Cindy rushed out the choir room towards them. "What the *heck* is wrong with you, for heaven's sake!" she hissed at Whitney, angrily. "She's afraid, can't you tell? Don't you have even an ounce of empathy? Honestly, you need to back off! I'm not letting you talk to her that way," she scooped Robyn off the floor and consoled her. "It's okay honey, we can go home, it's okay, it's okay…" stroking her back.

*Dammit,* Whitney fumed. She strode back to the choir room to apologize to Miss Abrams. *What a fiasco,* she thought, shaking her head. Tom had already departed with Cindy and Robyn; they were getting into the car. Miss Abrams looked entirely sympathetic. "It's okay, Whitney, these things happen sometimes," she told her, understandingly. "Sometimes, students just get too nervous. She's just going through a tough time right now."

Whitney exhaled, taking some deep breaths. Miss Abrams was right. *What was wrong with her brain?* Why the hell was she overreacting this way? she berated herself, feeling unmoored. Leaving Miss Abrams, she went down the hallway to the bathroom and opened her purse, searching for her vial of ANTm3. Finding it, she quickly whiffed a dose into her left nostril, then the right, tilting her head back, trying to hasten the chemical spray up to her sinuses. Blinking her eyes, she stared balefully at her reflection in the mirror, across the tiled sink. Tousled magenta hair, thick black eyeliner mocked her. *Who the hell was she?* she asked herself, clenching her teeth, agitated. She fled the bathroom, almost bumping into Luann and Jack. They shook their heads sympathetically, leaving the building.

Calm down, Whitney told herself. Go home. Make amends to Robyn, apologize to everyone. Be a nice mommy, she stewed inwardly, thoroughly frazzled.


That evening, she shut herself in her bedroom and called the Epilepsy Family Support Hotline, the phone number on the pamphlet Dr. Halpurn had given her.

"Hello, this is MaryAnn Leonard, how can I help you?" a pleasant female voice answered the phone.

"Uh…hello, my name is Whitney, I am calling for assistance, I have a seizure disorder and just needed to get some advice about how to cope with the stress…I think it is affecting me… may I speak with you?" she floundered, disjointed.

"Yes. Of course. You've reached the right place. You said you are having a seizure disorder…? Right now?"

"No, no, no…." she corrected herself, dizzily. *Did she just say that*? "I meant my *daughter* has a seizure disorder. I'm her mom. That's what I meant. I was hoping to talk to someone," she clarified, voice strained.

"You can talk to me," Mary Ann offered, gently, sensing Whitney's distress. A pause. "You can't manage this all alone," she stated quietly, "Why don't you tell me what's going on?"

"I uh…can't explain it, but something is very wrong," Whitney blurted out, close to tears.

# CHAPTER 22
# PORTILLO

Lowering himself down onto a mound of dry pine needles, loose dirt and dead leaves, Trent sat quiet in a stand of aspen and lodgepole pines gazing out across the Gallatin National Forest. Now October, a hint of chill hovered in the air, it was a perfect, sunny fall day in the Montana Rockies. Dapples of green, burnt orange and gold shimmered off the mountainsides in a million shards of light, creating a canvas of color that never ceased to astonish him. His heart quickened from the memories of this place and the melancholia it always brought forth. Janet. Montana State University, climbing and skiing in the Gallatin… He sighed heavily, thinking about events. After Portillo, everyone had gone home for shoulder season to regroup. Karis back to her family's place near Aspen, Whitney back to hers in Crested Butte. Ian and Alyn had flown commercial out of Santiago back to Seattle, where each had apartments somewhere in the sprawling metropolis. Shenti had departed, though he wasn't altogether sure where. The man was like a chimera, materializing whenever he called him with work then disappearing like a poof of smoke when on hiatus. He assumed Duncan had gone home to Steamboat right after they touched down at Eagle Airport.

It had been nearly fifteen years since he hiked up to this spot near Bozeman, compelled to meditate on what occurred in Portillo and what went so terribly wrong. He closed his eyes, letting his mind drift with rare introspection. Sifted through memories, reviewing abstract bits of conversation and exchanges with people he knew and had known, he allowed their voices to flit through his mind like feathers in the wind. The loss and emptiness of their wake was a crushing weight he carried deep inside, buried so far down it was nearly impossible to conjure. And juxtaposed with the brilliant and undulating beauty of the Gallatin, he felt particularly sensitive, emotional about the surreal duality of his tortured existence.

Janet and him…standing together, euphoric on top of Heaven's Peak in Glacier National Park…she, smiling, taking a picture of him, her voice awestruck by the stupendous scenery, light brown hair glowing in the afternoon sun. "The most beautiful places on Earth are always the most dangerous," she had said, eyes alive with excitement. He had chuckled in agreement, giving her an affectionate squeeze. She was right, of course. The most beautiful places on Earth *were* usually the most dangerous. And to see them was to dance with death, knowing in the back of one's mind that the next climb or the next ski run might be your last…

Meeting Janet Elsberg had been an unbelievable, life affirming gift when he first moved back to Bozeman after leaving the Czech Republic. After four years of cohabitating with Lech, working odd jobs around Cesky Krumlov; for a time as a custodian in the village museum, cleaning artifacts and glass cases filled with Nazi memorabilia from Hitler's occupation in the Sudeten, another as a waiter, which he was terrible at, preferring the solitude of the museum and its terrible history, he was ready to return home. Following the procedure with Dr. Belcic, his mind *had* healed; in so far as he was able to move beyond the trauma of Travis's death and his own broken bones and limited capacities, though he still had nagging residual problems, in which Dr. Belcic helped him with.

The doctor had given him a vial of medicine, telling him, "This is a neuro-stimulator; NS3, for your side-effects. It should help with the emotional changes you've been experiencing since the surgery." By now, they had been in contact regularly, establishing a patient-doctor relationship that bordered on almost friendship. Lech and several other guys on the bike racing team were also using the stuff too. Like him, they had been having problems with the procedure's aftermath, as well. Loss of empathy, extreme aggression, moodiness. That fateful year, everything imploded, the whole team was disqualified from participating in the Tour de France, turned out that NS3 *was* detectable in their urine, after all. The racing officials didn't recognize the compound, the whole debacle becoming a national scandal. Trent finally decided it was time to leave the Czech Republic and go back to Montana to start over again, rebuild his life. Got a job at Montana State University as an assistant coach with their ski team then rented a small apartment in town.

He met Janet, a program coordinator in the athletic department. Like himself, she had a passion for mountain sports and a love of outdoor adventure. Lovely, thoughtful, kind, he knew she was someone he could happily spend his life with. They dated for nearly two years, then moved into a new apartment together, near campus. Totally smitten, he was happier than he'd ever been his whole life. He wanted to marry her, even start a family. Went out and bought her the nicest engagement ring he could afford in Bozeman and gave it to her in a proclamation of love and adoration, opening his heart up, hopeful.

What started out as some minor mood changes after the procedure became more pronounced. He began using the NS3 more frequently, his lack of empathy and changing personality becoming an increasing source of frustration between them, fraught with friction and anger. Interactions with co-workers and people in his sphere became frequently awkward, even infuriating. And instead of telling her about the procedure and the medicine, he chose to hide it from her, a terrible miscalculation. As things escalated between them, she became more and more distraught, perplexed by his erratic behavior. Eventually, she told him she couldn't be with him anymore, couldn't live with his volatility.

He would use the NS3, then stop for a while, careening between states of fearlessness then fearfulness, compassion then dispassion, anxiousness then equanimity. It was a mind-bending rollercoaster to be on that made him dizzy with despair. She would appeal to him, tearful. "I think you may be bipolar- you should seek out help." He felt paralyzed in secrecy, unable to reveal his past activities, his dependency on the contraband chemical.

Marriage became out of the question; she rebuffed his proposal.

Brokenhearted, he left the athletic department and let her go. Said goodbye to all he hoped to build and all he imagined their lives would be. She moved out of their apartment; it was over. Shortly afterward, Consumco contacted him with a job offer that was too lucrative to turn down. He accepted their offer, finally giving up the NS3. Better to exist in an emotional state that was fearless, devoid of empathy, than endure the gut- wrenching ups and downs of the powerful drug.

Directing Consumco's extreme ski team came at a price, however.

Dominate. Win. No matter what.

He reflected on this year, the company's insistence that Karis and Whitney get the procedure. The women's dazzling athleticism and superhuman skiing would compel consumers to buy more beverages, snacks, insurance and apparel; turbocharge product sales. That was the whole point. If there was friction between the two, all the better- it made for exciting press. Press equaled sales. Sales equaled profit. Profit equaled job security. Simple equation.

By committee, Ian was recruited as their golden boy; ordained to win WESC by virtue of his own natural talent and showmanship, his fearless athletic prowess and daring moxie. Followers were enthralled by his bad-boy image and personal style, his mohawk and piercings, his cool tatoos and flamboyant clothing. From Theodore's perspective, he was considered untouchable.

Mason was recruited to compliment the group; an excellent, though second-tier athlete. The young guy would always be odd man out, Ian's wingman. Like many insecure athletes, it didn't take long before the constant grind and comparisons to Ian got to him, he began drinking and drugging, losing his edge.

The accident in Portillo had nothing to do with that however, Trent felt sickened by the loss.

And *he*, Trent Resnick, was puppet- master of them all. Disciple of Consumco, mercenary for the devil. It was the price he paid for his salvaged life, the cost of working in the most beautiful places on Earth.


Portillo. He had seen others die on the team over the years, it was part of the deal. You simply could not do the things they did without coming to terms with it, somehow. They had arrived the second week of June, converging on the ski area with a half- dozen other racing and freestyle teams from all over the world who had traveled to the Southern hemisphere to train and stay competitive. The Chilean playground, renowned for its massive snowfall and towering, twenty-thousand- foot Andean peaks, was a summer bacchanal of world-class celebrity skiers, paparazzi and jetsetters who happily shared lodging inside the legendary, exclusive resort just two hours northeast of Santiago.

Sven had arrived from Norway and immediately set off a photo blitz with Karis, of course, the two dancing and partying like it was 1999 in the lodge's glittery discotheques every night until one a.m... Mugging for the cameras, glomming over each other, dressed for the runway, glamorous and sexy.... Ian sulking behind his mirrored sunglasses at Tio Bob's apres ski. Karis, his on and off flame, grinding hips and chest against her tall, blonde, muscular burnin' hunk of love... Sports journalists darting around the buzzing restaurants and nightclubs, clicking photos of international ski champions and revelers in an alcohol- fueled zeitgeist of debauchery... posting them on social media with hedonistic abandon...Gucci, Pucci and all the rest...

He knew Whitney tried to stay out of the glitz and limelight, retiring to her room after training to talk to her parents and daughter's doctors. Mason had basically stopped communicating with everyone, spiraling down into a beer driven funk after practice, late afternoons. Trent came *this* close to kicking him off the team but restrained himself, deciding to give the kid a chance to pull it together. He had talked to Theodore about the situation, thinking *he* would *want* to fire him, but instead his boss said, "Let the guy flame out... He's an interesting character, we think our followers will enjoy watching what happens."

What a shitty thing to say, Trent had hung up the phone, thoroughly disgusted. Getting involved with the company had been his first original sin. Staying involved with Dr. Belcic, his second. Not listening to his *own* common sense, third. He paid for his transgressions in some way, every day.

On July twentieth, it snowed and snowed, a Pacific stormed inundating the ski area with almost four feet of powder. The steep, winding road from Santiago to Portillo was temporarily shut down, no one could drive in or out, they were essentially marooned in the Andes. The skiers were thrilled, naturally, it was like Christmas, birthdays and Easter to them. Endless powder, the party just getting started. July twenty-second, everyone woke up to hit the slopes, totally stoked; Mt. Aconcagua, Leguna del Inca, the iconic, yellow Portillo Ski Lodge absolutely slammed with snow. Theodore wanted footage, naturally. This was epic.

Setting out early morning in the cold, clear, dry air, quiet and still, with powder up to their waists, they caught the chairlift at the base and rode it to the top of El Plateau Garganta, midway up the goliath mountain. Getting off, they skied over to the base of Condor and caught the va et vient, sling-shot style, five-person poma to the very top.

The plan was to ski a line beneath the poma, and then traverse over to the enormous rock headwalls above El Plateau Garganta and ski off-piste between them. The vertiginous faces emptied out near the frozen lake, four thousand vertical feet below. Whitney, Karis, Ian and Mason would take positions above the headwalls while Trent stayed at the top, watching them descend, in pairs. Shenti and Alyn would be stationed in a warming hut near the base, using telephoto lenses to capture their lines.

The five of them pushed forward, breaking snow, Trent behind everyone else. All were outfitted with avalanche equipment and transceivers. Duncan had meticulously checked each piece of equipment before they had left the lodge, everything was functioning perfectly.

Stopping at the second headwall, Trent took out his binoculars. Two groups, Mason and Whitney, Ian and Karis, had separated fifty feet ahead. Karis yelled out to Whitney and Mason, "You guys go first, we'll ski next, after you!"

The two dropped in. At that moment, Trent saw the fracture line between the two headwalls. Instantly heard the thunderous crack reverberate across the slope with a sickening boom, the slab gave way. Whitney was already skiing straight down the fall line, her blue ski jacket bobbing up and down inside the enormous cloud of swirling snow, disappearing. As the avalanche collapsed down the mountainside, Mason completely evaporated, his olive-green parka devoured by the savage, roiling beast.

Frantically, he radioed for help, shouting over the din. Ski patrol, search and rescue and other ski teams immediately headed towards the site to help find them. He, Karis and Ian rocketed to the bottom, desperate to locate their bodies, where they might be buried.

Whitney had felt the mountainside give way and instantly deployed her airbag to help keep her afloat. Skiing towards the edge of the avalanche, she literally surfed its churning slough, the colossus nipping at her heels threatening to annihilate her. Staying on her skis, she raced to the bottom alongside it, avoiding the brunt of its maw. Emerging from the cloud of snow and debris, she was miraculously intact. Face white as a sheet, she was speechless and in shock. Trent and the others skied over to her, astounded.

Mason was gone.

Everyone probed the site for three full days, sifting through twenty-five feet of snow for any signs of his body. The transceiver too weak to convey his location, and it wasn't until July twenty-fourth that the rescue teams and their dogs finally located his cadaver and extracted it from its tomb of white cement. A Bell 407 transported his corpse to Santiago, Trent accompanied the body. Consumco sent the Gulfstream to fly them to Missoula, Trent stayed with Mason's family throughout the whole tragic episode, explaining what had happened, and why.

Why. Because it just *did*. That was life in the alpine, the odds just multiply. Trent frowned sadly, gazing over the forest, still seated in the aspens, brooding over the avalanche and the circumstances leading up to it.

Bothering him more was the disturbing revelation that Karis may have seen the fracture line, but not notified Mason or Whitney before they dropped into the face. He shuddered; the thought plagued him. But what could he do? He was already in so deep. There was no turning back.

Karis. Had they created a monster?

Standing up, he brushed the pine needles and loose dirt off his pants. Brushed away his misgivings and regrets. There simply wasn't time to dwell on this any longer, they had the National and World Championships to prepare for. He had to move on.

# CHAPTER 23
# PORTILLO

When it happened, she simply reacted. No fear, no thought, just the immediate response by her body to survive. Ski towards what she perceived to be the safest place on the mountain and outrun the monster. It was pure luck, of course, Whitney knew. No one really could outwit an avalanche. If it was your day to die, it would simply take you, that was a fact. She had just been more fortunate than Mason. Perhaps because she was skiing a few seconds ahead, further downhill, that had made the difference. Perhaps because he was skiing where the snowpack was deeper and heavier, that had been the factor that killed him. Whatever the circumstances, it came down to literally seconds between life and death. Likely, Mason deployed his airbag and fought desperately for survival, but it was no match for the avalanche, it didn't save him.

The thunderous crack of the slab giving way had hit her ears like an explosion, she instantly felt a rolling sensation like she was surfing down a waterfall and being sucked inside it from below and above. Automatically, she had yanked the strap of her ABS then pointed her skis straight downhill, skimming along the roiling, white tsunami, fighting for purchase. In a complete whiteout, with no visibility, she just kept going, going, going... All she remembered was arriving on a plateau somewhere beyond the mayhem, people shouting for her, shouting for Mason, completely disoriented.

Disaster. Too much to process, she was numb, dissociated. Asked for a ride back to the lodge on a snowmachine; someone drove her there. She immediately went to her room and huddled on her bed, staring vacantly at the beige walls. The worst part of the experience, besides losing a teammate, was facing the onslaught of public commentary that followed.

Calls from her own parents, then Luann and Jack, filled with horror and recriminations and pleas to return home. Stop competing! Just stop! *Stop*! Images of the avalanche had gone viral, the whole world instantly notified almost soon as it happened. Her cellphone lit up like a Christmas tree, every media outlet and newscaster wanting a story, a photo, a quote- anything. Even Alyn immediately started texting her, trying to get through. Consumco's marketing director demanding that Whitney give them exclusive rights to her story, that Alyn get an interview ASAP to promote the equipment she had been using during the avalanche. Overwhelmed, Whitney had turned off her phone, buried herself under the blankets and closed her eyes.

Trent pounded on her door, she finally answered it, he sat down on a chair near her bed and crossed his arms, silent. Didn't say a thing, just waited until she finally managed to choke out a few desperate words.

"Have they found Mason's body yet?" she asked haltingly.

"No, it's a huge area, snow is over twenty feet deep. Could take a while. I'll be leaving for Missoula to meet with his family," he had replied, dully.

She had just shaken her head, shoulders sagging, silent.

"You don't have to feel guilty about surviving," he told her, gently. "Nothing is your fault, nor Mason's, okay? It was an accident." What he didn't tell her was that he was getting keelhauled by the press, fellow coaches accusing him of being too cavalier managing risk, not protecting his athletes, exposing them to danger. The story was blowing up into an international shitstorm and he was at the center of it.

"Do you want to go home?" he asked her, head tilted back, staring off into space.

She'd been thinking about it, maybe she should.

"I don't think I can bear it," she told him, sighing. Just thinking about her mom and dad's faces, and everyone telling her to quit, the confrontations, the explanations the energy it would take to absorb all their outrage and mollify their fears; she would rather stay here.

"I'll come back here in a week or so, after the funeral arrangements. I'm not sure Mason's family will want me to be there, but I'll make myself available," Trent frowned, sighing wearily. "We're scheduled to stay in Portillo until September second, but you can do whatever you want. Take some time off, ski easy if you want, or fly home and regroup. Whatever."

She chewed her bottom lip, considering. "I'll stay here. Going home right now would be a terrible thing for me, I need space."

Trent nodded. "You may find this very disturbing, Whitney, but Consumco contacted me and said there was an enormous spike in AcyDgreen sales and other products since the avalanche. Alyn and Shenti have assured me they didn't post any of their footage of the accident, someone else must have. It could have been anyone in the vicinity. Anyway, the company is giving you a ten-thousand -dollar bonus. Just wanted to give you a heads up, so you were aware. I realize it's rather macabre."

"You're kidding me," she shook her head in disbelief.

"I kid you not."

She shook her head again at a loss for words, then told him, "The only person I want to talk to right now is Duncan. Could you text him for me? Ask him to meet me in the lounge?" she sat up against the headboard.

"Will do," he nodded. Standing up, he left the room.

"Hey kiddo," Duncan had met her downstairs. He sat beside her on the plush, leather sofa. "I brought you some tea," he handed her a white porcelain mug. They were in the hotel's main lobby by the windows that looked out across the treeless, majestic Andes. Several large outdoor swimming pools were down below; Inca Lake off in the distance, nestled at the base of the imposing mountains. "How are you feeling?" he asked her, deeply concerned.

"Remarkably alive, I guess you could say," she had replied, ruefully.

"I can only imagine. Don't really know what to say, other than thank God you survived. Very sorry about Mason," he shook his head sadly, lips drawn. "Yeah, it's terrible, I mean, his poor family…"

Whitney searched for words. To her ears, they rang hollow. She was unable to *feel* the sympathy she should- it was the procedure, she realized, recognizing the deficiencies it wrought upon her mind.

She tried to *act* and *sound* sympathetic when she spoke with him, still in a state of shock. MaryAnn Leonard had suggested she try doing that, if she was having difficulty empathizing. Weirdly, Robyn and her own brain disorders seemed to have merged during their consultations, it had become difficult to separate the two. MaryAnn had described how a person could instruct their brain say certain things, even if it didn't feel natural. Put on an act, so to speak.

Right now, things were a blur. She was losing her sense of place, of time. What was it called? She struggled to find the word. Dysphoria...

"I keep replaying the avalanche over and over in my head, trying to figure out how I missed the signs," Whitney told Duncan, frowning. "They were blasting all night long in the ski area, I assumed we were safe."

"They *were* blasting all night long. Into early morning too," Duncan told her. "You guys were right near the boundary outside the ropes, technically outside the area's safe zone. There must have been a fracture just below the cornice between those two headwalls. Trent didn't see it either, from his vantage point. We talked about it at length. He's devastated."

"I didn't know he could be devastated about anything," she replied, bitterly. "What *I* wonder is if Karis or Ian saw a fracture line, beforehand," she uttered, suddenly vibrating with anger.

Duncan paled visibly; the scenario too grisly to even contemplate.

Whitney took a deep breath, confiding, "My folks- who are accustomed to hearing about bad alpine accidents- are totally freaked out about this one. For Robyn as well. They're worried about her reaction, her ability to process the news...."

"Totally understandable," he replied, sympathetically. "No one would blame you for bowing out, if that's what you're considering," he added, carefully.

Whitney sipped her tea, thinking. She would speak to her folks, Hans, Zokas… Let them know she needed time alone to process the events and take it easy, here in Portillo. Duncan relaxed into the sofa, thinking, internally. Clearly, she needed more real support. He would try to help her; be a safe and supportive colleague. This tour was beginning to resemble a feeding frenzy inside a shark tank and he was starting to look forward to finishing it, the thought occurring to him.

"I had a friend once who used to say, "when in doubt, do nothing," she told him, half-smiling.

"Meaning…." he nudged, inquisitively.

"Meaning, I'm not going to make any quick decisions right now. I've got the rest of September and October to think about things, think about what to do. If I bow out, that's exactly what Karis wants. What she's wanted all along," she added bitterly. "I've worked too hard to just give it all up. I can't just sacrifice my entire career. But I'll consider it, if that's what my family needs," she ruminated, sighing.

"I think that's a wise approach," he replied, circumspect.

"The fact is, I'm not afraid. I'm not afraid of going back out on the mountains, or getting my skis back on," she stated, shrugging.

He found that remarkable but didn't say anything; she was an enigma. He supposed that was one of the things that attracted him, among other attributes. Hair almost back to its original brunette, no make-up, she looked almost like her former self. He wanted to hold her in his arms, comfort her, but resisted the urge to do it. It crossed a line of professionalism, and he didn't want to take that chance.

How is Robyn, if I may ask?" he broached instead, cautiously.

She told him, "I talk to her doctors regularly, they're monitoring everything, all her symptoms and side-effects…they increased her medication level, they're trying to reduce the frequency, duration and intensity of her seizures. There's some abnormal tissue in her occipital lobe that they're watching. We'll probably know more by this fall or winter."

"That's gotta be stressful," he said, "on top of everything else."

"I'm lucky," Whitney told him. "My parents have really stepped in to help me, even Luann and Jack have come to our assistance. So, I can't complain," she confided with a sigh. "Sometimes, I call the Colorado Seizure Support Network and talk to a woman named MaryAnn when I feel overwhelmed." She changed the subject quickly, "What are your plans for shoulder season? Are you going back to Steamboat?"

"Yes," he answered. "Stewart, the owner of the ski shop I help out at, needs me to do some remodeling before ski season starts. Says he's planning to retire in a few years, keeps asking me if I want to buy the place and manage it after he's gone." He added, grinning, "I'm considering it. Every year the place gets busier and busier, it seems like a good opportunity. I'd probably enlarge the retail space and add more inventory, then expand the guiding part of the business, too. Offer flyfishing, snowmobile tours, those types of things."

"That's really great, I'm happy for you," she told him, sincerely. *Maybe after this tour she could go see him...spend some time with him there,* she thought, optimistic.

He blushed, "I'm happy- and excited too. I'm taking some online business classes now, preparing for it. I think my days of doing this type of gig," he looked around the lounge, shrugging, "are numbered. I want to settle down, stay in one place."

Whitney enjoyed listening to him, he was so *pleasant*, so *normal.* She began to relax a little more, feeling better.

Duncan brightened, enthused, "I really love working with customers, you know? Helping them find the right equipment, helping them get hooked up with tours. I like the sense of community." He added, chuckling, "traveling for weeks in a van with a group of smelly skiers is starting to get old. *I'm* starting to get old."

"You are not remotely old, Duncan," she chided him, smiling. "This tour is making me *feel* old," he sighed, lightly. A young man and woman approached them. They had been standing in the lounge for some time, having drinks, talking quietly. The woman was dressed elegantly apres ski, she had an Argentinian accent.

Heartfelt, she told Whitney, "We heard about the avalanche. I am so glad you are alright. May I get your autograph?" she asked, hesitantly.

Whitney brightened. "Of course! Of course! I really appreciate your kindness and support. What would you like me to sign?" she asked, eyes lighting up.

The woman handed her a Portillo ski area map. "Would you sign this, please? My name is Letitia," getting a pen from her purse.

Accepting the pen, Whitney scrawled, "Letitia, it was a pleasure to meet you! Whitney Olson."

"Thank you *so* much, this means so much to me," Letitia told her, seeming a little dazed she was speaking with her. The man looked slightly embarrassed.

"You are *very* welcome," Whitney reassured her. "Have a fun vacation- be safe," she added, politely.

Karis sauntered into the lounge, she spotted them, striding over. "Oh my *God*! I have been *looking* all over for you guys," she stated, voice brittle. Lowering herself onto a tufted chair she shrugged her shoulders and exclaimed, phony solicitousness oozing from her voice, "I can't *believe* what just happened. How are you *doing?*" Glass of champagne in one hand, cellphone in the other, she simpered, "I feel just *terrible* about Mason." She sipped her champagne, sighing.

Whitney stared at her, face going white. Instinctively, she suspected Karis had seen the fracture line, sent them to their deaths.

It was a gut feeling.

But no proof. Her whole body instantly retracted, shivering.

"Hey," Duncan quickly turned to her, "How 'bout we get something to eat," he responded, throwing her a lifeline.

"Yes. Let's do that, she said, stomach flipflopping, feeling faint. He reached out to steady her, she took some deep breaths. After a few uncomfortable moments, the sensation passed.

Karis stood up, casually gliding away.

# CHAPTER 24
# PORTILLO

Trent called a meeting when he returned from Missoula. They all congregated around a large, circular table inside the airy and spacious dining room as groups of skiers shuffled around the coffee station, ordered breakfast, chatted animatedly and planned their day on the slopes. A young man wearing a brown hoodie and wool beanie with the logo "Icelantic" sat beside him. A sponsor, no doubt, Whitney surmised, evaluating.

"Good morning, everyone," Trent announced, holding court. "I want you to meet Noah Hynes. He hails from Whitefish, Montana, but I tracked him down in Fernie, thank heaven," he added, dryly. "He agreed to fly back with me yesterday afternoon."

"Hey, welcome," Ian nodded across the table, neutrally.

Duncan partially stood up and reached across the table, offering him a handshake.

Karis flashed Noah an angelic, alluring smile and fluttered her eyelashes. This morning she wore a robin's-egg blue sweater with delicate, white snowflakes scattered across it, Tiffany silver brace-let. Round diamond studs sparkled off both earlobes attractively. Sipping coffee nonchalantly, she ran two fingers through her tousled hair and glanced away, then back at him, assiduously. Noah's face flushed, imperceptibly.

Whitney's chest tightened. This meeting seemed so premature, so callous, she lamented, infuriated. The vibe seemed much too casual. As though it were any other day. Mason had just died, the unspeakable tragedy still at the forefront of her mind, and they were already courting his new replacement without a pause. Except for Duncan, she noted. Reticent, he had hardly said a word.

She had heard of Noah, of course, they all had. The guy had a huge reputation for skiing monumental lines and was frequently in the press, a real slayer. Short, reddish-brown hair, wind-burned face, probably from being in the mountains all the time, he looked about twenty-five years old. She greeted him politely.

Noah gazed around the table, "I'm really honored to be here with you guys," he told them all earnestly. "When Trent reached out to me, I was like; *Yeah*. I gotta take this opportunity. Can't pass it up." He added, "sorry about Mason, what a bummer, man. I had so much respect, so much admiration for the guy…. Anyway, I'm here for you guys. Here to help the team in any way I can," he finished, dipping his chin at Trent, affirmatively.

*We are not a team, and we do not "do" help*, Whitney burned internally. The comment was almost grotesque, given her suspicions about Karis. Fighting the the urge to blurt out something she would probably regret and maybe even get canned for, she restrained herself. Noah seemed liked a nice person, she conceded, obviously trying say the right thing, which was probably hard to do, under the circumstances. But this whole dog and pony show was offensive. *She* had almost been killed that day, *she* had barely survived the avalanche, and it wasn't much stretch to imagine them all sitting around drinking coffee, welcoming *her* replacement.

Too bad for Noah that he took that call from Trent, she thought, ironically. He may not live to regret it. She sipped her coffee, chewed a piece of toast.

Inhaling deeply, Trent folded his arms across his chest and pivoted. "I have information about the U.S. semi-finals and finals coming up at Jackson Hole in February, so listen up," he informed them, all business. They sat up, attentively.

"You'll each ride the tram to the summit with the other competitors," he stated. "There are four, pre-assigned runs from the top. We'll go there a week early so you can preview the runs, choreograph your descents. The judges will use a point system for scoring. The top two scoring males and females will go on to the finals, and those winners will go on to WESC. Duncan has reserved a condo for the duration of our stay," he added. "You've all done competitions like this many times before. But now, the stakes are much higher."

They waited, anticipating.

"WESC," he said flatly. "You guys need to understand that La Grave is a whole different category of freeriding than anything else we've done in the United States. Has anyone skied there before?" he asked, looking around the table, pointedly. All were silent.

"No. Then let me explain," he gazed around the table, voice deadly. "You will be faced with dangers unlike *anything* you have ever experienced in North America. There are no ski area boundaries. There are no trail markings. There is no avalanche control, no ski patrol. *Everything* is off piste. You will be skiing on glaciers with deep crevasses and unstable seracs. Navigating thousand- foot cliffs and icy couloirs. There are deep gullies and dense forests to navigate," he took a deep breath, "and highly changeable weather conditions. If you are trapped, stay put and wait for assistance. A typical route is over seven thousand vertical feet, so it can take time for a helicopter to locate you. Expect to complete one, maybe two runs a day," he finished.

They blanched, expressionless. It was important to look unfazed, cool.

"Now here's the kicker," Trent leaned forward, going on. "Unlike typical competitions, the judges will be awarding points on *your* singular, crafted descent. There will be no *practice* runs, no designated routes. It is up to *you* to select your *own* route down. Points will be based on the difficulty of your line and speed, your jumps and how well you negotiate the terrain. Mountaineering skills are absolutely necessary. Expect to abseil using fixed ropes and confront unexpected hazards along the way." His brows furrowed, "I advise you to examine the La Grave area maps and work on your rope skills over the next three months. If you don't think you are physically or psychologically up to the task, now is the time to bow out. Understood?"

They nodded gravely.

Dramatically, he looked around, announced, grinning, "WESC sponsors will award one million dollars to the winners. In addition, Consumco will give three hundred- thousand- dollars, a new Volkswagen Tiguan *and* a very lucrative, five- year endorsement contract to anyone on this team who takes first place."

Whooping out loud, they all exhaled in unison, exhilarated. Game on. They were *in*, his announcement just sealing the deal.

Whitney headed back to her room, dazed. Whatever reservations she had about continuing to stay on with the team had just evaporated. She would explain to her folks that she couldn't drop out, she had to compete. But she'd wait a while until things calmed down, sometime in October. Meanwhile, she'd transfer more money into their bank account to pay off Robyn's latest medical bills. Then call Hans and Zokas, get back into training, big time.

Noah caught up with her near the elevator. "Hey, I just wanted to let you know how sorry I am about Mason," he stated, eyes meeting hers. "I heard about what a close call it was for you," he added, conciliatory. She nodded back at him. "It was. But thanks, Noah. It's good to have you aboard. Good luck with everything."

He lowered his voice and asked her, "Say, do you have any advice for me, Whitney? I'm the new guy here, I'd like to avoid conflict, just do the right thing."

Biting her lip, she considered. What should she tell him? That their coach had sociopathic tendencies? That Karis was a predator? That Ian was a self-absorbed automaton? That they were total narcissists singularly out for themselves? That he should probably run for his life to save his skin?

For that matter, who was *she* to be giving him any advice? she winced, conflicted. Wasn't she just as awful, going along with them for the money and the fame?

Doing the "right thing" didn't count with this group, just staying in your lane and winning mattered, she had learned.

Noah was a talented skier though; he deserved an opportunity to compete, she thought. She shouldn't try to influence his perspective one way or the other, it wouldn't be right. She answered lightly, "Just be yourself, Noah, you'll be fine."

"Uh, hey thanks," he replied, voice uncertain.

She stepped inside the elevator, adding, "I would suggest you don't pet the lion, though. Sometimes it bites."

# CHAPTER 25
# OCTOBER

They each ordered a cup of coffee from the barista and found a small table to sit down at in the Capitol Hill coffee shop, a local hangout surrounded by walls of exposed brick, well-used books and pieces of artwork. Newspapers were cast about the bohemian looking establishment, some customers sat engrossed at their computers, a few people were talking. Alyn glanced outside. Overcast and gloomy this afternoon, some drops of rain pelted the window. Harris had good-naturedly agreed to meet her here, living not far from the neighborhood.

"Welcome back to land of rain and water," he told her wryly. "How long will you be back in Seattle?" he asked, removing his rumpled, tan corduroy jacket. Underneath, he had on an argyle knit vest, circa 1965 grad student. Brown horned- rimmed glasses completed the vintage look.

"I'm back through December, then I go back to Colorado," she answered him, genial. "Consumco hired me to write a bunch of promotional pieces for the U.S semi-finals coming up in January," she added, stirring a few grains of brown sugar into her coffee. "They just got a new skier named Noah Hynes; I'm supposed to write a feature on him next week. Most of it I can do from here, but I need to meet the guy, take some photos. So I might be going back sooner," she told him, explaining.

"They sure didn't waste any time finding a replacement," he responded dryly, raising an eyebrow.

"No time for crying over dead bodies," she replied, humorlessly. "The show must go on. These folks are tough, I swear they're made of steel."

"I suppose it comes with the territory. I mean, they're facing death all the time. Sorry to hear about Mason, by the way," he told her, gulping coffee like a person in the throes of caffeine withdrawal.

"It was horrible, and it's more than that," she frowned, lowering her voice, confidentially, "I've been traveling with these athletes for nearly a year, and they're the most uniquely dysfunctional, cagey people I have ever met in my life. I wouldn't even be surprised if his death weren't an accident, to be honest. Did you find out anything else about the ANTm3?" she asked him, with a hint of urgency.

"You're going to find this rather interesting, I think," he told her, leaning forward. "As I mentioned to you earlier on the phone, I contacted the University of Washington's Department of European History and International Studies and managed to get a meeting with a Dr. Petrovsky, there. Told his secretary I was a writer, doing research on the Czech Republic after the break-up of the Soviet Union. Would it be possible to speak with someone in the department?"

"Very clever," Alyn commented, impressed. "You always had a knack for figuring out how to meet people."

He grinned at her, "After you told me what was going on with Whitney, I'll admit, I was intrigued. Thought there might be a story there. I don't think you would have been so persistent if there wasn't. Anyway, I met with him on campus, and we chatted for quite some time. Oddly, he seemed very happy to talk to me. Like, here was some young guy who was actually interested in this bygone stuff. He looked about eighty years old, told me he used to live in Belarus, before he emigrated to the United States."

"Go on."

"So, I asked him lots of things about the former Czechoslovakia and the Czech Republic. About their military, their culture, their politics, etcetera. Told him I had heard rumors about their athletes, how the Soviets may have doped their cyclists, gymnasts, and other big-time competitors in the early nineteen eighties…. Was it true?"

"What did he say?" she prodded. Harris always enjoyed drawing out a story, building drama. It used to drive her crazy, when they worked together.

He took a deep breath, now more serious, "Professor Petrovsky told me that the Soviet military had a neuro-science research program that worked specifically on developing methods to eliminate the perception of fear in their soldiers so that they could be more effective on the battlefield. Implied that they did surgical procedures and used chemicals to achieve those ends. And that their professional athletes were involved, as well."

Suddenly enervated, Alyn's ears shot up. This *was* interesting.

He continued, "There were some high- profile international scandals at that time. Countries that had to drop athletes, as in the case of that Tour De' France competition we talked about earlier… the one that Trent, your ski coach, was training for in the Czech Republic, coincidentally."

"He wasn't training for it; he was just riding with guys who were. Isn't that what you originally told me?" Alyn clarified.

"Yes, I think you're right. It's been a while since we talked."

**264**

"Hmm… you said Trent came back to the States, not long afterward," she stated, intrigued.

"Yes. Although, by that time, the new Czech government had discontinued funding the research program. According to the Professor, there were too many unintended side-effects associated with the things they were doing. The soldiers were shooting each other, were suffering from severe mood disorders, that kind of thing. So, the military shut it down."

"*They were shooting each other?*" Alyn exhaled, taken aback. She thought about the ski team's frequent disregard for each other, their antisocial behavior. "It's an interesting piece of history, I have to say," she considered, finishing her coffee. "If nothing else, you probably made the professor's day by talking to him," she added.

"I enjoyed it. Here's the *really* interesting part of our conversation," Harris told her, savoring his next remarks, eyes glimmering, mischievous.

"Okay, lay it on me," she sighed, waiting.

"The program was reconstituted in Serbia. In Belgrade, to be specific," he said, meaningfully.

"*Really?* What else did he say about that?" Alyn pressed him. This seemed like too much of a coincidence to ignore. Whitney and Karis had gone there for a promotional conference early winter. At least, that's what they *told* her.

Harris replied, pointedly, "Only that the Serbs were much more lenient, that they allowed the neuro research to go on, unfettered. The government doesn't have as much money to support it, but the program receives private funding through other sources."

"Interesting. Did you ask him about the ANTm3? Did he recognize the substance?" she held her breath, waiting.

"I did ask him, but he said he didn't know about it specifically," Harris shrugged. "But he did say that he had heard about a neurotransmitter with a similar name, NS3; I believe, that was detected during the nineteen- eighties at that same Tour De' France competition…. he paused, "the one that the Czechs were disqualified from."

Alyn chewed her lip, pondering, "I wonder if ANTm3 is another iteration of NS3. Whatever it is, it would have to be undetectable," she considered aloud, "otherwise, it would be too risky."

"Believe me, I was surprised to learn this. Our meeting was a lark, I didn't expect to find out this much," Harris said, shaking his head. "There's a lot to chew on here, there's probably more to the story than we know. I think you should pursue it."

"I'm wondering if Whitney or Karis may have been sent there by Consumco to receive some kind of…I'm not even sure what to call it…treatment," she concluded. "There's no way of knowing, I'm sure they'll never tell me. Whatever it is, it's probably against the law."

"Thanks for all the intel," she told him, appreciatively. All this information would go into the journal she was now keeping.

"You're welcome, just another day in the life of a nosy journalist," he chuckled. "This is all pure speculation Alyn, you can't jump to any conclusions," he reminded her.

"I know. We never had this conversation, right?" she responded, laughingly.

"Right. Hey, you should come work with me again," he told her, brightly.

"I just might do that," she told him half-seriously. "Let's order some food, okay? My treat."

Back in Crested Butte, Whitney finally had an opportunity to take a walk that afternoon with her dad. Usually, he was enmeshed in the store, helping customers, answering phones, stocking shelves. Now that it was shoulder season, they weren't so busy, he could get away for a few hours. They drove up County Road 317 to Oh Be Joyful Campground and parked the car at the Slate River trailhead, their favorite spot to see fall colors.

Bright sunbeams reflected off aspen and scrub oak leaves, a million gold coins fluttering against the turquoise sky, a slight chill whispered in the air; snow could fly any day now. For a while, they just walked quietly along the riverbank, gazing at the fantastical explosion of autumn flame in the Gunnison National Forest. Water cascaded in ripples over shillings of slate grey and black rock in a playful dance of light. Fourteen- thousand- foot peaks cocooned the shaded trail and campground below in a protective forest of deciduous and needled trees.

Her dad spoke thoughtfully, his methodical, even strides matching hers. "We came here when you were just a toddler, do you remember?" voice nostalgic.

She sighed, replying, "I was so young then, I don't remember. It wasn't until I was older that I realized what a spectacular place this was- if that's what you're getting at."

"Your mom and I fell in love with the area," he inhaled deeply. "I suppose fate brought us here. And I suppose fate is what brings you to the place you're at too, Whitney," he said to her, somberly. Lately she seemed so conflicted. As though she were struggling with everything she said or did. Was it PTSD? he worried. Was it stress? He and Cindy discussed it at length, acutely aware of how much their daughter's personality had changed. How she vacillated between normal conversation and short-tempered, impatient exchange. How she seemed unconcerned about the risks she was taking and how it affected other people. Her change of hairstyle, make-up...her weight loss...

On the other hand, she had been incredibly attentive to Robyn while she was home, he contemplated internally. Taking care of her, paying her medical bills... It was a lot to handle, given that she was at the gym every day working out, then studying topo maps every afternoon. No one trained harder than she did, he acknowledged. Maybe he was just reading too much into things. She had told them that she would be staying in Crested Butte through December, which was encouraging.

As though reading his mind, she spoke haltingly, "Dad, I *have* to finish this competition. I've gotten this far- I'll get through the rest. I can understand why you and mom might be worried, but I think the most dangerous part of this tour is behind me... We've got a new film coming out called 'Ski Free Odyssey,' she said, animated. "I'll be earning royalties for the first time, from a *movie*... I feel like I've finally arrived to where I've always wanted to be in my life... Making a living skiing, doing what I love to do. I can't just give up now," she told him, plaintively.

"I know that. Your mom knows that" he replied, nodding. "It's partly our own damn fault that you're so great at what you do. We brought you here to this amazing place and raised you in these mountains, so it's no wonder you became a pro skier, we get it. But the mountains always have the last word," he stopped on the trail, "and they got Mason. *You* could be next."

She bit her lip, nodding. It was true. You couldn't sugar coat the danger. Best not to even try.

They walked along further, absorbed in the sound of flowing water, the rustle of branches in the breeze.

"I love you guys," she finally said, simply. It seemed like the only thing worth saying.

"We love you too, sweetheart," he returned, heavily. "There are things we don't have control of as parents. We're learning how to let go," he added, with a sigh.

"I know," she responded, thinking of Robyn.

On Tuesday, Robyn had another seizure again at school, this one considerably worse than others, previous. Mrs. Hennessey called her at the gym, immediately. The school nurse rushed into the classroom and assisted her through the brief, but intense episode. Whitney raced over in her car, ran into the building to get her. Robyn was still conscious, though very disoriented when she arrived.

Their drive to the emergency room in Gunnison was a blur of miles and ranchland, cars and trucks whizzing by; Whitney scarcely noticing them. Robyn whimpering in the seat, beside her.

She checked Robyn into the facility, heart pounding. Then waited several hours for the doctor's report.

She went back outside and sat in her car for several minutes and took some whiffs of ANTm3 deep into both nostrils, bracing herself for the next salvo. She would need all the compassion she could muster for what she imagined would come next.

"We did an examination of Robyn," the young doctor informed her, mid-thirties, light brown hair. "She's doing alright now, starting to feel better. Over the next twenty-four hours I expect she will be quite tired and need a lot of rest. I reached out to her pediatrician, we discussed her episode at length," he explained, voice concerned. "She filled me in on her medical history, sent over her charts. I see that Dr. Halpurn is involved in her ongoing care, as well." Whitney listened carefully, attentive. He went on, "Robyn should be seen by both doctors, soon as possible. They need to recheck her blood level and run more comprehensive labs in the neurology department this week," he added, firmly.

This episode could have been worse, she realized, somewhat relieved.

"I think you should be able to take her home in several hours, after she's completely stabilized," he finished, pleasant though businesslike.

"Thank you," she nodded, appreciatively. "I'll contact her doctors and get everything scheduled soon as possible," she told him, then added, swallowing, "It's just so unpredictable. I never know if I'm supposed to call 911 or take her to the emergency room myself. It's scary."

He nodded, sympathetic. "Seizure disorders are extremely stressful for parents and family members. It can be a long journey to figure out what is causing the seizures, what the best course is for managing them and finding a cure. Fortunately, you have an excellent pediatrician and neurologist. With their guidance, I think you'll find the answers. Best of luck," he shook her hand, warmly. "Here's my card, call me if there's anything I can do."

She thanked him again, grateful for his expertise and encouraging words. Although they were soothing, optimistic, her heart sank, she felt discouraged. Both she and Robyn were facing a frightening vortex of medical problems with no clear path forward. How much more could they endure?

On the drive back home, Whitney reached over, briefly caressing Robyn's cheek as she slept in the passenger seat, head drooped against the cold window. Black sky, miles of open road ahead, she steeled herself, jaw set, determined. She'd win that money. For Robyn, for her family, for herself.

# CHAPTER 26
# TETON'S CALLING

Christmas dinner was a feast of roast turkey and wild rice stuffing, root vegetables and cranberry sauce, followed by apple pie and sugar cookies that Whitney and Robyn had baked and decorated for the occasion. Cheerful, white twinkling lights lined the frosty windows of their cozy family room, a fresh Norfolk pine adorned with festive bows and colorful figurines sat splendidly in the center of it, casting a wintery glow. Hans and Zokas stood in the adjacent, open kitchen talking to Cindy, effusively thanking her for inviting them to dinner.

Both would have spent the holiday alone, eating cans of soup, they told her abashedly, as she scraped bowls of leftovers into storage containers and stowed them into the overflowing refrigerator. Whitney was hovering over the coffeemaker brewing coffee to sip by the fireplace. Tom was crouched in front it, jabbing at split-birch logs with the wrought iron poker, coaxing the fire along, listening to the babble of voices in the room. Robyn was curled up in the overstuffed easychair beside him, seemingly entranced by the red-hot embers and dancing flames beneath the metal rod. The group moved into the seating area to join them.

Hans reached into his jacket pocket and handed Whitney a little present. She guessed he had wrapped the box himself-- not an easy task, given his arthritic and gnarled hands. Touched, she undid the crooked, folded paper and tape, delicately.

"You didn't have to do this, Hans," she chided him, with a smile.

"It's for good luck," he told her, anxiously watching as she opened the diminutive, wooden jewelry box. Inside was a slightly tarnished antique silver reindeer pin, a piece from Austria that had belonged to his late wife, Marta. Whitney exhaled in surprise, taken by its charming beauty. Hans told her, "It belonged to my wife, I wanted you to have it. She would have wanted you to have it too," his eyes crinkled. "You can wear it in La Grave."

"Oh my gosh, thank you, Hans," she hugged him, effusively. "And thank you for all your help and friendship over the years, it means so much to me." Hans smiled bashfully, unaccustomed to so much attention. Whitney leaned down to show Robyn the silver pin. "See, this belonged to his wife, it's very special."

"Oooh, it's beautiful, mommy!" Robyn exclaimed, wide eyed.

"Someday it will belong to you, too." Hans told her, fondly.

Whitney sat down on the comfortable sofa in front of the flickering fire, Robyn jumped up snuggled with her, head in her lap, eyelids growing heavy as Whitney absently ran her fingers through her tangled hair and gently stroked her flushed, soft cheeks. Tom and Cindy settled in beside them. Hans and Zokas sat down on a pair of red and green plaid stuffed chairs across the pine coffee table.

"When do you leave for Jackson Hole?" Zokas asked Whitney, conversationally.

She answered, "I'll drive up to Frisco next week, Trent wants to ski some one-on-one with me in Summit before we fly to Jackson on January twentieth. Consumco is flying us there a week early so we can practice the course before the competition. They rented an Airbnb at the base, we'll be staying there until we fly on to La Grave. That is, assuming one of us makes it to the World Championships," she added, clarifying.

Tom leaned in, "Who do you feel is your biggest competition, at this juncture?" he queried, taking a sip of coffee.

"Karis, of course," she told them, "She's probably the best skier I'll compete against, but there will be other top women at the semi-finals. Alyssa Peters, from Oregon, Annette Stahl, from Wyoming, Chrystal Hays from Utah… I've skied against all of them these past several years and they're all phenomenal," she added. "It'll take everything I've got to make it to the finals."

"And the men?" Cindy asked her, tilting her head, curious. She had been so busy preparing for the holidays, this was the first chance she had to sit down, learn more about the National Championships.

"Great question," Whitney answered her mom. "Let's ask Hans- he probably has strong opinions about that," she nodded at him. "What do you think?" she asked him, deferentially.

Hans cleared his throat, a little raspy, "Quite honestly, I've been following the international skiers more than the Americans," he stated. "I think Renard Genet, from France, Felix Beisteiner of Austria, those two are going to be the ones to beat. Angelo Moretti, he's a contender too. They're all from the Tyrol, familiar with the terrain. Climbers. Same with the women," he told them. "Marie Aubaurer of Austria, Anna Fischer of Germany… Maybe even Carla Alarcon, from Chile. She's an exceptional skier and climber in the Andes, accustomed to that kind of alpine terrain, too. You'll have to keep an eye on her," he dipped chin at Whitney, pointedly.

Swallowing apprehensively, she concurred. Though the ANTm3 was helping her relate to her family and friends here more easily, the residual fear and anxiety provoked by the chemical had been surfacing, as well. Hans' comments reminded her of how dangerous the mountains were in La Grave. She couldn't help but feel a little nervous.

Robyn opened her eyes, asking sleepily, "mommy, when will you come back home?"

Whitney caught her breath, guiltily, "I should be back by the end of February, luv bug." A lengthy absence, a lot could happen between now and then. Once again, motherhood tugged at her conscience; misgivings about leaving. Trying to reassure Robyn, she told her, "When I return, it will be for a long time. Okay honey? I promise."

"I'll miss you mommy," Robyn's eyes fluttered closed again. Probably time to tuck her in to bed, Whitney thought. They both had to drive over to Luann and Jack's tomorrow morning to exchange Christmas presents. She kept Robyn's head in her lap for a few minutes longer, savoring the moment.

Zokas addressed Tom and Cindy, his Greek accent breaking through, "Wheetney and I have been climbing all summer long. She's developed incredible upper body strength and rope skills. I'm sure she'll be able to hold her own against the European women at WESC." Adding, confidently, "She's also mastered the front-double flip with a twist on the diving board. That should set her apart from most of the other women, in terms of her aerials."

Hans agreed, nodding, "I watched her perform one on the slopes this winter. She stuck the landing perfectly. I believe she's ready," he said to Tom and Cindy. "She will do great."

Both looked at Hans and Zokas. Tom spoke, "We appreciate everything you've done to prepare our daughter for WESC, we know she's ready as she'll ever be."

Unspoken, all knew a multitude of things out of Whitney's control could affect the outcome of her competition. Injury, illness, poor weather, bad snow conditions…that was the nature of skiing. Both Tom and Cindy would stay in Crested Butte throughout the competitions and watch them on TV with friends and coworkers. Over the past several years, it had become increasingly stressful to travel with her out of state, they preferred to stay home with Robyn.

Their conversation continued, Robyn's eyes closed, the fire settled down.

Zokas turned to Whitney, "How do the judges do their scoring?" he asked her, unfamiliar with the system.

Whitney explained, "Everyone begins their run with fifty points, automatically. The judges add points for difficulty, fluidity, line, speed, tricks, aerials, and turns. They subtract points for errors like stopping on the run, falling, lack of fluidity, lack of speed, poor jumping and loss of control." She added, "a skier can't exceed a hundred points on any single run. Each person will do three different required runs, and then the two highest average scoring competitors will compete against each other for the National Championship." She concluded, "The American champion will go on to compete at La Grave against the top international qualifiers in the world."

"Let's have a toast to our new World Champion," Hans announced broadly, holding his coffee mug up in salutation. Zokas grinned, joining him.

Whitney responded, self- consciously, "you guys are awesome, I really appreciate your support. I only hope that I can live up to your expectations." She stood up and lifted Robyn off the sofa, carried her into her bedroom, tucked her under the covers. Kissed her on the forehead.

*Please, no seizures tonight...*she closed her eyes, praying. She sat on the edge of her bed for a while, watching Robyn fall into a deep slumber. She needed time apart from everyone for a few minutes, the pressure of the competition, their comments weighing on her shoulders. Sometimes she wished she could just disappear for a while, have a desk job for a few days....

"You let your hair go too long between visits," Mervette admonished her, frowning. Chiffon had been overjoyed to hear from Whitney, booking her appointment the last minute. "We heard about the avalanche in Portillo. Oh my God, that is *so scary*. We're glad you're okay!" she had exclaimed breathless, over the phone.

Whitney told Mervette, regretfully. "I'm sorry I didn't come sooner, I was dealing with so much other stuff, there wasn't any time." She was sitting in a chair at the salon. "I think I need a different look. Any suggestions?" she asked the stylist as they gazed at her reflection in the huge mirror.

"How about platinum," Mervette offered.

"You mean like, *platinum blonde?*" Whitney gaped, skeptically.

"Yes! We could shorten the length, do some layers.... soften up the bangs... They've grown out, anyway." Mervette chewed her lip, evaluating. "We could lighten your brows, you could switch to a softer eye shadow, do some earth tones... go for a more sophisticated look. What do you think?"

*Outrageous.*

"Go ahead. Do it," Whitney crowed.

"You trust me?"

"Of course, I trust you," Whitney laughed out loud. Last time she changed her make-up and hair style, Consumco had given her a six-thousand- dollar bonus. *Why not* do it again? she thought boldly, anticipating the look on Trent's face. Priceless.

"My nails look terrible," Whitney lamented. "They're perpetually broken from climbing and skiing. Could they get a makeover too?" she asked, hopefully.

"Yes, indeed! Ambergris can fix them. We'll make you the most glamourous skier in the whole USA," Mervette replied, grinning. "Frisco's own pride and joy."

"Everything helps," Whitney grinned back at her. "Believe me, everything helps," she repeated. After she lost a few more pounds, she'd be perfect.


Jackson Hole. Revered for its fiercesome steeps and killer couloirs, rocky cliffs and stupendous views, it was considered the birthplace of freeriding, the place where skiers went to cut their teeth and test their mettle against some of the most challenging steeps in the country. Situated in the Grand Tetons of Wyoming, the ski area boasted over four thousand feet of vertical drop and off-piste skiing in vast swaths of extreme terrain. The town itself was a charming mix of cowboy esthetic and upscale, billionaire chic. Steak houses and fancy boutiques lined the narrow streets, sporting images of buffalo, antelope, ranching life and all things Western. Sprawling, cloistered estates sat on the edge of town, providing privacy for the wealthy seeking solitude, access to world class flyfishing and outdoor sports.

Consumco flew them into the small airport near town. Duncan had already arranged the transfers, mobile equipment storage and food delivery that they would require over the next several weeks.

The entire town was alive and energized leading up to the National Championships. Huge banners hung across the main street, announcing the upcoming event. Sponsors and media professionals had set up kiosks and vehicles around the ski area's snow-covered base and parking lot, staking claim for interviews, promotional videos and television newscasts. Duncan and Trent were already placing web cams along the course so that Shenti could live-stream the skiers as they came down the mountain. Alyn had just flown in from Seattle and was lugging around pounds of camera gear and computer equipment, planning her photo blitz for the next several weeks.

Annette Stahl, her coach and support staff had just arrived and were already practicing on the slopes. Chrystal Hays, Emma Whitstone from Washington State, Lauren Bell from Montana and Alyssa Peters were all scheduled to arrive soon. Jayden McIntye, from Lake Tahoe, would be flying in next week with her coach and several sponsors.

Ian was getting the lion's share of the attention. A sportscaster from ESPN was standing in front of him near the red aerial tram holding a microphone, asking him questions about his prospects for winning. A cameraman stood nearby with a huge lens over his shoulder, pointing it at them. Ian appeared characteristically cool and self-assured posing with his skis, plastered head to toe in sponsor logos. Standing offside watching them was Noah, looking a little uncomfortable, out of his element. Probably wasn't too thrilled about playing second fiddle, Whitney imagined, knowingly.

Pete Henderson from Wyoming, Chris Porter from Colorado, Jordan Swain from Utah and Luca Chase from California had also filtered into Jackson, hitting the slopes to familiarize themselves with the course as well. Heavy hitters Ezra Amash from Oregon and Josh Landen of Alaska were due to arrive later in the week, support staff in tow.

Whitney observed the throngs of people congregating, the spectacle unfolding with detached interest. She had stopped using the ANTm3 in late December, a renewed sense of invincibility and purpose re-igniting within her as she prepared for the task ahead.

Critical she let go of past setbacks and trauma, the avalanche, Robyn's seizures, she focused solely on skiing and competing, without distraction or fear.

Nothing would stop her, now.

# CHAPTER 27
# SEMI-FINALS

Nine a.m., Whitney and Karis loaded onto Jackson Hole's enormous aerial tram at the base of the ski area. Capable of holding a hundred skiers, the tram quickly filled with women competitors wearing stylish parkas and bright yellow identification bibs, helmets, gloves and goggles plastered with colorful product logos and sponsor decals. Event officials and media personnel jockeyed for position, ski boots and skis clunking against the hard metal floor. Voices rose with excitement and intensity as they pressed shoulder to shoulder inside the tram, waiting for the huge glass doors to slide shut.

With a barely audible hiss of forced air, the beast detached from the platform and started to smoothly ascend, leaving the massive structure behind. Suspended on cables dangling a hundred feet above the ground, it glided with surprising speed up the toothy, snow-covered peaks. A hush fell over the group as they gazed across the Bridger-Teton wilderness with giddy anticipation. In nine short minutes they would arrive at the top of Rendezvous Mountain.

This morning had been a crush of preparations that began at six a.m. following breakfast, painstaking discussions about ski equipment and strategy, the snow conditions and weather. Five inches of fresh snow had fallen last night, the officials notifying them that the first round of competition would go forward on Corbet's Couloir today. Trent and Duncan both agreed that Whitney and Karis should use shorter skis to manage the tight turns at its entrance, despite the deeper snow.

Trent told Whitney and Karis, voice granite, hard and unyielding, "Corbet's Couloir. The legendary eliminator. Once you drop in, make that first left turn *immediately*. It's critical, otherwise you'll hit the rock wall. Shift right into your next turn, or you'll hit the other side. Lose control, and you'll be crashing in a no-fall zone, so *don't*. We were notified early this morning that the judges wanted to start the competition with Corbet's because the snow conditions are good right now. Often the run is closed when it's too icy." The women nodded, silently. He went on, "once you're at the bottom of the couloir, you'll have a ton of speed. Ski left of the tram through the stand of trees, then do a back layout at the cliff drop into the chutes. At the base of chutes, there's a cat track. Catch that kicker and do a 720 into the next set of chutes as you head towards Amphitheatre. Stay high near the trees, on the ridge. Don't ski down into Amphitheatre, otherwise the judges will penalize you. Got it?" They both nodded. "ESPN will be flying drones overhead and livestreaming," he added. "Try to ignore them. I know it's distracting, but you can do it. Ski to the base of Thunder Quad chair towards the judges stands, and we'll meet you there," he finished. Whitney and Karis set their jaws, absorbing his words. Like high impact bullets, they hit their mark.

The tram glided to a seamless stop at the enormous steel platform on top Rendezvous Mountain, elevation 10,450 feet. Early morning clouds were congregated heavy and dense over the serrated peaks in a weather system far colder and windier than milder conditions at base. As they clambered off the tram onto the platform, particles of snow whipped their faces, breath freezing in the high alpine air. Whitney carried her skis down the ungroomed ridge several yards, then set them down in the deep snow and clicked into their bindings. They would be skiing in-bounds on Corbet's, roped apart from other recreational skiers on the mountain. A foreboding gash in the mountainside, Corbet's Couloir sat a slight distance offside the top of the tram and fanned out below a gigantic set of rock headwalls. Notoriously steep and narrow, it required skiers go airborne to enter it.

The women skied slowly down to its entrance and then paused, waiting for instructions from the event officials. The officials would radio down to the judges to communicate their positions.


Whitney gazed across the mountains. Much of Teton range was obscured by clouds, but she could still make out jagged edges of their massive forms cloistered behind the snowy ridge where she was standing. The officials informed the women that they had to wait for the clouds to dissipate, skies to clear. The delay seemed interminable; she grew impatient standing around in the freezing temperatures waiting for the judges to give them the "all clear." Karis, wearing bib number 6, looked impatient, too. Both had kept their distance from each other all morning, barely communicating.

Whitney heard an official call her name, she moved into place behind Jayden McIntyre, wearing bib number 3. Emma Whitstone, from Washington, would go first. Moving into position above the top of the couloir, she prepared to drop in.

The "go" signal was given. Emma dropped in.

Instantly airborne in the nearly vertical chasm for the first twenty feet, Emma contacted with the ground. Watching with binoculars, the judges scrutinized her every move. Cranking the first left turn proficiently, she quickly shifted her weight into the critical right turn, but lost control at the opposite wall. Tumbling head over skis, she cartwheeled down the narrow ribbon of snow like a rag doll between the two rock walls, finally skidding to a stop a hundred yards below. Limp, she lay prone against the snow, motionless for several long minutes.

*Was she alive?* Everyone held their breath, wide-eyed, frozen.

Slowly, she got up and gathered her skis and poles, as event volunteers who were stationed nearby skied over to help her. Gingerly, she made her way down to the base, her competition over. The judges radioed up, awarding her 7 points for difficulty, minus 3 for falling, minus 3 for an incomplete run. She received a total of 51 points.

From Montana, Lauren Bell stood poised above the couloir. At the signal, she launched off the edge, freefalling twenty feet. Grinding her first left turn hard and aggressively, she shifted her body into the right turn immediately, staying on top her skis. Shooting down into the chasm, she maintained her balance and continued descending at high speed. Whitney got a glimpse of her slender form entering the pine trees, then disappearing into the lower chutes. After twenty minutes, her score was relayed to the top: 82 points.

Going third, Jayden McIntyre from California approached the opening of the couloir. She paused. Whitney could see her confer with the officials. She backed away from the entrance, evidently taking herself out of the competition. A murmur went through the cluster of skiers as the officials relayed the information down to the judges. Still recovering from a knee injury, she had evidently decided at the last minute she didn't want to risk taking the run. Her score: 0.

In fourth position, Whitney slid into place above the couloir, waiting for the "go" signal. Hearing it, she pushed off the edge in a low, aggressive crouch, airborne for thirty feet inside the chute. Hitting ground, she grinded her first left turn with a powerful edge, then right, knees up to her chest. With a hard shift, she pointed her skis straight down, allowing gravity to drop her nearly weightless body to the fall line, towards the trees. Making quick, powerful dips and cuts around their snow-packed trunks, she prepared for the twenty-foot cliff drop, adjusting her body into perfect alignment. She launched off the huge headwall into a full back layout, legs perfectly symmetrical, arms balanced and outward, landing perfectly into a deep pillow of snow in a low, crouched stance. Still moving swiftly down the fall line through the gully's trees, she caught air off the cat track, effortlessly performing a 720 off its edge, landing with a confident thwump. Now she could see the bottom of the chairlift, the four judges watching her. With a long fluid arc, she swooped down towards them, gracefully. Ten minutes went by, her score was announced: 87 points.

"Fantastic run, Whitney!" Trent and Duncan beamed, congratulating her. Gulping air, she was still catching her breath. Trent handed her a pair of binoculars with a reassuring comment, "Hey, don't worry, kiddo. The judges are just being conservative, allowing room for more points over the next two days." Nodding, she stood beside them to watch the next competitor descend from the top.

Number 5; Alyssa Peters from Oregon dropped in. Whitney observed her attack the first two crucial turns and ski through the couloir, in control. Moving down the fall line, she cut precisely through the trees, knees moving quickly up and down, expertly absorbing the bumps and troughs in her path. At the cliff, she made a noticeable speed check to control her set up, then launched off its edge with a back- tuck somersault, landing on her skis. Forward and balanced, she cruised through the next set of trees into the lower chutes, deviating from the fall line for several moments. Regaining it, she headed towards the cat track and launched off its edge, doing a mule kick. Landing proficiently, she was almost at the bottom now. She skied towards the judges stand to join her coach. The two waited together for her score: 83 points.

Now Karis moved into position, poised at the couloir's opening. Whitney held her binoculars up, focused intently. At the signal, Karis dropped into the chasm going airborne several seconds, then landed, knocking out her first set of turns. Shoulders forward, body spring-loaded, she dug into her edges, rocketing through the rest of the couloir, perfectly. Skis forward, fast, fluid turns down the fall line, hips swiveling, knees dipping, she wove through trees, effortlessly. At the cliff, she popped off the lip with a back layout, body arched, arms extended, legs together. Landing with a poof in the deep snow, she bobbled, slightly off-center, nearly losing control. For a split second, Whitney wondered if she would crash. Quickly recovering, she got back over her skis and headed into the chutes towards the cat track. Here, she flew off the kicker with a 720, landing smoothly in the heavy snow. Now skiing towards the judges stand, she skidded over to Trent, Duncan and Whitney, bent at the waist, catching her breath.

"Great run, you crushed it!" Trent congratulated her, exhaling. The only way to score big was to be on the edge of control. And although she had almost lost it, she had gone hard on speed and jumps. The judges announced her score ten minutes later: 86 points.

Chrystal Hays, from Utah, entered the couloir and took a bad fall from the top, losing control on her first turn. Tumbling down the nearly vertical chasm in a terrible crash, the competition came to a halt as the ski patrol and paramedics attended to her. Whitney followed the events through her binoculars, watching them strap her injured body onto a sled then tow her body down the mountainside behind the snowmachine. An unfortunate development, everyone looked somber, concerned as they waited the additional forty-minutes for the officials to announce when the last competitor could take their turn. Annette Stahl, from Wyoming, had been patiently standing at the top the entire time, waiting for her chance to finally go.

Seemingly undeterred by the accident, Annette dropped into the couloir, free-falling the first twenty feet. Edging low and hard on her skis and making powerful left and right turns, she avoided hitting the rock walls on either side. As they watched through their binoculars, they could see her crouched low and forward over her skis, moving swiftly down the fall line towards the trees; her athletic, strong body navigating through the uneven obstacles like flowing water. Executing a front twisting somersault at the cliff-drop, she landed solidly in the loose snow and popped up, skiing through the chute's dips and gullies. Checking her speed at the cat track, a tiny error, she launched off the kicker and performed a 360 helicopter, legs apart, arms out in open position. Very showy. With a near-perfect landing, still pointing her skis down the fall line, she rocketed towards the judges stand, skidding towards her coach, all smiles. They stood and waited for her score. Ten minutes later it was announced: 86. She had tied with Karis.

At three-thirty p.m. the scores for the day were officially confirmed. Whitney; 87, Karis and Annette; 86, Alyssa; 83, Lauren; 82, Emma, 51. Chrystal and Jayden; 0.

The base of the ski area was a madhouse. Throngs of spectators, fans, vendors, sportscasters and bystanders all hit place like swarm of bees trying to get close to the competitors. Whitney and Karis were instantly inundated by press wanting autographs, comments, photographs and interviews. Fielding their requests with professional courtesy and politeness, they hung out near the judge's station while Trent spoke with officials, holding court. Shenti trudged around the parking lot shooting video of the women as they met with sponsors and greeted ski industry insiders. Alyn frenetically sent text to Consumco for real-time marketing. Ian and Noah jumped right in the action, talking and schmoozing with the crowd.

Whitney participated in the hullabaloo for as long as she could sanely manage, then exited the scene. Walking back to their rental house, she did a mental checklist. Call home, make sure things were okay, take a shower, eat some food…

Alyn called over to her, excited. "Hey Whitney, everyone *loves* your hair! I need a quote about your new look!"

Whitney grinned, giving her a thumbs up. "Sorry. Can't do it right now. I'm tapped. How 'bout later, okay?" she returned, and kept walking. She had to call home, check on Robyn. Her folks would be waiting to hear from her.

On the second day of competition, skiers and officials clamored again early morning inside the cavernous aerial tram, ascending to the top of Rendezvous Mountain. Two inches of snow had fallen that night, blanketing the slopes with a small layer of new powder on top a largely compacted base. Fifteen degrees Fahrenheit out, some low-lying clouds still hung over the area. The forecast showed clearing skies and mainly sunshine by ten a.m.

They would be skiing inbounds again, beneath the Sublette Quad Chair and Lower Sublette Ridge, then on to the base of the ski area. Trent's directives had been straightforward, succinct. "Once you get off the tram, ski down Rendezvous. Do your first 720 off the kicker, near the top of the chairlift. Ski towards Laramie Bowl and do a front twisting somersault off the headwall, into the bowl. At Lower Sublette Ridge, take at least two more jumps on the way down. Max out your points with a 720 and a backflip, otherwise you're out of contention."

Whitney and Karis both nodded, resolute, familiar with the drill. These were sequences they had been practicing since they arrived at Jackson, they were ready, stoked for the course. "We'll meet you at the judges stands," he finished, a little terse. Ian and Noah would be there, watching as well. They would be competing on the same course, next week.

Duncan had inspected the women's equipment that morning, making sure their bindings were properly adjusted and set, edges sharpened, bases waxed, boots intact. Ever since their trip to Silverton where Whitney's bindings had been tampered with, he had been keenly obsessive about double- checking everything. Whitney had run a finger over the metal edges of her skis right after breakfast. "Thanks for all your help, as usual," she told him, appreciatively.

"You got it," he had replied solemnly, cleaning a little smudge of dirt off her lightweight, graphite Leki poles. "I'll see you at the bottom."

Whitney's main adversaries at this point in the competition were Karis, Lauren Bell, Alyssa Peters and Annette Stahl. The other women had dropped rank quickly on the first day. Things could certainly change if someone got injured or sick, or had to withdraw, of course, but it appeared the best skiers had already distinguished themselves at this juncture. Shivering in the freezing cold, they stood on the summit of Rendezvous with event officials, the wind whipping up snow and stinging their faces, blowing through layers of outerwear like shards of ice.

Waiting for her turn to descend, Whitney watched each woman ski down the steep face towards Laramie Bowl and their first set of aerials. Swallowed up by the stands of trees and rock lined chutes, she only heard their last whoops of excitement as they disappeared. She felt indomitable, strong, fearless as she anticipated her turn, next. Clearly, the procedure was doing its magic.

At the official's "go" signal, she pushed off her poles and skied straight down the fall line, setting up for her jump near the top of the chair lift. Executing the 720 with perfect form, she nailed the landing and stayed precisely on the fall line, crouching low, aggressive, cutting through the dips and gullies with powerful turns. Gaining more speed, she sailed off the cliff, instantly tucking into a twisting, double front somersault. Unfurling herself a split second before the landing, she sunk into the heavy snow and popped out, knees up to her chest, still on the fall line. Now she was moving along a treed ridge, toward Lower Sublette, carving long, fluid turns preparing for her next jump, a mule kick, on the way down. Landing it, she set-up her next aerial; a spread eagle off a small knoll. Almost at the base now, she ripped straight towards the judges stand in tuck position, skidding to a stop beside Trent, Duncan, Ian and Noah, who were all holding binoculars. "Fantastic run!" they high fived her, levitating. She bent over, gulping air to catch her breath. "Thanks! It felt *great!*" she exhaled, thrilled.

Duncan handed her a pair of binoculars. She looked up the mountain to watch the others ski down. Ten minutes went by, her score was announced. 90 points. Trent turned to her, commenting, "Great run. You went for the double- front twisting somersault, I noticed. Gutsy move," he added dryly, glancing back up the mountainside.

She really took a chance, adding that extra rotation, he smiled inwardly. She was skiing to win, no doubt about it. A true competitor.

"I *had* to do it. Had to stay in the game," Whitney told him, explaining.

"Well, that aughta do it," he grinned, lifting his binocs again. They all watched as Alyssa, then Karis skied down Lower Sublette Ridge. Both had superb runs, swooshing towards the judges stands, arriving fifteen minutes apart. Karis came over to join them, waiting expectantly for her score.

Her single, twisting front somersault at the top of course had garnered fewer points than Whitney's double.

The judges made the announcement: Karis, 88 points, Alyssa, 85.

They all continued watching skiers come down the mountainside. Annette was clearly a top contender, making a show of force with her skillful aerials and powerful skiing down the fall line. Once again, she tied with Karis, obtaining a score of 88. Lauren had had an excellent run earlier that morning, garnering 83 points; consistent with her first run, the day before. Emma, Chrystal and Jayden scored 79, 76 and 75, successively. At the bottom of the group, they were in danger of being eliminated.

After all the scores were officially recorded, everyone headed over to the main lodge to do meet and greets, photo shoots and press conferences with their coaches and sponsors. Whitney ducked out from the party-like festivities after several hours, needing a break. Looking for Duncan in the parking area, she located him at the white rental van, putting away ski equipment and cleaning up around it. The area was littered with water bottles, folding chairs, coolers and fast- food wrappers, a sea of human detritus. Relieved to be away from the crowd, he waved her over.

"Hey! Congrats on an amazing day! You're the main story! How're you holding up?" he asked her, as he scraped bits of hard-ened snow from underneath some ski bindings with a screwdriver, brushing frozen crust off the ski. He set it down. She handed him her skis and poles, unbuckled her boots.

"Good, good, but I'm ready for a break. All that hoopla," she waved over in the direction of the lodge, "is a bit much, after a while. I wanted to thank you for taking care of all my equipment since we got here- it's such a relief. I can't shlep it all back to my room every day, so thanks again," she told him earnestly.

"Yep, it's safe here with me, under lock and key," he grinned at her, "no problem at all."

"I'm going back to the house- need to clear my head, call home. I'll make us some stir fry or something when you get back there," she offered over her shoulder.

"Sounds great! I need to put all this away, but I'll see you later," he called over to her, loading some boots into the van. Gleefully, he did a happy dance inside his head. Dinner with Whitney, *Sweeeeet!*


The third day of competition was essentially a showdown between Whitney, Karis, Annette and Alyssa, though all the women would be competing, the lowest scorers hoping for a lucky break. Pressure was building, a buzz of nervous anticipation coursing through everyone that morning as the event grew closer. Alyn was trying to corner Whitney and Karis for more photos, telling them, "They want fashion shots before the race!" Karis was snapping back at her, "Tell them it's not a *fucking race!*" as she applied more mascara. Shenti was at the kitchen table, groaning about not having enough music samples for all the video he had taken. Duncan was grilling Trent to see if the women needed skins to get over to Casper Bowl. Tensions continued spilling over as they ate breakfast and guzzled coffee. Karis was in a funk about yesterday's score. "I would have done a different aerial if I'd known Whitney was going to do a double," she complained, glowering. Trent was irate, absorbing her anger. This one was on him, he recognized, internally. Reviewing strategy with the two, he made an effort to mollify her.

"You'll be skiing Casper Bowl today," he informed them. "Greybull and Moccasin are the two runs that give you the best opportunity to showcase your steep skiing ability. You've both showed the judges your aerials over the past two days, they've seen them now. Unless you can pull something bigger out of your wheelhouse, I suggest you rip those courses like there's no fucking tomorrow. However," he looked at Karis meaningfully, "*you* may choose your own line, do whatever the fuck aerial you want, okay? It's *your* decision," he added, irritably. She looked at him, jaw open.

Clearly this morning was wearing on him, he seemed even testier than usual. What was going on? Whitney wondered, inwardly. Was he upset with Karis for some reason? Ever since the avalanche in Portillo, he had been on edge.

Trent went on, frowning, "The judges will be near the top of Casper Quad Chair, stationed at the bottom of the bowl. You'll keep going down Easy Does It. There's a big lip off the traverse at the top of the bowl for an aerial, so go for it. Take the Casper chairlift back to the top and meet me at the judge's station," he stood up, leaving the table.


Leaving the kitchen, Karis brushed by Whitney, she whispered harshly, "You *little* bitch!" She walked towards her bedroom.

Whitney stepped in her path. "You think you can get rid of me, but you *can't*. Mason may be dead, but I plan on sticking around for a long time, so better get used to it."

Karis shrugged indifferently, shut her bedroom door.


Again, they all took the aerial tram to the top of Rendezvous and got off, this time, traversing a half mile along the top of the narrow ridge towards Casper Bowl. Whitney dug her poles into the snow and pushed forward on her skis, inhaling deeply. Frigid air filled her lungs, stinging the back of her throat as she followed the group single file across the untracked snow. Sunlight reflected brilliantly off the slopes sparkling like tiny diamonds in every direction. Winds had calmed, temperatures were warming up to twenty degrees; it was a perfect day.

Breaking snow further up the second half of the ridge, the group finally arrived at the very top of the bowl, above a concave mountain face featuring a minefield of formidable rock headwalls and near vertical drop-offs. Whitney scoped out the terrain, analyzing the features.

There. She spotted it. A thirty-five- foot cliff between Beartooth and Greybull. Silently, she moved closer to it, inspecting the in-run, above it. Her eyes moved down the cliff, surveying the smooth slope of pristine powder, below. No one else appeared to be interested in the formidable precipice, perhaps they considered it impossible.

To her, it was irresistible.

Preoccupied with her own thoughts and strategy, she mechanically observed the first two women make their descents, shooting off the ridge's cornice, into the bowl. Skiing down Easy Does It in front of the judges, they each performed proficient aerials at the cat-track and descended beyond her sightline. She tuned out everything, except for the official's voices, waiting for her turn.

They gave her the signal.

She was off. Turning the opposite direction of the group, she rocketed away towards the lip of the cliff and went big. Body crouched down for the set-up, she popped off the lip, getting huge air into a double- back twisting layout. Fully extended, arms out, legs together, she brought it down, landing perfectly into a relaxed and crouched position. Still rocketing down the open bowl towards the judges, she prepared her next jump off the edge of the cat-track, executing a front- tuck somersault and landing on top her skis with ease. Now she was cruising at extremely high speed down Easy Does

It, catching air on a series of moguls, first an iron cross, then a 720 with a grab, absorbing the ground's impact; relaxed torso, perfect form on each landing. Hips forward, upper body quiet but balanced, she skied to the base of Casper chair and jumped onto it, heading up the rugged mountainside to meet Trent.

Trent turned to her, eyes glinting, he grinned broadly, "You'll need to get ready for the final round tomorrow, Whitney. Go down, do your meet and greets, then get back to the house to rest. You're going to need some time to decompress before the real mayhem begins. I'll see you later," he exhaled, shaking his head. Man, she frickin' *killed* it.

The final scores were confirmed and delivered by the judges by three that afternoon: Whitney, 99. Karis 89, Annette, 88. The rest were irrelevant. Nobody could touch that first aerial off the cliff that Whitney had done. Not even close.

Whitney and Karis would be skiing for the National Championship against each other. One would win one hundred thousand dollars and go on to La Grave. The other would stay behind.

## CHAPTER 28
# FINAL, JACKSON HOLE

T he sleek, blue A-Star 350 B3 lifted off the snow-covered tarmac from the base of Jackson Hole with Karis and Whitney. Two male event officials sat across from the women, their faces obscured by black colored balaclavas and dark goggles, listening to the pilot on their headsets as he hovered briefly over the open area near the heliport's maintenance building and small parking lot. Whitney felt the sudden lurch and weightless sway of the roaring machine as it turned quickly towards the mountains and began flying low along the Bridger National Forest, heading past South Hoback Ridge towards the top of Cody Bowl, south of the main ski area. Passing Rock Springs Bowl, she looked down, scrutinizing the cliff bands and rock headwalls sitting ominously beneath them, their jagged, sharp edges narrowing into snowy chutes. Sparsely spaced clumps of spruce and pine grew along the steep rocks, clinging to the mountainside, their branches an impenetrable tangle of green flora and dead stumps on the exposed granite.

They continued gaining altitude, Karis's face pressed against the heli's frosted window. Staring down into the snowy wilderness, her golden braids peeked out from underneath her bright red helmet, matching balaclava. Though impossible to see the expression on her face, her body language exuded supreme composure and confidence; the procedure preventing any semblance of inhibition or fear. Whitney too, gazed calm and nonplussed at the enormous bowls below, entirely at ease with the sway of the helicopter and foreboding cathedral of serrated ridges, cliff bands and vertical walls. A long cornice extended several miles across, with fragmented sections along the way. Maneuvering towards the highest arete, their pilot skillfully lowered the machine above the narrow ridge, hovering just long enough to discharge the skiers.

Barely wide enough to stand on, Karis and Whitney hastily exited the helicopter single file. Grabbing their equipment from the exterior rack they moved hastily aside to accommodate the spinning rotors and blowing snow. Both event officials grabbed their skis and followed quickly behind. Bodies crouched, chins tucked down, 10-knot winds pummeled their frames, knocking them off balance on the narrow ledge.

The pilot swiftly turned and swiftly flew back down to meet the four judges and videographer. They would return to this exact location to watch and film the women from above.

Trent had met with Karis and Whitney that morning looking pained. "The judges informed me that they want you to ski this course together. You'll take one run, that's it. Cody Bowl is a notorious avalanche zone, so bring all your avy gear." He had briefly attempted to dissuade the judges from the decision, but they had dismissed his appeal as overreaching and unnecessary; wanting to compare the women's descents side by side. He gave them specific instructions, "Ski off the center of Four Shadows, then down to Rock Springs Bowl. At the bottom near the forest, cut over to South Hoback and ski to the base. The judges will be evaluating your lines from the air." Adding tersely, "Only do the jumps you can safely manage with your backpacks on. That's an order."

Internally, he knew the two should not be skiing anywhere near each other. Neither of them had the mental nor emotional capacity for it. But the decision had been made, it was out of his hands.

Putting their crampons on, they hoisted their backpacks and skis over their shoulders. The four began climbing several hundred feet farther up the ridge towards Pucker Face, the very first run off Cody Mountain. Not stopping, they broke snow another fifteen minutes up the ridge to a second summit, No Shadows; a particularly narrow precipice with exposed rock. Sharp edges and icy surfaces tripped them up, making passage difficult. Continuing past No Shadows' vertical cliff bands and shaded cornices, they trudged carefully to the open chute at the top of Four Shadows. Here, they stood for several moments, evaluating the terrain. They could hear the A-Star's rotors reverberating across the mountains, already on its way back.

Whitney wore a bright blue bib with the number 4 across her chest, Karis bright yellow, with the number 6. They removed their crampons and stowed them in their packs. The officials began their safety checks with the women.

"Transceivers on; Check."

"Probes; Check."

"Shovels; Check."

They examined the women's backpacks, making sure their straps were secure, then reviewed the route one more time. Karis and Whitney clicked into their ski bindings and adjusted their boot clips and goggles. Wind blowing harder now, snow lashed around their faces. Thick, gray clouds were gathering at the summit. Almost eleven-thirty a.m., the helicopter came into view, hovering in the distance. The officials radioed to the pilot, making contact. The heli moved in closer, then gave a tail wag, almost above them. The officials gave the signal.

"Go!"

Simultaneously, the women pushed off the cornice, dropping into the concave, 55-degree chute. Racing down the untracked snow parallel with each other, skis pointing straight down, both shot over bands of granite lightly dusted with snow, bottoms scraping rock. They made only one single turn near the base of the bowl, launching off a large roller, executing side-by-side back -tuck somersaults then landing with a whoosh into deep powder. Popping up, they rocketed further down, attacking the fall-line with total abandon.

Still staying parallel at breakneck speed, they flew over uneven bumps and dips, both furiously trying to take the lead. Shoulder to shoulder, their bodies hurled downward, engulfed in a frenzy of swirling snow, jabbing poles in their wake. Whitney's thighs and lungs burned on fire, her heart pounded like a jackhammer on hyper drive. Like a jet engine on nitro, she was ready to explode. Setting her jaw in determination, she attacked the mountain like a projectile shot out of a cannon.

Coming up were a series of rock headwalls, just above Rock Springs Bowl. Whitney chose the right side of them, parallel the trees. On her left, she sensed Karis close by. Could hear her skis scraping crust, see Karis's slough next to her as she drew near. Suddenly even closer, Karis boxed her in near the wall of rock. Hurtling towards her, she was cutting her off. Now she was right in front of her, forcing Whitney into certain disaster. Staying in a low tuck, Whitney held her ground, desperate to avoid contact. In one split second, she would hit the wall, lose control. *Karis was forcing her into the rock! Oh my God, oh my God! She had to react! Now!*

In a last- ditch act at self-preservation, she cut hard left across the tips of Karis's skis. Karis lost balance and lost control, slamming headfirst into the wall. Ricocheting off it, her body catapulted down the mountainside, voice screaming in terror. Her crumpled form disappeared down a gully obscured by rock and debris. Whitney kept skiing forward, holding on, a blur of trees and snow flying by. Heading to the cat track, she skied towards South Hoback, carving a few last, broad turns down the long, steep ridge. Almost at the base now, she began to recover, head in an adrenalized fugue. The helicopter followed her partway down, then turned away to initiate a rescue mission for Karis.

Trent and the rest of their group were congregated, suspended. Seeing only Whitney, Trent froze. The judges had just radioed him, the accident was all on video. Karis clearly had tried to annihilate Whitney.

"We just got word, they're going back to look for Karis," he told her, stunned. "You just won the National Championship, Whitney. Congratulations!"

The press would be all over her in a few minutes, Whitney knew. Hurriedly, she borrowed Duncan's cell phone to call home. Her parents probably saw the whole thing on TV, they would be going insane.

No answer.

Excited, she texted her mom. "Just won National Championship!"

No response.

Maybe they were at the store, watching it with their customers, she thought, wildly. Probably Hans and Zokas were there too, everyone rooting for her. She called the store's landline. An employee answered, Kelli Pearson.

"Hey, I've been trying to reach my folks. Are they there?" she asked her, impatient.

"No. They had to leave. They're on their way to Children's Hospital, in Denver," Kelli told her anxiously.

"What happened?" Whitney almost shouted over the phone.

"Something happened to Robyn. That's all I know. They left in a hurry about two hours ago, said they were driving to Denver. I'm sorry I don't have more information," she stammered, distressed.

"It's okay, it's okay. I'll get a hold of them soon. Thanks," she told Kelli hurriedly, hanging up.

Trent had gone to talk to ski-patrol, he strode back to her. "They're airlifting Karis to Jackson Community Hospital," he told her, voice grim. "They said she's in bad shape. Broken femur, broken jaw, punctured lung, broken ribs. But she's still alive. *Motherfuck*," he swore suddenly, "I've gotta call her parents right now." He pulled out his cellphone. *Shit.* Another parental nightmare.

Pacing back and forth on the snow, Whitney overheard him talking to Karis's parents. She almost felt sorry for him.

She got a text from her mom. "We didn't want to tell you before you started your competition. Would have been disastrous. Robyn had very bad seizure, Dr. Halpurn told us to take her to Children's Hospital in Denver. We're on our way."

She texted her mom back. "I'll be there ASAP."

"I'm flying to Denver," she told Trent, when he got off the phone.

"*What!*" he exclaimed, face darkening with fury. He looked wiped out. Today was too much. They didn't pay him enough for this shit.

"I have to go. Robyn's going to Children's Hospital in Denver right now, I have to go," she repeated.

"Jesus Christ, you're kidding me!" he retorted, apoplectic. What a complete clusterfuck. Karis in the hospital, now this.

"I'll buy a ticket when I get to the airport," she stated, devoid of emotion. "Duncan can give me a ride. Take all my climbing and ski gear with you to LaGrave, I'll meet you there in two weeks," she told him flatly, clicking out of her bindings, picking up her skis and walking away.

"*Jesus,*" he shook his head, totally frustrated. This was all going sideways. A complete disaster, he agonized.

Ian and Noah better pull through, he grimaced dejectedly, shoulders sagging. Whitney would never make it to La Grave in time to compete.

Like sand sliding through his fingers, the World Championship was slipping away.

# CHAPTER 29
# ROBYN

S he hurried up the crowded escalator into Denver International Airport's main terminal and made her way over to the east exits of the building to hail a taxi. Standing outdoors in the covered concrete queue, a four-door compact sedan pulled up quickly. Tossing her duffel bag into the backseat, she shuffled inside, making eye contact with the middle-aged male driver across the rearview mirror. A green, paper pine tree air freshener dangled from it, forlornly. "Where to Miss?" he asked politely, starting the meter in the front console, beside his phone.

"Children's Hospital, please."

"That's in Aurora," he nodded, pulling forward in the long line of buses, SUVs and taxis.

"Yes. Thanks," she replied quickly, leaning her head back on the black vinyl seat, exhaling. Dark outside, they were already heading onto the freeway. Runway lights and planes taking off receded in the night. She had managed to get a six thirty-five p.m. flight out of Jackson, after pleading her case with the booking agent at the airport, paying an exorbitant price for a last- minute seat. Duncan had taken her out to the regional airport, they had discussed her gear in painstaking detail.

He reassured her as he was driving, "Don't worry. I'll pack everything you left behind. All your outerwear, your climbing gear, your ski equipment- I'll take it with us to France. You just concentrate on getting through this with Robyn, okay? Then call me soon as you book your ticket."

"I'll let you know which airport I fly into, most likely it will be Lyon," she told him, distractedly.

"That's fine. I'll pick you up when you get there," he told her, calmly.


The taxi driver turned off the main road and drove into a sprawling medical complex filled with dozens of massive brick and concrete buildings and parking lots. He dropped her off at the Anschutz Children's Hospital. A whimsical figure of child holding three colorful balloons sat on the front of the modern structure near the entrance. She walked inside. Vibrant painted birds and abstract designs covered the entire main floor inside the spacious atrium. A huge glass elevator was at the center of it, she hurriedly approached the guest services counter. It was just past eight- thirty p.m.

"I believe my daughter Robyn Olson just checked in a short while ago," she told the receptionist, a dark- haired woman, breathlessly.

"Yes. She's in the Pediatric Neuroscience Center," she replied, quickly. "Take the elevator up to the second floor and check in at reception. A visitor's concierge will assist you," she added, kindly. "I'll let them know that you're your way," she lifted her phone, punching some numbers.

"Thank you," Whitney exhaled, clutching her duffel. She rushed over to the elevator.

Cindy and Tom were there waiting for her in the Neuroscience Center's guest lounge, a quiet and comfortable area filled with plush couches and chairs. Lovely pieces of art depicting animals and nature were displayed on the walls, contributing to the soothing quality of the room. Both jumped up when they saw her, she rushed over and hugged them. "I got here as fast as I could," she spilled out, breathlessly. "What exactly happened?" she tossed her duffel on the floor.

Cindy answered, a torrent of words, "We were at the house this morning, starting to watch ESPN. Dad had just come back from opening the store, Hans and Zokas came over to watch the competition. Robyn got up and had breakfast, at the table. She finished eating and then sat next to me on the sofa. A few minutes later, she just slumped over and started jerking, completely out of it. I'm telling you- this was the worst seizure she's ever had. I called Dr. Halpurn right away, he told us to get to Children's Hospital. Made the referral soon as we hung up." She exhaled, "she isn't responding to the medicine. He said it's time to take other steps."

Tom interjected, frowning, "The staff said she would undergo some tests tonight. We were waiting for you to get here, before we met with them again. I'll let them know you're here," he stated, heading over to the reception desk.

Whitney's face froze. She told her mother mechanically, "Don't worry. Everything will be fine." Robyn will be fine." She picked up a magazine.

Cindy looked at her oddly. What a bizarre response, she thought, not saying anything. What the *heck* was going on with her? She sounded completely out of it. *And what did she do to her hair?*

Tom came back and said, "they'll meet with us, shortly." He looked at Whitney more closely. Her hair was platinum blonde. When did that happen? he furrowed his brows perplexedly.

She blurted out, "I won the National Championship!" the words sounded strangely antithetical inside the quiet lounge. "I won a hundred -thousand dollars!"

"Yes! Yes! We heard!" her parents both responded, a little disoriented. "We we're driving up I-285 when we got the news. Congratulations! they hugged her again, enthusiastically. "What happened to Karis?" Tom asked. "There was something on the news. Was she injured?"

Whitney paused. Evidently, they hadn't seen the accident on TV, otherwise they would have been completely off the rails. "She uh… she's in the hospital. It's on the video," she replied detachedly. "I have to go see Robyn," she stated, walking over to the reception desk. A man and woman wearing long white lab coats came out the double doors leading into the neuroscience wing. They greeted her. "Are you Robyn's mother?"

"Uh, yes," she answered, standing still.

"I'm doctor Latham," the man introduced himself, "and this is my colleague, Dr. Davis. We need to discuss your daughter's prognosis, the medical procedures she'll be undergoing. May we talk?"

"Yes, yes! Of course. My parents are here too." Whitney waved them over, disembodied. She couldn't *slow down*, her mind kept picturing Karis barreling towards her, skiing her into the wall… her body careening across the snow, the sound of her screams as she tumbled down the mountainside, crashing to the ground…. Nervously, she tapped her foot against the floor and chewed her lips, wanting to bolt. Somehow, she had to pull it together.

*Re-entry,* she told herself.

*Get it together, get it together,* she chanted inside her head. *Get. It. Together.*

"So, Robyn has what we would characterize as drug resistant epilepsy," Dr. Davis started, her voice had a pleasant, almost musical ring to it. African American, her hair was knotted at the base of her neck in an elegant chignon.

"Over the next several days, we'll need to run a series of tests to locate the source of her seizures," she explained. "One is called a video EEG, which requires that we put surgically placed electrodes on her brain. We will need your permission of course, in order to do the procedure."

The three of them nodded, slightly dazed.

Dr. Latham spoke, explaining, "We will also run a SPECT test, single-photon emission computerized tomography, that allows us to measure the blood flow in her brain during a seizure. This will help us with diagnoses. When Robyn was admitted this afternoon, she was in a very strong post ictal state- having difficulty speaking, disoriented, lethargic. Tomorrow morning when you visit her, she'll be more alert and able to communicate." He added, "you'll also meet with Dr. Laghari, the other neurosurgeon on our team. He can provide more information about her tests and what our next steps will be," he took a breath, "do you have any questions?" It was a lot to digest.

Whitney inhaled quickly, "do you think she will require surgery? What are the risks?"

Dr. Davis answered her, thoughtfully. "We have studied Robyn's previous EEG's and CT scans, which show that she had some abnormal tissue in her occipital lobe. Because her seizures have worsened

**308**

and have not responded to medication, there *is* a likelihood that surgery may be advisable. Sometimes there is a poor delineation between the grey and white matter interface in the brain, and that can disrupt the neuro pathways, causing focal cortical thickening. Lesions can interrupt and interfere with normal neuron behavior, as well. Here at Children's Hospital, we have found that surgical excision or resection can often provide good outcomes and profoundly improve the life of the patient." She took a deep breath, "however, there are risks associated with surgery, and that is something you have to consider."

Dr. Latham leaned forward, "she could experience problems with her memory, or her ability to understand and use language. One of the associated and significant risks with surgery in the occipital lobe is visual field defect, which is a consideration. She could lose some of her normal vision. Other risks are depression, mood changes, headache, and in some worse cases, stroke."

Whitney swallowed. Dr. Belcic's face entered her mind. Belgrade. The procedure. It all came back.

"On the other hand, if she continues on without treatment, she will unfortunately have developmental delays, worsening memory and thinking skills, possible depression and anxiety," Dr. Davis explained further. "And there is the risk of physical injury or even death if she were to drown, or fall, for example. You'll need to weigh those risks against the risks of surgery, which is always difficult."

Tom spoke up, apprehensive, "Tomorrow we can meet with Dr. Laghari and learn more about her condition. Let's not jump to any conclusions until we find out more and hear more from him." He looked exhausted.

"Absolutely," they nodded. Dr. Davis told them, "You'll be staying at our Family Resource Center, near the Neuroscience Center for the duration of her treatment, so we'll have many opportunities to meet again and discuss things." She looked around the lounge, "in fact, a guest liaison should be here soon. They'll help you get settled in."

It was getting late, fatigue washed over Tom and Cindy. Whitney's thoughts raced around in circles like a bicycle in a velodrome. *This is going to cost a fortune! I need to be training, how will I compete in France* with *Robyn in the hospital, oh shit, oh shit, oh shit!* She glanced at her cellphone. A hundred messages sat in her inbox. She started sifting through them.

Luann, imperious. "Would you please call and tell me what's going on. Is Robyn alright? You should *not* be going to the World Championship in my opinion. Kyle would be appalled."

Zokas, "hey, geeeve me a call. Hope Robyn's okay. Congratulations on your ween!"

Hans. Gravelly voice, formal. "Hello. This is Hans. I am worried about Robyn. Please let me know how she is, when you have the opportunity. Congratulations on winning the National Championship. I knew you would do it, Whitney."

Trent, terse. "Consumco needs you to call them ASAP. They need to discuss product endorsements and their advertising campaign for the new EnrG bar. Call them please. Then call me. By the way, I have a check for a hundred-thousand dollars with your name on it from the American Freeriding Association. Call me."

Alyn, "People magazine reached out to me, they want to do a piece about Robyn and you at the hospital. I told them I would get back to them right away, would you please call soon as possible... hope Robyn's okay."

Shenti, muffled. "Uh...hello Whitney...I heard about Robyn, hope you both are alright ...uh, good luck."

Naturally, nothing from Ian.

The messages went on and on. ESPN wanted an interview with her about Karis's accident, Sports Illustrated wanted to write a feature, Powder magazine needed a cover shot for their next issue....

Wearily she turned off her phone and padded around the Family Resource Center in her pajamas, getting acquainted with her new living quarters. It was surprisingly comfortable and well- appointed wing in the hospital, with a full kitchen and dining area, spacious lounge and workspace. She even had her own private bathroom. Suddenly ravenous, she dialed up food service on the hospital phone and ordered a ham sandwich and chicken soup from the cafeteria. They told her an orderly would bring it up shortly. Disappearing into her bedroom, she called Duncan.

"Hey, it's me. What's going on? I'm at the hospital."

"Oh jeez...hey, it's *nuts*. After you left Jackson they had a major party at the lodge, everyone stoked about your win. Disappointed that you had to leave, of course... Alyn and I got up and announced you had a family emergency. The press was all over that in a second, they wanted to know what was going on." He caught his breath, "Karis is at the hospital in Jackson, it's a mess. Trent and Alyn are over there right now, waiting for her parents to arrive. I can tell he's freaked out about you being gone. He put Annette Stahl on as an alternate for La Grave--just wanted to give you a heads up... The men's competition starts tomorrow. I'll keep you posted. Say, how is Robyn?" he asked, earnestly.

"She's having some tests done tonight. We're all at the Pediatric Neuroscience Center in Aurora, it's one of the best places in the country. Tomorrow we'll meet with another specialist. I'll tell you more later," Whitney replied, tired. She'd eat her food then go to bed.

"Glad you called. Good luck with everything," he added graciously, they ended the call.

*Thank God for Duncan,* she sighed, internally. He was an island of calm in a sea of crazy.


Dr. Laghari met with them at one p.m. in the neuroscience lounge, they all shook hands, sitting down in a huddle. He got straight to the point, "Our tests indicate that Robyn has occipital cortical dysplasia. We have determined that we can do laser interstitial thermal therapy, called LITT to destroy a small portion of her brain tissue. We'll use MRI to guide a laser to remove the tissue, it is less invasive than regular surgery," he informed them, a strong British accent. "She will need to spend the first night after surgery in the intensive care unit and at least four more nights in the hospital for observation and testing. We'll need to do a series of post- surgical tests and brain mapping to determine the efficacy of the surgery and its after- effects," he added, looking at the three of them. They were listening solemnly, wringing their hands. Whitney asked him, "Does this mean she can stop taking the medicine, afterwards?"

"Unfortunately, no. She will need to continue taking the medicine indefinitely, although that could certainly subside over time, as we would anticipate that her seizures should greatly diminish. Our child-life specialist will help her navigate her new, baseline state. Robyn will continue to need ongoing evaluations and medical care here to monitor her condition over the long term," he explained, his dark, almost black eyes meeting theirs, serious. East Indian, he had brown skin and exceptionally white teeth. Whitney found herself distracted by them in a puzzling way. She was having trouble concentrating, her thoughts misfiring, jumbly. He continued, "I have every reason to expect a positive outcome for her. She should respond very well to the surgery," he added, reassuringly.

Whitney nodded. "Can we visit her today?" she tried to sound normal.

"Yes, of course. You may see her soon. Check in with the nurse's station, they can direct you to her room. I presume we will be going forward with surgery?" he inquired, looking at the three of them.

"Yes," Whitney answered.

"Very good. Tomorrow morning, we will prep her for surgery and use general anesthesia, just so you know. She will be in the ICU afterwards, for recovery," he added.

Cindy asked him, anxiously, "What should we do for her after surgery? Will she be in pain?"

He answered empathetically, "Robyn's head will likely be a little swollen painful, she will need to use icepacks and painkillers and maybe some narcotics. It will be several months before she'll be strong enough to go back to school and engage in her usual activities. Our staff will make sure you are provided with all the information you need for her post-surgical care, following her procedure." He smiled, patiently, "I understand your concerns. We are all working together to make sure she has the very best outcome possible."

Cindy and Tom frowned, nodding. Whitney bit her lip, paralyzed. How could she possibly expect her parents to do all this for her and Robyn? Pay for all this care? She stared at the walls, immobilized.

Cindy confronted her in the cafeteria during lunch. "Would you please tell me what the heck is going on, Whitney?" she sounded angry. "You have been so...*emotionless* since we got here. I don't get it, and I'm not liking what I see. I can't do all the heavy lifting here; I need you to be more engaged with us. It's like you're not even on this planet, she added, frustrated.

"I'm sorry, mom. I really am."

You don't sound sorry."

"I *am* sorry," she pleaded, contrite. This hospital was suffocating, she needed to be in the mountains, preparing for La Grave. Cindy frowned and shook her head, irritated, eating her lasagna. "Bring a sandwich upstairs to your dad," she told Whitney, tiredly. "He's trying to run the store on zoom, the employees aren't used to him being away this long."

She stood in a bathroom stall and called MaryAnn. "I'm going crazy," she whispered into the phone. "We're at the hospital, Robyn needs surgery. I think I'm going insane."

"You are not going insane, Whitney," MaryAnn responded, instantly. "I watched your competition; you are under tremendous pressure. Anybody in your situation would feel that way," she added, sympathetically.

"I mean, I can't *relate* to people...or my family..." Whitney fretted. "My head is in two different places. If I don't ski and train right now, I probably won't win. If I don't win, I won't make money to pay for Robyn's medical bills. It's total madness," she ruminated. "I'm literally climbing out of my skin here."

"Listen to me Whitney, our organization has a counselor right there, in the hospital. Go talk with them. They can help you figure out a payment program and all that insurance stuff, they do it all the time. Promise me that you'll meet with someone there today," MaryAnn insisted, alarmed. "Okay?"

"Okay, I will," Whitney sighed. "Thanks for listening, I appreciate it," she hung up. Rummaging in her purse, she found her vial of ANTm3 and put it up to her nose, taking a deep, sustained whiff into each nostril. The spray hit the back of her throat with its familiar metallic taste, she exhaled slowly and leaned against the metal stall, waiting for the effects of the drug to kick in. *This* was what she needed. No counselor was going to fix her problem. How could they? She was a total wreck.

Wanly, Robyn looked up from the hospital bed as Whitney and her parents entered her room. Parts of her head had been shaved; several bald spots sat at the back of her skull. She sat propped up, under the blankets.

"Hey sweetie, it's mommy!" Whitney knelt by her side, kissing her cheek, tenderly. "Grandma and Grandpa are here too. We have a present for you." They handed her a soft, furry stuffed teddy bear. The three sat down next to her bed and visited with her, she looked tired.

"The doctors are going to take great care of you, honey. You won't feel anything during the whole procedure, okay?" Whitney told her soothingly, caressing her cheek. "We'll be here the whole time. And after you're all done, you'll be able to go home and rest. So don't worry about a thing, alright?" she added, anxiously.

"Did you win, mommy?" Robyn asked, sleepily, eyelids half-open.

"Yes, I did, honey."

"Wowee mommy, I knew you would," she proclaimed happily, hugging the bear.

"You get some rest now, we'll be right outside," Whitney told her. "Hans sends his love, so does Grandpa Jack and Grandma Luann. I talked with Miss Abrams and Mrs. Hennessey; everyone is excited to see you when you get home."

"I love you, mommy," Robyn's eyelids fluttered, then closed.

The days and nights at the hospital melted into one another, trips to the cafeteria, naps in the lounge, consults with doctors and nurses, visits with Robyn while she was awake. The surgery had gone successfully, she was released from the ICU and brought back to the neuroscience wing for recovery. Dr. Laghari was cautiously upbeat about her condition, he spoke to Whitney afterward by Robyn's bedside.

"She's doing very well at this juncture," he told her, they were four days out from the surgery, "I expect her swelling to diminish and for her pain to subside over the next several days," he stood next to her, examining her surgical site, covered with bandages. "She will need a great deal of rest over the next several months, it will likely take six months to fully recover. We always worry about complications after surgery, of course, and we'll need to do a series of brain mapping tests before she's discharged, including those for visual field defects. I would like her to stay here for at least another week, given that you live so far away," he concluded, nodding at Whitney.

A nurse entered, wheeling in a tray of macaroni and cheese, apple juice and an oatmeal cookie into the room.

"Will her vision be alright?" Whitney pressed him, chest constricting. It was what she worried about the most.

"It is possible that she may experience some visual deficits, however; you should know that the brain is an incredible organ," Dr.

Laghari reassured her. "With enough therapy, it can rewire nerve cells to allow undamaged brain regions to take over the functions of damaged ones. We see children who had previous neural deficits recover their ability to see, hear, read, learn a musical instrument, process information… I find it fascinating," he added, as he started to exit the room.

"What about fear?" Whitney asked him, suddenly.

"Fear?" Dr. Lagheri paused, "That's a huge area, unto itself. You'll need to be more specific," he looked at Whitney. "I heard you were a professional skier. One of our staff mentioned you just won the National Championship in free skiing. Congratulations. I must say, that's amazing."

"Thanks. I did," she replied, a little self-consciously. "What I wondered, is, uh…what if someone had, for example, um, a brain injury where the amygdala no longer felt fear--like the neurons no longer had a pathway to that part of the brain, anymore. Could they get that emotion back?" she stammered, wanting to talk to him.

"Hmm, that's an interesting way of putting it…" he considered, a little puzzled, "If some pathways are severed, other parts of the brain can learn to compensate for those deficits. We're always discovering new technologies and techniques for repairing brain damage, it's an ever-evolving field of study. In fact, we're learning that gene therapy may change the perception of fear and emotions within the human brain as well," he answered, helpfully. She appeared to be extremely interested in his reply.

Whitney frowned, "I just wondered… that's all…thanks."

"You're welcome," he smiled pleasantly.

Robyn had been asleep for the past twenty minutes, her eyes fluttered open. "I'm hungry," she announced, eyeing the tray. Whitney scooted it over and raised her up to a seating position in the bed. "Macaroni and cheese, today," she commented.

"It's cold," she lamented.

"I'll go downstairs and bring up anything you want. Do you want soup? A sandwich? How about spaghetti? Whitney offered.

"Chicken noodle soup. With crackers."

"Okay. No problem," Whitney smiled, cheerfully, the ANTm3 was doing miracles. She felt less disjointed, more empathetic, more *herself*. What would happen if she ran out of it, though? Would she have to contact Belcic? Get refills from Trent? she shuddered, thinking about the prospect.

"I'll bring back some soup and we can read books together, if you want," Whitney told her. "Or do some coloring. Or listen to music," she suggested, brightly.

"I want to listen to violin music," Robyn replied, emphatically.

"Okay. We'll find some on my cellphone when I come back, then," she hugged her gently.

Cindy and Tom were in the Family Resource Center, zooming with their employees. She popped in on them on her way down to the cafeteria. "Do you guys want anything? I'm going to get food," she offered.

"Not right now, we're working," Tom answered, glancing up from the computer. Cindy shook her head.

"Okay. I'll be with Robyn," she replied, ducking out. Later today she'd need to tell them she was going to La Grave. Her career depended on it.

Her phone pinged, a text from Trent. "Ian just won the men's division National Championship. Noah, second place. He'll be going to La Grave with us as Ian's alternate. Don't forget your passport, Whitney. We'll pick you up at arrivals when you get to the airport. Call me, goddamn it."

"How 'bout we listen to Beethoven?" she returned to Robyn's room with a tray of food.

"Yes! I love him!"

She googled Beethoven violin music on her cell phone. Raptly, they listened to his Kreutzer Sonata, while Robyn ate.

"What would you think if I took violin lessons with you and Miss Abram's when we get back?" she posed, thoughtfully.

"I love that idea, mommy. We could play together!" her eyes lit up, happily.

"We could. I love that idea, too," she agreed, nodding.

Sitting companionably for a while longer, Whitney told her, somberly, "I need to leave for France tomorrow to compete in the World Extreme Ski Competition. It's my last event. When I get home, I'll be with you for a good long stretch, just so you know. Grandma and Grandpa will stay with you here at the hospital until it's time to leave." She explained gently, "You're going to be fine. The doctors say you're doing really good; that the surgery went great. I'm sorry I have to go while you're here honey, but it's my job," she sighed, frowning. *It's how I'm going to pay for all this…*

"I know, mommy," Robyn took her hand. "Please don't die, mommy, we have to play violins," she stated plaintively, lower lip quivering. Tears formed in her eyes.

Stomach knotting, a coat of sweat flushed over Whitney's body. In eighteen hours, she would be boarding a United Airlines Airbus enroute to Lyon, leaving her daughter behind. Leaning over, she kissed Robyn's cheek and looked straight into her eyes. "I will not die," she told her, firmly. "I promise."

# CHAPTER 30
# LA GRAVE

D uncan steered the black Mercedes van through congested narrow streets, making their way through blocks of ornate and imposing fifteenth- century cream- colored buildings lining the waterfront. Trent sat beside him in the passenger seat tapping his foot distractedly against the floor as they cruised past the heart of Lyon's central district, heading southeast towards the Hautes-Alpes region in France. For several hours, Whitney slouched drowsy and jet-lagged in the van's back seat, gazing out its tinted windows at the small, charming villages replete with stone houses and narrow cobbled streets along the way. As the terrain grew increasingly more rural and rugged, she saw the majestic, towering mountains of Ecrins National Park loom ever larger above the terraced, snow-covered meadows. Mt. Blanc, La Meije, Verbier, Grandes Jorasses; legendary peaks she had always dreamed of climbing and skiing, but never had the opportunity to visit until now. Five p.m., the sun was setting, darkness settling in. Beneath the dusky shadows, massive hanging glaciers and toothy peaks lined the steeply walled valley. Trent turned his body to face her in the backseat. "How was your flight?" he asked, finally.

"I slept all the way to Frankfort," she answered a little fuzzily. "The five- hour layover there was no fun, but the flight on to Lyon was fairly easy. I'm totally zonked, though."

"I figured you would be," he replied, nodding. "Tonight, just get something to eat and get some sleep. If you have the energy, we can do some skiing tomorrow afternoon. You won't believe La Grave," he added, shaking his head. "There's this old-time pulse gondola that goes to the top, it's the *only* lift in the entire ski area. Takes thirty minutes to get to the glacier at the summit and half the day to ski down, I kid you not." He went on, "I spoke to the event officials- told them about your circumstances, asked them if we could move your competition slot to later this week. It'll give you some extra time to acclimate."

"Thanks. I could definitely use it," she replied.

"Here's the plan," he said, voice growing in intensity, "the heli will take you to the very top of Girose Glacier with the judges. They'll deposit you there, then track you down the mountain from above. Only two women per day will compete because the runs are so long. The two highest scoring finalists will ski Glacier de la Girose for the World Championship. The entire women's competition should take five days, weather permitting," he finished.

Trent sounded animated, agitated. Whitney's absence had totally stressed him out. The last several months he had come to realize Ian was not as proficient a climber as she was, that she was their best hope to win the Championship.

Whitney nodded, fatigue assailing her, his words a blur of distorted sounds.

"There's more we need to discuss," he went on, oblivious to her fatigue, "You'll need to select your route for the semi-final. Have you decided on one yet?"

Whitney nodded, "I have," she answered fixedly, "I'm going to ski Glacier de la Meije, descent des Enfetchores."

"Holy Christ," he frowned, "that's the most difficult, dangerous route on the entire mountain, Whitney. We'll have to see if the conditions are even safe enough to do it. It might not be possible," he added, shaking his head.

*Of course* she would choose Enfetchores, he thought inwardly. She was a ringer; it had just taken him a little extra time to figure that out.

"I've studied the terrain all summer long with Hans," she replied, voice stoic. "Memorized every classic route and established line I could get my hands on. The most successful descents have occurred in February when it's super cold out and there's ample snow. Conditions should be ideal right now. The avalanche danger should be relatively low," she finished, shutting her eyes.

Trent grimaced, he'd already witnessed enough mayhem and death this season. Never imagined he'd be trying to dissuade his national champion from skiing this suicide mission.

"By the way, how is Karis?" she inquired, detached.

"She's alive. But she won't be skiing again for a long time," he answered, dour.

Whitney shifted in her seat, "I'm up against the best European women on the planet here. Marie Aubaurer of Austria, Anna Fischer of Germany…Vivienne Aubert of France. The only way I'm going to distinguish myself with these judges is to ski the most challenging route better than anyone else. I did not fly out here to play it safe and fritter this opportunity away. To win WESC, I'll have to put every-thing on the line," she finished, resolutely.

She was right, of course, and they both knew it.

Duncan glanced through the rearview mirror at Whitney, lips turned down. He worried about her, though he couldn't say it, overtly. There was too much at stake for all of them. Over a million dollars, sponsorships, advertising contracts, her daughter's medical expenses. No wonder she felt so much pressure to win. Silent, he kept driving.

Trent was quiet, a few moments. "I have to think about it," he conceded, looking out the window, eyes faraway. La Meije loomed over the valley's expanse, its blueish white glacier nestled amongst the serrated rock cliffs, sinister and foreboding. If she skied it, she would be risking her life. La Meije was a notoriously dangerous mountain. Throughout history, many alpinists had died on it. Whatever the out-come, he would have to live with his decision forever. On the other hand, if she didn't ski it, she risked being overlooked by the judges, lost in a sea of killer women who were accustomed to these insane routes. Theodore would want her to do it. Of that, he was certain.

They were nearing La Grave now, the narrow winding road pass-ing by medieval stone chalets, the forested walls of the Alps drawing closer. Duncan slowed down and turned the van into a short drive-way, its tires bumping along the icy ruts. Parking in front of the rus-tic, traditional French chalet, he killed the engine and came around the side to help her out. Completely dark outside, Whitney grabbed her duffel bag and walked through the knee- high snow to the build-ing's entrance. Inside, Ian, Noah, Shenti and Annette sat at a large wooden table in the farmhouse-style kitchen. A tray of cheese and sausage sat in the center of it with freshly baked French bread and some grapes. A fireplace flickered in the adjacent room, the smell of burning wood wafting through the quaint and warm interior.

"Hey Whitney! Good to see you! Have some food, I bet you're exhausted," Noah called over to her, pointing to a chair. He smiled warmly. Annette greeted her, asking, "how is your daughter?" genuinely concerned. It was the first time she had communicated with Whitney since their competition in Jackson Hole. She had come as a back-up, thrilled with the chance to compete. Now it seemed unlikely, she would just have to observe the huge event. Whitney dropped her duffel bag on the floor and joined them, suddenly ravenous. "She's doing well, all things considered," she answered, sitting down. "My parents should be taking her home from the hospital soon," she added, relieved to be back with her teammates. Ian removed his earbuds and set his cellphone down, in a show of recognition. She reached for a plate, filling it with hunks of food. "Honestly, I'm exhausted, these last few weeks have been brutal," she admitted, taking some bites. The cheese was delicious.

"I bet." Alyn wandered into the kitchen, joining them. She asked Whitney, "Did you get my messages? People Magazine want an interview, Powder wants an interview; Consumco needs a photo shoot with the new EnrGBar." What she really wanted was to talk to Whitney about what happened at Jackson Hole. Karis's jaw was wired shut; she was totally out of commission. She needed Whitney to shed more light on the accident.

Lately, things had gotten so bizarre on the team that she had started writing a book about it, convinced they were doping. Karis had tried to *kill* Whitney.

"Can't do it yet," Whitney shrugged her shoulders, brain in a jet-lagged stupor. "In fact, I'm going to bed. Right now." She stood up.

"Which room is mine?" she asked, to no one in particular. Alyn rose with her, guiding her to the stairway. She pointed up the wooden steps. "Your room is second door on the right," she told Whitney. "Watch your head- the ceilings are low." She followed her up the stairs, whispering furtively, "I really need to talk to you. Can we *please* talk?"

"Can't do it now," Whitney told her again, stupefied. "I'm spent." She shuffled over to a diminutive sized bedroom. There was a twin bed with a white goose down comforter in it. Falling onto the mattress, she closed her eyes instantly and sank into the black nothingness of sleep.

They spent the next four days at the base of La Grave, immersed in a beehive of international skiers, fans, coaches and publicists who had descended upon the traditional French alpine village in a non-stop frenzy of photoshoots, interviews, podcasts and promotional activities. Paparazzi swirled around the competitors, morning to night as they milled at the base of the mountain with their entourages. Renowned alpinists Carla Alarcon of Chile, Heather Case of Canada, Gianna Presutti of Italy, and Ana Honneger of Switzerland were all there. The male champions, Slovenia's Anton Kovac, Italy's Angelo Moretti, France's Renard Genet, Austria's Felix Beisteiner were convened, as well.

Legendary skiers Anna Fischer of Germany, who had selected the Pan de Redeau, an extremely steep, cliff-filled run, and Marie Aubauer, who had chosen LOrciere de Droites, an exposed, technical route with overhanging glaciers and unstable seracs, held court amongst the media and fans. To be here was to mingle with ski royalty, these skiers far more experienced the Tyrol and Hautes-Alpes than any American. Whitney felt dwarfed in their presence.

Whitney and Ian did meet and greets with Consumco executives and sponsors in a dizzying blur of photo shoots, interviews, product endorsements and autographs. As they made the rounds, Vivienne Aubert, from France, finished her run on LOrciere de Gauche, "La Vaute," and came over to the timbered lodge to join them. A bevy of onlookers and photographers welcomed her, waving French flags, erupting into shouts and cheers for their country's national champion. Like the other top five women, she had scored in the low nineties and was predicted to be a finalist.

Early Friday morning, Trent and Duncan drove Whitney to La Grave's main heliport that serviced the skiing and climbing area in the Ecrins Mountain Range during the summer and winter months. Parking the van near the long, austere stone building they got out and unloaded her equipment beside the snow-covered pad. Gusts of light wind swept through the valley floor. Sixteen degrees Fahrenheit outside, a cluster of white cloud hovered over the summit of La Meije, obscuring the top thousand feet. Trent had begrudgingly relented to let Whitney ski Glacier de la Meije, descent des Enfetchores, after repeatedly analyzing the weather forecast and discussing snow conditions with local experts. They had assured him the course was viable, snowpack relatively stable right now. The seven -thousand-foot vertical drop was a frightening prospect for nearly anyone who viewed its avalanche prone walls. Except for professional ski mountaineers, few people ever attempted to go down it.

The judges, two men and two women from France, Austria, Switzerland and Italy, extreme ski champions and world- class mountaineers in their own right; sat waiting for Whitney inside the burly Bell 407, its blades rotating in a blurry roar. A French videographer from BBC sat perched at the window, his long, telephoto lens poised at the ready. Footage of her descent would be live- streamed throughout Europe, Asia, North and South America, in addition to other countries throughout the world. Whitney's sole objective was to make the descent down La Meije as dazzling as possible.

In four hours, Gianna Presutti would take this same helicopter to the summit. She would ski down her chosen route, the steep and formidable Glacier du Tabuchet.


Both Trent and Duncan had been up since dawn, checking all her equipment with obsessive care. "You'll be in radio contact with the heli pilot and me," Trent told her, tersely. "If anything happens, we'll send a rescue team to assist you. Your backpack is too full and heavy to do more than one single rotation in any aerial. This time, no double flips, understand?"

"Okay," she had nodded.

"Duncan, check her transceiver, make sure it's full battery," Trent chewed his left cheek.

"I already checked it multiple times."

"Check it again. And then check her pack. She needs to have three quarts of water, ten chemical heat packs and six energy bars. Rope," he stated, with a concentrated frown.

"I put a 40- foot rope inside her pack."

"Shovel. Probe, ice axe, headlamp."

"They're there," Duncan answered.

"Harness. Extra clips, nuts, carabiners.

"Check."

"Skins, crampons, RAD Petzl Kit, binoculars."

"Check," he replied, touching everything again, carefully.

Over the thundering noise of the helicopter, Duncan handed her her Atomic skis and Leki poles, then knelt down to click her electric boot warmers on. "Good luck," he told her, locking eyes. She nodded back. Face obscured by her balaclava and reflective goggles, she gave him and Trent a high five. Bright EnrGBar, 4Tress logos were emblazoned across both sides of her black helmet, her name printed in big block letters across her yellow identification bib. Han's reindeer pin was attached to her parka's lapel, she touched it for good luck. Walking to the helicopter, she gave a last departing thumbs up to Trent and Duncan, then climbed inside.

As they rose upward and lifted off, Whitney shivered nervously, each sway and dip of the machine bringing forth waves of anxiety and apprehension, the ANTm3 still coursing through her bloodstream. Though she had taken the last whiff of it in Denver over a week ago, the drug's side effects lingered on, hitting her with the unwelcome sensations at the worst possible time.

The heli hovered, depositing her atop the Glacier de la Girose. Up at this lofty elevation, the wind was blowing more forcefully, temperature a frigid three degrees Fahrenheit. Clouds undulated over the white expanse, the flat light making it harder to distinguish features on the snow. Ducking her head, she grabbed her skis and poles from the heli's exterior rack and shuffled away from its whirling blades and thunderous growl. Taking a moment to look around, she made note of the Belledonne Massif, Aravis and Thabor, the gaping crevasses that marked the Meije and Rateau Glaciers with their deep, sinewy gashes. With a deep breath, she clicked on her skis, adjusted her poles and then pushed off the snow, heading towards Enfetchores.

A trickle of trepidation crept up her spine, tingling her nervous system like an electric live wire. This run had the potential to be a whole new level of scary with the ANTm3, she exhaled, nervously. Gathering speed, she glided smoothly across the glacier, carving purposeful turns towards Couloir de la Meije. Immediately, she caught air off a large, natural feature, executing a graceful 360 rotation, landing flawlessly. Skiing swiftly down the fall line to the couloir, she stopped and snapped off her skis, retrieving her crampons from her pack with practiced ease. After attaching them to her boots, she clipped her skis and poles back onto her backpack and crouched down, clipping her harness onto the fixed rope. She lowered herself down quickly, abseiling into the hundred and fifty- foot couloir and dangled over the vertical drop, surrounded by walls of ice- encrusted schist inside the narrow tube. Descending efficiently, she kicked the tips of her boots into the hard packed snow and began going down the chasm with powerful, self-assured steps. To control her heart rate, she methodically counted numbers. One-two-three-four-five, inhale. One-two-three -four-five, exhale; remembering Zokas' instructions. At the bottom now, she felt a level platform of icy rock and paused to turn and look, assessing her position.

La Meije; the gigantic, concave glacier unfolded beneath her, its surface a maze of towering seracs and hidden crevasses glinting in the sunlight. She gasped, dwarfed by its size. Quickly, she undid her crampons and put them into her pack, retrieving her skis and poles, snapping them on. Unclipping her harness, she skied down the center of the glacier and veered right, making quick forceful turns in the deep, powder snow, avoiding the crevasses in her path. Slough blew up around her face, clouding her goggles. Relying on the internal map in her head, she rocketed down its face, making split-second decisions on the best and safest line. An enormous snow buttress loomed ahead at glacier's base, she instantly performed a perfect front- somersault off a medium-sized cliff before reaching it, her backpack's extra weight a noticeable impediment for gaining lift. Landing with a balanced "whumph" into the slope, she pointed her tips down and flew on, reaching the base of the buttress. She came to a stop. Almost forty minutes had gone by since she left the heli, she estimated. From this spot, she would begin the next technical aspect of the route.

Taking off her skis, she opened her pack and retrieved her crampons and ice-axe, again. She would have to boot climb a two-hundred and fifty- foot incline of snow and ice up a forty-degree narrow ridge on the side of La Meije to the next point of her route. Hefting her skis and pack onto her back quickly, she kept one pole in her left hand and ice axe in the other, thrusting them violently into the crusty snow and ice with each step up the mountainside. Legs burning, chest heaving, clouds and wind nipped at her heels, blowing white granules against her goggles. She was thirsty but couldn't stop. Couldn't look down. Four thousand vertical feet dropped beneath her, a staggering void of endless rock cliff and ribbons of snow and ice. The helicopter hovered above her, its dark and hulking form a constant companion. Terror flooded her body. It took every ounce of concentration to keep it in check, fend off a full-fledged panic attack.

Count. Breath. Don't look down, she muttered over and over.

At the top of her destination, she removed her crampons, attaching her skis while balancing on a knife ridge composed of steep snow and rock. Now, she would be skiing down the tongue of the glacier, a harrowing chasm of ice and rock wall that funneled thousands of feet below. Taking some deep swigs of water, she balanced herself on the ridge, preparing to ski down the fall line for the next two hundred feet. Making some hard kick turns, she dropped into the chasm, skiing down to the next fixed rope along the cliff wall. Another twenty minutes had gone by.

The route was narrowing to a single chute only several feet across. Aghast, she realized the fixed rope was missing.

*What the FUCK!* she almost wept. Her heart was hammering so hard she thought it would explode. There was another thousand feet of rock and snow below her on this section. This was the route, but the rope was gone!

She gritted her teeth. No rope. This was so utterly fucked! Still in her skis, poised at the top of the chute, she gathered her wits. Forty feet of rope sat coiled, in her backpack. She took off her pack and retrieved it, along her lightweight climbing nuts and carabiners. Tying a series of knots, she attached her harness to the rope and detached her skis. Putting her crampons back on, she grabbed her ice axe, reattached her skis and poles to her pack, put her pack on, and then began gingerly lowering herself down the chute. Placing a nut into a rock crag for protection, her hands numb from the exposure to the elements, she kept going. Loose snow rained down on her head from above.

Swiftly, she worked her way down the abyss. At some point, she would run out of rope and need to free climb the rest of the way down, if necessary. A terrifying thought, she considered, swallowing. She could probably stay put and be rescued, but it would be a shitstorm like none other and absolutely torpedo her chances of winning. And her parents would probably kill her, she laughed ironically, like a crazy person going to the gallows.

The word Hans had used kept running through her head. Desensitization, desensitization...What the hell was she doing here? she muttered, surreally, taking stock of her surroundings. Walls of white, rock and ice.

Five feet of rope were left on her abseil, she looked for a place to stand up. Scooting over to the lip of the chute, she found a small patch of snow and climbed onto it, sitting for a few seconds on her haunches. From here, she could see all the way down to the forest below. Taking some deep, calming breaths, she retrieved her binoculars and studied the terrain, searching for a line. The helicopter was still hovering above. Spotting an uninterrupted ribbon of snow that led to the base of the mountain, she put her skis back on and tucked away her crampons and ice axe, then traversed seventy feet over to an opening on the fifty-five -degree face.

With total relief, she dropped in, carving clean, powerful turns down towards the end of the glacier's spiny tongue. Here, barren larch trees greeted her as she flew into the snowy forest. An almost preternatural calm came over her now. She was through the worst of it, skiing through the tall trees with exact precision, gaining more speed by the minute. The forest opened to a wide glade; she saw a kicker on a mound of snow and crouched down for the set-up, executing a backflip, twist off its lip. Landing perfectly, she skied on.

Halfway down the mountainside now, she glanced ahead. A long, treeless ridge beckoned ahead; she used the opportunity to ski even faster. At the bottom of ridge, she entered another glade. Trees packed densely close together, she bobbed and swiveled around their trunks, branches lashing at her face. It took every ounce of concentration to ski through them without losing control. Arriving at a lower basin that funneled into a narrow gully, she skied rapidly through the thinning trees to a clearing. Here, she stopped momentarily to access her location, searching for the main road on the valley floor. The helicopter still hovered above her, its rotors reverberated noisily across the rugged expanse. She radioed Trent and Duncan to notify them of her location, then pushed off her poles and flew down towards the road. Within a matter of minutes, they pulled up in the van to meet her.

Trent's face was ashen. "I can't believe what I just witnessed," he shook his head, blanching. "Thank god you made it down that chute in one piece," he exclaimed, tersely. Duncan was speechless, eyes wide open like he had just seen a ghost. He grabbed her skis, clapped the snow off them. "Jeez, Whitney, that was totally insane! I almost shit myself, watching you."

"Well, I survived it," she announced brightly, in response to his uncharacteristic, profane candor. "It was the most terrifying run of my entire life though, I'm not gonna lie," she added, climbing into the van, still gulping air, chest heaving.

Trent stared at her with newfound awe. They drove back to the base, dazed, quiet.


For the rest of the week, they watched the remaining women competitors ski down their runs, impatiently pouring over the judges scores and comments with obsessive fervor. Word was out that Whitney had descended La Meije faster than any woman in history, that she had conquered the beast with more finesse than most Europeans. She held her breath, suspended. By some miracle, things were coming together.

On Friday, at five p.m. the judges announced the two top scores. Marie Aubauer, 96. Whitney Olson, 99.

She had just won the Women's Finals. Tomorrow, she would be skiing for the World Championship.

# CHAPTER 31
# LA GRAVE ~ THE WORLD CHAMPIONSHIP

Time; 11 a.m.

Altitude; 3568 m. (11,706 feet). North Facing Slope. Vertical drop, 2400 m.

Location: Top of Dome de la Lauze, Glacier dela Girose, La Grave, France. Technical Difficulty; Exposed Traverses, Complex route finding, crevasses.

Weather: Winds calm, 3 degrees Fahrenheit. Cirrus clouds, with sunshine. Forecast; dry, no precipitation.

Whitney stood still gazing out onto the magnificent and vast glacier, an open expanse offering seemingly limitless routes down its wide bowls and endless steeps. Spectacular moraines, chutes, ridges beckoned in the distance, promising an unforgettable day on top its cathedral of riches. Glacier de la Girose was considered possibly the biggest, boldest alpine ski run in the entire world, the crown jewel for those seeking epic lines, off-piste runs on planet Earth. Her radio crackled. A message from an event official came over the receiver.

"At 11:15 Marie will begin her descent," he announced briskly, with a heavy French accent. The man was stationed a quarter mile away, standing next to Marie on the other side of Dome de la Lauze. He continued speaking over the radio, "You are to start your descent at precisely 11:25 a.m. Good luck."

She responded, "Roger, message received," she glanced at her watch.

Ten minutes.

Marie had selected an entirely different route down the glacier, it was unlikely they would cross paths, the area between them so huge. It was only at the glacier's tongue that their routes would converge, a narrow funnel emptying down to narrow couloir, straight down the middle. At the base of the couloir, their routes would separate again as they each threaded down two goliath mountainsides plastered with trees, rock walls and vertical cliffs.

She had been dismayed to learn that the judges would be observing them simultaneously from a helicopter last night, the system conjuring terrible memories of when Karis had nearly skied her into the rock wall at Jackson Hole. Trent kept reassuring her it would be okay. "This is very different, Whitney. You'll each be descending ten minutes apart from different points at the top. And there's so much terrain, you probably won't even see her. After a period of discussion, Whitney felt better about the arrangement. The whole fiasco with Karis had been a unique one-off, it would never happen again.

Trent, Duncan and she had spent the whole afternoon yesterday sorting through her backpack, replacing the rope, nuts and carabiners she had left behind on Le Meije. Duncan drove to the local climbing store in the village to purchase the supplies, searching the exact items. It wasn't until early this morning that he had finally located a prusik cord, that she was ready to go. Standing atop the glacier now, the twenty-five- pound pack tugged at her shoulders. They had included more water, the extra weight reminding her of last week's near disaster. She hadn't communicated with anyone back home about it, too shook up by the terrifying ordeal to even talk about it.

Waiting for the official's command, she touched Han's reindeer pin on her lapel, prayed for good luck.


The official's voice crackled over her radio, it was time to descend. The Bell 407 hovered raptor-like over the glacier now, its rotors echoing across the mountain with a sinister, low frequency vibration. Pushing into the untracked powder, she accelerated quickly and skied over a series of uneven bumps and knolls, per-forming a back- tuck flip off a roller, landing squarely over her skis. Staying on the fall-line, she threaded her way down a narrow chasm with seracs on both sides, their towering edifices much too close for comfort. Getting past them fast as possible, she rocketed towards a snowy ridge that divided the glacier into two halves. The right side led to a nine-hundred-foot cliff, with no skiable route down, she remembered, picturing her map, internally. She stayed left, and zoomed down the glacier avoiding the treacherous rocks, clumps of ice littering the terrain. Now knee- deep in increasingly heavier and deeper snow, she made hard, short turns towards the glacier's tongue, slough flying up behind her.

She skidded to a stop at the top of a narrow chute that dropped three hundred feet to the glacier's next hanging plateau, ice scraping under her skis, catching her edges. Here, polar blue jumbles of ice, boulders and loose rock converged to a narrow opening, surrounded by rock wall. Pausing, she took several moments to consider her route down, side slipping to the edge of the chute and searching for a line. Spotting it, she executed a kick turn then glided off the chute's edge, launching thirty feet into the air. Dropping into the chasm in a low, crouched stance, she landed, driving hard, aggressive turns on her edges into the crusty snow. Establishing her balance, she flew down the remaining half of the chute at high speed, tips pointed straight down.

A voice was coming over her radio, shouting. Now two voices- male; female. French and Austrian accents. "*Emergency*! Emergency! Alert! Crevasse! Crevasse!"

She tried to decelerate. Inertia pulled her down further, despite her efforts to stop. Another male voice. Was it the pilot? she wondered, panicking. The heli was hovering almost directly above her head now, the sound of it deafening. She could barely understand anything they said above the roar.

"Marie fell into a crevasse! You must stop and render aid immediately!" the man commanded, over her radio. Now a female voice. Was it Marie? It was muffled, barely intelligible. "*Help!* I think I broke my leg!" The radio crackled with static, Whitney couldn't make out any more of the communications. On the plateau now, she was able to finally able to decelerate and stop. She searched for Marie's tracks, looking for any clues to where she was on the glacier. The pilot was speaking to her over the radio again. "We have contacted help. You must wait for the rescue team." The voice sounded French.

Whitney froze, not moving. Extricating her binoculars from her backpack's side pocket, she carefully searched the expanse of the snow looking for a crack, a fissure, a hint of translucent blue.

A single ski pole met her eyes, about forty feet away. A dark gash in the glacier. Was that it? she shuddered, adrenaline pulsing through her body. Clicking her own skis off, she thrust the rear tips into the snow and opened her pack, taking out her crampons and headlamp. Putting them on, she grabbed her rope and attached one end to her harness. With her shovel and ice axe, she moved gingerly forward one step at a time towards the crevasse, constantly poking the snow beneath her to feel for holes. She trudged back to her skis and backpack, bringing them closer towards it. Ten feet from the edge of the crevasse, she stopped.

She began digging a deep, horizontal trench in the snow, creating a trough for her skis to use as an anchor. Attaching the other end of her rope to both skis, she tied a tight knot. Placing her skis into the trench, she shoveled snow around them, packing them in tightly, so they were immobilized. Holding her ice axe, she crept towards the edge of the crevasse and scanned its dark interior.

Marie was at the bottom, her form a crumpled heap.

Bits of snow gave way around the sides of the crevasse, threatening to cave in. She shouted down. "Help is on its way! Are you alright?!"

Marie shouted back up with a thick Austrian accent, "I think my leg is broken! Please help me! I have a young child!" her voice anguished.

Whitney shouted to her again, "Help is on its way, they're coming!"

"There is icewater down here! I am freezing! I must get out *now*!" she yelled up to Whitney, frantic.

"Can you move away from it?" Whitney yelled towards her, urgently.

"I cannot move my leg!" she groaned, in agony.

"Give me a few moments! I have to get my equipment!" Whitney shouted down into the chasm, again.

"Please hurry! I am getting numb!" Marie shouted up to her, panicked.

Whitney stepped hurriedly back to her pack. Grabbing her Petzl kit, she opened it, clipping the looped rope to her harness. She shimmied back to the edge of the crevasse on her stomach. "I'm coming down!" she yelled.

Turning on her headlamp, she lowered herself into the dark, freezing void, using her ice-axe and crampons for purchase. Twenty feet down, she got to Marie. Both skis had popped off her boots, she was lying partly submerged in a foot of icy, rushing water. "Where's your backpack? Your ice-axe?" Whitney asked her, urgently.

"I think it's over there-- I can't reach it," Marie gasped in obvious pain with short, shallow breaths, pointing several yards away. Whitney spotted the dark green pack, partially submerged in the rushing water. Kicking the tips of her crampons into the wall, she worked her way over to retrieve it. Taking off her insulated gloves, she opened the pack, extricating Marie's rope, crampons, headlamp and ice axe. She would have to figure out a way to hoist Marie out of here.

Climbing back over to her, she handed Marie her ice-axe, then attached her crampons onto her ski boots in the icy water. "Grab my harness!" she urged her. Marie reached up, desperately grabbing at it with both hands. Teeth chattering, her body shivered uncontrollably in the freezing temperatures. Whitney grabbed two chemical warming packs out of her parka's pocket and tore them open. Shaking them for a few seconds to activate the chemical reaction, she quickly unzipped Marie's parka and thrust them into her inner lining, zipping it back up. Marie's lower body was soaking wet.

"I'm going to lift you into a sitting position," Whitney commanded, breathing hard. Pulling herself up the wall of the crevasse several feet, she pulled Marie's torso out of the water. "Place your strong foot into the Prusik loop and push yourself up now. I'm going to hook you to my rope and harness," she instructed, heart racing. "We'll both pull ourselves up the wall together with our ice-axes. Use your strong foot for climbing!" she ordered, voice heaving with exertion. The effort was brutal. It would take superhuman strength to get up the wall. They had to try.

"I'm too heavy to do this!" Marie cried, teeth chattering. "I don't have the strength!"

"You can do it! You *must!* You will see your child again! We are going up!" Whitney insisted, thrusting her axe into the wall and kicking her boots against it, determinedly. She had to get Marie out of the water. She could die of hypothermia.

Some voices yelled down to them.

They heard the thumping of helicopter rotors, felt its reverberation, above. The rescue team had arrived. Two men wearing harnesses began climbing down the crevasse. They approached Marie and Whitney. Quickly they attached their rope to the women. Another person at the top began lifting them up to safety. Daylight appeared at the opening of the shaft. A red and white helicopter hovered in the air. A long cable with a litter attached to it dangled below, swaying back and forth. The men grabbed the litter and held it in place, lifting Marie on. Strapping her expertly in place, they signaled the pilot.

Instantly she became airborne, body suspended in the sky. The helicopter flew off, transporting her towards the valley floor.

The men spoke to Whitney. "You are alright?" they asked her, with heavy French accents.

"I am," she exhaled, dazedly. "Thank you! Thank you *so* much!" she burst out, gratefully.

"Thank *you*, Whitney," they both said, solemnly. "You may have saved her life. She was in shock. Hypothermia sets in quickly."

They began shoveling snow to unearth her skis, helping her retrieve her equipment. One of the men gathered her rope and other items and put them in her backpack. "You did an amazing job," he told her, with admiration, adding, "We will ski down to the base with you."

"You don't have to," she told him. "I'll be okay, I can go by myself."

"Believe me, it is an honor," he smiled, "The people in France and Austria are very thankful for what you did." He shook her hand, earnestly.

"Okay, then," she replied, with a nod. Pushing off the snow, she pointed her tips straight and resumed skiing down the glacier. Euphoric, strong, indomitable.

Helicopter hovering above, the judges watched her descend.

# CHAPTER 32
# CRESTED BUTTE

Whitney and Robyn sat beside each other on some chairs, holding their violins. Miss Abrams sat erect, poised on the edge of her chair across from them, demonstrating to Whitney how to properly hold a bow.

"You need to hold it like this," she instructed, reaching over to adjust Whitney's thumb and forefingers, carefully. "The amount of pressure you use will affect the tone," she added. "It can take a while to get used to the hand position, it can feel quite awkward." She guided Whitney's bow across the strings, explaining, "This is open position. You can hear the timbre of each string as the vibration travels through the bridge and into the violin, creating sound," she sat back, observing her.

Robyn watched her mother solemnly, eyes shining. It was their first music lesson together.

Miss Abrams leaned over and placed a sheet of manuscript on Whitney's metal stand. "Learning how to read music is like learning an entirely new language," she stated, pointing to the staff lines. "There are many symbols used in notation. This one is called the treble clef," she explained, moving her finger across the paper. "The black dots on the lines are called notes," she added, Whitney squinted at them dubiously.

Robyn interjected, excitedly, "I can see them better now, mommy! The dots don't squiggle around like they used to!" she beamed, happily. Miss Abrams smiled benevolently, delighted to have her back in her studio. It had been a long break since their last violin lesson together and Robyn was obviously thrilled to be there with her mother. She had never seen her happier.

Whitney stared at the manuscript, confused. Learning to play the violin was going to be a lot more challenging than she anticipated, with new respect for Robyn's music studies. Miss Abrams reached for her hand, gently placing it around the fingerboard near the tuning pegs. Whitney struggled to hold her fingers in the correct position, it felt alien, uncomfortable.

"This is much harder than I thought it would be," Whitney burst out, frustrated. Her chin and neck were cramped from holding the instrument in place, her hand ached from grasping the bow. Her plan to learn Happy Birthday for Han's seventy-ninth birthday party in September didn't seem so cut and dried now anymore. She might have to sing it to him, instead.

Miss Abrams replied knowingly, "It never feels natural at first. You'll have to be patient."

Patience was not something Whitney was very good at. And ever since the procedure in Belgrade, it was terrible. Was this what it was like, when she first learned to ski as a young child? She tried to remember. It was so long ago…

Robyn piped up eagerly, "It's okay mommy, I'll help you with it at home, okay?" she looked elated. This was something *she* could teach her mom; she was so much better at it. Hair finally starting to grow back, the bald patches on her scalp where the incisions had been made were nearly gone. She had more energy and vitality than she had had in years. The surgery had been nothing short of miraculous.

"Okay," Whitney smiled at her daughter, taking a deep breath. She tackled the music again. Dr. Laghari had told her violin lessons were excellent for initiating Robyn's recovery, that the fret work and bowing would help redevelop her fine motor skills and mental acuity. Tremendously supportive of Robyn since the surgery, he and Whitney spoke regularly as she rehabbed. The fact that reading manuscript, listening to herself play could help reactivate, strengthen Robyn's aural and visual neuropathways damaged by the seizures prior to her surgical resection was very encouraging.

"Not only will Robyn benefit from reengaging with the instrument, lessons are something you both can do together. That in and of itself is extremely valuable," he told her.

She considered telling him about her procedure with Dr. Belcic, thinking maybe he could help her too. She recalled their conversation several months ago when he told her about the research he was doing while Robyn was in the hospital. How he and his colleagues were discovering new ways to cure seizures and brain disorders. Maybe he could take her on as a patient, she thought, with newfound hope.

Perhaps he could synthesize the ANTm3 for her in a lab if she provided him with a sample of it, she thought, feeling a little more optimistic. It might help her transition through the mood disorder until they found a way to repair her severed neuropathways, she crossed her fingers.

The only thing keeping her from asking Dr. Laghari for help right now was her reluctance to tell him about the procedure itself. It was simply too risky. There was too much at stake. Even though she often had the urge to confide in him, the procedure would have to remain her secret, for now.

Consumco's secret. Trent's secret. Karis's secret.

Otherwise, their house of cards would crumble.


Playing the violin would certainly help her too, Whitney figured. She would do everything possible to regain her empathy and compassion, find a way forward, no matter what.

Robyn's medical condition and her own issues required she find new ways to manage their interactions. New ways to communicate that were more empathetic, less combative. It would take time to adjust, but she was determined to overcome things.

She recalled a conversation with MaryAnn several months ago when she had been feeling particularly disconnected and irritable. MaryAnn had wisely responded, "You might *feel* impatient, angry or aggressive towards someone, but you can *choose* to respond differently with them. It's about being mindful with your reactions, controlling your emotions and behavior.

She was correct. Her own recovery required establishing new habits, taming her worst impulses. But she also needed to maintain a regular supply of ANTm3, establish the correct blood level of it as well.

She was deluding herself, she admitted, brutally. Truth was, as time went on, the whole situation was becoming increasingly difficult to manage by herself. She would have to get professional help, soon.

Though she tried to be thoughtful and considerate interacting with others, off the ANTm3, her mood was constantly in a state of tumult, flux. Alone with her broken circuitry, unable to share her plight with anyone, the money and professional success had shackled her to a prison of silence that was nearly unbearable. Really, how long could she live this way? The prospect of renewing contact with Dr. Belcic to obtain more of the drug and dealing with the clandestine aspects of it were unsustainable.

Instinctively, she knew that Trent had had the procedure as well. Experienced the same effects as her. It would explain why he acted the way he did, she thought, dreading what the future held.

She wondered if Duncan had known anything about it, and what had been happening on the team. An innately intuitive person, he must have sensed *something* was awry, she frowned, looking back.

Duncan was different, though. He treated everyone well, didn't gossip, didn't get sucked into the drama, he just did his job. For those reasons alone she doubted he was aware of anything illegal or unethical. Duncan had integrity. That's why she cared so deeply for him.

Miss Abrams interrupted her thoughts; she was speaking to Robyn. "Listen to the melody. It's very smooth and connected, the technique is referred to as 'legato.' Try drawing the bow across the strings like this," she suggested, elegantly demonstrating. Robyn watched intently, imitating her.

Whitney's mind drifted back to Duncan. They had been talking on the phone regularly since returning to Colorado from La Grave. Excited, he told her he purchased the ski shop from his boss in Steamboat and started remodeling the place. The construction was coming together he told her, he wanted to show her the place. "You should come visit, bring Robyn with you," he cajoled, enthusiastically. "I'll take some time off and spend time with you."

She had been hesitant about the invitation, apprehensive about jumping into a relationship. But she also realized how much she missed him. She could be herself with Duncan, he understood her. Reticent, she told him, "I'm not the greatest person to be with, these days. I'm struggling to adapt to life. It's hard being off the slopes, without the single- minded pursuit of trying to win a World Championship and stay alive," she confided, haltingly. "I guess..." she tried to articulate the way she felt, "life seems odd. Mundane, without all the adventure and risk I'm accustomed to. My moods swing all over the place," she added, explaining lamely. "Sometimes I'm difficult..."

She wished she could tell him the truth, instead of dancing around it. She *wanted* to tell him the truth.

That her brain was really screwed up, but she was trying to fix it. That when she was skiing, the world was ordered, simple; but when she wasn't, it was chaos... that she wanted to be with him but was also afraid he might reject her.

"I know," he had chuckled wryly, over the phone, reading her mind. "I've been on the road with you for almost two years, I get it. If I didn't understand what you're telling me, I'd be a real dumbbell, Whitney. I want to be with you, regardless. You're like family to me now. Besides," he added playfully, "I need you around to help run my backcountry guiding business. I'll even pay you," he laughed, teasing her. He could tell she was feeling low, he was trying to cheer her up.

"I think I would like that," she smiled over the phone. "And I do miss you." Life in Crested Butte was a little empty and colorless without his grinning face. She missed his steady hand, his kind and thoughtful manner. Duncan persisted, "I'll support your career, wherever it takes you. I'll look after Robyn, I'll be your guy for all seasons, Whitney. I understand how hard you've worked, what you've gone through. No matter what, I'll have your back. You'll always have someone around to check your bindings," he joked, half-serious. The tour had ended, so had his daily interactions with her. He missed her terribly.

She caught her breath, her heart quickening wildly. She imagined sharing her life with Duncan, being with him all the time. Could she do it? She would have to tell him everything. It was the only way forward.

"Okay, we'll come out. Robyn's done with school in three weeks," she conceded, heart swelling. "We can play Scrabble, gin rummy, all go out for ice cream."

"Sounds scintillating. Can we do anything else?" he asked, playfully.

"Yup, yeah...um, we could do other things."

"Do you mean like.... *other* things?"

"Yeeesss," she drawled, always the sport.

Duncan was like air, she always breathed easier when he was around. Somehow, they would muddle through, find happiness together. She was convinced.

"Can't wait," he replied, grinning madly over the receiver, doing cartwheels in his head. All along, he had dreamed of the day he could finally share how he felt about her, that she would feel the same. That he could show his love.

Miss Abrams concluded their lesson. "Please practice pages 1 through 4," she instructed Whitney. "Next week we'll review your progress." To Robyn, she said, "I'd like you to practice pages 28 through 30 and try to play the pieces legato." Robyn beamed at her, then slid off her chair.

They thanked Miss Abrams for the lesson and departed from her studio. Whitney told Robyn, "We're going to drive out and visit Grandpa Jack and Grandma Luann this afternoon. Let's bring our violins home first and have a snack."

"Okay, mommy, good idea," she exclaimed, happily.


Three months had gone by since Robyn's surgery at Children's Hospital, she was able to attend school again, through the remainder of the school year. Whitney walked her to class in the morning.

Mrs. Hennessey's face lit up when she saw Robyn arrive at her classroom door. Hugging her fiercely, she exclaimed, "I am *so* glad to see you!" She welcomed Whitney back.

"I am *soooo* glad to see you too!" Robyn eyes sparkled, grinning. She rushed over to her old desk.

"How has she been doing?" Mrs. Hennessey asked Whitney.

"Extremely well, all things considered," Whitney told her, buoy-antly. "She still has to take medicine, but the seizures have largely stopped. She feels so much better... she's able to play violin again, she can concentrate now... It's been a huge improvement. I'm *so* relieved, it's wonderful..." she exhaled, voice catching.

"I'm delighted to hear it," Mrs. Hennessey replied, marveling. "You've done a great job, Whitney. Helping your daughter... winning the World Championship. It's all so impressive," she added, heartfelt.

Several days of blissful normalcy went by, broken when Alyn contacted Whitney to arrange an interview with her in Crested Butte. She had stayed on in Frisco to finish editing her editorial about the World Championship for Sports Illustrated, instead of flying back home to Seattle after the team dispersed. She rented a SUV and drove down to Crested Butte, taking the newly opened Cottonwood Pass to see her. Rendezvousing at a local Italian cafe, they ordered some coffee and a pizza margarite, sitting down at a small table near the front windows of the bustling, popular restaurant.

"You're back to your natural hair color, I see," Alyn commented offhand, stirring some sugar into her coffee cup. Brunette, right?"

"I'm back to being me," Whitney nodded briefly, taking a sip. Alyn had driven an awfully long way to talk about hair color. Something was up.

"You left La Grave so quickly after winning, I didn't have a chance to talk to you," Alyn offered, affably. "I mean, the ink on your million- dollar check barely dried, and you were gone. I suppose you just needed to get away after all the insanity," she added, looking directly at Whitney's face, deliberate.

"I needed to get home to Robyn," Whitney stated, explaining. "She's been waiting for me for a long time." She fell silent.

Alyn nodded, there was a brief lull between them. She stated, "I heard you donated fifty thousand dollars to the National Epilepsy Foundation, another fifty grand to the Denver Children's Hospital. Very generous," she took a sip of coffee.

"It was the least I could do," Whitney replied, easily. The pizza arrived. She slid a big slice onto her plate. "I've started volunteering with the Foundation. We're teaching people recovering from seizure disorders how to ski and snowboard, just for fun," she told Alyn. "I'm starting a chapter here in Crested Butte. I plan to work hands-on with the patients, right at the ski area."

Alyn took a slice of pizza. She inquired, "What else are you doing these days? I bet Trent wants you back with Consumco. After Ian lost at La Grave, he probably needs you more than ever. Are you guys talking?"

"Occasionally. But I haven't quite decided what I'm going to do next, yet." Whitney turned her head slightly to look out the window. Some tourists walked by on the sidewalk. Mid May, patches of dirty snow and ice still clung to the pavement. The ski area had recently closed for the season, most of the shops were winding down. She looked back at Alyn, thoughtfully.

"For the first time in my life, I'm really evaluating things," she told her, answering. "Like, I've always skied for the love of the sport, for the freedom it provides. But I've recently realized that I don't have to *kill* myself for it. Literally." She chewed a mouthful of pizza, adding, "You know, I always felt like I had to prove myself, that my worth was based solely on what I *did*, or what I *achieved*. But I've learned that my worth, or my value, is really about *who I am*. As a parent and as a person," she shrugged her shoulders, trying to explain.

Alyn leaned towards her, earnestly. "It's interesting to hear you say this, Whitney. I had always hoped for this type of candor, introspection from you, for our readers." Perhaps, she could finally get Whitney to speak openly for a change. She held her breath.

Whitney sighed, "Well, I've finally had some time to think about things more carefully now, since the tour's over. I still have a lot of commercial obligations with Consumco, but additional offers are coming my way. Offers to do ski movies, judge competitions, do public speaking... The financial rewards have been incredible, it's changed my life. I'm finally able to afford my own home, pay off all Robyn's medical expenses, give back to my parents," she confided. "And I can focus more on being the mother Robyn deserves." She added, "I've also been thinking about what I can do to assist other female athletes with the issues of sexism, financial parity, mental health."

Alyn studied her, calculating. This was her opportunity to ask her the big question, Whitney's chance to come clean. She proceeded carefully, venturing obliquely, "I always meant to ask you about your trip to Belgrade, Whitney. How it went. When I talked to Karis, she told me you both did an appearance for Adventura Fibre Apparel at the new store they were opening." She waited, silent.

"Uh... yeah." Whitney replied, taken by surprise. She blinked her eyes a second.

"So how did it go?" Alyn asked her, casually.

"Oh fine, fine... We got a lot done. Um, the Serbs really liked the product... the grand opening was great..." Whitney stammered, squirming uncomfortably.

She was a terrible liar.

"Riiiiight," Alyn dragged the word out cynically, sighing, "look, Whitney, we both know something very bad was happening on that tour. And whatever it was, it almost killed you. I was around the whole time; I saw and heard a lot of things that were extremely disturbing. I have always wondered-- what took place in Belgrade? All this "help female athletes who have been victimized...No offense, but that seems a trifle ironic. *You* were victimized, Whitney, I know that much."

Whitney froze. She felt faint.

*What did you do in Serbia?*" Alyn pressed again, more insistently. She set her pizza down, stared across the table. She had come here for the truth.

Whitney sat quietly. When she spoke, her words came out slowly, "You suspected Mason was in cahoots with Karis, before he died, didn't you? Alyn. Why didn't you say anything to Trent? Or me?" she replied, deflecting the question, eyes narrowing. She wanted the truth, too.

Her response took Alyn off guard, it seemed they had reached an impasse. She lowered her voice, answering apologetically, "I did overhear the two of them arguing in the grocery store one afternoon. It struck me as very odd, but I decided to stay out of it. Like you, I was cowed by Trent and didn't want to get involved. Now, I'm very sorry about that," she added, voice wavering slightly.

Whitney exhaled; she sensed Alyn was honestly contrite. But the entire conversation had completely blindsided her, she wasn't prepared for it. The questions were potentially devastating. If addressed honestly, they could destroy everything she had worked so hard to achieve. Her World Championship, her income, her career, her reputation. The implications were simply disastrous. She stopped eating. Stomach churning, she felt sick.

Alyn pursed her lips, frustrated. Their exchange was not going as well as she had hoped. She had thought Whitney might be willing to talk, considering Karis had attempted to kill her no less; Trent protecting the vicious young woman all along. But that was only part of the story. *Both women* had somehow been involved in something illicit and dangerous. Of that, she was convinced.

She made another stab at getting information, countering gently, "Look, the truth will come out, Whitney. It's just a matter of time. I'll get to the bottom of this story if it takes me ten years. I'll investigate old documents, speak with other athletes, search Consumco's records…Right now, I don't understand all the moving parts, but eventually I'll connect the dots, publish an expose. What I observed made me extremely suspicious of their practices and what they were doing. If it's doping, steroids, you could lose everything. Your title, your money, your reputation… if it's something else, maybe not. There may be something you're missing, or unaware of. Talking to me would be a good thing for you to do. You have an opportunity to get ahead of this, before it takes on a life of its own."

*Goddamn her!*

Enraged, Whitney stood up from the table, placed two twenty-dollar bills on it. She had a nearly uncontrollable urge to strangle Alyn right then and there. Grab her I-pad from her satchel and smash it against the floor until it broke into a hundred pieces. The impulse was swift and violent, unlike anything she had ever experienced before. It took nearly several seconds to compose herself, steel her mind and body to calm down. *Calm down*, she told herself sternly. *Breathe.* Civility must prevail, no matter what.

Yes, she had been a victim, but it was complicated. She had benefited from Consumco's largess, as much as she had lost. No one was going to take away what she had worked so hard to achieve. No way. Right now, she needed to get out of here and get some air. This afternoon had turned her world upside down, everything spinning… spinning…spinning out of control.

Still seated, Alyn looked up. Her expression was one of concern, though stoic, resolved. "I'm staying nearby at the Antler Inn for several days, Whitney. Call me, okay?"

First thing in the morning Whitney called Hans. "I need to come over and talk to you right away, is that alright?" she asked him, voice shaking. All night long she had lay awake, anguished, ruminating over the new development. Robyn was at school, it was eight a.m. Her parents were already at the store, helping customers.

"Whitney, of course. Come on by. You sound upset," he answered, worriedly. "What's wrong?" he asked, voice cracking, it was early.

"I'll be over in fifteen minutes," she told him quickly.

They sat at his quartersawn oak table in his kitchen, a carved, wooden cuckoo clock sat above them on the wall, one of the few items he and Marta brought with them from Austria. The appliances were still circa 1980's, a black, potbellied woodstove emanated heat from the small sitting room. Old newspaper articles with pictures of her and Hans were strewn atop the table. He was cutting them out with scissors to put in his scrapbook. Clearing some space, he moved them into a pile.

"Do you remember that time we were skiing this spring, and you asked me if I had any fear?" she asked him, immediately, voice ragged. She looked utterly distraught.

He suddenly stopped what he was doing immediately and looked at her. His brows furrowed worriedly. Something was wrong.

"I recall mentioning it, yes."

Her voice broke, a flood of pent-up words spilled out her body, a reservoir bursting its dam. "They sent me to Belgrade. They did surgery to remove my sensation of fear.... A doctor..." she was sobbing.

He froze, uncomprehending. This made no sense, what she was saying. *Surgery*? For *skiing*? The words were freakish, they careened around the room like sinister molecules. He reeled, shaking his head in confusion. How could this be? Consumco, --her coach-- had sent her to Serbia to get a...a procedure? To remove her sense of *fear*? Monstrous.

His face flushed with rage, his shoulders sagged with sorrow, his eyes watered with sadness. "Whitney, have you told your parents?" his voice shook with emotion.

"No," she answered, voice breaking. He stared in disbelief.

"You must! You cannot keep this inside you. It will destroy you... A secret like this will poison everything," he stuttered, outraged.

"I am so *ashamed. Disgraced.* I can't face it." She looked shattered.

"Tell me what happened," he asked her quietly.

She told him.


"You were coerced," he told her flatly, softly. "What you describe is the very definition of coercion. You are responsible for your actions, but Consumco, Trent, the doctor...all of them took advantage of your weakness for their own gain."

"If I confess, I will lose *everything*," she mourned, stricken.

"No. You will regain your humanity. And that *is* everything. No one could live with that, without help. It would eat them alive," he uttered, exhaling heavily.

"How will I go forward?" she cried.

"Listen to me," he stated, his voice a rich timbre of wisdom, sage and experienced, "the hardest thing will be to tell those people you love. But you can do it, you are strong. You have already achieved the nearly impossible. Survived and *won* the World Championship. Lost your husband and helped your daughter regain her health. Now you can speak truth to power. There are likely other athletes who were victimized too. *Speak*, on their behalf," he urged, tremulously. "They will thank you, and people will understand." He reached across the table and grasped her hands, reassuringly.

Whitney looked around the room, tearfully. Pictures of Hans and Marta lined the walls. Standing together in front of snowy Mt. Blanc, smiling beatifically. In front of the Maroon Bells, grinning like two teenagers who just fell in love.

Sweet photos from earlier days when he was married to the love of his life. How much he had lost.

"I never told you about her last days," Hans sighed, following her gaze.

"I was much younger. You spared me," she replied, heavily.

"Yes. She was in unspeakable pain. Pancreatic cancer. She only had a few more days to live, even the morphine couldn't stop all the pain. She was unable to move, wasn't eating, wasting away. But she begged me to take her up to Lake Irwin one last time. Just so she could see it. Middle of December, sub- zero temperatures," his voice broke, "I bundled her up and carried her out to my truck, drove up Kebler Pass in the freezing snow. Put her in my sled and pulled her up the Pass, on my snowshoes. We sat together and looked across to Ruby Mountain Range at that gorgeous lake in total wonder. That was all she wanted, one last look," he swallowed hard. "I never thought I'd get over her death, I missed her so much. Wanted to die, too," he murmured, sadly. "She was my best friend on Earth. But I did finally get over it. It just took a long time. We all move through heartbreak and pain. But you already know that Whitney, you've had more than your fair share," he finished, heavily.

"I know, Hans," her eyes welled up.

"You will move through this chapter. And it may bring you places you never anticipated, along the way. You may be entitled to compensation from Consumco. People will support you. You'll see," he added, with gravitas.

"Alyn asked me to come forward, she came to see me yesterday. She knew something was very wrong."

He stood up, retrieved a box of saltine crackers from the cupboard. Placed a stack of them on a delicate, porcelain plate with a beautiful, five-point stag etched in the center of it. Marta's, no doubt, Whitney thought, moved by the tenderness of the gesture. Even in her absence, Marta's spirit, soul permeated everything he did. They nibbled a few crackers and sipped some earl grey tea. Sat quietly for a few long minutes.

"Will you talk to her?" he gazed across the table, asked her gravely.

She thought of Duncan, Robyn, her parents. Their future as a family, as a unit. So many years she had chased her dream, chased her aspiration and desires. But they were all that truly mattered. Those other things were just embers of a fire she had let burn too hot, too hard, too long. It was time to heal.

She nodded.

"Yes, Hans, I will tell her everything."